PRAISE FOR THE ART OF REMEMBERING

Exquisitely drawn... this relatable story pulled me in from the beginning, never releasing its grip until the end. You will be rooting for Ailsa with every turning page. **Peggy Lampman,** *award-winning author of The Promise Kitchen and The Welcome Home Diner.*

From the prologue to the very last word, Ragsdale commands the reader's attention with characters that are both complex and compelling. One by one she peels back the hidden layers of responsibility, expectation, and fame to expose the soft under-belly of Ailsa MacIntyre's life. Highly recommended. **Bette Lee Crosby**, *USA Today bestselling author.*

The Art of Remembering is a deeply moving story, one woman's evocative journey through the life she knows and the one she's lost. A beautifully woven tale of finding yourself all over again with a heartwarming conclusion that will leave you a little richer. **Rochelle Berger Weinstein**, *USA Today bestselling author.*

The body remembers even if the mind forgets. This is the essence of Alison Ragsdale's novel The Art of Remembering. Reading the book is like watching a Degas painting come to life and finding out what happens to the dancers after they leave the canvas. This is a luminous story about love...for a spouse, a friend, for music and for ballet—it's heartbreaking and yet joyous. **Amulya Malladi,** *Bestselling author of The Copenhagen Affair and The Nearest Exit May Be Behind You.*

From page one, Ragsdale brings the reader into Ailsa's world. As we get to know Ailsa and Evan, we are rooting for Ailsa as she tries to recuperate, a process which involves not only regaining her physical strength but also piecing together her personal life. **Heather Bell Adams**, *award-winning author of Maranatha Road.*

ALSO BY ALISON RAGSDALE

THE ART OF REMEMBERING

ALISON RAGSDALE

THE ART OF REMEMBERING

For information: alison@alisonragsdale.com

ISBN: 13:978-1-7330377-0-9

ISBN: 10:1-7330377-0-5

For all the exceptional individuals who have dedicated their lives to dance, and to all those who have supported them in the pursuit of their passion.

"And even this heart of mine has something artificial. The dancers have sewn it into a bag of pink satin, pink satin slightly faded, like their dancing shoes." – Edgar Degas

PROLOGUE

NEW YORK CITY, OCTOBER 2019

The curtain rose, and the stage at New York's Lincoln Center was in total darkness, as the tightness of Ailsa MacIntyre's pointe shoes cut off the circulation to her toes. The hard soles ran like familiar tightropes under each of her arches as she pulled her weight up through her supporting leg and into her core. She could defy gravity, ignore the crushing of her toe joints, and work through the throbbing pain that had been plaguing her for months, heavy above her left ear. She could float, ethereal and transcendent. She could do this.

Ailsa waited for the first violin to cut into the silence and the spotlight to split the blackness around her. Just as she released the breath she had been holding, the first high C slid across the soundless stage and the light snapped on. Its brightness instantly intensified her headache and she blinked several times to clear her vision.

Arms still at her sides, she lifted her head slowly and looked above the orchestra pit, high up behind the audiences' heads, letting her focus settle on a small red light in the control box.

The second and third violins picked up their line in the score and the fine hairs on her arms stood to attention, as always happened with Prokofiev. On cue, her right arm released and lifted away from her side as she slid her left foot out, pushing through the floor and extending the ankle and toes. It had begun.

The music began to fill her head, pushing down the drum of pain throbbing in her temple. Layer by layer of instrument, the orchestra built a platform for her interpretation. Each beat filled her, running through every vein, muscle and tendon like syrup, connecting her to the ground and yet blurring her own edges against the atmosphere.

As she moved around the stage turning, balancing, gathering momentum and controlling her breathing Ailsa knew, deep within her being, precisely where she needed to be at every pause and crescendo. Her body moved on autopilot and yet was not unmanned—the steps a familiar map that she had followed many times—moving the choreography forward and filling the space around her with shape, form, energy and emotion.

Her muscles propelled her reliably through her solo and as the audience applauded she felt the familiar rush of heat, and joy at the sound of their appreciation.

As her sides heaved, the oboe sang out—a thin note of intro-duction, teasing the other woodwind instruments as it lilted away toward the ceiling. As had been happening frequently over the past few weeks, the familiar notes sounded different tonight, as if the tones were being stretched on a wire, distorting as they sent a hot needle into her left eardrum. She blinked through the pain, ignoring the pattering under her breastbone, and tried to home in on the guiding melody.

The Corps de Ballet filtered onto the stage around her just as another stab to her head made Ailsa gasp, the pain now excruci-ating as it seared above her ear, flashing angrily up into her temple. Dragging her focus back to the next movement, she bent her knees to prepare for a series of fouetté turns.

Time instantly became suspended and she could no longer see the red light she used for spotting, the music now so distorted it was almost unrecognizable. As she struggled to locate the melody that would lead her through her next variation, the stage before her became smudged against the darkness of the audience.

The moment it took her to search again for the spotting light was a moment too many, and the screeching music moved on without her.

Three of the Corps passed across the front apron of the stage. Among them, her best friend, Amanda, turned her head, wide eyed as she looked back at Ailsa, who remained stationary.

Her breathing ragged, Ailsa locked on Amanda's eyes and shook her head. With an imperceptible nod, Amanda executed a series of châinés turns, her head whipping around as she stepped out onto each alternate foot, carving a full circle back to the middle of the stage. When she finally stopped, the line of her body and the long courtly skirt she wore created a blessed eclipse, sheltering Ailsa from the glare of the lights and the view of the expectant audience.

Squinting into the darkness, she tasted salt on her upper lip and as panic filled her chest, she turned her head toward the stabbing pain and scanned the wings. The company's Artistic Director, Mark Chambers, was beckoning her off stage, so, with all her strength, she slid her foot out to the side trying not to lose her balance. The floor seemed to be undulating under her shoe and she felt bile rising into her throat.

Amanda and the rest of the Corps had filled the stage in front of her, Capulets and Montagues in groups of three and five, their weaving lines and meticulously aligned Arabesques creating a curtain that Ailsa could hide behind as she slipped away from the last, unfulfilled bars of the movement.

She slid into the wing and Mark gathered her under her arms, barking at a stagehand to fetch water as she dissolved into his grip, her face slick and her throat constricted.

"What's wrong, darling?" Mark, acting as a crutch, maneuvered her toward the dressing rooms. "Talk to me."

3

"My head's going to explode." She pressed her palm over her ear and leaned on Mark's arm. "The music sounded wrong and I can't...I can't..."

Mark's hands dug into her armpits as she felt herself falling, then all faded to black.

BOOK ONE

Five months earlier.

Glasgow, May 2019

AILSA

A ilsa was running late and trying to get out of the flat in time to pick up a latte on her way to the studio. Glancing in the bedroom mirror, she tucked a long dark curl behind her ear, smoothed an index finger under each sky-blue eye then grabbed her bulky cloth bag, full of dance wear and pointe shoes, and rushed into the living room.

Scanning the space for her keys she caught her husband, Evan, frowning at her from the kitchen door.

"Sorry. I'm going to be pretty late tonight." She lifted the metallic bundle, from the dish on the dining table. "What're you going to do?" She slung the heavy bag over her shoulder and smiled at him.

Evan's dark eyes were cold.

"I'm going to scale Ben Nevis, then run a marathon before I come home and cook myself dinner." He snapped. "It's the same thing every Wednesday, Ailsa. Leave work, go to the pool for some laps, grab a beer then come home." He spread his arms. "Nothing different tonight."

"God, sorry I asked." Her face fell. "What's wrong with you today?"

Evan grabbed the newspaper, slid past her and slumped into one of the armchairs that flanked the fireplace. The morning light being dim in their ground-floor flat, his cheerful dark curls looked incongruous around the shaded angles of his face.

"Evan?" She stood behind the leather sofa that separated them. "Is this about last night?" She gripped the strap of her bag, her finger nails cutting into in her palm.

"You're already late. We can talk later." He flapped the paper at her.

The dismissive gesture brought her teeth together.

"Please don't do that." She sighed. "You know I can't leave if you're still angry." She dropped her bag on the floor, walked over and perched on the arm of the chair opposite him.

Evan let the paper fall to his knees, his bear-like hands balling the morning news into his fists.

"You always do that to me." His eyes flashed. "You make me feel like this bloody ogre, when all I'm trying to do is be smart, make good choices for the both of us." He released the paper and began smoothing the creases he'd made.

"I wasn't trying to make you feel like an ogre." Her cheeks were burning now. "I appreciated everything you said, but sometimes I feel dictated to rather than considered." She pushed her tailbone into the soft leather, willing her taut muscles to relax. The clock on the mantle said 8:15 a.m. leaving her only forty-five minutes to cross town, get changed and to the barre for her 9:00 a.m. ballet class.

"If you didn't behave like a child, I wouldn't have to treat you like one." His eyes were hooded.

Adding injury to insult, an arrow of pain shot up from her jaw into her hairline, sending her lurching forward and her palm flying to her temple.

"Hey." She sucked in a breath. "That was uncalled for."

A shift in his expression gave her a moment's hope then, his face closed again and he pushed himself up from the chair.

"What's wrong?" He gestured toward her hand.

"Another headache." She massaged the skin above her ear. "They're getting worse." The words out, she wished she'd held them back. His attitude to anything that pertained to her health was baffling, as if he was in denial about the possibility of her body not being the perfect machine required to power her career trajectory in the ballet company.

"You just need a decent night's sleep, or a massage or something." His face was stark of emotion and the chill in his voice made the hairs stand up on Ailsa's forearms. "Just go to class. We'll talk about everything later." He turned to face the fireplace, his broad back hunched under his dark sweater.

Ailsa stood up, sensing another defeat.

"Look, all I wanted to do was talk about the potential for us having children, but every time I bring it up you shut me down."

He stared into the empty grate.

"Evan?" She moved to his side. "We need to be able to talk about it." She laid her palm on his back feeling his warmth through the prickly wool.

When they'd married eight years earlier, both at the urging of her mother Jennifer, a former Prima Ballerina, and for the sense that it made for Ailsa's career, she and Evan had agreed to put off having a family for a few years. As time passed and she progressed within the company, eventually being made a principal a year earlier than expected, her deep longing for a child had only continued to grow, hovering inside her like a gathering storm. She'd been building up to talking to him about it again and the previous evening, her nerve lubricated by a couple of glasses of wine, she'd ventured there.

Now, she let her hand drop away from his back.

"Are we always going to find a reason not to do it?" Her finger tips were tingling.

"We agreed to wait." He turned to face her.

"I'm not saying it has to be right now, Evan. Just preferably before I'm fifty." She clamped her mouth shut.

His face colored as he stepped away from her, and he shoved his hands into his pockets.

"You're going from strength to strength in the company. You've only been a principal for a year. Why would you jeopardize that now?"

"But I'm thirty already." She pressed her eyes closed as he turned his back on her again.

"After everything we've sacrificed, all the time and energy we've put into your career, would you really just give it all up? Because you know, once you have a baby it's as good as over."

Her hands had begun to shake so she laced her fingers together, as her father had taught her as a child.

"That's not always the case anymore, and I'm not talking right away, but I'd like to stop when I'm still at the top of my game. Then we can start our family, love. Doesn't that count for anything?"

He shook his head. "We should wait at least another year."

An alarming high-pitched whine reverberated in her ear as, with a leadened stomach, she walked over and lifted the shoe-bag. Sliding it onto her shoulder she focused on his back.

"We need to keep the subject open. It's really important to me, Evan."

His back was now ram rod straight as he looked at his reflection in the mirror above the fireplace.

Ailsa pressed her lips together then glanced toward the door.

"Have a good day, O.K.?" A last modicum of hope that he might turn and look her in the eye kept her frozen to the spot.

"Yeah. You too." Rather than turn, he met her gaze in the mirror. "Don't skip your warm up because you're a bit late." He frowned. "You can't afford any injuries this season. Not if you want to go on tour."

There being no words that her disappointment could work

around, Ailsa simply nodded.

"And remember what I said about Richard. He turned to face her, his index finger directed at her middle. "He's not as stand-up a guy as you think he is."

At the mention of one of her dance partners, and good friends, Ailsa's remaining patience evaporated, but rather than wade any deeper into this quagmire, she avoided Evan's eyes and headed for the door.

Ailsa stood at the barre, sandwiched between Amanda, in front and Richard, behind her. The dance studio was musty, a film of condensation covering the windows and a cocktail of dust and rosin, the sticky crystals the dancers crushed under their pointe shoes for traction, hanging thickly around them.

Having used the rigorous barre exercises to work out her anxiety over the events of the morning, Ailsa's limbs now felt loose and ready to work. Her skin was pleasantly tacky and the only thing marring her elevated mood, as they completed the barre with the battements en cloche combination, was the undeniable onset of one of her headaches.

They'd been worsening over the past few months and, as the pressure of the upcoming tour continued to build, so their frequency was increasing. As often happened when she felt the pain, like a knife's edge slicing down her forehead and into her left eye, a flicker of anxiety followed, releasing dozens of butterfly wings in her chest.

Trying to ignore the storm gathering in her temple, she let herself be pulled along by the rousing music, swishing her leg forcefully from front to back passing through first position, creating an arc beneath her as her leg sailed up close to her nose and then into a high Arabesque behind her.

The piano thrummed from the corner of the room and the

ballet mistress, Hélène Thoreau, a recent transplant from the Paris Opera Ballet, paced in front of the wall of mirrors tapping a wiry thigh, her flimsy skirt clinging to her hips.

"One two three, two two three. Get those legs up." Her reedy voice was like nails against glass.

Ailsa winced at the strident sound, and when Miss.Thoreau turned away from them, Ailsa extended her leg and brushed Amanda's backside with her toe.

Amanda whipped around, a smile tugging at her mouth, her sleek blonde bun immaculate as always.

"Stop it." She whispered, slicing a palm across her throat." "Because I'm the one who'll get it in the neck." She grimaced and turned back to face the front.

Suppressing a laugh, Ailsa glanced over her shoulder to see the corners of Richard's dark eyes crinkling. He'd been her primary partner before she'd been promoted to Principal, and while she loved now working with the formidable Steven Owens, his immense talent and artistry having helped her grow as a performer, she missed the element of mischief that Richard had brought to their partnership.

He winked at her as she closed her feet into a tight fifth position, just as the music came to an end.

"Goody two-shoes." She whispered at Amanda's back.

Miss. Thoreau spun around. "Miss. MacIntyre. Please." She frowned, sucking in her sunken cheeks.

A wave of heat crept up Ailsa's sternum as she dipped her gaze to the floor.

"Sorry." She sucked in her lower lip, catching a muffled snort coming from behind her.

"People, we really need to focus. Only two weeks until the tour and so much still to accomplish."

Ailsa glanced across the studio to the opposite barre taking in her fellow company members; the rainbow of leotards, a mixture of black and pink tights, and layers of scruffy wool warmers wrapped around a forest of slender limbs. Ballet Scotland's entire touring company was taking this class and, with a full-length rehearsal of Sleeping Beauty immediately afterward, they were all destined to be in this sweaty space for many more hours.

"Crazy woman." Amanda hissed over her shoulder.

Ailsa's suppressed another laugh.

"Who, me?" She leaned forward and tucked the end of a stray ribbon tightly in to her inner ankle.

Miss. Thoreau held Ailsa in her gaze as she beckoned the company members toward her.

"Into the center please." She stepped back, her scrawny arms held in a wide second position. "I won't bite."

Ailsa tiptoed into the center of the room and took up her customary position at the back of the class. She grinned at Richard, who'd taken the spot next to her, and just as she was about to lean in and whisper to him, the ballet mistress tutted.

"Why not join me up front today, Miss. MacIntyre?" She raised her eyebrows expectantly.

Ailsa dropped her chin, tucked a stray tendril of hair behind her ear and carefully wove between the rows of dancers. She received several smiles and gentle nudges as she passed her friends, then slid into the front row next to Steven, her Prince Desiré.

"Welcome, Princess Aurora. I don't often have to invite our principals to come to the front." Thoreau widened her eyes, then her stern face crumbled into a smile as a few titters from the class brought the heat back to Ailsa's face.

Ailsa fidgeted with her leotard and grimaced at Steven, who was smiling broadly at her.

"Grow up." He mouthed as she stuck her tongue out at him.

"Right." Thoreau barked, snuffing out any potential for further mirth. "Port de bras."

~

Inside the noisy changing room, Amanda sat on the floor next to her, as Ailsa wound the silky ribbons around her pointe shoes and shoved them into the shoe-bag.

"Good class today." Amanda nodded to herself as she untied her shoes. "I nailed my triple pirouettes, for a change."

"I saw that." Ailsa smiled. "You're great at turning."

Amanda shook her head. "Not consistently. It's like I can do it, but only when I don't try too hard." She pulled a face, then their laughter mingled in the chilly room.

"Sounds like my life in general." Ailsa watched as Tricia and Samantha, two members of the Corps, trotted past them heading back to the studio, their skinny arms linked and their heads both neatly inclined to the left as if performing the iconic pas de quatre from Swan Lake.

Amanda frowned. "Trouble with the great dictator?"

"He's not that bad. He just wants the best for me." Ailsa bit her bottom lip and tugged the zip closed on the bag. "We were rehashing the same old stuff before I left this morning." She felt the levity of earlier begin to seep away.

She'd met Evan at a party on the Glasgow university campus when she was just nineteen, and had joined the Corps of Ballet Scotland a matter of weeks earlier, as a gauche young dancer. Evan's impressive height, sparkling brown eyes and reserved humor had drawn her in. The fact that this intelligent, handsome man, eight years her senior, was interested in Ailsa, had been seductive and she'd soon fallen hard for her confident and deter- mined suitor.

Amanda shifted closer, dropping her voice.

"Want to talk about it?"

Ailsa draped a wrinkled pashmina around her shoulders.

"He's so cross and closed off these days. He seems so deep inside his own head that he just doesn't hear me anymore." Her chest began to ache. "It's as if he sees me as another project to be handled." She leaned her head back against the wall.

14

Amanda nodded. "Well, you know what I think." She paused. "He needs some interests of his own."

Ailsa's mouth twisted. From early in their relationship, Evan had taken on the mantle of a protector, and guide. He had always been the one with the big plans and seemed to know instinctually what was best, for them both. Ailsa, an introverted mesh of insecurities and self-doubt, like many of her peers in professional dance, had gladly relinquished control but, as the years passed and she progressed within the company, gaining in confidence and maturity, Evan's ministrations had begun to feel more like being managed by him than married to him.

"Perhaps he's always treated me like this, but I just didn't notice it before?" She paused, the thought like a noxious worm burrowing its way into her middle. "I sometimes wonder if I even know what I think about things anymore. It's like he plasters his own thoughts on top of mine." She uncrossed her legs and extended them, circling each ankle until the ligaments popped. "He's over-involved in some things and completely inaccessible in others. We're sort of operating around one another at the moment." Her voice faltering, she smoothed her palms over her temples.

Amanda nodded. "You know what?" Her friend's cornflower-blue eyes were full of sympathy. "You need a break. Maybe a holiday away from all this." She flapped her hand. "Some time to reconnect." She pulled a tattered leg warmer over each foot. "Evan gets so wrapped up in what he wants for you, he forgets there's two of you in the marriage." Amanda frowned. "Shall I come over and slap him around a bit?" She flexed her bicep comically.

"No." Ailsa laughed, releasing the tension that had been building in her middle. "You're awful." She batted Amanda's thigh. "We'll sort it out. I just wish he'd take a big breath and relax now and then. We used to laugh a lot, you know." She eyed her friend who was pursing her lips. "What? We did."

Amanda pushed herself up from the floor, turned and held a hand out to Ailsa.

"You know I'm always here, right?"

Ailsa grabbed the hand and let Amanda pull her to her feet.

"I do, and I don't know what I'd do without you."

As Ailsa sat cross-legged on the floor at the front of the studio, watching the company rehearse the Prologue from Sleeping Beauty, she sewed a set of ribbons onto a pair of new pointe shoes. Princess Aurora was one of her most challenging roles and, despite having danced it numerous times now, performing the Rose Adagio in Act One, with the four Princes, still made her nerves tingle as badly as they had when she'd been a novice.

In front of her, Amanda and Richard led a small group in a courtly dance, as behind them the Corps formed neat rows, slicing past each other like graceful tectonic plates of humanity.

Hélène Thoreau floated across the studio, her face gathering color as the heat in the room rose.

"You're behind the music." She wagged a finger at Amanda, then gently corrected a stray arm on one of the newest members of the Corps.

Amanda widened her eyes at Ailsa, then dipped sideways into Richard's waiting arms, the back of her hand softly touching her opposite cheek.

Ailsa suppressed a smile, then felt the sharp darning needle prick her index finger.

"Damn." She stuck her finger in her mouth, tasting the mixture of dust and blood, and let it linger there as she watched the intricate human patterns continuing to form and reform in front of her. With Tchaikovsky's rich score trickling over her senses, Ailsa revisited the morning's confrontation with Evan.

His position on them having children was increasingly

unyielding whenever she ventured to bring it up now. While there was a part of her that understood him—her becoming a principal at just twenty-nine was no mean feat and much of that achievement she felt she owed to his sacrifice and support—his closed off position was hurtful and frustrating.

Now, as his words of earlier echoed in her mind, a brittle realization slid into place. The more years of their marriage that slipped by and the more he pushed the idea of children away, the more evident it became that Evan may never want what she did, and the thought was crushing.

All she'd ever wanted to do was make him happy and proud of her, and she wondered if he realized that so much of what she did, she did for him. He'd made many sacrifices for the sake of her career, put up with her crazy schedule; missing out on a trip to New Zealand to visit his cousin because he'd insisted on being at the post-performance party at the end of her first season as a principal, and a few years earlier he'd even refused a promotion that involved a transfer overseas. Despite all of that, for which she was unendingly grateful, what she needed from him now was much more profound.

As she watched the company finish the Prologue and Mark, the director, walk into the studio, Hélène's voice snapped her back to the present.

"Princess Aurora. Will you join us please?" Hélène pointed at the ground in front of her.

Mark looked over at Ailsa and smiled, then turned his attention to the busy studio.

"Right, you horrible lot. What's going on in here? I want to see it full out, no half-measures." He narrowed his eyes at the sea of flushed faces, then grinned. "Come on. What're you waiting for?" He pointed at the dancers. "Let's get this show on the road."

EVAN

E van shoved the glass away from him, catching the barman's eye.

"One more please, John."

The barman lifted the empty glass, his rheumy eyes scanning Evan's face.

"Not going home th'night?" He squinted at the beer tap, brown-black liquid sliding down the inside of the tilted glass.

"Nothing to rush home for." Evan shrugged. "She's rehearsing till late."

John nodded and slid the fresh pint toward him.

"Want something to eat then?"

Evan considered his options, a quick meal here where he was protected from the driving rain outside, or a dash home to an empty flat to forage for leftovers in the fridge.

"Yeah. Shove me that menu, will you?"

John slid the laminated card across the bar.

"The fish is good tonight. Caught fresh this morning."

Evan pushed the menu back.

"Decision made. Fish it is."

John nodded then walked to the register to punch in the order.

The pub was unusually quiet, the after-work crowd having left already and the small group of regulars that remained having scattered to the handful of warped tables at the edges of the room, rather than occupy the stools at the bar.

Evan preferred the Curlers Den to the other pubs that were dotted within walking distance of their flat on Dumbarton Road. Tucked into an alley, it tended to be missed by tourists, and those not familiar with the city, resulting in a slightly more reserved crowd who respected one another's occasional need for space and quiet. This being one of those nights, Evan hadn't joined Jerry and Stephanie, the two police officers he generally drank with. Not to appear rude, when he'd declined their invitation, he'd bought them a drink which they were now enjoying at a table in the corner near the fireplace.

Evan looked over and raised his glass to the couple, then turned back, his knees grazing the front of the bar. He leaned forward on his elbows and stared up at the TV mounted next to the impressive collection of Malt Whiskies that lined the top shelf. Assessing the bottles, he spotted a twelve-year-old Caol ila, the pale whisky from the Isle of Islay that was his drink of choice.

"John. Can I have a single?" He pointed to the bottle.

"Aye. Just a minute." John slid three glasses into the washer under the counter and turned to Evan. "Pushing the boat out, eh?" The older man smiled, his broad face folding into a mass of lines.

"Yep. Might as well treat myself." Evan ran a hand over his still-damp curls. The swimming pool had been a welcome break from the tension of work and now, as he watched John pouring the single measure, he could already taste the smoky burn of the light-gold liquid.

"So, what's new?" John tucked a dish cloth into his belt, his stomach bulging over his trousers and a sliver of shirt protruding from under his Argyle sweater.

Evan lifted the whisky glass and inhaled.

"Ah, that's the stuff of life." He sipped. "Hits the spot."

John began polishing a glass, waiting for Evan to answer.

"Nothing new really. Work's O.K. Developing a new App at the moment. Should be going into testing soon." Evan switched to beer.

"When's Ailsa off again?" John set the glass on the counter and lifted another from the sink.

"Couple of weeks." Evan rolled his eyes. "Asia this time."

John whistled softly through his teeth.

"Jeez-o. Lucky her." He dipped his chin. "How long for?"

Evan took a draft of beer then set the glass on a warped beer mat.

"About a month, I think." He twisted the glass, his lower lip protruding.

John's eyes widened.

"Do you never go with her?"

He gathered several clean wine glasses and began sliding their bases into the wooden racks that were suspended over the bar.

"I'm not invited."

Evan ran a finger down the side of his beer, leaving a clear trail on the sweaty glass. His level of dedication to shepherding Ailsa's career made being left behind while she toured the world with the company, galling.

"Oh well, I suppose when the cat's away…" John laughed, his thick fingers spread on the bar top.

"No, no." Evan felt guilt tug at his middle. "Not my style." An image of long red hair, a pair of green eyes locking on his, tapering fingers tracing a line along his inner arm made him blink several times.

"I'm only joking, pal." John's eyebrows danced. "Ailsa's a

gem. You'd be a nut to risk that." His face began to color, and he raked his fingers through the tufts of greying hair that floated out from above each ear.

Evan sat up straight.

"I know, mate. No worries." He patted the bar. "A person could starve in this place though. Where's my fish?"

"Ha. Right-o." John nodded, then walked away toward the kitchen.

Evan let himself into the flat. The hall was dark, so he ran a hand along the wall until his fingertips found the light switch. Flipping it on, he hung his soaking-wet jacket on the coat rack behind the door, walked over and tossed his sports bag onto the sofa and his keys into the dish on the dining table.

His phone had buzzed twice in his pocket on the walk home but he'd chosen not to answer it while the rain still pounded down, so now he pulled it out and checked the messages. Seeing two missed calls from the same number at his office he licked his lips, but instead of calling back, he tossed the phone onto the table.

In the bedroom he stripped, leaving his damp clothes in a heap on the wooden floor. The chill of the room made him shiver so he ran along the hall and into the bathroom.

Once under the powerful shower, he turned and let the warm water slide down his front. He closed his eyes and felt the hot needles pummel his face as the conversation he'd had with Ailsa that morning came back to him.

Over the last few months, he'd found himself being angry with her. Initially it was over trivial things, but more recently, his anger had morphed into a quiet resentment that simmered all the time. As he tried to pinpoint the cause, he couldn't find any one thing that would justify it, until an image of those green eyes was before him again, the way they rendered him still, pinned him down from over the partition that separated their cubicles at the office.

A bolt of clarity made him put a hand out and steady himself against the tiled wall. His breathing faltered and as he grabbed for the soap he missed it, sending the bar skittering between his feet.

"Fuck it." He leaned down and picked up the slippery oval, and as he began lathering his torso, Evan knew that in his heart he was already a cheater. Whether he'd acted on the impulse yet or not, his anger toward his wife was nothing more than a smoke screen he was hiding behind.

He pictured Ailsa's face, the hurt expression she'd tried to suppress that morning and her tremulous voice as she'd wished him a good day, and a new trickle of guilt slid down his back.

He knew how badly she wanted to start a family but his gut churned at the thought of her giving up her career, a path he'd so carefully planned and coached her along for almost a decade.

After everything he'd done to support her path to success, he just couldn't imagine Ailsa not dancing. He got a rush when he introduced her, or talked to strangers about what his wife did for a living, and he'd grown used to getting a better table at their favorite restaurant and their home being filled with flowers after her performances. It was also thrilling, occasionally seeing his name in the papers, and his face in the recent, two-page spread that had appeared in Dancers World magazine when he and Mark had persuaded a reluctant Ailsa to allow them into their home to do a lifestyle piece on her. Basking in that light felt good, and he deserved to be included, if only by association, in the small amount of celebrity that Ailsa had earned over the years. He wasn't ready to give all that up, even if she was.

Turning his back on the water, he stared at the wall and tried to visualize her pregnant; her washboard stomach bulging under a summer dress, her pacing in the bedroom with a wailing child in her arms, or them rushing to the pediatrician with every fever or rash that appeared, but he just couldn't picture himself in those scenes.

Evan turned off the water and stepped out onto the bath mat. Dripping his way across the cold floor, he yanked a towel off the rail, wrapped it around his waist then swiped a clearing in the foggy mirror and stared at himself. At thirty-eight he should be mature enough to accept her being away a couple of times a year, and not wallow in childish resentment. Moreover, he should be ready to have children, but rather than being open to it, he was allowing himself to be distracted by the lure of another woman. Someone who came from his world. Someone who was not only openly pursuing him but understood what he did, enjoyed what he enjoyed, more profoundly than his wife ever had.

The green eyes came back to him again. The confident red head's name was Marie. Her attention was flattering, and he couldn't deny his attraction to her. The truth was that when Ailsa left for weeks on end, he felt superfluous. Even if accompanying her on tour was completely impractical, his sense of being cast aside burned, and it was pushing him toward making a dangerous decision.

AILSA

It was after 11:00pm when Ailsa crept into the flat. Anxious not to wake Evan, she dropped her bags, tiptoed through the living room to the kitchen, drank a glass of water then made her way down the narrow hall to the bathroom. Inside, Evan's towel was in a heap on the floor, so she picked it up and folded it over the rail.

Pulling the pins from her bun she stacked them in the container she kept under the sink then dragged a brush through her hair. Enjoying the gentle tug of the bristles, and the tingling sensation trailing over her scalp, she caught her reflection in the mirror and frowned. Leaning forward she dropped the brush and patted the dark skin under her eyes, then placing her palms on her cheeks, pulled her face tight to smooth the fine lines that were forming around her mouth.

Dropping her hands, she stepped back and considered her face. Something had changed. Her eyes looked deeper set, her skin had an odd pallor and her cheek bones seemed more prominent. Ailsa frowned, the question that she'd been asking herself frequently over recent months resurfacing. Was she simply beginning to look her age or was something else, more concerning going on?

Her headaches were coming almost daily now, worsening at night, often making her delay going to bed. While she wanted to put them down to work stress, and the preparation for the tour, their increased intensity was making it harder to dismiss them so easily.

Tutting at herself she took a shower, cleaned her teeth then feeling her way down the hall, padded into the bedroom.

Evan's back was to her as she slid under the duvet. His breathing was slow and even, and his hair created an unruly dark pool against the white of the pillow case. She lay her head back gingerly and closed her eyes, not wanting him to wake as she might have a few months ago, to have him turn to her and ask how rehearsals had gone.

As her headaches had worsened over recent months she'd become worn down by them, made weary. Consequently, she'd been quieter than usual, and keeping him at a distance. It was clear that he'd noticed and when she traced things back in time, it coincided with his becoming more strident and closed off.

As she stared at the ceiling her chest felt tight, and tears welled up in her eyes. Even as they trickled down the side of her face she did nothing to wipe them away, rather, she let them come, their passage a promise of cleansing, potentially taking with them the fear that lived inside her most of the time now that something major was off-kilter with her carefully choreographed life.

Turning onto her side she tucked her hands under her chin and closed her eyes. The next day was Wednesday, over a week since they'd argued, and while things were still somewhat stilted between them, Evan had been making an effort to be more communicative. She appreciated his attempts at humor, and his asking her if she'd like to go out to eat one evening rather than pick at the meager contents of the fridge, but underlying those gestures his eyes had been vacant and he'd been checking his phone constantly as if he'd rather be somewhere else.

There were only a few days left until the company went to Asia and she wanted to leave things on a steady note rather than be worrying about every eye flicker or sigh she might pick up on their video chats. A month was a long time to feel anxious and insecure, especially being so far apart, and with the level of focus that performing required.

Pushing the weighted thoughts down, she bunched the duvet under her chin and tried not to ignore the pain that was ticking in her temple. There were very few windows of opportunity left for her to see her doctor before leaving, so resolving to call the clinic in the morning, she slipped into the controlled pattern of her yoga breathing and soon, gave way to the drag of sleep.

Having no idea how long she'd slept, Ailsa's eyes flew open. The pain was excruciating, traveling in scorching waves that pulsed from deep inside her left eye socket out toward her ear. Her breathing was shallow as she pushed herself up to a sitting position, careful not to wake Evan, who was gently snoring, his back still turned toward her.

She pushed the covers off and felt for her slippers with her toes but unable to find them, she stood on the chilly floorboards, her head leaden and her palms clammy. Lifting her robe from the bottom of the bed, she slipped from the room and headed for the kitchen.

With a glass of water in hand, her stomach flipped as she gulped down the cold liquid and willed the thumping inside her head to subside. Accompanying the pain was the inner whisper that was becoming familiar. At first it had been a tiny voice that she could dismiss with the dawn, a timely cup of tea, or a chat with Amanda, but lately the voice was becoming more insistent. *Something's wrong with you.*

Allowing herself to go to a dark place wasn't Ailsa's habit but something was telling her that she needed to pay attention to the voice, and soon.

~

Doctor Daniels, her stethoscope slung around her neck and her glasses shoved up into her mass of blonde curls—having done a rudimentary examination—leaned back in her chair.

"Nothing jumps out, Ailsa, though, I'd like to see you gain a little weight. You're down three pounds since your last check up." She scanned the paper on her desk. "Your heart sounds great. Blood pressure's normal. I can't see anything in your eyes or ears." She leaned forward and picked up a pen. "What I think you're experiencing are migraines, probably exacerbated by stress."

Ailsa felt a sinking in her middle, a confusing mix of relief and disappointment.

"O.K." She picked at the cuticle on her thumb. "It's just that the headaches are almost daily now."

"I understand." The doctor nodded slowly. "And you're going on tour when?"

Ailsa cleared her throat, the sudden urge to cry over-whelming.

"Thursday morning. I'm gone five weeks this time."

Doctor Daniels dropped the pen on the desk and stood up.

"Well, I think we need to do a full blood panel, give you a referral to a neurologist and get you on the list for an MRI." She paused. "We can draw the blood today, but we won't have the results until after you're gone. Obviously, the other appointments won't be until you get back." Her gentle brown eyes scanned

Ailsa's face. "So, we need to find a way to manage your pain until then."

Ailsa nodded. "That'd be great." She ran a hand into the hair over her left ear and pressed her fingertips onto her scalp.

"Do you think we should consider an anti-anxiety medication?" Doctor Daniels leaned against the desk, her long fingers wrapped around the wooden edge.

Ailsa shook her head. "No. I'm tired, stressed about the tour and not sleeping well, but I'm not anxious." She forced a smile, fighting the urge to blurt out her worries for her relationship, the cloying presence that followed her around, nipping at her heels each day.

"O.K. If you're sure." Doctor Daniels dipped her chin, a gesture which reminded Ailsa of her mother.

"I'm sure." She stood up. "Let's get the blood stuff in the works and when I get home I'll come in for a full road-test." Ailsa nodded. "Whatever you give me for the pain can't make me dizzy or knock me out, though. I have to be able to stay clear-headed, and dance." She slid her bag onto her shoulder.

"Of course. Migraine medication won't affect you that way." The doctor circled her desk and leaning down, scribbled on a prescription pad. "Take these at the onset of a headache and then if you can, start keeping a headache journal, note down when they start, if anything specific triggers them etcetera." She held the slip of paper out to Ailsa. "That information will be helpful to the neurologist."

Ailsa took the prescription. "I will." She tucked it into her bag. "Day One. Headache started when I saw the empty coffee jar. Headache escalated when I got drenched on the way to rehearsal. Head exploded when I was hanging upside down in a lift then my partner dropped me." She twisted her face comically.

"Funny lady." The doctor held her hand out.

Ailsa shook it. "Thanks. I'll see you when I get back."

Outside the morning sun was hovering behind lacy clouds and as Ailsa made her way along Broomhill Road, toward her car, she looked up at the sky. She caught her breath at a sharp stab of pain in her eye, so rummaged inside her bag and then slid on her sunglasses.

She and Evan had agreed to invite her parents over from Edinburgh for dinner that evening, and she was looking forward to seeing them. Evan had said he'd make a lasagna if she took care of the rest, and pasta not being Ailsa's forté, she'd gladly agreed.

As she pulled away from the curb, she turned right, heading for the supermarket near Partick Station, and with the radio playing quietly, she focused on the road, pushing her hunched shoulders away from her ears.

Evan had been oddly cheerful that morning so she'd chosen not to tell him she was seeing the doctor. She had mostly stopped telling him about her aches and pains anymore, as it only seemed to irritate him, and while the avoidance of the subject felt unnatural, she didn't have the energy to deal with the alternative.

Jennifer and Colin Campbell rarely came to visit them anymore as, with Ailsa's performance schedule, it was almost impossible to find time to make it happen.

Ailsa's mother, a former ballerina with the Royal Ballet in London, was a no-nonsense woman with strong opinions and a forceful manner, who now taught ballet and devoted hours to charity work. Colin, a successful entrepreneur and paper mill owner, while technically retired, seemed to work just as hard as he ever did consulting for the businesses he'd sold a couple of years earlier.

This evening, Jennifer was on top form, swirling the wine in her glass as she volubly addressed Evan.

"You need to leave the foil on the lasagna for the first forty minutes then take it off for fifteen, so the top browns evenly." She set her glass down then smoothed her butter colored hair, pulled back in a chignon at the base of her elegant neck.

Ailsa noticed Jennifer's diamond earrings catch the candle light as she turned to look at her husband. "Right, Colin?"

The corners of Colin's pale eyes crinkled as he caught Ailsa's gaze across the table.

"I'm not getting in the middle of this." He pulled his chin in. "I never mess with a chef." He glanced at Evan, who was scratching at the linen table cover, and Ailsa noticed her father's brow twitch at his son-in-law's sullen expression.

"It was delicious, Evan." Colin, spoke to Evan's lowered head.

Evan remained silent, his eyes cast down to his lap.

Ailsa reached over and touched his thigh.

"Love, Dad's saying he liked the lasagna."

Evan's leg twitched under her palm, so she pulled her hand back, a prickly sensation creeping across her sternum.

Evan's head snapped up. "Right. Sorry." He met Colin's gaze. "Good, good. It's my mum's recipe." He pushed his chair back and began collecting the plates.

Ailsa stood and picked up her plate.

"Sit down." Evan nodded at the chair. "I'll do this." He took the dish from her hand. "Just talk to your parents."

His correction like a slap to her wrist, Ailsa frowned.

"I can help you." She gathered the napkins as, ignoring her, Evan turned toward the kitchen.

Colin, seeming to sense Ailsa's discomfort, cleared his throat.

"So how long are you away this time, love?"

Ailsa turned to him gratefully.

"Almost five weeks. We're doing Shanghai, Hong Kong, Kuala Lumpur then Singapore."

Colin's eyes glistened. "We'll miss you."

Jennifer, seemingly oblivious to the mounting tension around her, had filled her glass from the water jug.

"So, what's the program?"

Ailsa folded the napkins and stacked them on the table.

"We're doing Sleeping Beauty for the full program then the triple bill includes a new piece, by Simone Mandon, called Color and Form, Gillman's Two Doves and then a contemporary piece called Switch.

"Who choreographed that?" Jennifer sipped her water.

"Mark." Ailsa smiled at her mother. "It's gorgeous. All flowy with lots of lifts." She sat back down. "Steven's such a good partner, I hope I can do him justice." She sucked in her lower lip.

"That's ridiculous." Jennifer snapped. "You are every bit his equal and you need to remember that."

Ailsa's breath hitched at the rebuke, as Jennifer rose from her chair.

Her mother, having lived in the ballet world herself, had steered Ailsa well in many respects, but her constant driving was exhausting, and Ailsa often felt she was neither the master of her own fate nor was she ever quite meeting the impossibly high standards Jennifer set for her.

"If you have the attitude of being less than him, it'll show in your dancing. You must learn to have more confidence, because you've done the work, you've paid your dues and you deserve every role you have." Her mother's eyes flashed.

Ailsa fingered the stack of napkins, waiting for her to finish.

"Ailsa? Did you hear me?"

Ailsa took a steadying breath.

"I could hardly fail to hear you, Mum. I know I've paid my dues, but Steven is a veteran. He's got years of experience on me at this level, and I respect that." She met her mother's eyes. "All I'm saying is that I still have a lot to learn, and he's a great partner for that."

"Well as long as you don't go letting him think he's above you. Ballet partners are like pets, Ailsa. You have to show them who's boss."

At this, Ailsa and Colin laughed simultaneously.

"Oh my God, Mother. Are you serious?" Ailsa stood and walked over to her father, who gently took her hand. "Tell me she's joking, Dad."

"I would, if I knew for sure." Colin smiled up at her.

"Oh, for heaven's sake. You two are such birds of a feather." Jennifer patted the air dismissively. "I didn't mean it like that, exactly. It was just a figure of speech."

This type of tirade was typical of her mother, especially if she'd had one of the rare glasses of wine she allowed herself and, unconvinced by Jennifer's back-pedaling, Ailsa widened her eyes at her.

"You're awful, Mum."

As her mother pursed her lips, Ailsa circled the table to meet Evan coming out of the kitchen with a bowl of berries and a jug of cream on a tray.

"Dessert anyone?" He smiled at them in turn, but Ailsa saw the strain in his face and that his eyes were darting around the room, as if he were being hunted.

EVAN

Ailsa had been gone two weeks and Evan was adjusting to having the flat to himself. The lack of the recent, pervasive tension between them had been a relief, and consequently, he'd twice invited friends over to play cards, happy not to have to consider whether they'd stay too late or be too noisy if she was already sleeping.

This evening he was going to the Curlers Den to meet some of the other developers from work, and the idea that Marie might be among them was causing his heart to skip—a cocktail of excitement and guilt sloshing around in his middle.

As he flicked through the clothes hanging in his wardrobe, he heard the laptop pinging, so grabbing a white shirt, he walked into the living room and settled himself on the sofa.

Ailsa's face materialized and, seeing him, she smiled.

"Hi, love. Glad I caught you." She looked tired. "I've missed speaking to you this past few days."

Evan buttoned the shirt, avoiding her eyes.

"Yeah. I've been putting in some late nights at work, and the time difference is a major pain." He raised his head and looked at his wife. "How are you?"

"Fine. Performances are going well." She nodded. "No disasters so far."

He leaned back and tucked the front of his shirt in.

"Good, good."

She frowned. "Are you going out?"

He stood up, lifting the laptop.

"Yep. Meeting some of the team at the Den for a drink." He set the computer on the dining table and tilted it back so that he was looking down at her. "So, everything's O.K.?" He glanced at his watch.

Ailsa's face fell. "Am I'm keeping you?"

Evan pressed his lips together.

"Don't do that. Don't make me feel bad for going out." He rolled the sleeve of his shirt over twice then repeated the motion on the other side. "It's just a drink or two."

Ailsa seemed to rally.

"No. I'm glad you're going out." She raked her hands through her hair, pulling it into a ponytail which she then released, letting the dark twists cascade over her shoulders. "I'm just tired, I think."

He focused on her face. Her pale eyes were darkly shadowed, as were her cheeks, and he could clearly see the signs of weight loss, all of which made her appear starkly vulnerable. He sat down, pulling the laptop closer.

"Don't over think it. You just need to take care of yourself, Ails. Have a spa day with Amanda, or go to the beach or something." He smiled at her. "You look a bit peaky."

Ailsa's eyes seemed to light up.

"We're off tomorrow, actually. There's a place near the hotel which looks good. We're going to take a yoga class then lie by the pool for a few hours." She smiled. "I miss you."

Evan nodded. "Me too."

"Well, I'd better let you get going to your wild night at the pub." She rolled her eyes. "Drink safely." She put her fingers to her lips and blew him a kiss. "Love you."

The words she deserved to hear stuck in his throat.

"Yeah. Me too. Bye for now."

The pub was busy, a rowdy crowd of students occupying one end of the bar both berating and supporting the two football teams that darted around the pitch on the TV screen. All the tables were occupied and as Evan scanned the room, looking for familiar faces, he spotted the long red hair.

Marie turned just as he approached the table and smiled at him.

His knees loosened and he sank into a chair next to her.

"The lads aren't here yet?" He looked around the room.

"No. I told them half-past so you and I could talk." She laid her hand on top of his, the contact making the hairs on his forearm stand on end. "Want a drink?" She leaned in, and the vanilla scent of her hair made Evan close his eyes.

AILSA

Amanda sat on the lounger next to Ailsa, a tall, frosted glass on the table and an open paperback balanced across her stomach.

Ailsa extended her leg and touched Amanda's calf.

"Hey. Do you want anything to eat?"

Amanda shook her head without opening her eyes.

"No thanks. So many noodles this week, I'm feeling it." She patted her thigh. "Richard will be complaining that I'm a heavy-weight soon." She smiled behind her sun glasses.

The pool on the roof top of their Hong Kong hotel, over-looking Kowloon's Harbor City, was quiet, with only a few other guests sitting under umbrellas, and some children splashing in the shallow end.

The morning heat of June was oppressive and, despite them being under a shaded canopy, it lay like a weight on Ailsa's chest. She'd taken a migraine pill after breakfast, but it was having little effect on the throbbing above her ear that was begin-ning to make her nauseas.

They only had an hour before they'd have to get ready for

class, and a combination of hunger and pre-performance nerves was churning in her stomach.

The location of the hotel was perfect as the Grand Theater, where they were performing, was a walkable distance through the air-conditioned shopping mall that made up part of the City development protruding into the harbor.

She and Amanda had adjoining rooms and had opened the communal door so that they could flit back and forth. Steven and the other company members were scattered along the same floor, and they'd been getting together on their nights off to eat out in the Cultural District, rich with tucked-away venues serving Cantonese delicacies.

The previous evening they'd met up with Steven, Richard, Samantha and a few other members of the Corps and had treated themselves to a lavish dinner in the famous restaurant atop the Hotel Icon, in Tsim Sha Tsui.

The sweeping view of Hong Kong had been breath taking, but Ailsa's had been particularly fascinated by the impressive contemporary art collection that lined the walls. The deep reds of the cast-paper murals, depicting local neighborhoods and stunning cityscapes of Hong Kong, from Victoria peak, had captivated her. As she'd stared at the work, she'd compared it to her own situation as a dancer. As an artist lay their soul on canvas, so a dancer laid their heart on the stage with every step, breath and gesture, presenting themselves to the audience as a gift—open for appreciation, judgment, and even derision.

When Steven had laughed at her slack jaw, she'd blushed.

"Think about it, Steven. There's little less terrifying than opening yourself up to this level of scrutiny. We should take out hats off to the artist, because he or she was brave enough to show the truth of themself like this." She'd pointed at the painting closest to her.

"Wow. I didn't know you were such an art aficionado." He'd poked her ribs.

"Oh, shut it, Owens." Laughing, she'd batted his hand away. "At least I'm not a total Philistine."

At this, Steven had guffawed, just as his boyfriend Jason came up behind them.

"What's going on here?" Jason had flopped down next to Steven and slung an arm around his shoulder.

"A lesson in art appreciation from Ms. MacIntyre." Steven had hugged her close. "She's a woman of many talents, and great depth, you know."

His words, while intended to tease, had been said kindly and she'd leaned in and kissed his freckled cheek.

"Thanks, Steven. I'll take that compliment."

Her head had been, mercifully, less aggravating, allowing her to immerse herself in the light-hearted atmosphere circulating between their tables and as the evening drew to a close, they'd all walked back to the hotel, arm in arm and singing the Sleeping Beauty score, as alarmed locals stepped out of the way and stared at the loud troupe of skinny foreigners making a spectacle of themselves.

Ailsa had laughed so much that her stomach muscles ached and later, when she lay on her bed, while Amanda video chatted with her mother, and her five-year-old daughter, Hayley, Ailsa tried to remember the last time she'd laughed until it hurt. It had been months, and the sad realization made her bite her lip.

Now, as she watched a small boy, perhaps six or seven years old, with tousled black hair and wearing bright green shorts, carefully tugging his sister's arm-floats on for her, she felt a pull of longing. The glare of their sweet little faces being too much for her, she turned on her side.

"Shall we head back?" She poked Amanda's calf again. "It's almost one and I need to get cleaned up."

Amanda stretched theatrically, her slender limbs showing signs of sunburn.

"I suppose so. I said I'd call Hayley again, so we'd better get a move on if I'm going to catch her before we go to class."

The friends packed up their belongings and took the elevator down to their floor. The room was pleasantly cool, and Ailsa lay on her bed letting her flip flops fall to the carpet, then pulled her knees up to her chest, enjoying the comforting stretch in her hips. Beside her, the alarm clock said 1:08 p.m. and as she calculated the time difference with home, she rolled over and grabbed the laptop from the side table.

Before calling, she went into the bathroom, brushed her hair and put some chap-stick on her lips. Her freckles had become more noticeable from lying in the sun and her face looked less sunken than it had recently. Smiling at her reflection, she grabbed the computer and sat on the sofa under the window, overlooking the harbor.

It rang several times before Evan answered. Despite the early hour, he was dressed, wearing a shirt she didn't recognize and his hair looked as if he'd been in a wind tunnel, sticking up on one side in an odd, cone-like shape.

She turned up the volume and smiled at him.

"What've you been up to? You look like you've been running for a bus." She laughed softly.

Evan raked his hair then shifted closer to the screen.

"Just busy doing stuff around here. You know." His voice was odd, as if he was controlling its volume.

As she scrutinized his face, she saw the high color in his cheeks and the beginnings of a four-o-clock shadow, unusual for Evan.

"Growing a beard?" She pulled a face.

"No. God. I just haven't shaved since yesterday." He cupped his chin then rubbed his hand along his jaw. "Gave myself a day off." He smiled. "So, what've you been up to?" His eyes shifted up above the laptop screen, then Ailsa watched him tracking something, a movement of some kind.

"Are you O.K.?" She adjusted the angle of her screen. "You seem weird."

"I'm fine." His eyes flicked down then up again and then, she heard it. If she'd had to guess, she'd have said it was a laugh, soft and muffled.

"What was that?" She leaned in toward the screen, her heart thumping so hard under her bathing costume that she could hear it in her ears.

Evan shook his head. "What?"

"That sound." She paused. "Is someone there?" She stood up, carrying the laptop to the desk across from her bed.

"No. Who would be here?" His face was unreadable, his eyes holding hers. "It's the TV."

Knowing that Evan, who detested watching TV, would likely never turn it on for the entire time she was away, a chill crept down her back and then, she heard the noise again.

"Evan, what's going on?"

At this, he stood up and moved over to the dining table.

"Nothing." He almost hissed, the intensity of his voice startling her. "Can't we even have a chat without some drama or other?" He gave an exaggerated sigh.

He was lying to her, there was no doubt in her mind, and the reality of that made her want to gag. As she watched, he continued to evade her eyes, trying to divert the conversation as one might with an obstreperous child.

"Don't eat all that greasy food. Everything's noodles or fried out there, isn't it?" He coughed into his fist. "And no wine, or night clubbing. Don't let Amanda drag you to those places, because you could twist an ankle or something."

His voice began to fade, slipping beneath the wash of emotions that were flooding her insides, and then it was as if she was falling from the top of a skyscraper, the wind being sucked out of her as she tumbled into emptiness, with nothing to save her from crashing onto the ground below.

The performance that night was a strain, her mind wandering back to the conversation with Evan, the staccato and prickly nature of his denial and their awkward goodbye. Now, as she stood on the stage of the Grand Theater, a full house of 1,700 people watching in the dark, Tchaikovsky's score, rich and melodic with its familiar lilting string melody, floated around her.

As the introduction to the Rose Adagio began, David, the senior principal who was dancing the role of her father, the King, turned to her, bowed gracefully and presented the four Princes from foreign lands, in order that Princess Aurora might chose her future husband.

It was a technically taxing act, demanding extreme control and balance, and yet calling for the youthful, whimsical nature of a sixteen-year-old ingénue. For Ailsa, one of the most challenging aspects of this adagio was moving from Prince to Prince, as each one of them handled her differently and her body must adjust to that with every switch she made between them.

Hearing her cue, she began the lively solo, a short series of neat pas de chat, pirouettes and grands jêtés en tournant as the Princes and the other guests at Aurora's birthday party watched in admiration. Her feet were light, the crisp, precise footwork being one of Ailsa's particular strengths. Then, she curtseyed to the four men and took up her position upstage right and, with her head now throbbing in synch with her heart, Ailsa pressed her eyes closed for a second and summoned her inner strength—she just needed enough to get her through this next couple of hours before she could go back to the hotel and fall apart.

The first Prince, a soloist called Adrian, was by her side. He was tall, wore a long jacket of oriental design and supported her left hand as she unfolded her right leg in a high développé à la seconde, her right arm in a graceful curve above her head. Then she let go of Adrian's supporting hand and held the pose for a second or two before turning to the next Prince. This time it was Richard, with his eyes twinkling under an elaborate turban. She repeated the développé and balance then performed the same combination with the next two Princes, Sasha and Billy, both of whom she'd danced with in various other roles.

Next came the most nerve-racking part for Ailsa. Adrian held her hand as she stepped onto pointe and lifted her left leg into a curved attitude behind her, her other arm rounded in fifth position above her head. Locating her center, she pulled up through her supporting leg, feeling the course of energy, the firing up of every tendon and nerve ending, conducting her body's electricity and momentum like an almighty motherboard.

When she was ready, she blinked at Adrian and released his hand, balancing on her own for one or two seconds until Sasha stepped forward and took Adrian's place, and her outstretched hand. Once again, she found her center, released Sasha's hand when she was ready and held the pose until Billy stepped in. Lastly, Richard repeated the movement with her until Ailsa, awash with relief at having managed this feat of balance, prepared for a pirouette and spun neatly four times, her waist encapsulated by Richard's steadying hands.

As she prepared for the next section, a fiery stab of pain on the left side of her face shattered her concentration. One second was all it took, and she felt the dip of panic as she stepped into a posé coupé turn, then straight into an arabesque, just a moment behind the music. Her supporting leg was quivering, but Sasha was there, his strong hands ready to circle her waist.

Gathering some momentum, she made up the time with Adrian, repeating the steps then dipping into a controlled penché, her body leaning forward as her leg rose behind in counterpoint, her hips the axis for the position.

Ailsa's heart was pattering as she repeated everything with the two remaining Princes, the pain in her face subsiding as she breathed with the music, keeping her eyes on her partners' and the black space that held the audience.

The remainder of the adagio went without incident, Ailsa being given a rose by each Prince before executing several pirouettes with each man supporting her in turn, then her final series of posé turns, cutting a clean diagonal across the stage—each step bringing her closer to the front of the apron.

The last section of the adagio was a grueling repeat of the attitude balances that she'd mastered at the beginning, and as she breathed into each one, searching for that sweet spot, where grace and strength meet balance, she managed to press down all other sensations, even the pain that was building again above her ear.

As she extended her leg into one final, beautifully placed arabesque, relief flooded her limbs as she then stepped back into a graceful curtsey, her work done for the moment.

The audience erupted in noisy applause and Ailsa and her Princes took their bows before exiting the stage—one act down and two to go.

Amanda handed her another tissue. Samantha and Tricia had come into their room for a drink directly after the performance and it had been all Ailsa could do to hold herself together until they'd finally left her and Amanda alone.

Now, Ailsa blew her nose noisily and threw the tissue into the half-full bin.

"I know what I heard. It was a person. A woman." She sniffed. "He had someone there." Her eyes filled again as her throat knotted, choking off further speech.

Amanda shifted closer to her and put her arm around Ailsa's shoulder.

"Look, I know I'm not always his number one fan, but that's a bit of a leap, don't you think?"

Ailsa swallowed, the skin around her eyes beginning to burn.

"Do you think it's possible it actually was the TV? I mean it wouldn't be out of the question, would it?" Amanda was grasping, and Ailsa loved her for it, but a deep sense of foreboding was filling Ailsa's insides.

"He never watches." Her voice hitched. "Hates TV."

Amanda nodded, moving to the top of the bed and leaning her head back against the padded headboard.

"Well, perhaps you need to take a day or so to let things settle down and then call him again. Be calm about it, not all accusatory, just ask him." Her eyes were bright. "What do you think?"

Ailsa shook her head. "I can't do that from here. Something like that, I'd have to do in person." She paused. "Besides, if he could lie to me today, he'd just lie again tomorrow." She folded at the waist, her face planting itself on her thighs.

"Hey. Come on now." Amanda was up and next to her again, easing her upright. "I think you're maybe jumping to conclusions because you've been having a hard time connecting recently." She moved the long curtain of hair away from Ailsa's cheek. "Plus, you're not feeling well. All these headaches, and not sleeping." Amanda handed her the tissue box.

Ailsa pulled a fresh tissue out and wiped her nose. Perhaps Amanda was right. She, Ailsa, could be over reacting. She was simply exhausted, and the headaches were draining her energy so, with all that, plus the hectic travel and performance schedule, she certainly wasn't at her most together.

She turned to her friend, mustering a watery smile.

"Thanks. I know you're probably right." She nodded. "I'll try to put a lid on it until I can talk to him, when I get home." She crumpled the tissue into a ball. "Evan might be a grumpy git these days, and yes, a bit of a control freak…"

Amanda's eyebrows jumped, then she rolled her eyes.

"But he wouldn't be unfaithful." Ailsa said it out loud, the statement more for her own benefit than Amanda's.

AILSA

Over the five days they'd spent in Kuala Lumpur, and the eight in Singapore, their last stop on the tour, Ailsa had struggled to talk to Evan and not refer to their odd call. Consequently, their conversations had been subdued and often days apart.

She'd tried to focus on what Amanda had said about there being other possible explanations for what she'd heard, but the odd sound in the background that day kept filtering through her mind.

As her stress level had increased, along with her consistent headaches, the music she was dancing to had begun to sound odd —the notes stretching, sometimes distorting so much that she found it hard to find the melody. The sensation wasn't constant, but when it happened it was frightening and disconcerting, so much so that she'd missed a couple of cues. Despite being shaken by what was happening, she'd chosen not to mention it to anyone, especially not Amanda, who was already worried about her.

Now, they were finally headed home, and she sat with Steven and Jason, in a busy bar at Changi airport, nursing the remains of a glass of wine. The noise around them was the typical airport meld of voices, unintelligible P.A. announcements, the distant rumble of aircraft landing and taking off and a dated musical sound track playing behind everything. The combination was proving a distraction to Ailsa, who's head was thumping at a six-out-of-ten on the pain scale.

She sipped her wine and winced as a child behind her let out a high-pitched squeal, the noise sending a needle of pain into her temple.

Oblivious to her discomfort, Steven was slouched on the dark leather sofa opposite her, his arm slung around Jason's shoulder.

"So, when are we going to have another shin-dig at your place?" Steven grinned at her. "You and Evan used to throw the best parties."

Jason nodded, his olive skin and thatch of black hair in sharp contrast to Steven's fair, freckled complexion.

"Everyone says that." Jason nodded. "But I've yet to be invited to one." He pulled his mouth down at the corners.

Ailsa set her glass on the table.

"You know, we haven't had any parties since you joined the company Jason, I don't think." She frowned. "God, it's been years actually, now that you mention it."

Jason pouted. "Well perhaps it's time you resurrected the tradition. Maybe when we get back?"

Steven patted Jason's thigh.

"He's not backward at coming forward, is he?" He smiled at Jason, then rolled his eyes at Ailsa. "Can't take him anywhere."

Steven's phone buzzed on the table, so he leaned forward and picked it up.

"Oh, it's my little sister. Seems like she might be in labor." He grinned, tapped a response and then showed the screen to Jason. "I hate being away when this sort of stuff happens." His expression clouded slightly as he shifted back in the seat. "But, Uncle Steven. I like the sound of that."

Ailsa smiled at him, imagining him playing horse with a small, fair haired child riding on his back. The image was incongruous with the disciplined, laser focused professional sitting opposite her. Her expression obviously giving her away, Steven was looking at her quizzically.

"What? Can't see me as uncle of the year?" His eyes held hers, his amusement evident.

"No, it's not that." She blinked. "I was just picturing it, actually."

As they were finishing their drinks, Amanda appeared in the bar. She waved, wove through the mess of occupied tables around them then flopped down next to Ailsa.

"God, I'm exhausted." She reached for Ailsa's glass. "Can I have the rest of this?"

Ailsa nodded. "Sure. I'm done."

Amanda drained the glass and checked her watch.

"When are we boarding?"

Steven spun around to check the board behind him.

"Nothing showing yet, but it shouldn't be long now."

Amanda settled herself on the sofa, pulling her bag onto her knee. She rifled through the contents then pulled out a sweet-faced doll in a fuchsia colored silk, traditional Singaporean dress.

"Look what I got for Hayley." She waved the doll at Ailsa. "Do you think she'll like it?"

Ailsa nodded, picturing Amanda's daughter, the curly head, the clear blue eyes, duplicates of her mother's, the smattering of freckles across the plump cheeks, resembling a precious doll herself.

"She'll love it." She smiled. "Guaranteed."

~

48

Evan was waiting for her at the arrivals area of Glasgow airport. Ailsa spotted him leaning against a wall across the concourse as she and Amanda walked through the glass doors.

Ailsa halted her progress and reached for Amanda's hand.

"He's here." She focused on his familiar outline, head dropped forward as he checked his phone.

Amanda squeezed her fingers.

"It'll be fine. Just breathe and don't dive in right away. O.K.?" She gently tugged Ailsa's hand back. "Give it a day or so before you bring it up." She met Ailsa's gaze. "Yes?"

Ailsa nodded. "O.K., Mum." She flashed Amanda a smile. "Call me tomorrow?"

Amanda nodded. "For sure."

Evan saw her approaching and as he broke into a grin, a wash of relief allowed her to exhale. As she dragged her bag behind her, he came toward her, arms wide.

"Hi, love. Welcome home." His long arms enveloped her, her face meeting the front of his jacket which smelled of coffee. She hugged him tightly then leaned back to take in his face. He looked well, a faint glow in his cheeks, his hair slightly longer than he usually kept it and his eyes bright as they focused on hers.

"It's good to be back." She stood on tiptoe to kiss him.

His mouth on hers, taut, almost reserved, instantly re-released the butterfly wings under her breast bone. *Stop it, Ailsa. Stop.* She tried to keep her voice even.

"Everything O.K.?"

He nodded, stepping back from her.

"Fine, fine." He took her bag in one hand and lightly held her fingers in the other. "The car's over here." He guided her toward the exit. "So, are you tired? How was the flight? It's been mad here. Work's a bitch at the moment. I feel like I live at the office." He paused, then forced a laugh. "I might as well have a camp bed over there."

As the door opened and they stepped outside the terminal building, the flash of cold made Ailsa catch her breath. The twilight was dim, a film of grey cloud cover making the sky appear opaque.

"God, it's chilly." She huddled in toward his side. "Scotland in June, eh?" Their laughter melded as he steered her on.

Evan was animated, plying her with questions but not waiting for her to answer any of them, so she let him talk and lead her through the rows of cars, the warmth of his hand reassuring. Normally, she'd have been the one talking ten to the dozen, volunteering information about her trip, the tour, imparting the most recent company gossip, but instead she let the cadence of his mood be her guide.

In the car, he was cracking jokes, weaving through traffic, his chatter non-stop as Ailsa, feeling the drag of fatigue, just nodded, interjecting with the odd 'oh yes' or 'that's great' until they reached home.

Once inside, he carried her bags to the bedroom as she dumped her coat in the hallway then flipped through some mail he'd left stacked for her on the table.

"Want me to make you something to eat?" He was standing in the hallway, his hands rammed into the pockets of his jeans causing his shoulders to rise, reminding Ailsa of the stance of a small boy, unsure of himself. She'd been away over a month, and there was always a short, getting-to-know-you phase when she got home after such a long tour. This was nothing more than that.

She shook her head. "No thanks. I'm shattered. I think I'll just have a shower and go to bed, if you don't mind?"

He walked toward her.

"Not at all, love. You do whatever you feel like." He took both her hands in his. "I'll make something for myself, then slip in later." He bent down and kissed her cheek. "I'll try not to wake you."

"Love you." She watched his face, a trace of something she couldn't identify crossing behind his eyes.

"Yep. Me too." He was already walking into the kitchen.

~

Having tossed her clothes into the laundry hamper then stood under the thundering shower until her taut muscles began to relax, Ailsa turned off the taps. Stepping out of the tub, she rubbed herself dry with a towel and was instantly struck by a strange smell coming from the soft cotton, a heady, almost cloying vanilla scent. Frowning, she held the towel up to her nose and inhaled. The idea that Evan had bought a new laundry detergent was unlikely, but this unfamiliar scent was somehow unsettling.

Her heart began to quicken as she pulled on her robe and tipped her head upside down to shake out her hair. As she raked her fingers through the tangled fronds, in the corner of her eye she caught a flash of purple on the floor behind the toilet. Righting herself, she reached down and picked up an elastic hairband with long, red hairs tangled around it. She stared at the band, as a bizarre swooshing sound filled her ears. Then a rush of heat moved up from her stomach, creeping across her chest to her face as she grasped the edge of the sink.

Her thoughts took flight, the worst kind of dark fantasies that she'd been denying ever since she'd first heard the odd sound, that damned sound that had started to invade her dreams. Suddenly the hairband became caustic on her palm, so she tossed it onto the floor. As her mind teemed with images of Evan, with a faceless redhead, that made her want to vomit, she heard a sound, an animalistic, guttural cry.

As she tried to take a breath, she caught sight of herself in the mirror. Her mouth was open and distorted, her skin scarlet, her wet hair stuck to her face, and as she tried desperately to focus on what she was seeing, she heard the cry again, coming from her own throat.

As realization prickled along her limbs, so the towel she had just used became toxic. She kicked it across the floor, her hands shaking so badly she could hardly manage to tie her robe around herself. Then, the tears rushed in and as she slid to the floor, a mass of hurt trapped her against the cold tiles as she gasped for air.

She wasn't sure how long she'd been sitting there when Evan knocked at the door.

"What's going on in there?" He tapped again. "I heard a weird noise."

She tried to steady her breathing, her heart threatening to split through her breast bone as his voice, urgent, concerned, made her want to scream.

"Ailsa?" He banged the door loudly. "Are you O.K.?"

She rolled onto her knees and pulling herself up against the bath tub, sat on the edge, her damp hair cascading around her shoulders. Her breaths were coming in short bursts, the pain in her head pulsing in time with them. One, and two, three and four, she counted, trying to slow them down.

"Ailsa. What the hell's going on in there?" He sounded angry now and the edge in his voice was like a shot of adrenaline. She stood up and, shoving her hair away from her face, opened the door.

"Jesus, you had me worried." He looked flushed. "What's wrong?" He frowned and reached for her. "Are you ill?"

Ailsa snatched her arm away and locked her eyes on his. From some inner font she found the strength to control her voice, and spoke quietly and deliberately.

"No, Evan I'm not ill, but I do feel sick, now that you ask."

His face turned ashen and he stepped back as if she'd slapped him, then shoved his hands deep into his pockets.

"What do you mean?"

Ailsa slid past him and walked into the bedroom, her heart thumping wildly. He followed her, keeping a few paces behind, and as she sat on the edge of the bed, he leaned his back against the door frame then quickly stood upright again, as if the wood had scalded him.

"I found a hairband in the bathroom." She kept her eyes on his, hers steady and, for now, dry.

He shifted his weight to one hip and shook his head, but his face told her everything she didn't already know.

"Who is she, Evan." Ailsa re-tucked the robe across her chest, the thought of being exposed in front of him, nauseating.

Evan stepped to the side, his mouth working on itself but no sound coming out.

"Evan?" She shifted on the bed, grabbing the duvet into her fists, the seconds ticking by like the countdown to an execution.

Finally, he cleared his throat and moved toward her.

"Stay away, please." She held up her palm. "Just tell me who she is, and how long." As a half-formed thought clarified itself, she released her grip on the duvet and jumped up, tugging the edges of the robe tightly at her throat. "Christ. She's been in here too, hasn't she?"

In a second she had crossed the distance between them and with her free hand in a fist, thumped his chest.

"How could you do this to us?" Tears were blinding her, the saline seeping in between her open lips. "I can't believe you, Evan." She gasped for breath. "You total shit."

Evan grabbed her fist, his hand like a great bear-paw encapsulating hers.

"Stop it, Ailsa. Just take a breath, will you?" He held her firmly until she jerked away from his grip. "Calm down and we can talk." He looked down at her as a parent might on a child having a tantrum in the shopping mall.

"Don't speak to me like that. I'm done with you telling me what to do." She swiped at her nose with the back of her hand.

"You've given up that right." She jerked a thumb behind her. "When you brought her here, to our home, into our bed, you lost that right."

Evan's hand went to the back of his neck as he watched her, as if girding himself for the next hit.

"It wasn't like that. It's not like that." His eyes were darting around the room. "You make it sound so…" He stopped.

"So what? Calculated? Dirty?" Ailsa sniffed.

Evan was shaking his head as Ailsa, desperate to cover herself, grabbed a pair of sweat pants from the chest of drawers and pulled them on under the robe. Turning her back on him she put on a T-shirt and yanked a sweatshirt from the cupboard.

When she turned to face him, Evan was still standing in the same spot, his socked feet frozen to the floorboards.

As she raked her hair back into a pony tail, her fingers felt numb so she released the wet twists and shook her hands out, willing the blood to flow back into them. Her headache was now reaching a crescendo, a nine-out-of-ten on the pain scale, but she didn't have time for that kind of pain right now. She had something much more insidious that was eating her up, from the inside out.

She took a deep breath.

"You have to tell me what happened. Evan, look at me please."

He lifted his chin and met her gaze.

"Do you work with her?"

He nodded.

"Have I met her?" Bile surged into the back of her throat.

"No. She just started a few months ago. She's a developer." He moved toward the door, as if looking for an escape.

"What's her name?" Ailsa lifted her robe from the floor and began folding it, a reflex that once she'd started felt ludicrous under the circumstances.

"Ailsa." He held a hand out to her.

"What's her bloody name?" She tossed the robe onto the bed.

"Marie." He swiped a hand across his mouth. "Her name's Marie."

Ailsa heard the name, played with it for a few seconds, imagining a winsome redhead, all arms and legs, wearing a cheesecloth skirt and running theatrically through a meadow.

Despite herself, she laughed, then despising herself for caring, she blurted.

"What's she like? Some ethereal, waif type?" Her voice cracked.

"No. She's nothing like you..." He instantly looked alarmed by what he'd said, his eye's widening as she pushed past him and moved along the narrow hall to the living room, her heart ripping a little more with every step.

"I'm not staying here." She lifted her handbag from the sofa and searched for her phone.

"Where are you going?" He was close behind her, his proximity making her skin crawl.

"To Amanda's." She searched for the number and with a quivering finger hit the call button.

"Don't go. We need to talk." He held a hand out, then, seeing her expression, dropped it to his side.

She shook her head as Amanda's voicemail kicked in and, trying to keep her voice steady, she spoke.

"Hey, it's me. I need you to call me back as soon as you can. O.K.? Please call me back." She hung up and set the phone on the coffee table.

"Ailsa, please."

"What's there to talk about?"

Heat pulsed across her back, so she tugged off the sweatshirt. Her head was pounding at a nine on the scale and the image of thick blood, coursing through her veins, made her blink, the thumping of her heart pushing her pain toward a ten.

"It didn't mean anything." Evan's use of the well-worn cliché made her wince.

"How long?"

He frowned. "Why?"

"How long, Evan?" She shouted.

"A couple of months." He licked his lips.

"How many times have you brought her here?" She fanned the room with her palm.

"A couple." His chin dipped and finally she saw what looked like shame.

He shifted his feet. "Three. O.K? Three times." His voice was low.

Ailsa nodded, letting the information percolate. Three times this bitch had been in her home, contaminating it with her presence, and as she looked around the space that had once been her sanctuary, the devastating sense of loss made it hard to breathe.

"It's all gone." She blinked to clear her vision. "Everything we built. Everything we dreamed about, fought for, together. You've destroyed it all." She forced a swallow. "I hope it was worth it, Evan."

Evan moved toward her and this time she has no energy to bat him off. He reached for her hand.

"I'm sorry. I'm so in the wrong." His voice was thick with emotion. "I don't ..." He stopped. "I'm sorry."

Spent, she slid her hand from his and looked up at the dark eyes that had held her heart for so many years.

"I can't be here anymore."

Evan tried to take her hand again just as her phone rang. She picked it up, moved past him and headed for the bedroom.

"What's going on?" Amanda sounded out of breath.

Ailsa's throat clamped shut and all she could manage was a strangled cough.

"Ailsa?"

"Can I come?" Ailsa forced the words out, willing herself not to cry again.

"Come here? Of course. When?"

"Now." She was pulling some clean clothes out of the cupboard, absently shoving them into the bag that was as yet unpacked from her trip.

"Right now?" Amanda sounded shocked.

"Yes. Now."

"Absolutely. Do you need me to come and get you?"

"Yeah." Ailsa nodded in the silent room.

"I'll be there in half an hour. Just hang tight, O.K.?" Her friend's gentle voice was threatening to make her lose control all over again.

"Thank you." Ailsa choked out the words.

EVAN

E van sat on the sofa, the emptiness of the room like a tight band around his chest. Ailsa had left a couple of hours earlier and he still hadn't moved, frozen to the spot and letting the room darken around him.

Their confrontation had been brutal, and shocking. Not that he'd ever have been ready for the way she looked at him, the cold fury and then the raw heartbreak he'd seen in her eyes.

He'd always been able to talk her around, smooth her feathers, but this thing he'd done was bigger and more destructive than anything he'd ever done in his life, and he'd not only done it to her, but to himself.

The clock on the mantle chimed ten times and the metallic sound snapped him out of his stupor. Pushing himself up on leaden legs, he shuffled into the kitchen, filled a glass with water and drained it before filling it again. With the fresh glass, he went back into the living room and switched on the overhead light.

Unsure why he was checking, he picked up his phone and stroked the screen. No messages. Not surprised, he tossed it onto the sofa and paced across to the wide window that overlooked the garden behind the building. In the dark of the night he could barely make out the outlines of the trees, the lighter color of the footpath that wound around the edges of the small area of grass, and the shape of the wooden bench where Ailsa liked to sit and read in the warmer weather. The thought of her out there, a long scarf draped over her shoulders and her head buried in a book on anatomy, or some dancer's biography, brought a lump to his throat.

He pulled the heavy curtains closed and walked over to the drinks cabinet. Taking out the bottle of Caol ila he poured himself a double measure then sank back onto the sofa. Once again, he leaned over and checked his phone and seeing the flashing symbol for a missed call, his heart skipped. Grabbing it up he typed in his password and saw that his mother had called, most likely checking that Ailsa had made it home safely.

The thought of Diana, his sweet-natured mother, ever learning what he had done made him close his eyes. She would be thoroughly ashamed of him and, if she knew the truth, he suspected she might take Ailsa's side over his, she adored her daughter-in-law that much. At this precise moment, beneath his guilt and shame, Evan was grateful that his father, Michael, a stalwart family man, having passed away fifteen years earlier, was no longer around to see the mess his son had made.

Rather than call Diana back, he typed a quick text: *She's home safe. Will call tomorrow.*

Once he'd hit send he saw a new text flash up, surprised to see that it was from Amanda. There were three words, stark on the screen: *YOU STUPID FUCK!!!*

BOOK TWO

Glasgow, August 2019

AILSA

When Ailsa had gone back to the flat to pick up a few more of her belongings, she and Evan had spent a steely half hour together. He'd asked her to stay, but as quickly as she could manage it, with a couple of bags of clothes, toiletries and her laptop, she had made for the door.

"Can't we please talk?" He'd looked disheveled, her eyes drawn to the splotch of something red on the front of his shirt.

"I can't, Evan."

As she'd turned to leave, he'd called after her.

"Can we at least agree not to let our parents know what's going on? Not yet, anyway." He'd sounded nervous.

As she'd considered the fall out of her mother finding out, Ailsa had simply nodded.

"Fine. For now." She'd left him standing in the hall as she'd bumped her bags along the outside corridor and across the street to her car.

She had been staying with Amanda for six weeks now, sleeping on an air mattress on the floor in Hayley's little room.

Their hectic class and rehearsal schedule, and planning around Hayley's needs, had left little time for the two friends to do much more than get through the packed days, and their performances at night.

Hayley lived part time with her father in Dundee and the rest in Glasgow, with Amanda. Amanda's mother, Sally, helped care for Hayley and stayed at the flat with her granddaughter whenever Amanda was on tour. Since Ailsa had moved in, Sally had come over several times and much to Ailsa's relief had refrained from asking too many questions about what was going on at home. Ailsa presumed that Amanda had brought Sally up to date and asked her to be discreet, which was yet another reason to be grateful to Amanda.

Ailsa had taken on as much of Hayley's care as she could manage with her schedule, and the two had become even closer. As Hayley's Godmother, she'd always felt a special connection to the little girl but the past few weeks had deepened their bond considerably, with Ailsa finding time to take Hayley to the park across the street, doing her hair for her and reading to the child until she fell asleep in her arms.

Amanda would often come in the morning to find Hayley asleep next to Ailsa, on the air mattress, her daughter's blond curls mingled with Ailsa's dark tresses—a piebald rope draped over the pillow case as the book they'd been reading lay abandoned on the floor.

Now, on one of their rare nights off, they sat on Amanda's bed with Hayley sandwiched between them, the TV flickering in the dimly lit room. Hayley's two toy ponies were wrapped in tea towels and she was trotting them up and down her thighs as Amanda sipped her cocoa.

"He's a wanker." Amanda silently mouthed the third word, grimacing at Ailsa over the top of her daughter's head. "You need to do what's best for you now."

Ailsa nodded, stroking the floral duvet cover, her cup of cocoa going cold next to her. Over the weeks she'd been staying with Amanda, Ailsa had spoken to Evan several times and while

Amanda knew that she'd been in touch with him, and that he'd been asking her to meet him, she hadn't told Amanda how frequently he'd been calling.

Deep inside, beneath the mess of pain and anger, Ailsa missed her husband and the life they'd built. The threads that held them together, while shredded, weren't severed yet and even though she had not forgiven him, the time apart had made her think about her own actions and what, if anything, she might have done to cause this. But, as she tried to find reasons to make allowances, to even begin to forge forgiveness, she was reminded of how dismissive he'd been when she'd tried to tell him what she was feeling.

Now, as she stared at the TV screen, the whole thing felt like some colossal fugue of screwed-up events, a self-perpetuating melody where one misunderstanding had sprouted another, and another, until they weren't seeing or hearing each other at all. While she wouldn't take on responsibility for what he'd done, she did recognize that she'd changed toward him and that, if nothing else, was keeping the door in her heart open to him.

Amanda set her cup down, making Ailsa jump.

"Hayley, love, you need to go to bed now. It's really late." She stroked a gilded curl out of the little girl's eyes.

"No. I want to wait for Aunty Ailsa to come too." Hayley looked at Ailsa, her pastel eyes beseeching.

"No, darling. Mummy and Aunty Ailsa have grown up things to talk about. I'll tuck you in." Amanda eased off the bed and held her hand out to her daughter. "Come on, munchkin. I'll read you Peter Rabbit, if you like?"

Hayley pouted, but awkwardly slid off the bed with a pony still gripped in each hand.

"Can I have marshmallows?" She looked up at her mother.

"No. You've already cleaned your teeth," Amanda cooed. "Tomorrow, O.K.?"

Hayley nodded and at the door turned back toward Ailsa.

"Night night."

Ailsa's heart swelled.

"Good night, Pickle. I'll come in and kiss you soon." She waved as Hayley's tousled head disappeared through the door.

A few minutes later, Amanda came back in and flopped onto the bed.

"So, what are you going to do?" She leaned her head back against the headboard. "Are you going to see him?"

Ailsa considered the weighted question, twisting a strand of hair around her finger. Whatever she decided, and whatever happened with her marriage in the future, for now, Evan was still her husband. Avoiding him, while easier on her soul, wasn't going to fix anything.

"I think I'll have to, at some point." She licked her lips. "I can't pretend he doesn't exist for ever."

Amanda was scowling. "I could. Very easily."

Seeing Amanda's exaggerated expression, Ailsa felt a bubble of humor rising, something that had been comatose within her for weeks. She reached over and poked Amanda's cheek.

"You are the best, and you crack me up, but I can't hide any longer and, I can't sleep in Hayley's room until I retire." She smiled at Amanda's look of surprise. "I need to face the pile of doo-doo that is my life, and sort it out."

As Ailsa considered what the next day held, and when she might have time to meet Evan, she mentally ran through everything she had to do: ballet class early in the morning, then a meeting with Mark to talk about the October tour in the States, followed by an appointment with the company chiropractor, whom she'd been seeing for months now but who'd been unable to help with the headaches. Then, they had a rehearsal of Romeo and Juliet for a few hours, leaving her just enough time to dash back to Amanda's flat for something to eat and a quick shower before heading into the theater for the performance of Swan Lake. As her tightly-packed schedule raced through her mind, Ailsa felt the squeeze of it all like manacles on her wrists.

She came alive while dancing, loving the freedom she felt inside the movements, being at one with her limbs, the music, and the floor beneath her, but the other elements of her life as a performer were beginning to wear her down. Aside from the incredible physical demands of her job, she lived with the constant fear that she might falter somehow, become injured, begin to slip just enough to let someone new, younger and stronger, into her precarious slot. The pressure of this brutally competitive business was taking its toll and recently, to her surprise, she'd begun resenting it.

Sometimes, when she was in class, watching all the newbies —hopeful young dancers with wide eyes and an endless supply of shiny ambition—she'd try to pinpoint the one, the dancer who'd eventually take over her position in the company, one role at a time, letting her step back to where she could dance simply for the love of it, as she once had. The prospect, while making her nervous, wasn't entirely unwelcome anymore.

Turning to her friend, Ailsa spoke quietly.

"Amanda, do you ever think about doing something else?"

Amanda's eyebrows jumped. "Something else?"

Seeing her friend's expression, Ailsa backtracked.

"Oh, never mind. I'm just tired."

Amanda shrugged, then slumped down against her pillows.

As Ailsa sat in the quiet room, a shard of pain zapped across the left side of her face making her wince. She sat up straight and circled her neck, feeling the familiar grind at the base of her skull.

Oddly, since being with Amanda and Hayley, the headaches had been somewhat less frequent, something that Amanda had noticed and had vocally attributed to the lack of Evan, in Ailsa's daily routine.

While scared to admit it, Ailsa had been tempted to agree

until the previous afternoon when she'd had an almighty eight on the pain scale, this time accompanied by the sound of whooshing, like waves breaking in her ear. It had rocked her so much that she'd left rehearsal and gone outside, her sweaty back pressed up against the wall of the studio as she'd tried to breathe through the mire of pain and unnerving noise in her head.

Mark had come outside, startling her.

"God, you scared me." She'd batted his arm, playfully.

Obviously not taken in, he'd put a manicured hand on each of her shoulders, his grey eyes brimming with concern.

"Darling, what's wrong?" "Are you injured?" He'd scanned her body like an X-ray machine, his immaculate salt-and-pepper hair not moving in the breeze that was cooling Ailsa's prickling skin.

"No. I'm O.K. Just tired." The lie had tasted bitter. Mark was more than her director, he was her mentor and friend, and he deserved better from her.

He had lingered for a few moments until Hélène had popped her head out of the door asking him to weigh in on something, mercifully saving Ailsa from further questions.

Now, she slid her fingers into her hair and pressed her scalp, her nails sharp against the skin above her ear. The surge of adrenaline that often accompanied the pain in her head made her skin tingle as she recalled having cancelled the MRI appointment Dr. Daniels had arranged for her. The doctor had sounded worried, but Ailsa had stuck her heels in saying that she'd reschedule in a few weeks, when things settled down. As distracted as she was with everything going on at home, the last thing she needed was to find out that there was something more serious going on than just stress. Despite her wish to banish these headaches once and for all, she was terrified to face whatever truth her body was trying to communicate. No, for now, denial was all she could manage.

Amanda's brow was wrinkling as she reached out and squeezed Ailsa's arm.

"Suffering again?"

Ailsa shook her head.

"Not too bad. Manageable tonight." She let her hand drop and her head rest against the headboard. "I think I have to call Evan back." She closed her eyes, waiting for Amanda to protest. Instead, she heard her friend sigh.

"Yeah. I suppose so."

As Ailsa heaved herself up from the bed, a loud knock at the front door made them both jump.

Amanda's eyes narrowed as she slid from the bed, grabbing her robe.

"Who the hell's that, at this time of night?"

Ailsa shrugged, picking up the cup of cold cocoa, and following her friend out into the hall. As she hovered behind Amanda, Ailsa recognized the dark outline through the glass panel of the door. Her heart skipped a couple of times and her voice caught in her throat as she whispered, "God. It's Evan."

EVAN

E van sat on the sofa in Amanda's living room. It was chilly
and the smell of whatever spicy dish they'd cooked for
dinner lingered in the house.

The contempt he'd seen in Amanda's eyes when she'd
opened the door, and the protective way she'd positioned herself
between him and Ailsa, her hands on her hips and her chin
raised, had made his skin prickle.

"What are you doing here?" Amanda had glared at him.

Ailsa had moved out from behind her friend then and laid a
hand on Amanda's arm.

"It's O.K." She'd seemed calm. "Let him come in."

Amanda had huffed then shoved the heavy door open to the
living room.

"You can go in there." She'd pointed, then turned to Ailsa.
"Are you sure?" Amanda's back had been to Evan, but he'd felt
the anger emanating from the narrow shoulders.

"Yes. I'm fine." Ailsa had nodded. "Thanks."

She'd looked at Evan. "Give me a few minutes."

Relieved, he'd stepped inside the dark living room and patted
the wall to locate the light switch.

Ten minutes later he was still waiting for Ailsa to come back. His knees bounced as he clasped his hands between them and his eyes were gritty from lack of sleep. Since Ailsa had left, he'd been waking up at odd hours, wandering around the flat and reading into the wee hours of the morning. Now, frustrated at being made to wait, just as he was about to go find her, Ailsa appeared dressed in jeans, and a sweatshirt he didn't recognize.

"Hi." He stood up. "Sorry for just turning up, but you weren't calling me back about getting together and I…"

She held her hand up.

"I know. I wanted to call when I was ready." Her face looked drawn. "But here you are, so…" She walked past him and sat on the armchair, crossing her legs under herself. "It's late, Evan. What do you want?"

Evan felt his face warming, this situation that had made sense to him an hour earlier now seeming rather melodramatic. He took in her expression, closed off, almost impassive.

"We need to figure out what to do."

At this, she leaned forward, her elbows on her knees.

"We don't need to figure out anything. *I* need to figure out what I'm going to do next." Her eyes flashed. "As far as what you do, it doesn't concern me."

Her words struck his chest like darts, making him lean back.

"Ailsa, I'm sorry. I'll say it a million times if I have to." He rubbed his hands down his thighs, the denim feeling tacky under his damp palms.

She shook her head, the small movement all but imperceptible.

"I'm sorry too." Her words promised to release the knot of guilt hovering under his diaphragm until he saw her eyes. "I'm sorry you felt the need to tear us apart, for the sake of a screw or two."

Evan shifted on the sofa, crossing and re-crossing his legs, then mustering his resolve, he tried again.

"Don't talk like that." He eyed her. "You can't just toss all the blame into my lap and turn your back on us."

Ailsa made a sound he'd never heard before, a cross between a harsh laugh and snort, as she unfolded her legs and stood up. "I know I'm not perfect. I've made my share of mistakes." She paused, "But whatever the cause, Evan, you need to own what you did." She walked to the fireplace and began shifting the figures in Hayley's frog collection around on the mantle. "Until you do, I don't know what else there is to say."

He shuffled through the various scenarios he'd imagined, how this conversation would unfold, but none of the arguments he'd practiced in the car on the way over felt as if they had any teeth now. Steeling himself for the inevitable, he stood up and faced her.

"O.K. I own it. I fucked up, royally." He pulled his hands out, palms up. "But we need to try to fix this, Ailsa. Not just abandon everything we've built together." He saw a flicker of acknowledgement in her eyes. "We've made it through all your work challenges, sacrificed so much to get you to the very top of your career, and we did that together. We've a shared history, more than a decade together. We've got a lovely home, a good life. That's worth something." He paused, trying to get a gauge on her thinking. "It's you and me against the world, Ails. Always has been." He gave her a half smile, raking his hair away from his forehead.

She pulled the sleeves down on her sweatshirt, her hands disappearing inside the bulky fabric as she stepped back from him, her cheeks now rosy. She held his gaze, chewing on the inside of her cheek.

"Come home, love. Let's at least try." He stepped carefully toward her. "I deserve that much, don't I?" He reached for her hand but she pulled back. Afraid he was losing the tentative ground he'd gained just moments before, he whispered. "We owe it to ourselves, don't we?"

Ailsa lifted her hand and bit at the skin around her thumb. Her eyes were darting from his face to the door, the lids flickering as if she was watching some kind of internal movie. She remained silent, so Evan seized the moment and gently moved her hand away from her mouth.

"We love each other, Ailsa. You know that's true." He brushed some hair away from her eye. "Let's try to get back to that."

She let her fingers linger for a few moments in his then she stepped away from him.

"Why would I come home? What's to say you won't just do the same thing again." Her eyes glistened. "Every time I'm at work, on stage, away on tour, I'll be wondering whether you're with her." She jabbed a thumb over her shoulder. "The trust is shattered. I'm shattered." She pressed a palm to her chest and her voice broke. Seeing his moment, he lunged forward and wrapped his arms around her. To his relief, rather than pull away she leaned into his chest, her hand gripping his sweater, as the sobs came. "You chose her." She hiccupped. "You chose."

The truth of her words weighed heavy on him as he patted her bony back.

As her crying gradually subsided, feeling his power returning, Evan maneuvered her into a chair then went to the kitchen to get her a glass of water. When he came back into the room, she was standing at the window, her cheeks flushed but dry.

He held the glass out to her, but she shook her head.

"Listen to me." She spoke quietly. "The only way I'd even consider coming back is if we go to marriage counselling first." She folded her arms across her chest.

Evan frowned. This was a twist he had not anticipated.

"Counselling?"

She nodded.

"You know what I think about all that stuff." He set the glass down on the coffee table.

Ailsa stood her ground, her eyes fixed on his.

"That's the only way I'll even talk about coming back. I'm serious." She widened her legs, her stance now reminiscent of a miniature super hero.

Trying not to smile at the image, Evan nodded. "O.K. then. I submit. We'll go to bloody counselling if that's what you want."

Ailsa's eyebrows jumped. "Really?"

Evan nodded, knowing he was beaten. "Said so, didn't I?"

She bit her bottom lip then lifted her chin. "Right."

Testing the waters, he smiled at her. "Will you come home now?"

She shook her head. "No. If I come, it'll be when I'm ready."

Her eyes had dark shadows under them and seeing her painfully thin frame, drowned by the baggy top, Evan felt a twinge of concern.

"How are you feeling?" He frowned. "You've lost weight."

She twisted her hair into a rope at the back of her neck. "I'm fine."

She turned back toward the fireplace, tugging at the front of the sweatshirt.

"So, when will you come?" He pressed her, reluctant to leave without something concrete agreed between them. "Tomorrow?"

Ailsa turned to him, her eyes clear, her mouth resolute.

"When I'm ready."

Evan drove through the dark streets, a driving rain now making it hard to see. His neck was stiff and his stomach rumbled loudly as he steered past a parked car, and as he considered the success of his mission, he allowed himself a moment of triumph. Ailsa had as good as agreed to come back, and if counselling was the carrot that he had to dangle, then so be it. If he knew his wife, she'd be happy if they went to a few sessions and then he was sure she'd be home by the end of the month.

If he wanted to keep hold of the life they'd created, and retain the status and acknowledgement that went with it, there could be no more mistakes on his part so, he'd have to make it clear to Marie, that they were done. Even as he thought about her, the lustrous hair, the rowdy laugh, the long, shapely legs, this intoxicating woman who was the living antithesis to his waif-like wife, Evan felt the loss of Marie like a bereavement, and the flash of pain it gave him took him aback.

AILSA

A month later, September had crept in and Ailsa had been back at the flat for a few days. She'd moved into the spare room and was spending much of her time at work, either performing or rehearsing for the impending U.S. tour.

While things were tense when they were both at home, Evan had been making a marked effort—cooking for her when she came back late, doing the laundry and offering to come and pick her up so she wouldn't have to drive when she was tired. Ailsa was giving him credit for the gestures, but it still stung every time she imagined him with Marie.

Ailsa had located a marriage counsellor, nearby on Douglas Road. A willowy brunette, around fifty years old, Deborah Cunningham had a gentle manner, her Irish accent softening the often-tough messages she was imparting. They'd had eight sessions so far and Ailsa found the neutral territory of the bright, sparsely furnished office a liberating space.

Evan, however, had been less open or communicative initially, making sarcastic comments under his breath and embarrassing Ailsa enough that, after their third appointment, she'd called Deborah to apologize.

Deborah had spoken gently.

"I appreciate the call, Ailsa, but you're not responsible for how Evan behaves."

The statement had been a revelation to Ailsa, the truth of it like a light bulb flashing on.

During their first session, Deborah had asked them both why they'd decided to work on their marriage, rather than part. Ailsa had cited her feelings of gratitude toward Evan, sadness at where they'd come to and a sense of duty to try to repair things. For Evan it had been about his desire to preserve the life they'd built, so the effort and time they'd put in wouldn't feel wasted. Ailsa had found it both revealing and sad that neither of them had mentioned love.

Now, sitting on one of the Scandinavian style sofas, next to Evan, with Deborah waiting patiently for her to answer, Ailsa finally felt able to talk about how often he dismissed her.

"Whenever I try to talk to him about something that he doesn't want to discuss," she hesitated, "I'm dismissed like a troublesome child."

Evan made a grunting sound causing Deborah to shift her gaze to him.

"Evan, do you want to say something?"

"That's bullshit." He thumped back in the seat. "Sorry, but it is."

"Which part?" Deborah's eyebrows lifted.

He leaned forward again.

"She doesn't realize how hard it is to be her wingman. It's a full-time job. She has all these needs, and her career is so demanding that it takes both of us to sustain it at this level." He floated the flat of his hand next to his temple. "So what if sometimes we don't talk about our feelings all night." He paused, raking his fingers through his hair. "Honestly, it's exhausting."

Ailsa's stomach dipped at his assessment of their relationship.

"So, we're talking about Ailsa's work again?" Deborah tipped her head to one side.

"Well, you know what I mean." He slumped back against the cushion.

"I'd like to take it back to the relationship itself, if I may?" Deborah turned to Ailsa. "Work aside, why do you think Evan chose to be unfaithful?"

Ailsa recoiled, a mirage of images of Evan with the redhead flashing unforgivingly through her mind.

"I think his need for control, the deafness to certain things that are important to me, treating me like a frustrating job, all kind of built up, making me withdraw a bit." She could feel the vein in her neck pulsing. "I haven't been as communicative, or affectionate with him, so…" She paused, balking at the idea of talking about anything more intimate in this setting.

Deborah eyed her over her glasses. "So, you feel responsible for Evan being unfaithful?"

She'd exposed herself, was embarrassed by the level of scrutiny, but instead of turning to Evan before she answered, she held Deborah's gaze.

"Not responsible, but willing to acknowledge that my behavior may have contributed, in some way." She felt her tongue begin to stick to the roof of her mouth so reached over and took a long draft of water from the glass on the table at her side.

Deborah turned to Evan, crossing her long legs.

"So, Evan. How does hearing that make you feel?" She kept her face blank, the hazel eyes on his face as he fidgeted, his fingers linked awkwardly between his knees.

"Yeah." He nodded. "What she said is true. She was different. Quiet. Really cold." He glanced over at Ailsa.

At his willingness to relinquish any responsibility, Ailsa's reluctance to address intimacy evaporated.

"Is that what you got from her, Evan? Warmth?"

He looked startled.

"Yes. No. I don't know." He frowned. "Marie didn't ask for anything from me. She was easy to be with, her own person." His voice rumbled, discomfort creeping across his face. "We had a lot in common. I could talk to her. She was an equal." He held his palms up.

Ailsa pulled in her breath. She was teetering on a cliff edge, her gathering anger like a fireball under her diaphragm and, before she could stop herself, she shouted at him.

"Well, I'm sorry you don't think of me as your equal, Evan, but did you ever consider that you're the one who made me this way?"

She heard Evan's keys in the lock. He was early and the prospect of them being home together for an entire evening caused a pit to form in her stomach.

"Hey." He called from the hall.

"Hi." She continued slicing an onion, her hands trembling. "You're early."

Evan walked into the kitchen and, as he might have some months earlier, moved in close behind her and circled her waist with his arms. The contact was like a bolt of static making her twist around and step away from the counter. She caught the surprise in his face and, despite a pin prick of guilt, held her ground.

"Too soon." She tucked her hair behind her ear as he held his hands up, an odd smile pulling at his lips.

"S'O.K. I get it." He stepped back. "Shall I light the fire? It's getting nippy out there." He shrugged his coat off and, walking into the living room, slung it over the back of the sofa.

Ailsa turned back to the chopping board, trying to let go of her irritation at him not hanging the coat on the rack, which was just a few paces away behind the front door. How quickly he'd reverted to behaving as if nothing had happened, as if he hadn't blown them to smithereens.

Biting back her frustration she called over her shoulder.

"I'm making Stroganoff."

Evan appeared in the doorway. "Brilliant." He beamed. "You're a doll."

Two hours later, they sat opposite each other, their empty dinner plates stacked at one end of the table. The fire was glimmering behind him as Evan stretched, his mouth opening into a wide yawn.

Her headache beginning to escalate, Ailsa had eaten barely half of the small portion she'd served herself, so Evan had finished it for her, as was his habit. Now, she watched him sit back, loosening his belt.

"That was great." He smiled. "A real treat."

"Good." She stood and picked up the plates, walked to the kitchen and loaded them into the dishwasher. As she rinsed her hands, a surge of excruciating pain made her suck in her breath, and as she grabbed the edge of the sink waiting for it to subside, she sensed his presence behind her. Turning, she saw him leaning casually against the door frame, staring at the front page of the daily paper.

Earlier that week, as they'd been scheduling another appointment with Deborah, she had asked Ailsa when she was next leaving the country. Ailsa had told her about the U.S.A. tour which was now only a matter of days away and Deborah had squinted at them.

"I think it'd be a very positive thing if Evan came along. Even for part of the time, because you're making progress and I'd hate to see you fall back because of a long separation." She'd tapped the pen on the arm of her chair. "Think about it and let me know what you decide."

They hadn't spoken about Deborah's suggestion since and

now, with only days until her departure for New York, still conflicted, Ailsa braced herself—tossed the dishcloth into the sink and took a breath.

"So, have you thought any more about coming on tour?" She tried to keep her voice casual.

"Actually yes. I asked Gus if I could have a couple of weeks off." He paused. "He's fine with it."

Ailsa's eyebrows jumped. "Really?"

"Yeah. I can take two weeks, but then I need to be back for the second week of October. Got that big App coming out of QA testing." He leaned over, lifted an apple from the bowl and bit a chunk off it.

Ailsa eased past him and walked into the living room. The embers were glowing pink in the grate, so she backed up to the fire, feeling the welcome heat through her jeans.

Evan had followed and was watching her, his cheeks pulsing as he chewed.

"So, what do you think?" He spoke around a mouthful of apple.

Ailsa closed her eyes momentarily, the sight of the masticated fruit making her wince. When she opened them, he was frowning.

"What?" He looked offended.

"You realize we're leaving on Thursday. That's three days away and you have no ticket or anything."

Evan's face darkened.

"Look, do you want me to come or not?" He bit another chunk off the apple. "It's no hardship for me, either way."

Ailsa clenched her fists. If this was going to work out, they had to put in equal effort. The fact that she wanted to slap his petulant face right now was neither here nor there.

"If you can get on a flight, then yes, come." She picked up the poker and shoved it into the embers, sending a shower of sparks up around the wooden handle. "It's New York first, for a week or so." She placed the poker back in the stand. "So, shall I tell Mark?"

Evan nodded. "Yes. Tell him to count me in."

As she stood up, another wave of pain in her temple caught her off guard making her sway. She reached out and steadied herself against the mantel, her heart racing. Evan's mouth was moving but she could hear only the lashing of waves behind a high pitched squeal. Squinting at him, trying to make out what he was saying, she felt the pressure lift from her ear drum as if a tiny hole had appeared letting the ocean drain away.

He was frowning. "Did you hear what I said?" He walked toward her. "Are you all right?"

She saw the concern in his eyes and for a moment, a second, wanted it to be genuine, more than anything in the world.

"You need to go to bed." He put an arm under hers. "You look shattered."

Guiding her down the hall, Evan made to bypass the spare bedroom but feeling the momentum he was creating, Ailsa pulled back.

"No, Evan. I'm going in here." She stepped away from him, turning toward the spare room. "Good night."

She caught the flash of annoyance in his eyes as she went inside and softly closed the door.

EVAN

They'd been in New York for five days and things were still strained between them. Ailsa had become grey skinned and all but monosyllabic, eating like a bird and barely sleeping, and her appearance worried him. The potential for her to become really sick could possibly affect her ability to perform, maybe even threatening her place on this tour. He should've been more sympathetic, but frustrated at being relegated to the sleeper-sofa, when he'd hear her moving around the bedroom in the night, he'd feign sleep rather than ask her what was wrong.

He had been to see both programs the company were performing at the Lincoln Center and then, rather than sit through them again, had started spending his evenings in the city, checking out some local bars.

Marie had texted him several times and while he'd replied, he'd kept things brief saying only *In New York,* or simply, *What's Up? You OK?* She wouldn't always reply to his terse messages and when she left him hanging, he would swear and toss the phone down.

This evening he'd been tired, so rather than go out had taken a bath and then ordered room service. When Mark called the room, Evan was on his third glass of wine and had dozed off in front of the TV. When he opened his eyes, it took him a moment to register where he was and, fumbling for the remote, he hit the mute button then picked up the receiver from the side table next to him.

"Hello?"

"Evan, it's Mark."

"Hi. What's up? Aren't they still on stage? Evan rubbed his eyes and checked his watch. It was nine fifteen. "Or are you just bored?" He chuckled.

"Evan. Listen to me." Mark was terse. "It's Ailsa."

The ballet company director had been a friend for a decade, having nurtured and coached Ailsa as she progressed through the ranks of the company. Evan, though occasionally resentful at the feeling that there were three of them in the marriage, was grateful to Mark for his attention to Ailsa. His wife was one of the youngest principal dancers in the world and he knew how much of that she owed to Mark.

Aware that Mark was still talking, Evan tried to clear his foggy head.

"What's wrong?"

"She had another headache, but worse this time, then she passed out backstage."

"What?" Evan pushed himself up from the sofa, the effects of the wine making him rock back on his heels.

"We called an ambulance. We're at Mount Sinai emergency room and she's had a CT scan."

Evan swallowed. "Why?"

"The doctor was concerned about her symptoms. She was having trouble speaking and they suspected a stroke, but I think they've ruled that out." Mark paused. "She's in with the doctor now, but she asked me to call you. They're taking her for an MRI."

Evan stood in silence, letting the word *stroke* permeate as he stared across the living room of the suite. Heavy curtains folded around the bulky air conditioning unit that sat under the double-wide window overlooking Madison Avenue, the thrum of which he imagined he could still hear.

As he tried to focus through the fog of alcohol, Evan wished that he was at home in Glasgow, on familiar ground, where he'd know what to do.

"Evan, are you there?" Mark hesitated. "You need to come."

Evan felt a lump of offense forming at the back of his throat. "Why didn't she call me?"

"She did, but it went to voicemail. Then they said we couldn't use our mobiles from the hospital room, so I popped outside, while she's with the doctor." Mark coughed.

Evan walked into the bedroom, skirted the bed, picked up his mobile phone and hit the power button. The screen came to life. He checked the settings. Silent mode. There, on the home screen, was the symbol indicating a voice message.

"Shit. I'll be there as soon as I can get a taxi." He patted his pockets searching for his key card.

Back in the living room he slid his feet into the shoes he'd kicked under the coffee table, then scanned the dimly-lit space, momentarily frozen to the floor. There was no roadmap for this.

"Just be careful getting here. I'll wait with her." Mark's tone was warmer now.

Evan called the concierge and requested a taxi, grabbed his coat; slammed the door behind him and rather than wait for the elevator, thundered down the stairs.

The night was cool and the covering of low clouds was obscuring the moon, turning the light an eerie grey. As he stepped outside, the doorman, wrapped in a heavy great-coat, greeted him.

"Cab sir?" The young man stood between two parked cars, scanning the stream of oncoming vehicles.

THE ART OF REMEMBERING

"I think they called one." He jabbed a thumb over his shoulder.

The buzz of activity on East 45th Street, the constant movement of cars and taxis and the steady flow of passersby, laughing and calling to one another, all faded away as Evan fished his phone out and called Ailsa's mobile. It went straight to voicemail as he'd guessed it would.

As the minutes slithered by, he listened repeatedly to the message Ailsa had left him. Each time he heard her shaky voice, he wanted to kick himself for not checking his phone earlier.

Just as he pressed play for the sixth time he saw the doorman flag down a cab and as the vehicle drew to a halt, the young man opened the door for Evan.

"Thanks." Evan pressed a folded bill into the outstretched hand and slid into the back seat.

"Mount Sinai emergency room. And please hurry."

Thirty minutes later, all the time tapping his phone on his thigh and watching the kaleidoscope of lights on Madison Avenue sliding past the window, Evan was standing in a small, dimly lit room in the hospital wrapping his arms around Ailsa's spindly frame.

"It's all right. I'm here now." He whispered into her hair.

Mark patted his shoulder and then backed discreetly away, waving off Evan's thanks.

Oblivious to Mark's departure, and her distancing herself from Evan seemingly forgotten, Ailsa clung to him. She buried her face in his chest, her back moving in waves under her thin sweater.

Taken aback by her willingness to let him hold her, Evan was afraid to move, but after a few moments, she eased away from him and swiped at her cheeks with her sleeve, smudging the exaggerated stage make-up into a dark mess under each eye.

"What's going on?" He tried to smile.

She took a step back, squared her shoulders and blinked.

"Apparently I have a brain tumor. It's in the temporal lobe."
Her hand cupped her left ear. "It's about two inches in diameter."
Her voice was now eerily calm. "They said it looks operable."
She stared at him.

Evan's stomach rippled. The shock of the word *tumor* made
him lightheaded again, as if the effect of the wine had come back
for a second round.

"God. Ailsa." He hesitated. "Is it—I mean do they know…?"
Evan was choking on the word that had flooded his mind. The
word, that even when whispered, had the power to crumble
bones and extinguish spirits.

Ailsa seemed disconnected from what she'd said as she
looked around the room, and she didn't appear to have any more
information, or if she did, she wasn't sharing it.

"Does Mark know what's going on?" Evan focused on the
corner of her mouth as she chewed her lip.

She shook her head. "No. The doctor told me when Mark
was outside calling you. I don't want him to know, Evan. I don't
want anyone at the company to know yet." She tucked a strand
of hair behind her ear.

"Of course. Whatever you want." His stomach clenched.
Always the solid, practical one in the relationship, his unaccustomed uselessness felt heavy and, needing a task, however
insignificant, he lifted her coat from the low chair next to
the bed.

As quickly as the fear had flooded Ailsa's eyes it was gone,
and in its place was confusion.

"Can this be real?" She spun around and then swayed, grabbing for his hand, then turning her back on him she obediently
slid her arms into the coat that Evan now held up for her.

He watched her, as he had a thousand times, slip her hand
underneath her long hair and release it from the wide collar.

Turning back toward him, she tugged at her lapels and
waited.

He met her questioning eyes, willing something sage or comforting to come to mind, but he had nothing. He'd known that she'd been having headaches for months, and now he felt the press of overwhelming guilt at not paying attention when she'd talked about it.

He moved closer to her. "We'll find out more when..."

She scanned his face, and her total vulnerability touched him. Once again, he wished he could find the right words. She deserved that. Instead he resorted to giving directions.

"I want to talk to the doctor, before we leave." He ran a hand over his hair.

She nodded. "He's coming to tell me what the MRI showed. He asked if I wanted to wait for you, before he told me about the...about the results of the CT." Her eyes filled. "I wish I'd waited for you."

"You probably should have, but it's O.K. now." Evan wrapped his arms around her again, this time feeling more resistance in her wiry frame.

As he held her, Ailsa's crying gradually abated until she took several deep breaths, straightened up and, shoving the hair away from her damp cheeks, she met his gaze.

"I knew." She sniffed. "Deep down, I knew something was badly wrong. I was just afraid to face it." Her voice cracked. "Evan, what if...what if it's...?" She closed her eyes. "Cancer."

She had given the word life. As long as it had been inside his head it hadn't been real, but now it floated from her mouth like a cartoon speech bubble, rising up between them obscuring his view of her face.

He tightened his grip around her back.

"It won't be. It can't be." His voice was ragged. "It isn't."

Apparently locking onto his words, she nodded.

"Right. Right."

Evan's legs began to tremble. He must keep it together. After everything he'd put her through, Ailsa needed him to be strong now.

"When is the doctor coming back?" He glanced at the clock on the wall above the narrow bed.

"Not sure." She whispered.

"Why don't you lie down?" He gestured toward the bed.

"I'm not tired." She shook her head.

Evan held her away from his chest.

"Listen to me. I think you need to rest. Just for a bit. Just for a few minutes."

Two hours later Evan sat on a hard plastic chair and Ailsa lay on the bed, still wrapped in her coat rather than the blankets that lay folded near her feet. She had turned to face the wall and he could hear her sniffing. The sight of her small body, curled into a half moon and quivering under the bulky coat, was pitiful so he lay down and wrapped himself behind her, pulling her closer to his stomach.

She shifted back into him and lifted his arm over her side. He could at least hold her, if not protect her from whatever information was coming into this room along with the doctor, so he closed his eyes and waited, counting the rapid beats of his heart.

The footsteps were brisk, the shoes that approached squeaking on the highly polished floor. Evan jumped from the bed and seeing the white coat, touched Ailsa's shoulder, gently turning her over.

"Mr. and Mrs. MacIntyre?" The face was ruddy.

A tall young man with bright eyes and unkempt dark hair, his white coat looking as if it had seen better days, the doctor held a folder in his hand.

"Sorry that took a while. We had to page a senior radiologist to read the films." He smiled. "Wanted to be sure we got the right answers for you."

Evan caught the doctor's expression and it gave him a lift of hope. He nodded at the young man as Ailsa sat up on the edge of the bed and steadily smoothed her mussed hair, her eyes huge above the smeared make-up.

"So, it appears that the tumor is a benign gangliocytoma. It's very rare, but often presents in the temporal lobe. Of course, we can't be one hundred percent sure it's benign until we've done pathology, but ..."

Evan could no longer hear him. *Benign.* He spun around to see Ailsa fold over at the waist and bury her head in her hands. Her shoulders pulsed as he sat down next to her on the bed and as he laid his hand on her back, his vision blurred.

The doctor had stopped talking. Evan filled his lungs to bursting and tried to focus on the kind face.

"As I said, it's in a tough spot, so removal could be complex, but we have some terrific neurosurgeons if you decide to have surgery here in the States." He spoke to Ailsa, whose face was still firmly planted in her hands. "Mrs. MacIntyre?"

She nodded against her palms.

When she didn't respond, Evan grimaced at the doctor.

"It's O.K. Totally understandable." The doctor turned to Ailsa. "Mrs. MacIntyre, this is good news."

"Ailsa, the doctor's talking to you." Evan rubbed her back as her breathing began to level out.

Sitting up she wiped her coat sleeve across her face and shook the hair out of her eyes.

"Yes." Her voice was little more than a whisper. "It's good news." She paused, scanning the doctor's face. "So surgery is my only option?"

The doctor nodded. "Yes. From what we can see in the films, that's the recommended course of action."

As Evan watched her mouth twisting, Ailsa seemed to be taking in the information.

"How soon? I mean, when do I need to have it removed?" She cupped her temple and as she did this, Evan recognized the movement as something she'd been doing frequently over the past few months. Once again, his conscience prickled at his lack of empathy.

"I'd recommend as soon as possible. I'll prescribe a steroidal anti-inflammatory which may help to shrink the tumor enough to alleviate, or at least lessen some of your symptoms, but you shouldn't wait. The longer the tumor is there, the higher the risk of permanent damage to the surrounding tissue."

Evan, feeling momentarily extraneous to this crucial conversation, cleared his throat.

"So, what about risks? What are we looking at?"

The young man nodded.

"Well, there are several risks associated with this type of brain surgery, not to alarm you too much, but there's a potential for a blood clot to form, possible infection or bleeding in the brain. Seizures and potentially stroke." Seeing Ailsa blanch, he paused. "These are all worse-case scenarios, Mrs. MacIntyre. Don't dwell on that list." He smiled kindly. "You're young, strong and otherwise healthy. You stand an excellent chance of a full recovery."

Letting the intimidating list sink in, but not wanting Ailsa to see his face, Evan stood up and rubbed his chin.

"And what about after surgery? What's the potential for complications?"

"There's always a chance of complications but I see no reason to expect any."

Evan, shook his head, not wanting to be placated with less than the full picture.

"But what are the possible things she'd be facing? Will she dance again?"

The doctor stepped back, adjusting the stethoscope around his neck.

"Because of the position of the tumor, there could be a degree of hearing loss, a speech impediment or even memory loss."

At this, Ailsa's eyes filled again.

"God." Her voice cracked, and Evan moved back to the bedside and took her hand in his.

"It's all right. We just need to know what to expect." He stroked her fingers. "Information is power."

An hour later, with the medications the doctor had mentioned in hand and the list of risks and potential surgical outcomes swirling between them like smoke, they walked unsteadily down the long corridor toward the exit.

Evan reached down and made to take her hand, but this time she wouldn't let him.

"Let's go back to the hotel and we'll figure everything out." He sighed.

She looked up at him, her expression one that he didn't recognize.

"This isn't something we can simply fix, Evan." She pulled her coat around herself. "Not even you can do that, this time." She gave him a watery smile and walked away.

AILSA

Ailsa stared at herself in the mirror. The bathroom door was closed behind her, but she could hear Evan moving around the suite. He'd been hovering ever since they'd got back from the hospital but unable to reassure him, she had retreated to the quiet of this room

The information the young Doctor had given her circled her mind, foreign and disquieting. The procedure was called a craniotomy and tumor excision. She'd need a minimum of a week's stay in hospital, followed by three to four months to recover, depending on the outcome. Then there was the chance of recurrence if they couldn't get it all, potentially requiring further surgery or even radiation. As it all filled her head like some unfamiliar score, her heart clattered beneath her breast bone.

Underneath the fear of all the unknowns, ran a trail of dread. After everything that had happened, the last thing she could handle was Evan telling her what to do again, suggesting what might be best or moving her in a direction she was as yet unsure about. This thing that was happening was happening to her, and while its ugliness terrified her, and she needed his support, she wanted to feel the weight of control in her own hands.

Her temple throbbed, despite the pills the doctor had prescribed, and now that she knew the cause of the debilitating headaches, the pain seemed all the more vicious. Shining above the magnitude of the pain, however, was the word *benign*. As she considered it, Ailsa frowned. Was there truly such a thing as a benign brain tumor? The doctor had told her that despite the label, this mass of cells was invasive and life threatening. Depending on the outcome of the surgery it also possessed the potential, in its damaging wake, to change the course of her life forever. That this sinister growth, that threatened to alter the very shape of her universe, could be referred to as benign, was the quintessential misnomer.

She dragged a brush through her hair feeling the bristles scrape against her collarbones. Her face looked the same as it had that morning, before she knew what she knew now. Her skin, paler than usual, shone under the overhead light that highlighted the scattering of freckles over the bridge of her nose and cheek-bones. It was her face. Nothing had changed on the surface. And yet inside her head, under her scalp and the bones of her skull, there had been a change. A handful of cells had split, then split again, gathering momentum as they stuck together, working overtime to create an unwanted presence that had already grown to the size of an apricot, and the apricot had begun to alter her, well before she'd been aware of its presence.

As she cast her mind back to the changes that had crept up on her over the past year, so much of what she'd been experiencing made sense now. The crippling headaches and sleeplessness, the whooshing sounds in her ear, the trouble keeping rhythm and the bizarre distortion of music, were a jumble of jagged-edged jigsaw pieces that finally fit together. She'd also grown increas-ingly uncomfortable in groups, often refusing to join Amanda and her other friends in the company for drinks, or gatherings after work, and most recently there was surges of anger, boiling over when she'd least expect it. A good portion of that she'd attributed to the rift Evan had created in their marriage, still gaping and raw, but sometimes she felt overwhelmed by it—as if she might lose control.

She stared at her reflection, her mind going back to the night she'd arrived home from Asia, but unwilling to relive that gut-wrenching altercation, for the thousandth time, she pressed her eyes closed and continued brushing her hair.

In her mind's eye she could see the stark white sphere that had shown up on the MRI, like a ghostly photographic negative. Coming face to face with it had been shocking. The edges of the growth sliced into the gentle greyness around it and despite its cuckoo-like status, the tumor had stared out from the screen, audacious in its right to be there.

As she opened her eyes and laid the brush on the edge of the sink, her hand went up to her left ear. Running her fingers up into her hair she pressed them into the side of her head. Lurking deep under her fingertips was the enemy. What had happened to initiate this anomaly? Why had this happened inside her head? As she pressed harder, her fingernails dug into her scalp divining the damaging ball of cells.

Evan knocked on the door, startling her.

"You O.K. in there?"

Ailsa took a deep breath and shook her hair back over her shoulders.

"Yes. I'm just…thinking."

"I've made tea. Are you coming out?" His tone was upbeat. Forced.

Leaning forward she ran her index finger over each eyebrow, wiped under her eyes and sniffed.

"Yes. I'm coming."

∽

Knowing that she could not keep the truth from Mark any longer, and despite it being after midnight, Ailsa called him. He'd been awake and was obviously shocked, his concern coming through as anger before melting into sympathy.

"What the hell? How was this not picked up before now?" He huffed.

"What were you thinking, keeping this from me for so long?" She felt the well-placed barb of his words.

"I'm sorry, Mark. I know this is the worst timing for this to happen." She gulped down her tears and Mark, obviously hearing her struggle, immediately softened.

"Nothing is more important than your health, darling. Just let me know what you need from me, and you'll have it."

"Thanks, Mark. You're the best."

After talking through the logistics of her understudies taking on her roles for the rest of the tour, she hung up and flopped on the bed, Evan watching her from across the room.

"All right with Mark?" He looked tired, his eyes darkly shadowed as he crossed his arms over his chest.

She nodded. "I think so."

Feeling drained, Ailsa rested for a few minutes then, knowing that Amanda would be frantic, called her friend and asked her to come to their room.

Fifteen minutes later, hearing the tap at the door, Evan picked up his jacket just as Amanda walked in.

"I'll leave you to it." He nodded at Amanda, who grunted a hello in return. "I'll be down in the bar checking on flights."

Things were still extremely prickly between Evan and Amanda, and Ailsa felt the tangible fizz of tension as the two passed in the doorway.

"Flights?" Amanda's face was ashen. "Tell me all of it." She took both of Ailsa's hands. "Everything."

Ailsa filled her in on the diagnosis as Amanda's eyes filled.

"Jesus, you poor thing." She sniffed. "All those damn

headaches, I knew you should've seen the doctor again. How much pain have you really been in?" She blinked several times then took a deep breath, not waiting for Ailsa to answer. "What can I do?" The watery eyes now brimming with determination. "There must be something?"

Ailsa hugged her friend.

"Nothing, I'm afraid. We're going home as soon as we can get a flight and then we'll find out what comes next."

Amanda sat cross legged on the sofa as Ailsa paced the room.

"Mum can mind Hayley and I'll come and stay. I mean, if you want?" She looked at Ailsa, the tip of her nose now rosy. "I'll take care of you."

Ailsa felt the love emanating from the face she knew so well.

"Thank you, petal. I appreciate that, but Hayley needs her mum and I'll be fine, after a few months. My mum can help, and there's Evan..." She caught the frown fold Amanda's brow, so Ailsa sat down next to her. Part of Ailsa wanted to melt into her friend's arms and ask her what to do, but more than anything now, and for the foreseeable future, she needed to rely on her own strength.

When Evan came back up to the room, Ailsa was lying on top of the bed, a wash cloth over her eyes to help ease the pulsing pain that had rendered her speechless after Amanda left.

"Hey. You all right?" He tossed his jacket on the suitcase stand.

Ailsa nodded, feeling the cloth slip onto the pillow. She sat up sending a rush of blood to her head, and so closed her eyes against the sensation that she might faint.

Evan walked into the bathroom and washed his hands while she sat on the edge of the bed, trying to regain her equilibrium.

He stood in the doorway.

"So, it looks like we can get on a five p.m. or a ten p.m. flight today." He frowned. "I mean tonight." He shook his head. "You know what I mean."

She nodded. It being almost 3:00 a.m., he meant that coming evening. As she fought to focus, the sound of breaking waves gradually subsiding now she was sitting still, the idea of getting on a plane for a lengthy flight made her stomach churn.

"So the latest flight is at ten?" She said.

He lifted his phone and began scrolling on the screen.

"Yep." He raised his eyes. "Want me to book it?"

She nodded. The few hours grace she'd have to let her mind settle, hopefully get some sleep and prepare to face the journey, and what was waiting on the other end, was crucial.

"I'll do it now."

She stood up gingerly, a hand pressing down on the top of her head.

"Thanks, Evan." She saw him smile. "I'm glad you're here."

Evan had ordered room service for breakfast and Ailsa was soaking in the tub when she heard the knock at the door.

"I'll get it." He called from the bedroom.

She pulled her knees up and slid down further, letting the warm water flood her ears. The weight of the water felt good, like warm blankets on her stomach, chest and limbs so she closed her eyes and tried to imagine floating in the Dead sea, as she had done a few years ago when the company had toured the Middle East. After the tour, she and Amanda had taken a short flight to Jordan for a few days off in a beautiful hotel. They'd slept on the beach under fluttering umbrellas, read books, eaten when they were hungry and floated on their backs in the buoyant water. The tingling of her skin had made her laugh, and now, as the Epsom salts fizzed around her aching muscles, she tried to recapture the sense of relaxation she'd had back then. Back when this reality was as yet unknown to her.

Evan rapped on the door making her sit up abruptly, sending water sloshing over the edge of the tub.

"Are you ready to eat?" His voice was close to the door. There was a time when he'd have walked right in but now, with their fragile truce still in its infancy, she was glad that he'd respected the closed door.

"Give me a few minutes. I'll be right out." She rubbed herself briskly with a towel then wrapped the huge white bathrobe around her, folding the sleeves up several times in order to release her hands from the excess fabric. She combed out her hair and cleaned her teeth—her face was flushed from the heat of the bath water—a healthy rose-colored glow shining on her cheekbones. She smiled. Today, at this moment, no-one would ever guess that she had an uninvited guest inside her head.

When she emerged from the bathroom, Evan had poured her coffee and taken the steel domes off the plates of food he'd chosen for them.

"There you go." He pointed at an anemic looking omelet, all whites with patches of greasy spinach through it, and three small arcs of melon.

Ailsa eyed it, feeling her stomach buckle.

"I'm not really hungry." She grimaced. "But thank you."

Evan sat at the table and flicked open a white napkin.

"You have to eat." He stared at her. "Come on, sit down." He gestured toward the other chair. "It's just eggs." He pulled a plate of pancakes closer and began pouring dark syrup on them.

Ailsa breathed away a wave of nausea.

"I can't, Evan." She pressed a hand to her chest. "Maybe later?"

"Come on. Try." His eyes flashed. "It's such a waste."

She shook her head, a wave of irritation rising up into her throat.

"You eat it then, if that's what you're worried about."

"That's not what I meant." He waved his fork at her. "Just try some."

Ailsa's insides shrank away from her own outer edges, as if he was vacuuming the bravery right out of her, so she forced her shoulders back and breathed deeply.

"I'll eat later, when I'm hungry." She lifted the steel lid and placed it back on top of the sad-looking omelet. "So, the flights are confirmed?" She picked up the cup of coffee and settled herself on the small sofa that sat against the wall between the living area and the bedroom.

Evan shoveled a forkful of pancake into his mouth, then waggled his fork, telling her to wait.

Irritated, she raked her fingers through the long, damp strands of hair that were making her back feel cold, even through the thickness of the robe.

"Yep. So, we have a good part of the day to kill." He lifted the jug of syrup. "These things are like sponges." He said, soaking the remaining pieces of pancake.

"So, do you want to do something?" She pulled the belt tighter around her middle. "We haven't really had a chance to see much of New York." She turned to look out the window, noticing that the light was a silvery blue.

Evan nodded. "If you're feeling up to it, we could get out a bit. Maybe go to MoMA or for a walk in Central Park?" He swiped the last of the syrup up on a triangle of pancake and shoved it into his mouth.

Ailsa tried not to watch him chew.

"MoMA would be nice. Apparently they have Monet's Water Lilies, and Van Gogh's Starry Night at the moment. I've always wanted to see that." Even as she said it, Ailsa was struck by the ludicrous notion of them considering sightseeing while she had an alien burrowing its way into her brain and for a second, she wondered whether they'd both really taken in the shocking information as truth.

Evan shoved the chair away and tossed his napkin onto the empty plate.

"Van Goch's not one of my favorites, but worth seeing, I suppose." He stuck his little finger nail between his teeth, making a sucking sound. "It's probably too cold for the park today anyway."

~

Wrapped in her long wool coat, with a knitted hat pulled down over her ears, Ailsa half walked half trotted next to Evan, trying to keep up. Their hotel was on Madison and 52nd, but having decided to visit MoMA last, and feeling like walking, they'd cut up West 52nd then made their way south, along 6th Avenue, as Ailsa took in the hum of activity around her.

This city had a beating heart that underwrote every street corner and skyscraper, and Ailsa loved the rhythm of that life, pulsing under her feet. Her headache was a four on the scale, but as she looked around her, the noise of the city almost managed to drown out the now constant waves breaking in her ears.

On the corner of West 50th, a young man sat on a large tin can, battering a set of upturned plastic buckets with drumsticks. He wore fingerless gloves and his mottled coat and lace-up boots looked like Army issue.

Ailsa stopped, tugging on the arm of Evan's coat to halt his progress across the road.

"Wait. I want to listen." She smiled at the man who seemed to have heard her, his dark eyes glittering in recognition. Despite the noise inside her head, the rhythm he was creating with the rudimentary tools was mesmerizing, like the pounding of torrential rain on a tin roof, the speed of his playing and the truth of the beats seeping through Ailsa's skin, flooding her veins and leaching into her ice-cold insides. The trills and rests, the syncopation and breaks were expertly timed and without realizing it, she began moving her feet, her heels rising and falling and her arms swinging at her sides in time with the strikes of the wood on the plastic. For a moment, she felt as if she had left the bitter truth of her situation behind, and was one with this thrilling sound that had no elusive or discordant notes for her to chase.

Wanting to share this feeling, she looked over at Evan, who was talking to an attractive woman, leaning toward her as he pointed to something on the map she was holding out. She was smiling as he shook his head and then, sending a bolt of pain into Ailsa's chest, they laughed together. It seemed effortless for him to charm a complete stranger into laughter, have an easy repartee with someone he knew nothing about, when lately he couldn't find a way to relate to his own wife.

As she watched him point down the street, Ailsa pushed out her breath. If there was any chance of them making it through this mess, let alone through the next months that held so many unknowns for them, both individually and as a couple, they'd have to find a new way of relating.

Pulling her out of her reverie, Evan came back to her side and grabbed her hand.

"Come on. I'm cold."

"Not yet." She eased her fingers out of his. "He's incredible. Just listen for a few minutes."

Evan scowled. "We'll catch our death out here." He hunched his shoulders and shoved his hands into his pockets. "Ailsa?"

He spoke to her profile as she stood still, focusing on the drummer's eyes, willing him to continue.

"Come on, you shouldn't get too cold."

She took a deep breath, her eyes locked on the drummer's. The young man smiled at her and nodded, as if giving her permission to go and Ailsa reached into her handbag and pulled out her wallet. Finding a twenty-dollar bill she folded it over twice and dropped it in the upturned cardboard box that had a handful of coins and other notes in it. As she dropped the money, she heard Evan huffing.

"Thank you. You're so talented." She called at the man, as he continued to play. "Really brilliant." She grinned as he tapped his forehead with a drum stick.

"Thanks, Miss." He beamed. "You have a great day now."

"You too." As she turned to go, the leaving was almost painful. Such moments of honest pleasure seemed few and far between these days, and Ailsa was reluctant to let this one go.

Evan was hopping from foot to foot on the corner as she walked up next to him and looked around her, waiting for the reprimand, the sigh of frustration that she knew would come.

He looked at her and widened his eyes.

"Twenty. Really?"

She kept her face expressionless.

"Yes. Totally worth it."

He frowned.

"Let's get moving. My arse is frozen solid."

They walked on down West 50th, weaving through the steady flow of bodies, business suits and laptop cases, bulging carrier bags from Saks and tiny turquoise squares from Cartier, a mixture of elegant shoes and heavy boots passing them as they dipped into a couple of different doorways to let others pass and to re-wrap their scarves. The bitter cold was sliding inside her clothes and Ailsa's feet were beginning to turn icy.

Having passed Radio City Music Hall, then turning onto 5th Avenue, Ailsa pulled Evan to a stop. A few hundred yards ahead towered Atlas, protecting the entrance to Rockefeller Center, with its art-deco buildings spearing the sky like stylish fingers.

"Wow. It's so huge." She stared at the bronze statue, the impressive figure standing on one, muscular leg, the broad shoulders supporting the sphere of the heavens. As Ailsa felt the weight of her own situation, pressing on her shoulders, Atlas's fate seemed precariously close to her own. She blinked several times, paying silent tribute to his endless struggle and praying that she'd cope with this next challenge in as heroic a way.

Evan was checking his phone, and rather than wait, Ailsa turned and looked over at the Neo-Gothic spires of Saint Patrick's Cathedral, something inexplicably drawing her in. She'd rarely attended Church, of any affiliation, but the thought of standing inside the silence of a magnificent house of God such as this began to feel welcome, if not oddly essential. She put her hand on Evan's arm.

"Can we go in?" She jutted her chin toward the impressive building.

Evan's eyebrows jumped. "What? Inside?"

She nodded. "Yes. I want to see it."

He scanned her face then shrugged. "O.K."

They crossed 5th Avenue and walked toward the towering wooden doors, set under a dominating stone arch, and as they passed underneath it and stepped inside the cathedral, Ailsa sucked in her breath. The classical beauty and sheer height of the ceiling made her tip her head back, taking in the golden light that shimmered from the rows of ornate chandeliers hanging above them.

She spun around to see the stained glass windows set high up in the wall behind her, over the door they'd just come through, noting that even the dull light of the day outside seemed to transform to an incandescent form of itself as it streamed through the intricate panels of colorful panes.

"God, it's stunning." She whispered to Evan, who was staring up at the ceiling.

"Pretty impressive." He nodded. "Shall we go?"

"Not yet. I want to walk through." She ducked past him into the central aisle, the marble floor glistening under her boots, and as she headed toward the altar, the rows of ornately carved pews ran away from her on either side. As she walked, she trailed a finger over their gleaming dark surfaces, leaving a trace of her presence on their backs.

She was aware that Evan was following her, so ducked into a pew and sat down. Unsure of the protocol, she knelt on the low platform, leaned her elbows on the shelf in front of her, pressed her fists against her forehead and closed her eyes. She tried to empty her mind, push the sound of the waves and the mounting pain down, and let in whatever might come.

As her thoughts settled, she searched her heart, her lips moving as she silently prayed.

If you can hear me, I know it's been a long time. I may not deserve your attention, but I need your help. I'm in trouble and I'm asking you please to give me a second chance. I know I can do better with this life than I've been doing, if you will only give me more time. If you can do that I won't waste it. I'll be a better person. If you help me get through this, I won't let you down. I promise.

Within a few moments, she was aware of Evan moving in next to her.

"Are you praying?" He sounded incredulous, his mouth close to her ear.

She nodded against her fists, pressing her eyes tighter. "Shhh."

Here, in the dark silence, she was listening for something. Waiting for a whisper, a voice she might know, some soothing tone or string of words that would make everything all right, but there was nothing. The drag of disappointment made her press her lips together.

"This is all a bit…" Evan halted.

She opened her eyes and sat back on the bench. It took her a second to readjust to the light and as she stared at the beautiful altar, surrounded on three sides by carved stone arches, supporting more spectacular stained-glass windows above, her eyes filled. Without looking at Evan, she found a tissue in her pocket and wiped her nose.

"Are you finished?" His voice was low.

She nodded, shoving the tissue away.

"Feel better now?" He was smiling, but there was a hint of sarcasm in his voice.

"As a matter of fact, I do." She glared at him, her face growing hot. "Evan, whatever it takes I'm going to get through this." She stood up, indicating that she wanted to get out of the pew. "You needn't support everything I do, but please don't make fun of me."

He shifted his knees to the side to let her out.

"Oh, settle down. I wasn't being shitty."

She pulled her gloves on and waited for him to stand up, then she turned toward the door. "Let's go."

It was 2:45 p.m. when they let themselves back into the hotel room, and the air inside was chilly, so Evan pumped up the temperature on the thermostat. They'd cut their tour of MoMa short as Ailsa's headache had begun to escalate, and after they'd spent just a few minutes in front of the Van Goch masterpiece, she'd leant on Evan's arm and asked if they could go back to the hotel.

Evan had spoken to the hotel manager about their circumstances and she'd agreed to let them have the room for an additional day, so they had time to rest and pack before leaving for the airport.

"Shit, it's so cold in here." He tugged his coat off. "Shall I order us something hot to drink?"

Ailsa nodded. "Tea would be great."

He tossed his coat and gloves onto the sofa and lifted the phone.

"Want anything else?"

"No, thanks." She slid out of her coat and then pulled off her boots, rubbing one foot on top of the other, her toes sticking together with the cold.

Evan ordered the tea, switched on the handful of lamps around the room and then drew the curtains on the grey afternoon sky.

"That was good, today." He spoke over his shoulder. "Hope we didn't do too much?"

She shook her head. "No. It was fine. I enjoyed it. I'll take some more pain killers, though." She sank onto the sofa, popped the pills into her mouth then checked her phone, seeing a missed call from Amanda. "Oh, I missed Amanda." She held the phone up as Evan passed her, heading for the bathroom. "I'll give her a call back."

Before she could make the call, he turned back into the room, his face twisted into a scowl.

"Don't call her, or she'll want to come and see you." He leaned his shoulder against the doorframe. "You're tired and you need to pack, and rest before we go."

Ailsa let the phone drop to her knee. "But I want to see her before I leave." She saw his shoulders slump. "Would you mind if she and I had an early dinner together?"

He scanned her face, as if looking for a crack in her resolve that he could wriggle into. Ailsa kept her expression steady, her shoulders back and her chin up.

"O.K. But tell her she can't stay for long. She always stays too long."

Ailsa rolled her eyes. "She does not."

"We need to leave here at seven at the latest." He pouted. "Latest."

She nodded as she pressed the call-back button.

There were several rings before Amanda answered.

"Hi, are you O.K.?" Amanda sounded concerned. "When you didn't call me back, I thought…"

Ailsa kept her voice light. "What, that I'd kicked the bucket already?" She laughed.

"Don't say that." Amanda's voice was thick with emotion. "I was worried."

Ailsa pulled her feet up under herself.

"Oh, I'm sorry. My phone's been on silent for a while. We went to St. Patrick's cathedral and then to MoMA." She ran a hand through her hair, feeling the knots the wind had created catching her fingertips. "You could spend a week in that place and not see everything." She let her head drop back against the cushion behind her.

"We missed you in class today. Everyone was asking what was going on. Mark was very good—telling them just enough to be plausible and to stop them creating their own stories."

Ailsa nodded in the silent room, relieved that Mark had held true to their agreement that he would not tell the company anything other than that she was unwell and wouldn't be finishing the tour.

"Did anyone question it?" Ailsa bit at the cuticle around her thumb.

"No. Well, Steven wanted to know exactly what he meant by unwell, but Mark just said that it wasn't his place to discuss your private business and that he'd tell everyone more when he knew more himself."

Ailsa nodded. "Good old Mark."

Amanda sighed. "I'm not sure I agree with all this secret keeping though. Everyone is concerned about you, and they might be upset when the truth finally gets out." She paused. "Would it really be the end of the world if they knew what was going on?"

Ailsa lifted the remote control and turned on the TV, immediately muting the volume. Amanda's concern was valid and while

she, Ailsa, wished that she felt confident enough to be trans-
parent about her condition, the idea of all her friends knowing,
being sympathetic and scared for her, was more than she could
handle right now. Tears were hovering under her every breath
and she had no residual courage to share.

"You're probably right, but I think I might feel better about it
when we know exactly what's coming." She extended her legs
and crossed her feet on the low table in front of her. "Once I
have a date for surgery, and maybe some idea of when I'll be
back to work, it'll feel less dramatic to tell people."

"Yeah. I suppose I can see that." Amanda sighed. "I switched
performances with Harriet tonight, so can I come up, or is the
gatekeeper already at his post?"

Ailsa laughed. "No. Come. Let's have an early dinner
together up here." She scanned the room. "I don't feel like facing
the restaurant."

"How about I come at five? We can order something and chat
for a bit." Amanda whispered. "Don't tell Evan, I'll just turn up."

"I've already told him." Smiling at Amanda's mischief, Ailsa
stared at the TV screen as a red car sped around a treacherous, cliff-
side road sending clouds of dust up in its wake. "See you at five."

"Great. Do you need me to pick anything up for you?"

"No, thanks. I'm fine." Ailsa smiled. "Just get your backside
up here so we can talk."

Evan had retreated to the bedroom, leaving the women alone
with their meal. Ailsa was grateful to him for being sensitive and
had quickly relaxed into the company of her friend, their heads,
one blonde one dark, close together as they slouched on the sofa,
their feet up on the coffee table.

They'd ordered Cesar salads and shared a glass of white

wine, Ailsa sipping occasionally and Amanda gulping down more than her share. The act of sharing it had felt good, even if the taste had been bitter to Ailsa, the medication she was taking seeming to affect her sense of taste.

Now, Ailsa padded back and forth from the bedroom, where Evan was watching football, packing her case as Amanda talked animatedly about their class that morning.

"The petit allegro was brutal. All cabrioles and brisés." She huffed. "But I was done in before we even started the barre, today." She laughed. "Too much partying last night after the show."

Ailsa laughed, folding a sweater into the case. "Sorry I missed it."

"You're excused." Amanda pursed her lips. "But only because you have a brain tumor."

Ailsa stopped in her tracks, the joke landing squarely on target. Mustering all her energy, she feigned shock, widening her eyes and pressing her palm on her chest.

"God, Amanda."

Amanda's face fell.

"Oh, shit. I didn't mean it." She jumped up from the sofa and crossed the room. "That was..." Her face was flushed.

Ailsa released her breath and laughed loudly.

"I got you, you silly bugger." She hugged Amanda tightly as Amanda, batted her away, laughing again.

"Damn, you got me good." She tutted. "Not lost your sense of humor then." She grinned.

"God, I hope not." Ailsa shook her head.

Amanda took up her post on the sofa, a cushion behind her head.

"Tricia was asking after you, and Richard, or course." She rolled her eyes. "I think he's a little in love with you." She grinned at Ailsa. "Oh, and Steven made a point of asking if there was anything you needed." She looked wistful. "He's such a nice guy."

"He is." Ailsa nodded. "I feel bad keeping this from him." She cupped her ear, feeling the heat coming from her skull.

"Don't. When he knows what's been going on, he'll totally understand." Amanda's eyes looked filmy. "Everyone will."

An hour later, Amanda was emotional as she slipped her shoes on.

"So, call me when you get home. I'll be worrying about you traveling." She hugged Ailsa tightly. "Let Evan do everything and try to sleep on the plane." She sniffed. "I love you, girl."

Ailsa hugged her back.

"I'll be fine. I'll phone from home and everything will be O.K." She stepped back, seeing the strain in Amanda's face. "You'll all be back in three weeks and then we'll spend a weekend together. Bring Hayley, and we'll have a pajama party at my place." She grinned.

At the mention of her daughter, Amanda's pained expression relaxed. "She'd love that, the wee madam. She might never leave, because you know she prefers you to me." She rolled her eyes.

"I don't think so." Ailsa prodded Amanda's shoulder. "You're super-mum."

"Fly safe, love." Amanda kissed her cheek. "Be strong and let me know if his majesty in there needs his back-side kicked. You know I'd love to help you out with that." She pointed to the bedroom, at which point Evan called out.

"I heard that."

They both covered their mouths like little girls.

"You know I mean it." Amanda shouted back. "So, take heed."

Ailsa gently shoved her friend out the door.

"Go. I'm tired and I have to finish packing."

"See you soon." Amanda held onto Ailsa's fingers. "Bye."

"Bye, sweet friend."

~

The morning after they got home, Evan went out into the hall to call his mother, and Ailsa steeled herself for the phone call she had to make to her own parents. As she dialed, hoping that her father would be the one to answer, her fingertips were cold, chills rippling down her back as she tried to rehearse how she'd tell them the news.

She was relieved to hear her father's deep voice.

"Hi Dad, it's me." She pressed her back against the wooden ribs of the dining chair, the slight discomfort anchoring her.

"Oh, Ailsa, love. Where are you calling from?" His voice was cheerful. "Still in New York?"

Her throat began to tighten as she shook her head.

"No, actually Dad. We're home." She pressed her eyes closed, imagining his face, a frown creeping across his forehead.

"Home?" He paused. "Why… I mean, you just left a few days ago." She heard him clearing his throat and then, in the background, her mother asking who he was speaking to.

Ailsa pressed her shoulders back and shook the hair out of her eyes.

"Dad, first of all, you need to know that I'm all right. O.K.?" She waited for him to speak.

"O.K." He paused. "Go on."

Ailsa spilled the news with as little drama as she could manage, playing down the worst of the potential risks and complications. Colin remained silent, letting her get through it, typically thinking of what she needed at this moment rather than himself. As she finished, and he was still quiet, her heart flip flopped, imagining him having collapsed on the floor, clutching his chest.

Shaking the melodramatic image from her mind, she spoke quietly.

"Dad. Are you all right?"

"Yes. We're O.K." He covered the microphone and said something to her mother, but Ailsa couldn't make it out. "What do you need us to do, love? Shall we come?" Now Ailsa heard Jennifer clearly, her voice high pitched.

"Why isn't she in New York, Colin?" What's going on?"

To her surprise, her father shushed her mother, not something Ailsa ever recalled having happened before and despite her jangling nerves, she covered her mouth to stifle a laugh.

"Dad?"

"Yes, love. Sorry. Just tell me what you need."

Ailsa explained that they would be scheduling appointments with various neurosurgeons and that she'd keep him informed as soon as they had any more information, or potential dates for the surgery. The last thing she felt able to deal with was her parents visiting, especially when she and Evan were still so fragmented and awkward around one another. Her parent's presence would only serve to inflame the already tense atmosphere.

Colin was calm, keeping his voice controlled as he briefed Jennifer on the situation, until Ailsa was saying goodbye.

"So, I'll call you in a few days and let you know what's happening, Dad."

Then, she heard a sound that made her grab the table. As he said her name, Colin's voice cracked, his breath coming in ragged bursts. Ailsa thought her heart would split in two and then, she heard her mother's voice again, this time full of fear.

"Oh, Colin. Come on, my love. Please don't do that."

Ailsa pressed her eyes closed, waiting for her mother to take the phone.

"Ailsa, darling? It's me." Jennifer spoke gently. "Don't worry, Dad's fine. We're both fine." She halted. "We just need to get you the best doctors there are out there, and we will. Don't worry about a thing. All right?"

Ailsa nodded silently, the force of nature that was her mother, at times overwhelming, was now reassuring.

Finding her voice, Ailsa croaked. "Thanks, Mum." She paused. "I love you both."

"Us too, darling. Us too."

Due to the complexity of her surgery, and the need to find the most qualified neurosurgeon, they had scheduled appointments with three specialists, but the soonest they could be seen had been two weeks out.

Each morning Ailsa checked the calendar, and as the cloned days slithered by, she was chewed up by conflict, impatient to move forward and yet afraid of what was to come. Her headaches were relentless and as the pain built so her energy faded.

In an attempt to retain some kind of normalcy, she had gone to a ballet class at a dance school in the West End, but unable to bear the oddly twisted clattering of the piano, or the proximity of the other dancers, she had slipped away and retreated to the sanctuary of the flat.

Despite her efforts not to dwell on them, the doctor's' warnings of the risks involved with surgery played over and over in her mind, a word-worm squeezing out any other train of thought. She'd tried to tamp them down with music but the notes that emanated from her earbuds, instead of providing the comfort that she had relied on in the past, now sounded like razor blades hacking at her ear drums.

That morning, after Evan left for work, she'd done a series of stretches then switched on the TV, muted the volume and curled up under a blanket. Daytime programs that she'd never seen before had her mesmerized, the flickering screen a comforting presence in the quiet flat. As the morning passed, she rose only to use the bathroom and to pad back and forth to the kitchen for food and drinks.

Her fingers were raw from her constantly chewing the skin around the nails and her stomach felt mutinously empty, despite her steadily feeding the insatiable appetite that the steroids were provoking.

By 1:30 p.m. the light outside was still dull and as she walked into the kitchen, she shivered. It was less than an hour since she'd eaten a sizeable lunch, but her stomach was growling. Chewing her lip, Ailsa pulled the loaf from the bread box, cut two thick slices and pasted them together with a layer of peanut butter. As she cut across the sandwich, creating two equal triangles, fat tears plopped onto the backs of her hands. This appetite was winning the battle with her customary, cast-iron willpower. She thought she could already feel the difference in her clothes, a new layer of flesh having appeared around her waist, but there was nothing she could do other than eat. Dropping the knife onto the counter top she squeezed her eyes closed.

Evan had caught her foraging in the kitchen the previous afternoon.

"I suppose you should eat if you really need to, then get the weight off later, when you're back to work." He'd stood behind her, throttling the newspaper which he'd rolled into a tube.

"But I can't stop it, Evan. It's like this animal inside me that's never full."

She'd slapped her palms down so hard on the cool marble that it had sent prickles of pain up her arms and into her face.

Evan had walked over and hovered by her side as she sobbed into a tea towel.

"All right, but try to manage it. It'll be so much harder later, if you can't."

She'd hadn't missed the thinly shrouded judgment in his

words.

Now, she carried the plate back to the sofa and crawled under her blanket. Glancing at the clock she calculated how much longer she'd be alone. The solitude was peaceful and she felt a tiny jolt of dread at the thought of hearing Evan's keys in the lock.

She bit into the bread, the salty sweetness of the peanut butter spreading across the roof of her mouth as she made a mental note to clear away all her dishes before he got home.

Evan was pacing around her like a territorial lion. When he'd got home, she'd cooked a light meal and then he had cleaned up the kitchen. Their conversation at the table had been stilted, brittle, as they both avoided the subject that was consuming their every thought.

The theoretical nature of her surgery was hardening around the edges, the reality of what she was to face becoming clearer as each day passed, and as she gradually became sicker the more restless Evan was becoming.

Now, as he walked behind the sofa for the umpteenth time, Ailsa looked back at him.

"Sit down. You're making me nervous."

She glanced at the clock, calculating how much longer it would be until she could take another pain killer. The strong medication was only skimming the surface off the now incessant pulsing in her temple, but she still counted the minutes as time stretched elastically between doses.

"I might go for a walk." Evan turned abruptly and lifted his jacket from the back of the sofa. "Do you mind?"

Jolted by his obvious desire to get away from her, she shook her head. "Not at all. But it's chilly out there."

He pulled the jacket on and wound a rough-knit scarf around

his neck.

"S'O.K. I won't be long." He dropped a kiss on the top of her head.

The door clicked behind him and Ailsa let herself exhale. Her conflicting emotions were exhausting—wanting him around and yet being grateful that he'd gone—but this contradiction in her feelings about him was becoming more commonplace.

As she leaned her head back against the cushion a hot arrow of pain shot across her face, into her jaw and down the side of her neck. She clenched her teeth against its rippling progress then, as it gradually began to subside, she rose to find her pills.

By 9:30 pm Evan was still not back and facing the inevitable shadows of her suspicion at his oddly timed departure, Ailsa went to check if he'd taken his keys. Seeing them missing from the dish, she texted him. *You OK? I'm heading to bed.* After a few moments a reply bloomed on her phone. *Go ahead. Coming soon.*

She tossed the phone onto the table and pressed her eyes closed, but beneath her frustration, as shadowy images of Evan, standing on a dark street corner waiting for someone, floated through her mind, buried beneath them was the agonizing question of how much she actually cared anymore.

Dragging her feet, she gathered the scattered papers up from the coffee table, stacked them under the TV remotes then dimmed the overhead light. Her eyelids were leaden as she scanned the room then, balancing her weary body, she stroked the wall on her left as she walked toward the bedroom.

The following morning, Ailsa came out of the bathroom and could hear Evan on the phone. He was in the kitchen and as she approached, he hadn't seemed to notice her standing in the doorway.

"I'm scared, Mum. What if I lose her to this?" Evan was facing away from her but Ailsa saw him shake his head. Diana's voice hummed against Evan's cheek, but Ailsa couldn't make out what her mother-in-law was saying.

"After everything we've been through, this is just…" He paused as Diana's voice rose. "I know that, but she's so fragile. I'm not sure she's strong enough, and it'll all fall on me, as usual."

Ailsa's hand went to her mouth as she stepped back from the door. Him voicing the apparent burden of being with her, especially in the light of what he'd recently done, was like a fist to her middle.

She spun around and headed back to the sofa. Grabbing the blanket, she tucked it tightly around her thighs and picked up the book that she'd been reading the same paragraph of for the past two days.

Evan walked into the room and smiled at her.

"Mum sends her love."

Ailsa nodded without taking her eyes off the letters that were blurring on the page.

"Good shower?" Evan lifted the newspaper from the dining table and headed for the armchair at the fireside. "Ailsa?"

She dropped the book onto her leg and stared at him.

"You don't think I'm capable of dealing with this." Her fingers fluttered over her ear as Evan slowly folded the paper and dropped it into the basket at the side of the chair.

"That's not what I meant." He sighed.

A surge of adrenalin lifted Ailsa from the seat, and before she knew it she was standing over him pinching her hips and feeling the bite of her nails in the softening flesh.

"I'm stronger than you think, you know." She paused. "In the battle of me, versus this time bomb in my head, where's your money?" Her voice cracked.

Evan shook his head.

"Just settle down. You misunderstood." His eyes were shrouded, the skin around them seeming looser than usual. "Take a breath."

While he scanned her face, as quickly as it had sprung up, Ailsa's energy dissipated. All the impetus that had moved her to this spot was gone as she released her grip on her hips, aware of the blood rushing back into her fingers. Whether she wanted to or not, she needed Evan now, and any strength she had she must preserve in order to get through this next few months. The prospect of another argument was draining, so she slipped onto her knees and sat down on the rug.

"Just have some faith in me, please."

He leaned forward, linking his fingers between his knees.

"I will, but you've got to be strong, Ailsa."

His didactic tone made her lean away from him.

"I can do this, Evan. I'm going to be O.K."

Seeing him look somewhat unseated, Ailsa was overcome with the longing to get something off her chest. Something she'd been thinking about ever since her diagnosis.

"I think I should make a will."

Evan blinked at her.

"Um, O.K." He wiped his mouth with his palm. "But do we need to talk about this now? It'd be better…"

She cut him off.

"Yes, we do. Because who knows what might happen, and by then I may not be thinking as clearly as I am now." She willed her heart to settle as she watched him shift in the chair.

"Well, we'll need to see a solicitor then." He blinked.

"I thought I'd ask Dad's guy, John Bellamy."

Evan's eyebrows jumped.

Her defaulting to her father on something that Evan would naturally feel was his responsibility was obviously making him squirm.

"So, you've got it all sorted, then?" He pointedly dropped his gaze to the floor.

"Not really. But it's been bugging me for the past few days." Emboldened, she continued. "Even more so now, since I heard you talking to your mum."

Evan's eyes snapped up to meet hers.

"What do you mean?"

She leaned forward on her elbows.

"You said something about losing me." She saw him flinch. "It's O.K., Evan. It's not like I haven't thought about it too." She paused. "If we're realistic, we know there's that chance."

His eyes were glittering now, the reflection of the flickering fire lighting the dark brown irises.

"I didn't mean you to hear that." His voice rumbled low. "It's just that sometimes I need to talk to someone who..." He hesitated then leaned down and touched his fingertips to hers.

The contact was startling and suddenly, made almost breathless by how much she wished that they could rewind a handful of months and get back to the time when being in his arms was the only place she'd felt safe, Ailsa got up. She held a hand out and he took it, pulling her onto his lap.

"You can talk to me, you know. I won't fall apart." She whispered.

Evan silently wrapped his arms around her waist and as he pulled her closer she felt his breath across her throat.

Four weeks after her diagnosis, time punctuated by doctors, consulting rooms and a slew of tests, they met the third neurosurgeon. He was a small-framed man with clear blue eyes and a shock of silver hair, and as Ailsa sat opposite him, her eyes had been drawn to his Irish, Claddagh wedding ring, the two golden hands gently holding a heart between them. It had struck her as romantic, and somewhat whimsical, for a man so pre-eminent in his field, and it had instantly humanized him.

Mr. James Sutherland had talked them through all the test results and showed them the now familiar MRI films that illuminated the tumor's startling presence. He had gone over Ailsa's diagnosis, answered their numerous questions, and stressed again the potential post-surgical complications. Hearing once again that she could be facing a speech impediment, hearing or even memory loss, was just as chilling as the first time.

Now, sitting opposite him, Ailsa was reprocessing all the information, as Evan fidgeted in the chair by her side.

Sutherland cleared his throat. "What you've been experiencing is typical. When the gangliocytoma is located in the temporal lobe like this, headaches often get worse after exertion or exercise. The sound distortion too, is classic with this type of situation."

Ailsa nodded silently as he closed the file on his desk.

"Do you have any other questions for me?"

Ailsa turned to Evan who, without meeting her gaze, looked at Mr. Sutherland and shook his head.

"No. We're fine."

Sutherland nodded. "Shall we talk dates?" He glanced at his laptop. "I have an opening at the end of next week."

Ailsa felt herself being sucked into a vortex, a dark space where she'd have no purchase, no control of her own trajectory, but as she forced herself to take a deep breath, something shifted inside her. Just as Evan began to speak for her she leaned forward, put a silencing hand on his leg and focused on the surgeon's eyes.

"I'll work around whatever time you have available." She forced a smile.

"Wonderful." Sutherland smiled at her. "Just what we wanted to hear.

EVAN

The night before her surgery, Ailsa sat opposite Evan at the dining table. Having pushed an omelette around her plate, a shadow of something clouded her eyes as she twisted her napkin into a rope and dropped it next to her glass.

"What's up?" He nodded at the untouched food.

"I'm scared."

His heart lurched, as this was the first time she'd said it out loud.

"I know. But you're going to be all right. Better than all right." He watched her suck in her bottom lip. Whatever else had come and gone between them, at this moment he needed to be the voice of reason and keep her on an even keel.

Ailsa avoided his eyes and nodded.

"What if the worst happens, I mean what if I end up like some kind of zombie?" She turned to look out of the window, the November night sky coal-black.

"You won't." He shook his head. "And if you do, I'll book you into the nearest care home." He waited, as her eyes flicked back to his and then, seeing his face, she smiled through her tears.

"Bastard."

Evan grinned. "There will be no zombies in this house. Understood?"

She nodded. "Seriously though, what if something goes wrong and I end up worse off." She searched his face.

Evan pushed some salt grounds into a pile with his thumb.

"You need the surgery. There's no alternative." She was waiting for him to look at her, but now he avoided her eyes. What he'd seen there he had no comfort for, as right now his own fear was threatening to choke him.

After a few moments of silence, Ailsa stood and picked up her plate.

"I know I have no choice, and I'm trying not to go to the dark places, but it happens sometimes." She turned away from him. "I'll get through this."

The surge of relief was tempered by a sinking in his stomach at her use of the word I.

The hospital seemed quiet as they pulled up outside the long building. The weak sunlight was making little to no impression on the windows—multiple rows of dark eyes that rose above the grey concrete base of the structure.

A handful of cars were scattered throughout the parking area as Evan pulled into a space and switched off the engine.

"Ready to go in?"

She was staring out of her window, her shoulders moving with her deeply drawn breaths.

"Yep." She nodded and then let her forehead touch the cool glass.

"Come on then." He opened the door as a blast of cold whisked his breath away.

Having checked in and found her room, Evan put the small

suitcase on the end of the bed. Ailsa was pacing around, checking if the windows opened, pulling back the curtains, all the time twisting her fingers into knots as she moved.

"Sit down." He patted the bed. "Try to relax."

As he heard the ridiculousness of his statement, her hooded eyes met his.

"I know. Poor choice of words." He felt his face grow hot. "Just come and sit."

Ailsa rounded the bed and perched on the edge of the narrow mattress.

"I can't stand the waiting. They just need to come and get on with it."

"They said you should get into this." He laid his hand on the faded gown that was folded on the pillow.

"I know." She snapped, and then bit her lower lip. "Sorry." Evan shook his head.

"No problem." He paused. "Do you want some water?"

She looked up at him. "I'm not allowed any."

Evan felt newly inept. "Oh, right. Sorry."

She shook her head. "What a pair we are." There was a glimmer of a smile as she spoke and with it, relief washed through him.

Soon after a brief visit from Mr. Sutherland, who looked completely different in his scrubs and surgical cap, Ailsa's vital signs had been monitored; an IV port had been inserted in her arm and she'd signed numerous pages of permissions and consent forms. Now, the orderly stood in the doorway. An older man, his scrubs were taut across his ample middle and a mat of thick, silver hair was brushed back from his weather-worn face.

"Ready to go, Mrs. MacIntyre?"

"Yes. I think so." She turned to Evan and with her eyes

locked on his, nodded. "See you soon."

Evan cupped her face in his palms and kissed her. Her cheeks were dry, her eyes clear and as he pulled back he saw a flash of determination, a reminder of the rope of strength that he knew had supported her this far.

"See you soon." Evan held onto her fingers as the orderly released the lock on the bed's wheels.

"We're off to see the wizard." The man winked at Evan.

As the bed moved away from him, Ailsa's fingers slipped out of his and Evan's heart tore in two.

Evan stood at the end of the ICU bed and breathed in the scent of bleach. Ailsa was surrounded by a bank of blinking monitors, numbers flashing and electronic beeps keeping him alert to her breathing, her heart beat and the level of oxygen in her blood. He'd learned a lot by simply observing the nurses coming and going for the past twenty hours.

He hadn't been allowed to stay in her room overnight, but they'd let him come in for a few minutes at a time, so that he could hold her hand and speak to her.

Now, as he looked around, the room was grey. The walls, floor, ceiling and even the paintwork, which he presumed were once white, were all grey and apart from the noise of the machines tracking his wife's vital signs, it was quiet.

The whole neurosurgery ward was quiet. He'd done laps around it while Ailsa was in surgery and he'd noticed that most of the rooms had their doors firmly closed; as Ailsa's now had, protecting the individual struggles going on inside.

Evan's jacket hung on the back of a chair at the bedside and his phone lay like a rock in the pocket of his jeans. Simply by its presence it seemed to be demanding that he call someone; his mother, who was sitting vigil in her flat in Glasgow, or Ailsa's parents, who lived nearby in Stockbridge. Having waited with him for most of the night, and knowing that Ailsa was stable, they had left only two hours earlier to get some much-needed sleep.

Evan patted the phone, but until he had more news, there was nothing he could tell any of them that they didn't already know. Since coming out of the recovery room, Ailsa had opened her eyes a couple of times. She hadn't spoken or acknowledged his presence, but the doctor had said not to be concerned. Apparently, she would slide between various states of consciousness at this stage and Evan was just to be patient.

Her diminutive frame was motionless under the blanket. Her head was wrapped in bandages, heavy with Aladdin-like folds, and one twist of dark hair scarred her cheekbone, while her feet formed a perfect 'V' shape under the covers. Her arms were dwarfed by the tubes and blood pressure cuff that engulfed them on either side of her as she lay, vulnerable, child-like, her eyes shut tight against the starkness of the room.

Evan ran his palm over his rough chin. There was a metallic taste in his mouth from all the coffee he'd drunk, and he was desperate for a shower. He leaned over and stretched out his lower back, his tall frame feeling cumbersome in the small room and, as he looked down, even his feet seemed comically big against the shiny floor.

Ailsa had the smallest feet he'd ever seen, on an adult. Her custom-made ballet shoes were minute, which he loved to tease her about. She'd laugh and say 'well, you know what they say about small packages'.

She looked angelic, despite the bulky bandages, her face smooth and her skin porcelain-pale. Her hands lay loose at her sides, the right one partially open and her fingers curved, as if waiting for his. As he contemplated winding his fingers through hers, a voice inside his head saying *would she want you to, anymore?* held him back.

Now, as he took her in, she looked peaceful. He wanted her to open her eyes and smile at him, like she used to, and yet, in an inner corner of himself, he was also afraid of her waking.

Mr. Sutherland had advised them that there were any number of scenarios that could be expected after surgery, but that she would need at least three to four months just to regain her physical strength. The surgeon had warned that she might continue to experience issues with processing sounds and even spoken words, for some time.

Evan shuddered. He and Ailsa had talked through the various risk factors and tried to rationalize them. There had been tears, shaky moments when he'd expected her to fall apart, but ultimately Ailsa had mustered her strength, telling him that he could count on her to make the fastest recovery on record.

A sound from behind startled him. He swung around to see Amanda, recently back from the States, standing in the doorway. Her fair hair was pulled back in a tight ponytail, her narrow frame stooped under a heavy black coat, a long-handled bag hung over one shoulder and she held a small bunch of tiger lilies.

She whispered. "Can I come in?"

Evan stood up, pulled his sweater down at the sides and nodded.

"Of course." His nerves were already frayed, so the prospect of another dose of Amanda's anger was more than he could manage.

Amanda placed the flowers on the small bedside table, and then walked over to him and patted his arm briefly. The contact quickly turning awkward, she moved away, and as she avoided his eyes, it was clear that he was still on thin ice.

"How're you doing?" She finally looked over at him.

"As you see." He stepped back and did a mock bow. "I've seen better days."

To his surprise, Amanda smiled.

"Nice bow. Very Prince Charming." She slipped out of her coat. "It's bloody cold out there."

"Uh huh. November in Edinburgh. A real treat." He grimaced. "Did you take the train?" Evan eyed the large floral cloth bag that Amanda had dropped on the floor near the door.

"Yep. Not a bad trip." She looked over at the bed. "So, how's she doing? Any updates?"

"No. Stable, for now. She's opened her eyes a couple of times, but apparently we just wait."

Amanda walked over to the door and lifted the bag.

"Hayley sent her a treat." She rooted around inside it and then pulled out a KitKat. "But you might as well have it." She held the chocolate bar out to him, her face impassive.

"Thanks." Evan took the offering. "I'll save it for later."

Amanda rounded the bed and stood next to Ailsa's head.

"She looks so young." She turned to face Evan. "I wish we knew how long she'd be like this."

Evan sank into the narrow chair on the opposite side of the bed.

"You and me both."

Amanda and Ailsa had been close friends since their first week in the company and Evan had watched their friendship develop, surviving performance highs, disappointments, promotions and injuries. They had moved through the ranks together and had been promoted to Coryphées during the same season. When just eighteen months later, Ailsa had been made a soloist, Evan had wondered if there might be some hidden resentment in Amanda, but in all the time he'd known her, he'd never seen any sign of it.

"How's the munchkin?" He smiled.

"She's fine. She's with Mum." Amanda nodded.

When Amanda brought Hayley to visit them, Evan would sometimes spend time playing with the little girl, building forts out of cardboard boxes or chasing a football around the garden.

Hayley's deliberate way of enunciating her words, and her tendency to boss him about, amused him. While he couldn't quite imagine being a father himself, he enjoyed her visits.

"She sends you a hug."

Evan smiled. "She's a spitfire, for sure."

Amanda nodded. "Like mother like daughter, I suppose."

They sat on opposite sides of the bed and took turns dozing and fetching drinks from the vending machine in the waiting area. As the hours slid by, two different nurses came in and out of the room to check Ailsa's vital signs, switch out the IV drip and register the readings on the monitors.

Evan had been for a couple of short walks to get a break and then, when Amanda insisted, he'd dashed over to the Campbell's flat for a shower and to change his clothes.

Leaving Ailsa had caused his anxiety level to go up several notches and by the time he got back to the hospital he was breathing heavily.

"Any change?" He tossed his coat onto the chair and leaned over his wife.

"No. She's not moved." Amanda stood up and stretched out her back. "These chairs are awful." She grimaced.

Evan leaned down and kissed Ailsa's cheek.

"Go for a walk. I'll call you if anything changes." He watched as Amanda lifted her coat and slid it on.

"Do you want me to get you some food?" She slung her bag over her shoulder.

"No. I'm fine. Thanks." He shook his head. "Can't get anything down at the moment."

Amanda turned at the door.

"She's going to be fine, Evan."

He nodded. "I know."

AILSA

Ailsa's eyelids were locked down, and something was tugging cruelly at the left side of her head. There was an odd smell, like lemons, or something else she couldn't quite place, and the air that she breathed in was frigid. As she strained to hear, a series of distant beeps pinged consistently to her left—an unnerving sound that seemed to be linked to her breaths.

She forced a dry swallow, the sides of her throat sticky, as if they'd been glued together, and her heart beat dully in her ears as the volume of the beeps faded in and out.

Her sense of her body was numbed, her limbs like dead weights, and as she tried to force sensation into her fingers, their disconnection and refusal to respond to her directions sent a bolt of fear into her chest.

Her breaths began coming faster as she pressed her lips together, willing some clue to her situation to materialize beneath her eyelids.

As she once again tried to assess the receptiveness of her body, mentally connect with her musculature, her spine and limbs, now there was an undercurrent of pain, a blurred rather than sharp sensation, but she recognized it.

Her confusion building in time with her fear, she licked her chapped lips then, using all the energy she could gather, forced her eyes open.

It took a few seconds for her focus to clear then, above her, she saw a strange ceiling, rows of square white tiles, like an army of pock-marked faces, lined up cheek to cheek. She blinked, her eyes gritty as if all the moisture had been sucked from them, leaving two dry stones in the sockets. She blinked several times more until gradually the lids moved more easily, allowing her to focus on the yellowish light above her head.

Her hands were cold, and as she tried to move them, her fingers felt loose and rubbery. A stream of unconnected thoughts filled her mind, the unfamiliarity of her surroundings making her want to shout for help. Her breathing now ragged, she sucked more air into her lungs, and with an almighty effort lifted her right hand up in front of her face feeling something snag the back of it. Startled by a shooting pain, she made a fist, stretching out the tension around the cannula that was taped tightly to her skin.

Her heart was now battering its way out of her chest, as she let her hand fall again, the effort of holding it up too great to sustain. She was exhausted, adrift in a strange place and wanting desperately to find her footing but as she tried to focus, drag herself out of this bizarre dream, her mind remained clouded, as if the space around her was smoke-filled.

Letting her head roll to the left, Ailsa felt a stab above her ear, more distinct than before. Her instinct was to put her hand to her head but once again she felt the tug of the I.V. She tried to swallow past the nut of fear that was making it hard to breathe and as she turned her head to the right, she saw him.

The room was dim, but a man was sitting in a chair, his long legs splayed out in a wide V shape and his chin dipped to his chest above his crossed arms. As she stared at the outline, the sound of his throaty breathing was clear, and the realization that she was not alone made her heart rate pick up, even more alarming than the sensations that were now trailing along her limbs, like electricity beetling through her veins.

Desperate to place herself somehow, she glanced down and saw an unfamiliar, pale blue blanket and beyond it a plastic footboard at the end of the bed. On her right side, there was a rail, like those she'd seen on a cot, or bunk beds, and as she moved her hand out slowly, wanting to touch the metal to see if it was real, the man in the chair shifted. His head jerked upright as he pulled in his legs and abruptly stood up.

Her heart now near exploding and her vulnerability cloaking her in sweat, Ailsa made another fist, this time with her left hand, and tried to push herself up in the bed. Then, she felt his hands on her, one on each shoulder, keeping her down. She wanted to scream but her voice wouldn't come, so she squeezed her eyes shut and tried to go rigid under the pressure of his unwanted touch.

Then, she heard her name, faint but recognizable.

"Ailsa?"

That was her name he was saying and yet his voice made it feel as if it no longer belonged to her. Pressing her eyes tighter shut she tried to will him away, to picture her own room, the safe space that she knew, but no images came.

After a few moments, the pressure on her shoulders gradually released, so forcing her breaths to come more slowly, she opened her eyes again.

His face was close, the dark eyes scanning hers like search lights.

"Ailsa?" He spoke quietly. "It's me, love." He paused. "Evan."

Evan. She knew that name. A memory sparked in her mind but as Ailsa tried to keep hold of it, the pull of sleep was suddenly overwhelming. She tried to say his name, ask him where she was, where her parents were, but felt herself being dragged under a powerful ocean. Then, she heard her name again, this time louder, but she couldn't stay.

~

Ailsa felt clouds lifting her body, like a bed of soft cotton underneath her, floating her through a clear blue sky. The lemon smell was back, stronger this time, and the sound of beeping was louder than before. She tried opening her eyes again, this time able to do so more easily, and as she touched her thumb to her finger tip, she was jolted by a voice, close to her right side.

"You're awake."

As he leaned over her, she tried to place the blurry face, the mop of hair that fell into one of those dark eyes, the smile. As the features floated in front of her, a whisper from deep inside said that this man could help her, so she wet her lips and took a breath.

"Where am I?" Her voice sounded distorted, crackling with static like an old radio.

"You're in the hospital." He sat on the edge of the bed and she felt his hand slide over hers, the unexpected contact making her pull away.

He released her, as if touching her had burned them both.

"What…" Her voice failed her this time, so she swallowed and tried again. "What's happening?" She stared at the face, its edges taking shape as she blinked repeatedly. "Why are you here?"

He stood up slowly, placing a palm flat on his chest.

"It's me. Evan."

Ailsa saw fear in the eyes she now knew were familiar. An image of the two of them holding hands made her blink and suddenly she was certain that this was not someone to be afraid of. As he remained stationary, hand still flat on his chest, she felt a surge of pity and shifted in the bed. With the movement her hand went up to her head finding a spongy mound rather than her hair. As she fingered the foreign surface, searching for something that resembled her own body, her pity for him dissolved and the hairs on her arms stood to attention.

"What's the matter with me?" She turned and saw the blinking monitors next to the bed. "Why am I here?" Her heart was surging into her throat as she tried to push herself up from the pillows behind her.

"Don't move. Let me call the doctor." Evan spun around, skidded toward the door and pushed it open.

"Hello?" He shouted into the corridor, holding the door ajar behind him so that she could still see him from the bed. His presence, his grip on the string that was connecting them, felt tenuous, but something she didn't want to let go of. He was all she knew in this strange place. He mustn't leave her yet.

"Nurse?" He called again.

A tall woman in scrubs with a stethoscope slung around her neck appeared in the doorway. She held an electronic tablet close to her chest and her pale eyes looked tired.

"Yes?" She bobbed her cropped blonde head and then smiled.

"She's woken up." He spoke quietly. "But she seems disoriented."

The nurse nodded and slipped past him.

"Well, hello there." She laid the tablet on the bedside table and leaned over Ailsa. With gentle pressure she eased Ailsa back against the pillows. "Just relax, m'love and let me take a look at you."

Ailsa stared at the woman as she lifted a small flashlight.

"What's..." Ailsa croaked.

"Just follow the light for me."

With no apparent option, Ailsa obeyed, her eyes tracking the small beam of light back and forth.

"Lovely. Now stick your tongue out for me." The nurse lifted the stethoscope from around her neck and plugged it into her ears as Ailsa stuck her tongue out, foolishly probing the air.

"Great. Now breathe deeply for me." The nurse leaned in and placed the silvery disc on Ailsa's chest, the shot of cold shocking her.

Evan stood at the far side of the room, his back pressed against the wall until the nurse turned to him.

"Looks good." She nodded. "Now, Mrs. MacIntyre, can you tell me what day it is?" The blonde head hovered at the end of the bed as the woman addressed Ailsa.

Feeling as if the words had slapped her hard, Ailsa grabbed the blanket, her eyes flicking from the nurse to Evan, still standing in the corner. A million muddled thoughts were cascading through her mind, but the word *Mrs.* bubbled loudly to the surface.

"Mrs. MacIntyre?"

Ailsa's head was beginning to throb as the force of her fear gathered momentum.

"Can you tell me what day it is, Mrs. MacIntyre?" The nurse walked back to Ailsa's side and reached down to feel her wrist.

Hearing a pulsing in her ear, unsure if it was her heartbeat, Ailsa eyed Evan once again, then turning her head toward the nurse, she shook her head.

"What did you call me?" She panted, her skin beginning to feel tacky.

The nurse slung the stethoscope back around her neck.

"Mrs. MacIntyre?" The woman glanced over at Evan, who was frowning.

Ailsa shook her head again. "That's not my name." She flashed a panicked glance at Evan. "I don't know what day it is." She lifted a hand and touched her bandages again. "What's the matter with me?"

Evan walked to the bedside.

"You're recovering from your surgery." He glanced at the

nurse, seeming to ask for some sign of encouragement. Instead the woman was scanning the tablet she'd picked up from the table. "They took out your tumor." He hesitated. "Mr. Sutherland said it went well."

Ailsa stared at Evan. Tumor? The shocking word reverberated around her, a misnomer, surely a mistake.

The nurse gently eased herself in between Evan and Ailsa. "Ailsa. Do you know who this is?" She pointed at Evan.

Ailsa's eyes jumped between their two faces, and as she tried desperately to give them what they were asking of her, her lips rippled and her face dissolved.

"I know him." She sobbed. "But I don't know why I'm here." She jabbed a finger at the nurse and then overcome by the need to escape this place, reached down and yanked the blanket off. Her angular knees stuck out from the hem of the hospital gown and her skin shone opalescent under the overhead light.

Wishing she might sink back into the oblivion of sleep, she appealed to her friend.

"I want to go home, Evan. Where's Mum?" She hesitated. "Does she know I'm here?"

The nurse held Ailsa firmly around the shoulders and spoke carefully, close to her ear.

"Ailsa. Who is that man?"

Ailsa's strength was waning.

"He's Evan." She sniffed against the nurse's shoulder. "I go out with him."

Evan looked rocked by her words as the nurse gently settled Ailsa back against the pillows and smoothed the sheet over her chest.

"Evan's your husband, pet."

The word husband lanced her chest and Ailsa lurched back up, her head now pounding with the exertion of resistance.

"Where's my dad?"

The nurse held Ailsa against her chest and stuck her chin out indicating the button on the side of the bed.

"Mr. MacIntyre, press the call button."

Evan reached over and pressed it.

"Now go to the nurses' station and tell them to page the doctor." She whispered over her shoulder. "Go now, Mr. MacIntyre."

Ailsa looked up at the ceiling tiles again. She had counted them from one edge of the room to the other and was now working her way back to the door. Something seemed to be rocking the bed, and in order to resist sleep, she focused on the checked lines over her head.

A few minutes earlier there had been a cold sensation in her arm and now the nut in her throat was less choking.

Evan was standing in the corner of the room whispering with the doctor.

The nurse had called Evan her husband. His angular face, the eyes and the tight curls were known to her, but husband? A version of Evan was present in her consciousness, but only as someone she was dating. She knew his voice, his breath and his touch—although it disturbed her to be touched by him today—and even though she couldn't piece together the explanation that he'd given her for her presence here, she also knew that she trusted him, but could she love Evan? Love him enough to marry him?

When she tried to summon a memory, perhaps a flowing dress and veil, delicate flowers, or a ring, there was nothing but blankness, adding to her mounting sense of panic.

She shifted against the pillow and lifted a hand to her head. Once again, the lumpy bandage felt odd and intrusive under her fingertips.

Evan had said that she'd had a tumor removed. Ailsa frowned, the fear the word engendered was numbing as she tried saying it out loud. Tumor. Her mouth felt slack, the word cumbersome on her tongue.

She let her arm flop back to her side, her muscles like lead and the effort of moving draining her. As she closed her eyes, even her eyelids were aching.

In the merciful dark, Evan spoke again, and the doctor replied, but Ailsa didn't know the doctor's voice. He had talked to her a little while ago, when the nurse called him into the room, and he'd been kind. She liked his face, but it was new to her, his grey-blue eyes, below the smudged glasses that he'd shoved halfway up his forehead, had been distracting as she'd tried to focus on what he was saying, the thrum of her heart constant in her ears.

"Ailsa. Can you tell me where you are?" He'd looked down at her, his cool fingers pressed into her wrist.

"No." Her voice was still rough and speaking made her cough, sending rows of burning ants crawling up the side of her head.

"You're in Edinburgh, Ailsa. At the Western Hospital." He'd glanced at Evan across the room. "We removed your tumor successfully."

Edinburgh. The notion of being in her hometown had filled her with a mixture of relief and confusion. Then, there was that word again, the sound of it sent a chill through her middle.

"Tumor?" She'd blinked, watching his face melt into a blur and then clarify again.

"Yes. You've been unwell for quite a while. Do you remember the headaches, Ailsa?"

When he'd said the word, Ailsa did remember. The memory of the vice-like pain that would clamp around her head, making it hard to rotate her eyes in their sockets, had been clear.

"Yes." The nod she'd tried to give became a chin dip. "I remember those."

The doctor had asked her to follow the tiny light again and then told her to hold her hands out in front of herself, palms up. She'd done it, although she'd been unable to stay that way for more than a few moments before her arms sagged.

"All right. Just rest now. We'll talk again in a little while." He had patted her leg and walked back to Evan in the corner, where they stood now, their heads close together.

She opened her eyes and caught a flash of blue light, high up in the corner of the room. Curious, she turned her head to follow it. It looked like a firework, bouncing off the dull walls, evading the track of her eye. She lifted her hand and reached out toward the spark but wherever she looked, it moved, a sliver of time ahead of her gaze. She wanted to touch it, hold it like a sparkler stick on bonfire night, so she stretched her fingers out, but her hand passed through the light trails. Disappointed she looked over at Evan who was staring at her, his mouth slightly open.

"What is it, Ailsa?" The doctor was back at her side.

"A sparkler." She ran her tongue over her lips. "Up there." She flicked her eyes to the left.

He turned and spoke to the nurse who had appeared in the doorway. Ailsa tried to focus on what he was saying but the room's edges were fading, her visual field shrinking to a bull's eye and as the sounds around her became sludgy, their voices faded and sleep won out.

EVAN

E van sat in the waiting area outside Ailsa's room. It smelled of burnt toast and the floor was tacky under his shoes. Half a sandwich lay on a cellophane wrapper on the chair next to him, its dried edges curling upwards like wings, and the coffee in the paper cup he held was cold. He stared into the black fluid, where a reflection of the harsh overhead light floated on the surface.

He'd called Amanda's mobile and suggested she go home to Glasgow, until they knew what was happening. The last thing Ailsa needed at the moment was another face to confuse her, and while Amanda had sounded dubious, to his relief she had agreed.

For the last couple of hours, he'd been on an emotional seesaw, one minute elated that Ailsa had come through the surgery then, just as quickly, crashing to the ground because there was something new to deal with. Her memory being affected was one of the worse-case scenarios that Mr. Sutherland had prepared them for but now that it was apparently a reality, all the coping strategies that they'd talked about, should this happen, like using photo albums, pieces of clothing and letters they'd exchanged to jog her memory seemed inane and impractical.

While she remembered him, even saying his name, she'd forgotten that they were married. How much more of their existence together had been left in the operating room? Now, as his wife slept fitfully nearby, Evan was afraid to scratch the scab off that particular question. While, to his shame, there were things he'd prefer she didn't remember, had their entire timeline together been erased with the swipe of the scalpel?

He had called Ailsa's parents to tell them that she'd woken up, and they were on their way back to the hospital. Jennifer had been curt on the phone when he'd tried to explain what was going on. Ailsa's mother had intimidated Evan, when they'd first met. He'd felt as if he was being assessed as a potential husband from the first time they'd talked, and Jennifer's pointed questions about his career, his living arrangements and his ambitions had been intrusive, verging on insulting.

Colin had been equally inquisitive but had asked more shrouded questions, couching them with statements like 'When I was your age I was so focused on travelling I almost let my career plan get away from me. Do you have a long-term plan, Evan?'

Evan smiled into the coffee cup as he remembered the first, awkward dinners at the Campbell's chic, Stockbridge house. In the high-ceilinged, pastel-colored living room, replete with original artwork, French antiques and priceless Persian carpets, he had felt like a tugboat moored next to a row of sleek yachts. He was big, clumsy and slightly disheveled, despite Ailsa's efforts to tidy him up. Back then, he'd hardly been out of Scotland in his twenty-nine years and, oddly, when he'd talked about it, even the career he loved as an I.T. developer had sounded dull and tedious.

As these bi-monthly evenings with her parents went on he had begun to feel more relaxed with Colin, but there was something in Jennifer's manner which suggested that she remained singularly unimpressed by her petite, refined ballet-dancing daughter's towering lump of a boyfriend. Evan had soon deduced that one sure way to win Jennifer over would be to advocate for Ailsa, push and encourage the career aspirations that the formidable woman held for her daughter. It had taken a few years, but he'd eventually sensed that Jennifer considered him an ally in this regard but, despite that commonality, there were still times when he felt somehow less than what they had hoped for, for their daughter.

As he considered how fortunate he'd been that Ailsa had agreed not to share with her parents the fact that he'd strayed, he dropped his chin to his chest and rolled his head in a half circle, feeling the taut muscles pulling behind his shoulder blades.

He stood up, gathered the sandwich and threw it into the bin along with the coffee. Running a hand over his chin he turned to see Colin walking toward him. The older man was pale, his coat hung loose about his shoulders and the dark skin under his eyes showed the strain of the past two days.

"Evan." Colin smiled and patted Evan's back.

Evan gestured toward the sitting area.

"Let's chat for a bit, before we go in. Where's Jennifer?" He glanced behind Colin.

"She's in the ladies' room. She'll just be a minute." Colin rolled his eyes.

Evan nodded and sat as Colin, settled opposite him.

"So, our girl's having some problems." He eyed Evan, waiting for more information.

"She's been awake, speaking etcetera," Evan cleared his throat, "but it looks like there's been some affect to her memory." He heard footsteps and turned to see Jennifer approaching. Her cream coat swung around her slim calves and as he watched her progress down the corridor, Evan felt irrationally angry at the sight of her elegant high-heels, which seemed jarring and incongruous under the circumstances. She had draped a Burberry scarf around her neck, her pearly hair was brushed back in a tight twist and large diamonds flashed in her earlobes.

Evan watched as his mother-in-law slipped the scarf and coat off, handing them absently to her husband, before bending to peck Evan's cheek.

"Evan. How is she?" Her breath was minty.

Evan swallowed. This wasn't how he'd imagined this scene. He'd pictured them all sitting around Ailsa's bed while she lay peacefully, enjoying the family banter and talk of when she'd be going home. Now, he looked at her parent's expectant faces and, for some reason, felt responsible for the predicament their daughter was in, as if he had covertly invaded her brain and planted those errant cells, fed and watered them and then watched them grow into the catalyst that had brought all this about.

Forcing the notion from his mind, Evan pushed his shoulders down.

"She's resting. She was distressed, so they gave her something to help her sleep." He felt Jennifer's eyes land on him like searchlights from across a darkened pond.

"What do you mean exactly by distressed?" She leaned forward in her chair and clasped her long fingers around her knee.

"She was a bit confused about where she was and seemed to have no memory of having a tumor, or surgery." He paused. "Mr. Sutherland said it's possible that there's been some damage to the temporal lobe which is affecting her memory. He called it potential retrograde amnesia." He watched as Jennifer's eyes flicked to Colin's.

"Is it permanent?" She spoke to her husband, a note of panic in her voice that Evan had never heard before.

Irritated by her seeming dismissal of him, Evan spoke deliberately.

"We don't know yet." He went on. "They're going to do

another functional MRI when she wakes up and then they'll be able to tell us more."

Colin nodded and pushed himself out of the chair, walked to the window and thrust his hands deep into his pockets. Jennifer watched her husband and, for once, seemed to have nothing to add.

Evan stared at Colin's taut back, Evan's momentary irritation with Jennifer seeping away.

"What's the functional MRI again?" His father-in-law spoke to the darkening window.

"It measures brain activity by detecting changes in blood flow." Evan hesitated, as neither Colin nor Jennifer were reacting to what he was saying. Flicking his eyes between them, he went on. "From what I understand, they use contrast dye and then show her certain images and play sounds to her. When she responds to the images or sounds, various areas of the brain light up as blood flow to that region increases." He hesitated. "I think they can gauge fairly accurately if any areas aren't responding." Evan swallowed. The idea that areas of Ailsa's brain might remain unresponsive hadn't sunk in until he'd just regurgitated the explanation that Mr. Sutherland had given him a short while ago. The concept of Ailsa having been deeply or—God forbid— permanently changed by all this chilled him as the word *unre-sponsive* hung in the air.

Colin turned to face him. He looked dazed as Jennifer stood up and joined him at the window.

"Will she know us?" Jennifer wrapped her manicured fingers around Colin's forearm and to Evan's surprise, she looked scared.

"She should. She knew me—she just couldn't…" Evan stopped.

"Couldn't what?" Jennifer stared, her mouth slightly open.

"She didn't remember that we were married." Evan flinched

at the odd-sounding statement. Even as he said it, it felt too removed from reality to be given credence.

Colin's eyes snapped into focus.

"Seriously?" He shrugged Jennifer's hand off.

Evan nodded, as shock clouded his father-in-law's face.

"I'm sure it's only temporary." He tried to smile. "She was asking for you, Jennifer."

At this Jennifer seemed to spark back to life.

"Can we see her now?" She lifted her coat from the chair.

"I'll go and find out what's going on." Evan rose and as he passed, he patted Jennifer's arm. She didn't flinch or resist the contact, as he thought she might, but instead she placed her hand over his and squeezed his fingers.

"Thanks, Evan."

AILSA

A ilsa lay on the narrow examination table. The room was frigid and the thin blanket that the nurse had put over her legs wasn't heavy enough to stop her shivering. Her head was thumping and she wanted someone she knew. She wanted her dad.

The doctor had told her that she needed to have an MRI. She couldn't remember having had any before, but he assured her that she had.

"You're a pro, Ailsa." He had laughed. "You know more about these machines now than I do." He'd nodded at the long white tube behind her. "Just relax and these lovely ladies will tell you what to do."

Two nurses stood at the door leading to a long glass kiosk. One of them was the blonde woman who'd been in her room a while ago. Ailsa stared at the cropped head and wondered how easy it must be to have hair that short. She had long hair that took ages to dry when she washed it. The momentary flash of recall shone like a beacon. She had long hair. Such a simple thing, but something she knew to be true inside this fog of uncertainty that had swallowed her up.

The other nurse, a short woman with a red ponytail and blue scrubs, was now at her side, sliding a block under her knees.

"This'll help take the pressure off your back." She had an accent, but Ailsa couldn't place it. It didn't sound like her own, the vowels being flatter and the R's more pronounced.

Ailsa nodded against the flat pillow under her head.

"We'll put these goggles on you, so we can show you pictures when we talk to you from the control room, then we'll put this little cage over your face too, to help you stay still."

The woman leaned over her, a pair of clear goggles and a white plastic contraption in her hands.

Panic spiking through her veins, Ailsa's hands went up to protect her face.

"Do I have to wear those?"

The nurse laid the items on a small trolley next to the table and lifted Ailsa's hand.

"Try to relax. It won't take long, and we need these pictures to see what's going on." The cold fingers felt intrusive against her own clammy skin and Ailsa slid her hand away.

She stared at the red ponytail, now dangling over the nurse's left breast, and something stirred in her middle.

"Where's Evan?"

"He's waiting in your room. The sooner we get you in there the sooner you'll be out and back to him." The redhead jabbed a thumb toward the tubular machine.

Ailsa twisted to look at the cylinder afraid that she couldn't do this, allow them to slide her inside the white coffin, her face behind a plastic cage.

"How long?" She looked back at the nurse.

"Inside? About forty minutes." The nurse turned toward the control room window and signaled something, the ponytail now dangling between her narrow shoulder blades.

Ailsa pressed her eyes closed. The room was closing in, the walls pressing against her.

146

"Let's get on with it then." She whispered.

The nurse leaned down and spoke close to Ailsa's ear.

"Just try to relax. You'll be O.K."

Twenty minutes later, looking through the plastic cage, Ailsa lay inside the narrow tube. She'd been asked to wiggle her fingers and toes, purse her lips and stick her tongue out while the machine clicked and banged around her. The proximity of the tube was cloying and the impulse to sit up, to grab the sides and push her way out was making her sweat.

Now she stared at a mirror, only a few inches from her face. The cage made it impossible for her to move her head as images flashed on the mirror in quick succession—a flower, a plate of food, a mountain, a child in a stroller. The sight of the baby made her heart jolt as she blinked furiously.

As per the nurse's instructions, she pressed the controller in her hand as the images kept coming. A snow-capped mountain then a red car, then a river with white frothy waves followed by a tangerine sunset. She took a shallow breath, trying to focus on the images and not the disquieting, thumping vibrations of the machine around her.

The nurse's voice crackled inside the earphones.

"O.K., Ailsa. Now we're going to show you pictures and I'll tell you the name of each item. You'll need to click if the two things match. Understand?"

Ailsa tried to nod.

"Yes. How much longer now?" Her mouth was dry.

"Almost there. About another ten minutes and you're done."

Ten minutes might as well have been ten days as her eyes blurred behind the goggles.

Evan was standing in the room as she was wheeled back in.

"Hi, love." His eyes were tired.

She scanned his face. What was different about him? He looked older, and Evan was always clean-shaven, so the dark shadow on his chin was new. Something else that she knew for a fact was like a light bulb going on in her head.

On the opposite side of the bed her mother and father stood, shoulder to shoulder. Their faces were drawn, and her father's nose was red.

"Mum, you're here?" Her whole body awash with relief, Ailsa extended a hand toward them. "Dad?"

Jennifer's serene mask crumpled and she turned abruptly to the wall, digging in her handbag for something. The flash of emotion that she saw in her mother's face wrenched at Ailsa's insides, and while she waited for Jennifer to recover her composure, Ailsa felt her father take her hand. His hand trembled as he captured her fingers in his. Whatever had happened, she had caused this uncharacteristic and emotional reaction in them both, and she was desperate to comfort them.

"I'm sorry, Dad. It's all right. I'm O.K."

"You had us worried there, for a while." Colin squeezed her fingers. His face was flushed, and his eyes were glistening.

The healthcare assistant pushing Ailsa's wheelchair coughed, as if to announce his presence.

"Right, we need to get you back in bed." He positioned the chair next to the bed and lifted the blanket from Ailsa's knees. "Put your arms around my neck and we'll lift you up."

The man was tall and narrow, built like a runner. He wore a long chain with a small gold disc on it and as Ailsa obediently reached around his neck, she smelled coffee. He circled her waist with his arms and lifted her effortlessly from the chair up onto her feet. She hadn't stood up for a while so being upright made her unsteady and as she swayed, he held her firmly, taking much of her weight on his forearms.

"Well, you're just a featherweight." He spoke above her head and she heard the smile in his voice.

Supporting her under each arm he turned and seated her on the edge of the bed, then helped her swing her legs up, folded the covers over her and smoothed them across her hips.

"You take care now." He patted Ailsa's hand.

"Thank you, Eric." Ailsa read the name tag on his shirt. "You're very kind."

The man smiled at her and then over at her parents, who were now sitting together at the far side of the bed.

Ailsa's face colored, embarrassed that neither of them seemed to acknowledge Eric's presence.

Evan was once again standing at the outer edge of the room. His shoulders rolled forwards and his head hung, almost apologetically. He looked exhausted.

"Evan?" She watched as he raised his chin. "What time is it?"

He pulled his phone from his pocket.

"It's ten to six." He walked over and perched on the edge of the bed. As he reached for her hand, Ailsa took a breath and didn't pull away this time. She'd seen the hurt in his eyes the last time she'd flinched from his touch, and she had hurt everyone enough for one day.

He smiled at her, his big hand over hers.

"How're you feeling?" His brow was wrinkled and his dark eyes weren't looking into hers, they were scanning her bandages.

"I'm tired." Breathy and banal, the statement was all that she could muster.

Ailsa turned to her parents. They were oddly quiet, sitting vigil as she fidgeted, adjusting the gown that had become twisted and was now pulling tightly at her neck. The tape on her hand tugged as she moved and the cannula shifting inside her vein sent a shard of pain into her bicep.

She didn't want to be here any longer. There were so many questions that she needed answers to, and the sooner she could go home she was sure the sooner all this would make sense.

Evan released her hand and got up, then yanked at his sweater. She didn't recognize the sweater. It was brown and had a half zip going up under his chin. She liked it.

As she waited for someone to break the awkward silence, Ailsa could no longer hold herself upright. She let the muscles in her neck release and relaxed back against the pillow.

"Can we just go home now?" She eyed her parents. "Mum?"

Jennifer looked startled by the question and pulled herself up from her slump.

"Well, I don't know darling. What did the doctor say?"

Ailsa's last sliver of strength faded as she shook her head against the pillow.

"I don't know."

Evan had circled the bed and now stood at the end, looking down at her.

"It'll be a few more days. You need to heal and rest." He glanced over at her parents. "Then we'll go home, and you can start to get your strength back."

Ailsa frowned, confused at the idea that Evan would come home with her, her parents never having allowed him to stay over before. She saw her father's eyes become shrouded by his heavy brows.

"Can Evan come home with us, Dad?" Ailsa chewed her lower lip, the gesture a hangover from childhood nervousness.

Colin's mouth clamped shut and he smoothed the hair over his right ear.

Jennifer looked up at Evan and shook her head as he stepped around to the bedside and lifted Ailsa's hand again.

"You'll come home with me, Ails. To our flat." His pupils were enormous as Ailsa took in his words and tried to make sense of them.

"Our flat?" She frowned.

"Yes. Our flat in Glasgow."

Evan stood over her, his eyes questioning. What he'd said

had been clear, but the meaning behind it was shaking her to her core. She looked over at her parents, but seeing nothing there, other than their blanched expressions, she turned back to Evan.

He let her hand slip back onto the blanket.

"We've lived there for almost nine years. We moved in six months before we got married." His voice was flat, defeated, his obvious pain and disappointment grabbing at her middle.

Ailsa felt as if she were falling, a funnel-cloud of fear threatening to suck her in and consume her, but as she battled the wave of questions flooding her mind, she focused on Evan's face. Married. They were married. It must be true, because he wouldn't lie in front of her parents, but as she struggled to digest the information, her eyelids fluttering with the effort of controlling her desire to yell 'I don't remember', she saw his expression.

With everything she didn't know, she did know he was on her side, and she didn't want to upset him anymore. Wanting desperately to do at least one good thing amidst this mess, she grabbed his hand.

"I'm sorry. I just don't remember everything clearly." She tugged on his fingers trying to get him to look at her until eventually, Evan met her eyes.

"It's all right. Just rest now." He patted her hand and as he turned away she saw his face slacken.

Everything she had remembered since waking up in this place suddenly pressed in on her, the smell of the room; the coolness of the stringent air, the spongy bandages around her head and the needles in her skin, the cloying closeness of the MRI machine to her face, the doctor's pale eyes, the red pony tail. She pressed her eyes closed and felt herself rocking, as if she were lying in a row boat as the river undulated beneath her. She gripped the bedcover, trying to steady herself, her fingers clawing the blue blanket into her fists.

"I'm sorry." She gulped. "I'm just so tired."

She felt a cool hand close over hers and opening her eyes saw her mother, the pearly hair in the trademark bun and the blueness of the eyes, mirrors of her own, glittering as they traced her face.

"Sleep, darling. We'll sort everything out later." Jennifer lay her palm lightly on Ailsa's cheek, her mother's touch instantly calming. "Just sleep now."

EVAN

E van sat opposite Mr. Sutherland, in the stuffy office. The
light was waning outside the narrow window and Evan
realized that it would soon be a full forty-eight hours since he
had slept for more than a few minutes.

Ailsa sat next to him in a wheelchair. She had wanted to walk
to the office, from the room she'd been moved to on the
neurology ward, but Eric had insisted that she ride in the chair.

Evan had been shocked to see her so unsteady on her feet,
unable to stand without support, and he wondered if he had not
heard that part of the briefing they'd been given. She was dizzy,
nauseous and exhausted, all of which he could understand—but
watching her struggling to walk, even with Eric's strong arm
under hers, had knocked the breath out of Evan. It had reminded
him of programs he'd seen on TV about veterans in rehab clinics
battling with their broken bodies.

As Ailsa had eventually folded at the knees and sunk into the
waiting wheelchair, Evan had closed his eyes and visualized her
in the middle of a darkened stage, spinning in a series of fouet-
tés. Her body was held, perfectly centered, her supporting foot
moving up and down onto pointe as her working leg whipped out

in confident circles, creating just the right amount of momentum to turn her on the axis of her supporting leg, her head spotting sharply to the front.

Whatever role she was performing, Ailsa made the choreography look like it had all been her idea, despite its complexity and the often brutal demands on her body. As he looked over at her, he struggled to rationalize his conflicting emotions. The bloated-faced, bandaged and blanket draped woman in the chair next to him was that same talented dancer, but for now, she needed help just to walk a few steps.

Mr. Sutherland was talking and Evan realized that his exhausted mind had wandered and that he hadn't heard the last statement.

"I'm sorry, what did you say?" He must focus, as every word was critical.

"It's possible that Ailsa's episodic memory has been affected by the surgery." Mr. Sutherland leaned back in his chair. "You'll be able to remember most things in a general sense Ailsa, for instance how to make tea or tie your shoes; who's Prime Minister and what country you live in, but you could have problems remembering specific events in chronological order, like what year you left school or when you visited specific places." He hesitated, a silver pen sliding back and forth between his fingers. "For instance, you remember Evan—that you love Evan —but you didn't remember that you are married."

The word *love* lingered awkwardly in the room and Evan glanced over at Ailsa who was frowning, her fingers twisting the blanket over her knees.

"Your physical skills shouldn't be affected permanently. Once you've fully regained your strength, in a few months, you'll be able to move around perfectly normally, and even dance as you once did." The man's smile was warm but it seemed lost on Ailsa, who now stared out of the window.

"Where will I dance?" She spoke to the glass, her voice tremulous.

Mr. Sutherland glanced at Evan, handing him the verbal baton.

"In the studio with the company, and at the theatre." Evan reached over and tucked a strand of hair behind her exposed ear.

Ailsa met his gaze and frowned, her eyes enormous under the wad of bandages.

"Theater?"

Evan's throat tightened. The idea that she could have forgotten that she was in the ballet company tore at him. If she had forgotten that entire section of her timeline, the chances were she had lost a lot more.

Mr. Sutherland cut into the silence.

"Sometimes distant memories are easier to access than more recent events. You might remember your childhood, growing up and things involving your parents etcetera, more easily than what happened a few months or even weeks ago. It's known as Ribot's Law." He met Evan's gaze and Evan nodded, giving him permission to continue. "The events closest to your illness and surgery however, could be gone forever."

"Why?" Ailsa's voice was stronger. Whatever the trigger had been, she was now engaged in the conversation.

"Because the neural pathways of the newer memories aren't as entrenched as those of the memories you've been accessing for years." He smiled. "It's like each time you access an old memory you're making it stronger. Do you understand?" He leaned forward, slid the pen onto the desk and linked his fingers over a file.

Ailsa nodded.

"But if I really try to get them back—the newer memories I mean. Can I?" Evan felt his heart clench as silent tears slid down her cheek.

Mr. Sutherland picked up a box of tissues and held them out to her.

"You can certainly work on it. The best way to do that is to help the memories along with reminders like photographs. Listening to music you enjoyed is particularly good, or seeing and holding articles that meant a lot to you—like ballet shoes or your wedding dress." He smiled at Evan. "That can speed up the rate of recall."

Evan felt a lift of hope.

"So there can be recall. It's not all gone, forever?"

Sutherland pulled his mouth down at the corners and frowned.

"It's possible that some of it will come back, with time and effort, Evan. But every case is unique and honestly, we have no way of knowing for sure."

Evan leaned back in the chair and felt the wooden frame dig into his back. He'd take it. He'd take a maybe, however tentative at this point.

"You'll have to be patient with yourself, Ailsa." Sutherland stood up behind his desk, the movement an eloquent indication that the meeting was over. "And you'll have to be patient too." He turned to Evan. "Ailsa might be anxious and depressed. She could have problems being in loud places, or feel uncomfortable in crowds and public spaces."

He turned back to Ailsa.

"It's like your brain's filter is a bit clogged. You'll have to be careful not to overload it for a while."

Evan nodded and yanked at the neck of his sweater which was making him sweat in the over-warm room.

"Just keep focusing on your rest, Ailsa, on keeping up your strength. But keep moving too. We don't want your muscles to atrophy." He extended a hand toward Evan who, taking his cue, rose from the chair and responded in kind.

"You'll stay here for a week or so and I'll be checking on you daily."

Evan stood behind Ailsa's chair and gripped the rubberized handles. They felt tacky as he tightened and loosed his fingers around them.

As the wheelchair began to move, Ailsa held a hand up.

"Wait. I have a question." She turned her head and looked up at Evan, then back at the doctor.

"Of course." Mr. Sutherland nodded.

"Could I ask you in private?" She lowered her head, as if ashamed of her tacit request for Evan to leave.

Mr. Sutherland looked alarmed.

"Well, you can. But..."

"Ailsa, I'd rather stay." Evan spoke to the top of her head.

Ailsa reached across her shoulder and put her hand over Evan's.

"I'm sorry. It's just..."

Evan, deeply stung and tingling with embarrassment, withdrew his hand from hers.

"It's fine. I'll wait outside." He nodded curtly at Mr. Sutherland and walked out of the room into the stark corridor.

AILSA

Ailsa heard the door close and with it, the hold she had on her emotions gave way. Her face crumpled again and tears fell freely, making her head throb, as she tried to gather herself enough to speak.

Sutherland sat opposite her, his hands clasped loosely between his knees.

"Just take a breath." His tone was warm. "This is all very overwhelming."

Ailsa nodded, wiped her nose and exhaled, willing her stomach to stop lurching.

"I don't remember him—I mean being married to him." She stared at Sutherland's glasses, catching a glimpse of her reflection, all bulky and white. "And how am I supposed to go home with him when I don't know where that is?" Fresh tears pushed into her sinuses.

"I know it's frightening, Ailsa. I can only imagine what you're feeling, but Evan is your husband." He sat back and crossed his legs. "He's been with you through all this and he'll help you when you get home." He smiled at her. "Just give it time and trust yourself." He nodded. "You'll know what feels right soon enough. The brain is a marvelous and mysterious thing." He nodded. "You've a lot of healing ahead of you, so just let your body guide you."

Suddenly inspired by an idea, Ailsa sat upright.

"Could I go home with my parents for a while? Just until I feel stronger?" She heard the pleading quality in her voice, only a touch embarrassed by it.

Sutherland shook his head.

"I'd advise that you get back to your normal life as soon as possible. The chances of further recall and faster healing are much higher if you're in your own environment."

Own environment. The phrase made her clench her fists. Her whole point was that this place, this flat in Glasgow where she and Evan lived, that she had no mental picture of at all, was not home as she thought of it now.

As she was about to protest, Sutherland leaned forward and patted her knee, reminding her of something her father might do.

"There's an art to remembering Ailsa, but if anyone can master it, you can. Just be patient, keep your chin up, and you can always call me if you need to."

Ailsa sensed, as she had earlier, that her time was up, so wiping her nose she found a smile.

"Thanks, Mr. Sutherland." She held out her hand. "Thank you."

Two days later, Evan came in earlier in the morning than he had before. He looked stressed, his eyes darting around the room and his hair disheveled.

Ailsa pushed herself up in the bed, conscious of the night gown she wore having drooped down her chest. With a palm protecting her breast bone, she watched him shed his coat and drape it over the visitor's chair.

"How are you today?" He leaned in and, to her relief, kissed her forehead rather than her mouth.

"All right." She saw his eyes go to her hand which still held the night gown in place.

"Are you in pain?" He frowned, pulling the chair closer to the bed.

"No, actually." Ailsa responded before she'd given her answer any thought and the words out, she felt the lift of surprise. This was the first day since waking up in this strange new reality that the dull ache in her head had left her.

"Great." Evan smiled. "Because I have a surprise for you." He was smiling, but Ailsa heard something tentative in his tone, and her moment of light began to dim at the prospect of more surprises.

Evan was staring at her, obviously waiting for a response.

"What is it?" She smiled for him.

"Amanda's here and wants to visit you." His voice was silvery.

Ailsa heard the name and with it her nerves began to jangle, as it meant she was about to be tested again. Evan had talked to her about Amanda, asking her if she remembered dancing with her. Ailsa knew that Amanda was a friend from when she was younger, but further to that, there was little she could recall.

He kept talking about the company and how much everyone there missed her, but she couldn't put that information into context, so had pushed it back under the more immediate things she knew she must try to remember.

Evan's smile had faded at her silence, and now he was frowning.

"Ailsa?" He held her gaze for a few moments before trying again. "You two are thick as thieves." He rolled his eyes, making her unsure whether he was happy about Amanda coming, frustrated by it or simply by her, Ailsa's, lack of response.

Afraid to disappoint him anymore, she lied.

"I know."

His smile was back, but a little less bright and he placed his hand over her free one.

"That's great. She's dying to see you."

Anxiety clutched at her throat as she tried to pull up memories that included Amanda. Surprisingly, the first thing that came to mind was them floating in an ocean, laughing at their toes as they emerged like mismatched pebbles from the surface of the water. She frowned, trying to drill further into the memory.

"Can I tell her to come in?" He stood up, shifting the chair back to the wall.

"She's here now?" Ailsa heard the quiver in her voice.

"Outside the door, frothing at the mouth." He grinned.

Her pulse picking up its pace, Ailsa leaned forward slowly, tugged the nightgown down at the back and settled against the pillows. Seeing his stance, there was little she could do to avoid this next scenario and whether or not she had the right memory associated with Amanda, it was all she had to go on.

"O.K." She stared at the door. "I'm ready."

Evan opened the door and Amanda walked in. She was smiling, carrying a bunch of tiger lilies and her long fair hair was loose around her face.

"Oh my God. It's so good to see you." She placed the flowers on the table next to the bed, and Ailsa braced herself for the inevitable contact. "How are you feeling?"

Amanda leaned down to hug her and despite herself, Ailsa flinched. Instantly, she felt Amanda stiffen then pull away, looking wounded.

"Sorry, I didn't think…" Amanda stuttered, stepping back from the bed. "I…"

Seeing the distress in the kind face, a face that she knew was a friend's, Ailsa held a hand out.

"It's O.K. I'm sorry. It's just that…" She fumbled for something to say, a word or two that would dispel the awkwardness she'd created.

Amanda was shaking her head, an empty smile fixed on her face.

"No. It's my fault." She shook her head. "I always dive in without thinking."

Ailsa looked over at Evan, hoping there might be a cue, or a clue as to what she should do next, but he was staring out of the window, his back to her and his hands deep in his trouser pockets.

She looked back at Amanda, who was hovering at the bedside.

"Sit down." Ailsa pointed at the chair in the corner. "Please."

A visible flash of relief taking over her, Amanda dragged the chair a little closer to the bed and sat straight backed on the edge of it. Her eyes were flicking back and forth from Ailsa to Evan, who had crossed the room and was heading for the door.

"I'll go for a walk. Let you two talk." He looked at Ailsa. "O.K?"

Ailsa felt the tug of fear at the prospect of being left with someone, friend or no, that she knew so little about, but his expression spoke volumes—he expected her to deal with this.

"Yes." She nodded, her head like a lead weight against the bank of pillows behind her. "Fine."

As the door closed, Ailsa rolled the top of the blanket back and forth, willing herself to come up with something, anything other than the floating toe image, but the more she tried the more her mind seemed to shut her out.

When Evan had talked about Amanda, he'd said she was a friend from the ballet company, but those words had no significance for Ailsa. A company of strangers was no company at all, so as she looked at Amanda, who was talking animatedly about that same company, she tried to focus on the words she was hearing rather than their meaning. Steven. Classes. Richard.

Rehearsals. Tricia. Nothing specifically held her attention. Now Amanda was talking about Mark and then, she spoke of Hayley. At that, Ailsa felt a flicker of recognition. Hayley. As she played with the name, she was rewarded with the flash of an image of blonde curls, cherub cheeks and sticky little fingers, that made her catch her breath.

"Hayley." She said it out loud, stopping Amanda's flow.

"Yes." Amanda looked surprised. "She misses you. She wanted to come, but I told her it was too soon." She reached out tentatively and touched Ailsa's fingers. "Maybe next time, eh?"

Feeling the cool hand on hers was not disturbing this time. Amanda's presence was beginning to calm her and, letting herself relax into the feeling, Ailsa turned her hand upward and squeezed Amanda's fingers.

"We're great friends, aren't we?" She stared into the pale-blue eyes and saw a flash of pain. Her gauche statement floated between them as Ailsa leaned forward. "I'm sorry. I'm just so…"

Amanda was shaking her head as she stood up.

"Hey. It's fine. You probably need me to shut up anyway, so you can get some rest."

Ailsa shook her head.

"No. Please. I didn't want to upset you."

Amanda patted the air.

"No worries. Really." She smiled. "Just rest now and I'll see you soon." She turned to the door.

Willing herself to come up with something kind she could give her friend to take away with her, Ailsa said "Wait."

Amanda turned back to face her.

"I'll be better next time." Ailsa nodded. "I'll remember more."

Amanda yanked her bag up onto her shoulder.

"You're fine. No hurry." She smiled. "I'm not going anywhere."

~

Six days later, Ailsa sat in the car waiting for Evan to load her bag into the back. Her coat, one she didn't recognize, was wrapped around her against the December cold and her head, now free of the bandages, was covered with a soft floral scarf that Evan had bought for her.

She lifted a hand and, through the gauzy scarf, fingered the row of staples that protruded from the side of her head. They felt foreign and ugly as she counted them, moving her fingertips from the bottom of the incision up to the top. Under her skin, surgical screws had bitten into the bone in order to moor back in place the circular flap that had been cut out of her skull, much like the lid on a can of soup. The feel of the wound under her fingers made her shudder, adding to her mounting self-consciousness. Not only was the inside of her head messed up, but so was the outside.

She shivered, the extreme cold causing the exposed area around the wound to ache. She badly wanted to go home and had been anticipating this day, and yet dreading it at the same time. Going home had been all she could think about, but when she did think about it her mind defaulted to her bedroom at her parents' house in Stockbridge—the floral wallpaper that she'd chosen when she was fourteen, the kidney shaped dressing table with the crisp cotton skirt that Jennifer had ordered specially, and the soft toys lined up along the top of the mirrored wardrobe. That room made her feel safe, cocooned against the world and released from any sense of obligation to be anything, or anyone, other than who she was.

Ailsa understood that she lived in Glasgow now, with Evan, her husband, but she couldn't picture the flat he'd described to her, which along with her trepidation of what awaited her there, made her feel even more lost. She also knew that her inability to see their home in her mind's eye hurt him, but she was doing her best to put so many broken pieces back together. Evan said he understood, and that she mustn't put too much pressure on herself, but even as he said it she'd seen the shadow cloud his eyes and the way that he pinched his lips together.

Evan slammed the boot closed, walked around and got into the driver's seat.

"Ready?" He gave her a tentative smile.

"Yes." She nodded. "Let's go."

Her parents had come to see them off, and Ailsa had struggled not to cry as she hugged them tightly, then watched the dark Mercedes slip away from the hospital, inside it the only people she felt truly comfortable with. They'd promised to come and see her as soon as she was up to it, and it had been all that she could do not to ask if they could come now, today.

The drive from Edinburgh to Glasgow was taking a long time. Ailsa wasn't exactly sure how long it would have taken normally, but Evan was driving so cautiously; avoiding potholes, staying in the slow lane and waving people past him that it had begun to feel interminable. While his care of her was touching, being in the car was disorientating and she wasn't sure how much longer she could take the slow, lurching movements that were making her nauseas.

"You can go faster you know." She watched him flicking his eyes up and down to the rearview mirror, as if they were being followed. "I won't break."

Evan remained focused on the road.

"I don't want to push it. It's the first time you've been in a car since your surgery." He glanced at her. "Sutherland said it might bother you."

Ailsa yanked at the seatbelt which was claustrophobically cutting across her throat. The other cars on the road all seemed to be too close to the side of their Volvo and as they passed, it looked as if the other vehicles were veering toward them rather than giving them the space they needed to get by.

As they pulled up first next to a lorry and then to a double-decker bus, she closed her eyes, aware of her heart pattering wildly.

Evan stopped at a red light.

"You doing O.K.?"

"I'm fine." On an impulse, Ailsa reached over and patted his hand as it sat on top of the gear stick.

Evan said nothing as she turned to look out of her window at an SUV next to them. A small girl was strapped into a car seat in the back and was waving a book above her head. In the front the mother was speaking to the child in the rearview mirror and laughing. Ailsa could just hear the distant thump of a bass, perhaps a song the little girl loved and one they often listened to when they went somewhere together.

Ailsa's memory prickled, yielding an image that gave her a lift of joy. When she'd been young, her father had consistently played the same cassette in the car. Classical Pops it had been called. With the visual came the memory that her first exposure to classical music had been in the back of her parents' Citroen as they drove from Edinburgh into the Highlands to spend a long weekend in some stately home or castle.

As she stared into the car next to her, enjoying the clarity of the recall, Ailsa played with the memory. She remembered wanting to go to a seaside bed-and-breakfast or a campground like her friends at school did. She'd been jealous of those families, and had coveted their uncomplicated and fun-filled holidays, while she toured historic buildings and cathedrals in far-flung corners of the Highlands.

They'd had fun too, though. It wasn't always stuffy or boring, but her parents had never made a destination choice based on child-friendly facilities or entertainment. That just wasn't their modus operandi.

The Volvo jolted into gear and as the car with the little girl inside moved slightly ahead, a worm of loss burrowed into Ailsa's middle. She raised a hand to wave and the child caught the movement and flapped her book as the SUV slid away, easing into the lane ahead of them.

Tears pressed behind her eyes surprising her. Not wanting Evan to see her face, she dropped her head and leaned forward to retrieve her handbag from between her feet.

"What do you need?" He glanced at her.

"Nothing. A hanky, that's all." She rummaged inside the soft suede bag until she found a small plastic envelope of tissues.

"You all right?" Evan checked his mirrors and guided the car into the outside lane.

"Yep." She blew her nose, scrunched the tissue up and shoved it up into her coat sleeve, as her mother had taught her. She recoiled at the feel of the dampness next to her skin and as she watched the traffic surging around them it struck her as ludicrous that she couldn't clearly remember being married, or the home that she and Evan lived in, and she presumed been happy in, for almost a decade and yet she remembered to tuck her snotty tissue up her sleeve, despite hating the practice. As the absurdity of her situation took hold she was caught by a burst of laughter, and then the laugh turned into a snort.

"What's going on?" Evan looked alarmed. "Do you need me to stop?"

Momentarily, the laughter took over as powerfully as the tears had, just a few moments earlier. Her diaphragm was taut, and as her body rocked with the force of it she grabbed the seatbelt that had ridden up across her neck again and pulled it down to her lap.

"I'm sorry." She gasped. "It's just crazy." Tears trickled

down her cheeks. "I'm losing my marbles." She gasped, wiping at her face.

Evan glanced over at her and broke into a smile.

"What's so funny?"

"The tissue. The stupid snotty tissue." She coughed sending a zap of pain up the side of her face.

"What do you mean?" He was laughing with her now, his relief tangible inside the car.

"I hate the feel of wet tissues and I remember that." She took a deep, steadying breath, trying to calm the force that was crushing her stomach muscles and making it hard to breathe. "Of all the things that I need to remember, that's what I got." She thrust her arm out and pulled the sodden mass from her sleeve. "Sodding snotty tissues."

Evan laughed loudly and, glancing in the side mirror, changed lanes again.

"Well, beggars can't be choosers." He looked over at her and winked. Ailsa felt that this gesture was familiar and along with it came the joy of a shared moment of release. There would more of these moments, she was sure, but for now, as their laughter melted into a comfortable silence, a twinge of sadness returned at the loss of all those moments that had undoubtedly passed between them that she might never remember again.

The entrance to the tenement building on Dumbarton Road was long and dark. A tunnel with ceramic tiled walls, the narrow corridor cut through the depth of the sandstone structure leading out to a shared garden at the back. As they navigated the space, Evan held Ailsa firmly under her left arm, her bag slung over his opposite shoulder.

She studied the ground, her breath escaping in smoky puffs. She could smell coffee and something meaty, like stew, and she counted the tiles as she passed through the tunnel—twenty-four, twenty-five then the broken one, twenty-six, and then a broad front door stood facing her on the right. As she steadied herself against the wall it struck her like a lightning bolt that she'd remembered the broken tile and, with a rush of achievement, she yanked on his arm.

"The broken one." She pointed over her shoulder as Evan searched for the right key.

"What?"

"The tile. I remembered the broken tile." She smiled up at him as he slid the key into the lock.

"Brilliant. Little victories, eh?" Evan nodded and shoved the heavy door, holding it open for her as she stepped carefully over the threshold. He tossed her bag onto the floor in the hall and taking her arm again steered her inside.

The room was bright and warm. A tan leather sofa ran between the living room in front of it and a long farmhouse dining table behind it, separating the two spaces. The fireplace on the far wall, with the white surround and brick hearth, had a deep leather armchair at either side of it. There was a basket overflowing with newspapers next to one of the chairs and mounted above the mantel, was a mirror. Slightly offset, the black screen of a TV reflected the afternoon sunlight as it spilled through the window and onto the dark red Persian rug.

While unfamiliar, it felt good in here. Peaceful and lived in. Ailsa scanned the room and then, feeling her legs begin to wobble, aimed for the sofa, guiding Evan with little tugs on his sleeve.

He helped her take her coat off and settled her on the seat, then shoved two cushions behind her back.

"All right there?"

Her stomach was quivering from the effort of walking the few steps from the car, and the weight of his hands on her shoulders was steadying.

"Uh huh."

"I'll stick the kettle on and make us a cuppa'. Don't move now."

"Don't worry. I'm too tired to budge." She ran a hand over her forehead surprised to feel it clammy, considering the bitter cold outside.

Evan walked out of the room and soon she could hear dishes clattering and water running. As she looked around her, anticipating enjoying the first hot cup of tea she'd had in days, Ailsa felt a rumble low in her stomach.

"Evan?"

His head popped through the doorway.

"What's wrong?" He was frowning.

"Nothing. I'm hungry." She pressed a hand into her stomach.

"Really?" His eyebrows lifted. "What do you fancy?"

"Um. I don't know." She shrugged. "Toast?"

Evan saluted. "Toast it is. Sit tight."

Ailsa looked around the room again taking in the golden light from the wide paned windows, the high ceilings and the glittering chandelier that hung above her head. Two dark wood doors cut into the ivory wall to her right and as she looked at them, she realized that she had no idea what was behind either. Bedrooms, a bathroom, a cupboard? She had no clue. She was blank, and the thought that she knew so little about her own home shook her.

She closed her eyes and mentally traced her way around the room hoping that something would loosen a memory, but nothing came.

A few moments later, Evan walked in carrying a tray. A china mug with a tendril of steam curling up from it sat in the center along with a packet of biscuits.

"Here you go. Toast's coming."

Ailsa looked down at the biscuits.

"What're those?"

Evan halted on his way out of the room.

"They're Bourbons."

"Bourbons?" She lifted the dark brown package onto her lap. "Do I like these?" She stared at the unfamiliar lettering.

Evan took a few steps toward her.

"You hardly ever eat them, but they're your favorites."

Her brief moment of achievement with the tile slipping further away, Ailsa laid the packet back onto the tray and swallowed. She didn't know what her favorite anything was right now, or even what she liked, never mind loved—the person in front of her, the place she lived, the clothes she was wearing— and the fact was, she may never get those certainties back. As she looked over at Evan, she wondered if he could read her mind, but she had no way of knowing because she wasn't sure how well they'd known each other, how deeply their thoughts had been connected.

After only half an hour of sitting on the sofa, the familiar feeling of motion sickness was creeping up on her again.

Evan was sitting in one of the armchairs across the room, his head dipped toward the screen of his laptop.

"Evan?" She spoke softly, regretting her intrusion on his obvious need to check on work, or whatever he was so absorbed in, then she frowned, trying to remember what he did for a living.

"What's up?" Evan looked over at her.

"I need to lie down."

He nodded, tapped a few final keys and closed the laptop.

"Right. Let's get you to bed."

Ailsa let him hoist her up from the seat and, with one of his hands under her armpit and the other spread under her palm, he led her carefully down the corridor toward a closed door.

She hesitated at the panelled door and reaching out, placed her hand on the white glossy frame.

"Is this the bedroom?"

Evan nodded.

"Yes, it's our room."

Suddenly afraid of the unknown space beyond the door, and the implied intimacy of being in there with him, Ailsa took a deep breath.

"Can I use the bathroom first?"

"Of course. Sorry, I wasn't thinking." His face suddenly flushed. "Come on, we'll get you cleaned up."

Inside the brightly lit bathroom Ailsa held on to the towel rail as Evan thrust a hand under the water that was gushing into the big white tub. She looked around the room waiting for something, anything, to come back. The space was pleasant enough, the walls a soft aqua and the floor covered in warm beige tiles, but it all felt foreign to her. Undiscovered.

Evan turned off the taps.

"Right, let's get you undressed." He touched the zipper of her hooded sweatshirt.

Ailsa's body went rigid as the ticking of the zip, making its progress toward her waist, filled her head.

"Wait." She placed her free hand on top of Evan's.

"What?" He gaped at her.

"I can do it myself." A knot of emotion was forming at the back of her throat.

Evan frowned.

"I don't think so. You can hardly stand up at the moment." His dark eyes assessed her as Ailsa struggled to find an argument that might support her assertion.

He sighed.

"Come on now. Don't be silly. Let me help you."

She watched Evan's brow crease as he opened the front of her sweatshirt and then slid it off each arm. Despite her dread of what was about to happen, she had no choice but to surrender. She couldn't resist his manipulation of her limbs any more than she could his logic.

As her clothes accumulated in a small heap on the floor, Ailsa felt her face glowing. He was gentle, but as her body became more and more exposed to the air in the room, and to Evan's gaze, she wanted to crawl under a rug and close her eyes against her helplessness.

Once she was naked, he draped a towel over his shoulder and then led her to the edge of the bath.

"In you get."

Evan supported her under her arms as she stepped into the bath and then clinging to him she knelt and then folded her legs underneath her. Once seated, she crossed her legs, feeling the cold of the cast iron against her skin. The water felt good, warm, soothing her raw nerves. The level was shallow, sitting just below her belly button, and as she wrapped her arms across her chest, goose bumps rose along her forearms.

"Can you fill it up more?"

Evan shook his head.

"Not supposed to get you too hot. Raises your blood pressure." He smiled. "Come on, I'll wash your back."

He picked up a flannel and began soaping it and as he worked the rough cloth over her shoulders, she leaned away from the pressure of his hand.

"Too hard?"

Ailsa shook her head. She didn't want to make him feel bad, but her skin prickled when, as he rinsed off the soap, his palm made contact with her back.

As she closed her eyes and waited for this uncomfortable process to be over, Ailsa tried to analyze her reaction. She was self-conscious about her nakedness and yet she knew that he was her husband, a trusted person that she had obviously been intimate with. She must have loved him, and been this vulnerable

173

around him many times before, but the feeling of exposure was mortifying.

Having dried her off and helped her into her pajamas, Evan walked her into the bedroom. The bedside light glowed a soft amber and the paisley duvet had been pulled back in an expectant way, her presence anticipated.

"Can you get in?" He leaned over and helped her sit on the edge of the bed.

Ailsa pushed herself carefully back onto the mattress and tried to swing her legs up, but Evan's hand was instantly there, under her calves. Something inside her wanted to resist but instead she relaxed into his palm and let him help her, grateful for this last injection of strength as her own threatened to give out entirely. The bath had been exhausting.

The pillows were piled up high against the headboard and as she leaned back Ailsa yelped.

"Oh my God." A web of pain stretched across her skull.

Evan jumped. "What's wrong?"

She lifted a hand to her temple as the pain spread cloyingly over her face.

"My head. I can't lie back." She gasped.

Evan slipped a hand under her arm and lifted her torso forward. Leaning behind her, he propped two pillows up in an inverted V and then placed the third across their base, forming a triangle.

"Try that." He eased her back against the soft mound.

Ailsa felt the support of the top of the V behind her neck, raising her up enough to keep the pressure of the pillow off her head. Relieved, she exhaled, relaxing into the bed.

"Yes. That works. Thank you." She tried to smile at him, but Evan wasn't looking at her as he smoothed the duvet and then draped her robe over the end of the bed.

She watched as he folded her clothes neatly and then came

around to lift a book from the opposite side of the bed, before walking back to her side.

"I'll just be down the hall." He smiled at her. "Call me if you want anything."

As she nodded obediently, Ailsa was overcome with relief that he was obviously not going to get into the bed with her.

He leaned over and kissed her forehead, his hand on the bedside light switch.

"No. Leave it on." She pulled the duvet up to her chest.

"On it is."

For the first few days, simply moving around the flat had felt insurmountable and Evan had to insist that she get out of bed and walk around the living room every few hours. While she knew he was right to badger her, she'd begun to dread his coming into the bedroom to get her.

The previous day, when she'd said she was tired after only a few minutes, he'd teased her.

"Come on, you spend hours a day bouncing around in the studio. This is a piece of cake."

Ailsa had stared up at his expectant face, but nothing had come to her.

"I don't remember that."

Evan had tutted under his breath and continued walking her around the coffee table.

He had been patient with her, cooking; shopping and cajoling her through each difficult day and night. Her gratitude toward him was undeniable but her constant and unavoidable reliance on his help was fraying her nerves. So much felt out of her control at the moment but above everything else, the act of bathing herself, an innately private exercise, was the hardest sliver of independence to surrender.

Each evening, Evan would fill a shallow tub, undress her like a baby-doll, use the flannel on her back, neck and limbs, making sure not to wet her healing head, and then dress her again in her night clothes. All the while she would stare over his head, not making eye contact with those dark brown pools.

While she knew that she could not realistically cope without him yet, the indignity bothered her at such a fundamental level that she was afraid she'd been less than gracious with him once or twice.

She'd been home for a week, and now, as she used the toilet, having helped her inside, Evan was waiting outside the door. He'd insisted that she not lock it and she could hear him breathing, as if his face was pressed up against the wood.

"I'm fine, honestly." She chimed at the door. "I'll shout when I'm ready to come out."

She breathed in deeply, fighting the now familiar rocking motion that made her grab the sink to steady herself. Even if she felt like hell, being alone in here was good. She hadn't been completely alone since before surgery and this was the first time in days that someone hadn't been touching her, pricking her with needles or invading her space. She wasn't ready to give up this tiny slice of liberty yet and so she stood still and assessed herself in the mirror.

Her face was so swollen, blown into a moon-like round by the steroids and the weight she'd gained, that she barely recognized herself.

She blinked at the stranger before her. They had shaved a section of her head for the surgery, starting above her left ear and reaching a few inches up toward the crown, leaving her with a lopsided, punk-like mop of dark hair that she'd secured with a band on the right side. She pressed her fingertips to her mouth at the sight of the mess that was once her aquiline head.

Turning her gaze away from her reflection, Ailsa leaned down and opened the cabinet under the sink. There were rows of bottles and tubes with names that she didn't recognize. A tray full of makeup and several small triangular sponges sat next to a tub of face powder, and three different round hair brushes were stacked next to a hairdryer. Nothing that she saw sparked any kind of recall and as frustrated tears welled in her eyes she slammed the door shut.

She looked down at the pajama bottoms she was wearing. They had a small floral print on a grey background and as she grabbed a handful of the flannel material she gritted her teeth wondering when she had bought them, where she'd bought them, why she'd chosen flowers rather than checks or stripes.

Closing her eyes, she pressed her hips against the sink and let the tears come. Every sensation felt alien, even the wetness on her face. She wanted to lie down, but that hurt. She was still battling the demanding appetite and even although she was on an ever-decreasing dose of steroids, the medication was still messing with her sleep and her mood.

As she opened her eyes again, she gripped the sink with one hand and wiped her face with the other.

"Ailsa. Are you O.K.?" Evan's voice was close to her back.

"Yes. I'm fine." She pressed her eyes closed.

She could hear him moving outside the door, so she took a deep, steadying breath.

"Evan?"

"Yes?"

She turned to face the door, suddenly knowing what she needed.

"Can I have the phone?"

She heard a floor board creak.

"The what?"

She rolled her shoulders back.

"The phone."

"Is everything all right? Let me in." He sounded cross, and as she watched, the porcelain door handle began to move.

"No." Her heart quickened. "Please. I just want the phone."

After a few moments there was a tap on the door. She moved closer and opened it a couple of inches, just enough to allow Evan's hand to slide through and pass her the handset.

"What's going on?"

She took the phone from him and closed the door again.

"Nothing. I just want to call my parents."

She heard him sigh.

"Why didn't you say?"

She forced herself to swallow and stared down at the buttons on the phone.

"Evan?"

"What?"

Ailsa closed her eyes again and made a fist with her free hand, digging her fingernails into her palm.

"What's Dad's number?"

She heard him sigh. "Just press star then seven. It's saved in speed dial."

She looked down at the key pad, the numbers blurring. Star seven. That was all that separated her from a little comfort.

EVAN

E van sank into the warm water. The big claw-foot bathtub
had been Ailsa's choice when they'd renovated the bathroom. He'd resisted at first but acquiesced when she'd pleaded
and now, as his long legs stretched out fully and his back settled
against the curve of the tub, he was glad they'd done it. He'd
never owned a bath where he hadn't felt scrunched up before, so
had become accustomed to showering instead. Now, however,
his whole body ached and the warm water surrounding him was
blissful.

Ailsa had been home for ten days and while it was good to
have her back, it was zapping his energy. The first days had been
different than Evan had anticipated. Aside from the memory
deficit they were dealing with, he'd been prepared for her to be
exhausted and in pain, but he hadn't been ready for her general
weakness and unsteadiness on her feet.

He'd taken three weeks off work to care for her, but seeing
her still struggling with basic tasks, he was anxious that it wasn't
enough time. She needed so much physical support that he was
afraid to leave her for more than a few moments and while he

knew that after everything he'd done, he owed her this, he'd begun to feel trapped.

Ailsa's attention span was limited to a few minutes, regardless of what she was doing—reading, staring at the TV screen or even talking with him. She was still unpredictable, her emotions swinging from tearfulness to forced jollity, leaving Evan feeling unprepared for whichever version of her he'd be presented with that day.

He was feeling cooped up and as a result, his mind had been wandering back to Marie. As he'd bathed his wife that night, caring for her as a parent might, in his mind's eye he'd seen Marie's lithe, healthy body, the sinewy legs, the mane of red hair wet against her back, and he'd wondered how his life had taken this bizarre turn.

The muscles in his neck twinged so Evan rolled up a hand towel and crammed it behind his head, then lifted the half-full whisky glass from the bath caddy that spanned the tub. He hadn't been drinking at all since they'd got home from Edinburgh, but tonight he could allow himself to because his mother was on her way over.

Ailsa was napping under a blanket on the sofa and Diana was bringing dinner for them all. His mum had been a blessing, popping in every other day from her flat in Huntly Gardens, bringing treats for Ailsa to eat. Diana loved to bake and since his father had passed away, she seldom had anyone to cook for anymore.

It had been both odd and fun to watch his wife sampling his mother's baking, snapping pieces off shortbread and nibbling the corners of biscuits, as if tasting everything for the first time. They had established that she liked Bourbon biscuits and dark chocolate the best, but definitely hated custard creams. If he were honest, he was growing increasingly concerned at the amount that Ailsa was still eating, but he'd pushed the worry down. When Diana was with them, it was close to the only time he saw his wife smile these days.

Evan sipped the whisky and let the amber liquid burn its way down his throat. He'd missed this taste.

Ailsa was still easily upset. Everything she couldn't remember seemed to sting her so viciously that the things she did remember were getting lost in her disappointment. Despite his own frustration at everything she'd forgotten, he kept telling her how well she was doing, but, truth be told, he was running out of energy on that score.

Their chronology together was totally mixed up. She seemed comfortable with him, trusted him even, but then she'd look blankly at him when he'd mention their honeymoon in Paris, or a friend they hadn't seen in ages, and he'd bite his tongue. He was trying not to overload her with data, as Mr. Sutherland had warned him not to, but having her home had lulled him into a false sense of normalcy and occasionally he forgot to edit himself—only to be met with a blank stare.

Evan set the glass back on the caddy and lifted a flannel, soaked it in the water, wrung it out and laid it over his eyes.

The most concerning thing for him was Ailsa's inability, or rather unwillingness, to talk about the ballet company. Following Mr. Sutherland's instructions, Evan had held back, not pressing her too much about the many things that she'd still got little memory of, but on her third day home, they'd spent a while looking through their wedding album. While she hadn't seemed to recognize any of the pictures, she'd been calm, nodding as he talked her through the week they'd spent in a quirky, courtyard Auberge in Montmartre. He'd described them walking along the Seine, touring The Louvre and the Bois De Boulogne, and stopping to eat at cafés. She'd asked a few questions and while it obviously remained unfamiliar, she'd seemed to take it all in as fact.

When he'd moved on to a pile of programs from the Theatre

Royal, with photographs of her on stage as Odette, Juliet and
Giselle, none of the characters or costumes seemed to resonate
with her and she'd stared at the pictures as if she were looking at
a stranger. Eventually she'd simply asked him to put the
programs away. He hadn't ventured to go there again since, but
the gap in her memory of her greatest accomplishment, the thing
that they'd both worked the hardest for and at the expense of so
much, rattled him. It was the ultimate cruelty that her tumor had
delivered.

Outside the bathroom door, Evan heard shuffling. He lifted
the flannel and sat upright, straining to hear.

"Ailsa?"

The door slid open a couple of inches.

"How long will you be?" She whispered.

"Not long. Do you need to use the toilet?" Evan tossed the
flannel onto the caddy and looked around for his towel.

"No. But can I come in?" She sounded tentative.

She had often sat on top of the toilet lid and talked to him
while he was showering, but she'd never asked his permission to
come in before.

"Of course. Just a sec." Feeling oddly self-conscious, Evan
hauled himself out of the water and wrapped a towel around his
waist. "Come in."

Ailsa slipped into the room, walked slowly across the tiled
floor and stopped next to the towel rail. Her right hand rested on
the rail while her feet formed a perfect one hundred and eighty-
degree angle, and her knees were pulled up tight inside her
leggings.

"You look like you're at the barre." He nodded at the rail.
"Ready for your plies?"

Ailsa snatched her hand back as if the rail was white-hot, and
stuck it in the front pocket of her sweatshirt.

"I'm sorry. I don't remember that." She turned unsteadily

and, with her fingertips stroking the wall on her left, she moved carefully toward the open door.

Evan frowned, tightened the towel, and pushed down his irritation at the sight of her walking away, as his next string of thoughts played out. If she couldn't find her way back to ballet, something so seminal not only in who she was but in who they'd always been as a couple, could she find her way back to him? The idea that she might not was disturbing but then, glimmering behind it, balancing his fear, was the possibility that her inability to recall certain events in their life could turn out to be his get-out-of-jail card.

No sooner had the thought occurred to him than he shook his head. Things would play out the way they played out and there was nothing he could do to influence that, one way or the other.

He jumped out of the tub and walked into the living room. Ailsa was negotiating her way around the coffee table, heading back to the sofa.

"I didn't mean to pressure you."

She wouldn't look at him.

Evan stood in the middle of the room, suddenly feeling ridiculous. The towel was slung low around his waist and the water dripping from his body had begun to make a puddle on the stripped pine floor.

"I shouldn't have snapped at you." Ailsa lowered herself onto the edge of the sofa and looked up at him. "It's just that it won't come back, all that stuff." She looked young and heart-breakingly vulnerable. "I know I did it. I know I was there. I see the pictures. But I just can't get it back, in my mind." Her eyes were huge, beseeching.

Feeling contrite, Evan moved over and sat down next to her.

"I'm sure it'll all come back eventually." He put his arm around her and kissed the side of her head.

Ailsa accepted his kiss and then turning her face into his shoulder, took a deep breath.

"I remember the way you smell."

He felt her lips move against his skin.

"It's like sandalwood."

Evan shifted on the sofa. He'd been sleeping in the spare room for weeks, so continuing to do so after she got home wasn't unexpected, but now, the simple intimacy of this contact, her very proximity and willingness to touch him, was tough to take. For a second, he was tempted to kiss her, but deep down he knew she wasn't nearly ready for that, and, if he were honest, he wasn't sure if he was either, so, he gently disengaged from her and stood up, adjusting the towel.

"I'll be back in a bit. Don't want to leave a water mark on the couch." He winked and then turned back toward the bathroom.

AILSA

Ailsa stood at the living room window overlooking the garden and scanned the perimeter of the open space. It was tiny but perfect, with a small but adequate stretch of lawn, surrounded by dense herbaceous borders and thick rows of heather. The low, dry-stone walls that surrounded the flowerbeds were crumbling here and there, but that only added character.

As she looked outside, a memory sparked. Many of these old tenement buildings had been converted into new flats, decades ago. In this one's case, they had retained the original courtyard garden behind, leaving its residents a sanctuary to escape their homes to during the better weather. She suddenly knew that this had been one of the reasons they had liked this flat and, as the snippet of fact solidified itself, she smiled.

The wooden bench was empty as were the neatly edged flowerbeds that sat at the four corners, framing the now brackish lawn. The tall trees that bordered the far side were stark and leafless, and a lone squirrel dug furiously at the base of one of them.

December was drawing to a close and the garden was appropriately asleep. Ailsa closed her eyes, pressed her forehead to the glass and tried to picture the trees, summoning the color the blossoms might be when they bloomed, but nothing came. She opened her eyes, frustrated that her bruised mind could so easily reveal one thing and yet stubbornly shroud another.

Evan was working on his laptop in the bedroom and she was giving him some space. It had been over three weeks since she'd come home, and she was disappointed that she wasn't feeling stronger. Twenty steps to circle the kitchen, twenty-two around the dining table, forty-eight to complete a lap around the living room, and this was her new reality.

Now, as she stared out at the garden, Ailsa thought about what a tremendous support Evan was, her coach, carer and friend. He'd ferried her back and forth to various follow up appointments, and seldom complained about the time it always took. Deep in her heart she knew that she could never get through this without him but, underneath all that, what bothered her was her inability to feel truly close to him.

The nights were still the hardest. She would lie awake, her mind sparking between one train of thought and another as the light sank and rose again behind the curtains. The room still felt unfamiliar and being on her own fanned her anxiety, so she had asked Evan to move back into the master bedroom with her, two nights earlier.

She felt awkward and at odds with her body, and having him touch her was still uncomfortable, so the thought of any kind of intimacy was more than she could bear. She had registered the hurt in his face when she'd gently made it clear that all she wanted was his presence in the bed, for now, but to her relief, Evan had simply nodded.

The first night that he'd come back into their bed he'd propped her up on the pillows, kissed her cheek, turned his back on her and promptly begun snoring.

Ailsa was aware that she was hard work at the moment and could see Evan struggle at times. He seemed to love her, and as she watched him taking care of her needs, she desperately wanted to feel that same love for him. For the present though, all she felt was a deep sense of gratitude.

Now, as she watched the little squirrel tear at the frozen soil, Ailsa wished that she could wind the clock back. If only she'd known that one day there would be a string of lacy gaps in her history, she'd have been better about taking pictures, writing things down, making a point of solidifying the precious moments in time that tended to slip away as soon as something new took their place.

She pulled her heavy sweater down over her hips and bit at a hangnail. So much of her recent past was lost, she wondered if it would mean that she had been altered as a person. If we are a direct result of our experiences, would it follow that having lost a set of those experiences she was ultimately a different human being?

An image of the theater programs they'd looked at when she'd first come home made her blink. She'd seen herself right there on the glossy paper, in striking stage make-up, wearing costumes she didn't recognize and, as Evan had turned the pages, it had been like watching a movie of her identical twin leading a life she'd once aspired to. She'd gaped at the pictures, feeling her heart tearing a little more with each new image, until she'd pleaded with him to stop. Now, as she thought back to that moment and the mass of her reality that was gone, the hole that had been left in her felt cavernous. The outline of her past had been damaged, and she was terrified that no matter how hard she tried it would never be repaired.

Behind her she heard the living room door open. Evan stood holding his laptop in front of him like a tray.

"You O.K.?"

She nodded.

"Yep. Just looking at the garden. I can't wait for spring. I like to sit out there." She smiled.

"Yes, you do." He looked pleased. "You and your favorite books."

She made her way to the sofa. There was a pile of books on her bedside table and now as she pictured them, Ailsa remembered reading the one with the purple cover that sat on the top of the stack, titled Dance Anatomy. She couldn't remember much about its contents, but she did remember the feel of it in her hands.

"Do you want anything before they get here?" Evan set the laptop down on the dining table, arched his back and dug his fists into the lumbar muscles.

Today was the first time she would be seeing Amanda since that awkward visit at the hospital and this time, she was bringing her daughter too. In preparation, Evan had shown Ailsa several pictures of Hayley playing in their back garden, kicking a football with him, sitting on the wooden bench with Ailsa, and then another with the little girl grinning from inside a bouncy castle. Ailsa's favorite photo had been one of Hayley asleep on a pile of blankets inside a bright studio. Several dancers were pictured behind her in leotards and Basque skirts, obviously rehearsing something. Evan had pointed to a thin woman, back to the camera and wearing a tutu, and said 'that's you, rehearsing Odette.' Ailsa had looked at the bony shoulders, the pink tights and the neatly wound dark bun and just nodded. Her heart had sunk when the image brought nothing back.

The doorbell rang, startling her out of her reverie. Evan closed the laptop and ran a hand over his hair.

"Ready to face the enemy?" He smiled.

"Ready." Ailsa tucked her headscarf in tighter behind her head, and squared her shoulders.

∼

Amanda sat at the fireside. Her hair flowed around her shoulders and she nursed a cup of coffee in her lap. Hayley was on the rug with Evan, putting the large pieces of a jigsaw puzzle together as Ailsa smiled nervously at Amanda, and lifted the plate of biscuits from the coffee table.

"Want another?"

Amanda laughed.

"No. Yes, but no. Not if I want to keep my job." She rolled her eyes and lifted the cup to her mouth.

Ailsa frowned and picked up a biscuit.

"These are my favorites." She bit into the Bourbon as Amanda's eyebrows shot upwards.

"Well, good for you, girl. Go for it." Amanda laughed and balanced her cup on the broad arm of the chair.

To her left, Hayley let out a squeal as she fit a large corner piece of the puzzle together and Ailsa winced at the noise.

"I got a corner, Uncle Evan." The little girl's face glowed as she looked up at him. "Your turn."

"O.K. Let's see, does this bit go here?" Evan held up a piece of puzzle and turned it around before laying it in the middle of the carpet.

Hayley giggled.

"No, silly. It's an edge piece."

Evan reached over and stuck his finger into Hayley's ear sending her into a fit of giggles. The laughter rose in volume as Evan continued to tickle her until she let out an almighty scream, the noise driving deep into Ailsa's head like a bolt of lightning.

"Ahh." Her hand flew to her temple, the wail out before she could stop herself.

Amanda stood up and put her cup on the table.

"Hayley, keep it down please. Too much noise." She leaned down and moved a curl from her daughter's eye. "Tidy up now please."

Amanda's simple gesture made Ailsa catch her breath. So

gentle, so innate, and yet the unconscious movement of the child's curl had displayed such ownership that Ailsa could hardly breathe.

Dropping the half-eaten biscuit onto the plate, she pushed herself up from the sofa.

"I'm sorry, but I need to lie down for a bit." She watched as Evan stuck his tongue out at Hayley and then stood up.

"That was my fault, Amanda. I started it." He winked at the little girl.

Amanda waved off his apology and walked back to her chair, as Hayley began gathering up the puzzle pieces and putting them back in the box.

As Evan offered Ailsa his arm, she noticed that he wouldn't meet her eyes, and as she wrapped her fingers around his forearm, she felt his muscles flinch.

Ailsa turned to Amanda, and as they passed she reached out a hand.

"I'm sorry. I just can't take loud noises yet." She met Amanda's eyes.

Amanda got up and leaning in, kissed Ailsa lightly on the cheek.

"Don't worry about it. She's way too noisy anyway." She shook her head. "We'll go for a walk while you rest, and she'll calm down."

Evan was silent as he helped her into bed. He formed the inverted 'V' with the pillows and then pulled a blanket over her legs. She caught his fingers before he could pull away.

"I'm sorry, Evan. I just…."

He looked down at her and blinked several times.

"It's just hard, you know?" He stared at her.

"I'm letting you down, I know." She sniffed.

He nodded once, turned and left the room.

Ailsa wasn't sure how long she'd been resting when the bedroom door eased open. Her heart lifted at the thought that

Evan might be coming to check on her. Instead, Hayley's small tousled head peaked around the door.

"Aunty Ailsa, are you sleeping?" She pushed the door a little further and stepped into the room.

Ailsa pulled herself up against the pillows and shook her head.

"No, Pickle. I'm awake."

Pickle. It was an odd word, but even as she said it she knew it was her pet name for the child, and the memory itself was as welcome as the little girl was.

Hayley twisted the hem of her corduroy skirt in her chubby fist and waited.

"Do you want to come in?" Ailsa patted the bed.

Hayley turned to check behind her then bolted to the bed and climbed up next to Ailsa.

"Sorry I made a noise." She crawled into Ailsa's side and leaned her head on her chest. The soft curls spread across Ailsa's sweater, the scent of talc and chocolate bringing a nut of emotion to her throat. "Mummy said you have a bad head." Hayley folded her hands on the blanket covering Ailsa's legs.

"I do. But it's going to get better soon." She wrapped an arm around Hayley's shoulder, pulling her closer. "You smell like chocolate."

"I ate lots of biscuits and Mummy said I was a piglet." She giggled.

Ailsa planted a kiss on the top of the mass of curls.

"You can have as many as you like."

Hayley snuggled in and as Ailsa looked down, the child slipped her thumb into her mouth.

"Are you tired, Pickle?"

Hayley nodded, yawning widely around her thumb.

"Will you sing to me?"

Ailsa frowned, struck by the unexpected question, and unsure if she could sing in tune.

Hayley lifted her chin and looked up at her.

"Sing Puff. You know, the one about the dragon and the string?"

She didn't know what song the child meant and as Ailsa began to worry that she was about to disappoint, yet again, she caught their reflection in the mirror opposite the bed. Her God-daughter was buried in her arms, resting, trusting her, and suddenly inspired, Ailsa spoke.

"How about you start singing and then I'll join in?"

To her relief Hayley nodded, removed the now slightly puckered thumb from her mouth, pushed herself upright and pursed her rosy lips. She sang the first line of a song then pausing, looked expectantly at Ailsa who, still waiting for her vault of a memory to yield something, simply nodded.

Not discouraged, Hayley continued. The little voice rang into the bedroom and Ailsa closed her eyes, concentrating, hoping that something might come to her.

Another verse later, Hayley audibly gulped in some air and then stopped at what felt like the end of a chorus. Ailsa opened her eyes and before she could think about it sang the last few words with her.

Hayley clapped her hands together and smiled.

"You did it." She grinned at Ailsa.

In the doorway, Amanda's head appeared and just behind her, Evan was beaming. Ailsa and Hayley continued singing as their audience gave them thumbs-up and then a round of applause when they finished. The sound of their clapping hands sent a thrill down Ailsa's back. That was a good sound.

A week later, Ailsa stood in the bathroom and stared into the mirror. The staples had been removed from her wound a few days earlier and she'd been afraid to touch her head afterward, but getting home to stand fully under the shower, to finally be able to wash her hair, had brought her to tears.

Her scalp was tender, and while she could feel the deep indentation of the incision line lying between the four hard bumps of the surgical screw heads, the feel of her fingers on the skin was a good pain.

Now, she assessed her lop-sided appearance in the mirror. Three-quarters of her head looked normal and the other quarter looked like a scene from a bad horror movie. Making a snap decision, she opened the cabinet, pulled out a pair of nail scissors and grabbing a long tress, sliced it off and tossed it into the sink, then separated another handful and cut. She worked quickly, sectioning off the long strands and cutting until her hair was hanging around her jaw, ragged but already less freakish.

As she carefully trimmed the hair near her wound, the movements became mesmeric and gradually she blended the rest into the shorter length until, before she realized it, the sink was overflowing and her head had emerged as a gamine oval with a covering of dark waves. She stood back and took in the new look. It felt light, uncomplicated. She liked it.

Cleaning the hair up she stuffed it into the bin and then rinsed the stray strands down the drain. Simple as that, she had taken back control and changed something, made it better. If only the rest of her life was that easily fixed.

EVAN

E van heard his mother-in-law sigh, so lifted the phone away from his ear. Jennifer was coming that afternoon to stay for a few days and he was trying to go over all the instructions they'd been given by Mr. Sutherland. Jennifer was obviously frustrated with the softly-softly approach the doctor had recommended, but he ploughed on regardless.

"She must still rest, but get some physical exercise too. Most importantly, she needs to have her memory stimulated, but gently." He stopped, not sure if Jennifer was still listening.

"I know how to take care of her, Evan, but I won't pander. I'll be honest with her. She needs to get on her feet, start exercising and getting her life back on track." She paused. "Mark won't hold her spot forever."

Evan heard the blood rushing in his ears and once again lifted the phone away from his face before he answered.

"It's not a question of pandering, Jennifer. We all want her to get back to her life, but she isn't capable of moving at a faster pace."

Jennifer began to protest, but he cut her off.

"And as for dancing, she doesn't remember her career, the company or most of the people, and we mustn't push it, O.K.?"

She huffed. "I know. But that whole thing just seems so odd to me."

It was no mystery that his rigidly disciplined, former ballet-dancer mother-in-law was a graduate of the school of tough love, but seemingly that wasn't the way to move Ailsa forward, despite what he or Jennifer might want.

"It's odd to me too, believe me." He let his head drop back and stared up at the ceiling. "But it's what we're dealing with. It is what it is."

Jennifer made a choking sound.

"That's a fatuous statement, simply created to let people shake off their responsibility to take action."

He felt the reprimand like a slap on the wrist and the temptation to tell her to stuff her help where the sun don't shine made him bite down on his lip.

"Jennifer, we just have to let her take things at her own pace, however frustrating." He closed his eyes, the image of her pinched mouth and coiffed hair reminding him of a beautiful but hard-hearted cartoon character.

"Well, I'm sure I'll be able to get her moving, one way or another."

Evan opened his mouth in a silent scream.

That evening, Evan hefted Jennifer's large suitcase along the hall and into the guest room. If he'd had his choice he'd have moved Diana in for a while, but Ailsa had understandably wanted her own mother.

Jennifer stood behind him in the doorway.

"Thanks, Evan." She pulled the silk scarf from around her

neck, releasing a waft of musky perfume, and tossed her leather gloves onto the small dressing table under the window.

Evan had dusted the room and changed the bedding and now, as his mother-in-law assessed the space, he hoped it would pass muster.

"Everything O.K.?" He lifted the suitcase onto the end of the bed.

"Oh, don't put it there. You'll dirty the bedcover." Jennifer patted his shoulder as she walked passed him and out into the hall.

Silently counting to ten, Evan set the case on the floor and followed her into the living room.

Ailsa was on the sofa with a pile of cushions behind her, smiling up at her mother.

"Thanks for coming, Mum."

Jennifer sat next to her daughter and tucked a short curl behind Ailsa's ear.

"It'll be fun, darling. We can have girl time while the master of the house is out all day."

Ailsa nodded.

"Are you letting your hair grow back?" Jennifer cupped Ailsa's cheek.

Evan, standing behind the sofa, shook his head and made a cutting motion across his throat.

Jennifer frowned at him.

"Well it won't go up in a bun if she keeps it this short."

Evan rolled his eyes, walked into the kitchen, bypassed the kettle and opened the cabinet in search of wine.

AILSA

Ailsa watched her mother filling the washing machine, an image that rewarded her with a glimpse of her childhood. Jennifer's long elegant back was bony, the points of her vertebra visible through her cashmere sweater, and the visual tweaking Ailsa's curiosity, she reached across herself and fingered her own neck, feeling for the same bumps of bone under the skin. She wasn't sure if she'd really noticed her mother's extreme thinness before. Perhaps she had but had forgotten it, which would just be one more thing to add to the ever-growing list of missing details from the past.

As Jennifer continued to lean forward, pushing various items into the machine, the shape of her mother's back sparked something else in Ailsa. Suddenly, her memory handed her a picture of herself performing, a swan in the final throes of death, down on the floor with one leg tucked underneath herself, her torso folded over the extended leg, her feathered tutu forming a pool of white around a slim thigh as her fingertips fluttered downwards and finally brushed the stage.

Her breathing quickened, but rather than mention what she'd seen in her minds-eye, she pressed her lips tightly shut.

Jennifer had been staying with them for four days now and Ailsa had, for the most part, gracefully accepted the passing over of the reins of her mundane routine from Evan, to her straight-talking mother.

"Your whites aren't very white, you know." Jennifer sighed. "You need to change your detergent."

Her mother slammed the door and punched the button on the washer, then turned to Ailsa and smiled.

"So, shall we go for a little walk today?" She pulled her sleeves down over her wrists and then smoothed her immaculate hair.

The thought of navigating a busy pavement, passing people who might stare at her healing head, was overwhelming, so Ailsa shook her head.

"Not today. I'm not feeling up to it."

Jennifer's brow creased.

"Fresh air is good for you, darling. You need to walk, too. Then maybe we can start to do a few barre exercises together?" She extended her arms to second position and beamed at her daughter. "Evan said that Mr. Sutherland said…"

Ailsa cut her off.

"I'm not up to it." Seeing her mother smart at the harsh correction, Ailsa softened. "Look, the cold hurts my head." She fingered her scalp. "Maybe tomorrow?"

Jennifer dropped her arms and pursed her lips, a telltale sign of her displeasure.

"Fine. But you can't hide in here forever."

"I'm not hiding, Mother." Ailsa heard the pout in her voice, like a reversion to childhood. "I'm just healing."

After a few moments, Jennifer patted Ailsa's cheek dismissively.

"What shall we have for lunch? A nice salad?"

Ailsa was hungry. It seemed that she was still hungry much of the time. There was a deep trough inside her and no matter

how much she ate, it was never satiated. At breakfast, she'd had
a huge bowl of muesli and then, braving her mother's disap-
proving expression, a slice of toast ladled with butter.

As he'd left for work that morning, thinking that Ailsa was
out of earshot, Evan had whispered to Jennifer.

"Call me if you need anything."

Her mother had snorted and then half whispered back.

"What, like another truck load of butter?"

Evan hadn't responded but Jennifer's words sliced through
Ailsa like a knife, and she had retreated to the bedroom without
saying goodbye to Evan.

As soon as her mother had gone to shower, Ailsa had slipped
into the kitchen and made herself another slice of toast. She'd
stuffed it down listening for the bathroom door to open, as she
wiped the telltale crumbs from her cheek like a rebellious child.

Now, at the dining table, Jennifer set a plate in front of her. A
small wedge of avocado and some tomato slices were artfully
fanned across a modest pile of lettuce, and a handful of carrot
sticks and three stalks of celery were stacked on the side of the
plate. Knowing the futility of protest, Ailsa looked at the food
and then at her mother.

"What?" Jennifer sounded wounded. "It's a balanced lunch."

Ailsa lifted her fork and stabbed a piece of avocado.

"You'll need to slow down on the eating. You've gained
quite a bit you know." Jennifer passed her a slice of fresh lemon.
"None of your costumes will fit." Her mother smiled benignly as
the barbed words hit home.

Overcome by the feeling of having lived her whole life in a
costume that she wanted to take off now, Ailsa bit into the
avocado letting the creamy coolness still her tongue.

It was obvious that aside from Jennifer's jabs at the subject,
her mother was tortured by not talking about her dancing, but
Ailsa couldn't give her the satisfaction. Not because she didn't
want to ease her mother's discomfort, but because Ailsa didn't

know what to say. So much of what she knew to be true still felt cumbersome and unwieldy when she tried to slot it into any kind of timeline. The photos, theater programs and other reminders that were scattered around the flat, rather than stimulate memories, served only to remind her of everything she had forgotten, but rather than making her sad anymore, it just made her uneasy. These shadows of things that flickered in her peripheral vision seemed to hold memories that threatened to hurt her and, for now, the safest course of action was to say nothing, push them down and wait it out.

Jennifer was watching her.

"Is it all right?"

Ailsa nodded.

"Fine, thanks."

Jennifer turned her plate around several times, positioning it carefully in the center of her knife and fork. As Ailsa watched her mother, she was rewarded by a memory of her doing that same thing at every meal. Colin would tease Jennifer, saying it was like a dog turning around in its bed three times before it lay down.

Ailsa smiled around her fork.

"What is it?" Her mother was squeezing lemon juice onto her salad.

"Nothing."

Jennifer started eating and so Ailsa swallowed the food, and welcomed the silence that blanketed the room.

A few hours later, Evan's keys clattered in the door. Jennifer was in the bedroom on the phone, so Ailsa got up, balancing herself against the back of the chair before walking carefully into the middle of the room. She wanted to see his look of approval of her being up rather than lying on the sofa.

"Hello." She smiled at him.

"Hi. How was your day?" He leaned down and kissed her cheek, the smell of sour smoke on his jacket. "How's your mum?" He widened his eyes. "All ship-shape?" The comic twitch of his eyebrows made her laugh.

"Yes. All fine." She touched her fingertips to her hairline.

Evan set his laptop down and lifted the whisky bottle from the cabinet. Ailsa instantly shook her head and jerked a thumb toward the bedroom.

"You're joking?" He spoke in an exaggerated whisper, swinging the bottle across his body. "Why?"

"She gets uptight about it, you drinking every night." Ailsa grimaced. "Says it's a bad habit."

Evan closed his eyes and she saw the tension in his jaw as he placed the bottle back down.

"Is it O.K. to have a bath, or is that prohibited too?" His eyes were hooded.

"Sorry." She reached out and placed her hand on his arm, but he shrugged her off and strode down the hall, heading for the bedroom.

The next day was to be Jennifer's last before heading home, and though Ailsa had enjoyed much of the visit, she was ready for her mother to leave. The jibes about her weight, her hair and her getting back to work had burned through Ailsa's skin like well-placed drops of acid, leaving her sore both inside and out.

Despite this, Ailsa was feeling physically stronger, and as her body began to become her own again, so her confidence was growing. Now, as she poured coffee for them both, she added a generous splash of milk to hers then carefully carried the cups into the living room.

Her mother was standing at the window, looking into the garden.

"It's quite a pretty spot really, isn't it?" She took the cup Ailsa offered.

"Yes. We're lucky to have it." Ailsa nodded. "Many of these flats had their gardens torn out when they were renovated." The statement floated out without any conscious thought and in response, her mother smiled at her.

"Yes. I know." She paused. "It's good that you remember that."

Ailsa rolled her eyes. "I do have some memories you know. I'm not a total blank." She gave her mother an exaggerated smile.

Jennifer balked, then her expression shifted to one of resolve.

"Darling, I need to talk to you about that." She walked to the sofa and then beckoned to Ailsa.

Ailsa walked over, but rather than sit, she perched on the arm of one of the armchairs.

"What is it, Mum?"

"It's about your ballet, the whole not remembering thing." Jennifer held her gaze, a frown wrinkling the perfect forehead. "I know I'm not supposed to press you about it, but it just seems too bizarre." Her eyes were magnetic, making it impossible for Ailsa to look away. "You must remember something, after all the years…" Her voice faded.

Ailsa shifted on the seat, trying to formulate a response that would effectively end this conversation.

"Look, I'm doing the best I can. Some things are coming back, some are stubbornly not." She said. "I know I danced. I do have some memories of being in classes years ago. Of Amanda and I." She paused. "But even with the evidence before me." She swept her free hand around herself. "I still can't bring the more recent parts back." She tapped her head. "It's not that I don't want to." The untruth felt hot on her tongue, and with it came a question. There was no doubt that the trajectory of her career was mostly lost to her, but even the slivers of memory she *had* been handed of herself performing, she'd chosen not to share.

As she scanned her mother's face, Ailsa realized that by

keeping those slivers to herself, she was retaining a modicum of control, not only in her grasp of the past, but of what path she might choose in the future. Unsure of what that might be, and wanting to resist the railroading that was beginning to feel familiar, she felt the rise of what could only be described as excitement.

Emboldened, she sat up straight and smiled at her mother.

"Who knows? Maybe I won't go back to performing." Her momentary bubble of power burst as Jennifer's face froze.

"What are you talking about?" She jumped up, sloshing coffee on her pastel skirt. "Oh, damn." Jennifer set her cup down and hurried off to the kitchen.

Seeing her mother's reaction hacked at Ailsa's resolve, and wanting what had been a mainly positive visit to end on a good note, she followed Jennifer into the kitchen, where she was dabbing her skirt with a wet cloth.

"Listen, Mum. I know I loved what I did. I mean, I must have." She hesitated. "If it's meant to come back, it will. If not, then I'll just have to create a new path for myself."

At this, Jennifer brightened, tossing the cloth into the sink and facing Ailsa.

"Well, you've done the work, Ailsa. You've earned some professional courtesy, I'd say. And as long as Mark knows you're trying, really putting the effort in to rehab and training, I'm sure he'll give you some more time." She nodded decisively.

Deflated at her mother's inability to grasp her point, Ailsa sighed.

"Right, Mum. I'm sure you're right."

BOOK THREE

Glasgow, February 2020

EVAN

Seven weeks after coming home, Ailsa still hadn't voluntarily talked about dancing, or the company. Evan had warned Amanda not to labor it when she visited, and he had done his best not to bring it up too much after the last time when Ailsa had shut him down in the bathroom. He had no idea what had gone on between her and Jennifer, but as him not mentioning dance left Ailsa calmer, much as it rankled, he'd let it go.

As her general mood seemed to be lifting, he had even taken the large cloth bag full of pointe shoes from the back of their wardrobe and hidden it in the cupboard next to the fireplace, fearing that discovering it could send her back down an unhealthy spiral. But, as the days slipped by and the cards and flowers still trickled in from Mark, and other friends in the company, none of which produced much sign of recognition, Evan was growing increasingly frustrated by this loud silence within her.

The incident with her hair had really shaken him. The day she'd walked out of the bathroom with a do-it-yourself pixie cut, he'd been shocked into silence. She had always been paranoid about getting haircuts, telling the hairdresser exactly how much she could take off just the very ends. Not having varied the same long locks for as long as he'd known her, her outline was now so altered that he still caught himself doing double takes when she came into a room.

Now, he stood in the kitchen and stared out at the still Spartan garden. When it arrived, March would bring things back to life, and soon the weather would be warm enough for Ailsa to sit out in her reading spot.

He had been back at work for four weeks and while he was relieved to be out of the confines of the flat, the feeling of disconnection from Ailsa's days was disconcerting.

Since Jennifer had left, Ailsa was coping well with being left alone. He'd call her most afternoons, and Diana had been popping in regularly to bring her lunch. Ailsa enjoyed those visits and Evan was sure that it was because his mother made no demands on her. Diana chatted about the weather, what was on the news, cooking, and about Evan. Ailsa felt calm around his mother, and he was grateful for that.

Amanda had brought Hayley round as often as she could, and a couple of times had even left the little girl with Ailsa for an hour or so while she ran errands. It had gone well both times and, as Ailsa had reported to him when he got home from work, had inevitably ended up with them either singing or listening to music. Glad that Ailsa was responding to the child, Evan had set up the wireless speaker and loaded Ailsa's phone with a selection of songs that he knew Hayley loved.

He'd come home the previous day to find Ailsa standing at the window in the living room, a blanket wrapped around her and the window thrown wide open. He'd been shocked at how cold the room was and had scolded her.

"God, Ailsa. You'll catch your death." He'd closed the window and taken her frigid hands in his, rubbing her fingers back to life. "What're you doing?"

She'd shaken her head, letting him warm her hands.

"Just listening." Her smile had been dreamy.

"To what?" He'd guided her to the sofa and then turned up the central heating.

"Beautiful music. It was coming from outside, or maybe upstairs." She pointed at the ceiling.

Evan couldn't hear anything so had just nodded, and diverted the conversation to his day at the office.

The lack of physical activity and her increased appetite had softened Ailsa's edges. Her hipbones no longer protruded from beneath her leggings, her shoulders were less jagged and her face had a slight curve to it, the angular cheekbones and jaw covered with a new layer of flesh that made her look younger than her years.

Evan was trying not to mention her eating for the moment, but the one time he'd almost blown it was at breakfast a few days earlier. When she'd asked for it, he'd shoved the butter dish across the table to her and watched as she'd spread a wedge of it thickly on her toast.

Ailsa had caught his expression and frowned, the toast suspended in front of her mouth.

"What?" Her eyes flashed, challenging him.

"Nothing." He'd shaken his head. "You're obviously enjoying that."

"I like butter. So shoot me." She'd stuck her tongue out at him in a disarmingly playful way, and they'd both laughed the momentary tension away.

Today was Sunday, and Amanda was bringing Hayley over mid-morning. They'd decided it was time to take Ailsa out on an adventure and he had booked a table at a bistro on Ashton Lane that they'd always loved. He was concerned that a restaurant might not be the best place for her yet, but, despite her concern over still wanting to cover her healing head, Ailsa seemed keen to go.

Behind him the TV flickered above the fireplace, and as he

turned, he saw a volcano erupting, white-hot lava flowing across the screen. Ailsa now habitually had the TV on with the volume muted, as she still had trouble dealing with loud noises. Evan picked up the remote and turned the set off just as she emerged from the hall.

She had abandoned the sweat-gear she'd been living in for weeks and wore a long woolen dress. The gentle curves of her new body under the silver-grey wool, the short hair and the touch of color she'd added to her lips were all mesmerizing.

Evan smiled.

"Wow. Look at you."

She blushed, batting the air.

"Got to start making an effort sometime." She smiled and smoothed the dress over her hips, then frowned. "Am I getting fat?"

Evan shook his head. "Don't worry about that now."

Grabbing her coat, he slipped it around her shoulders as she gently leaned back into his touch. He turned her to face him, letting his hands linger on her shoulders, and Evan felt the first stirring of attraction he'd had in months. As he took in her face, fresh, open, happy, his stomach dipped with the certainty that she wouldn't look at him that way if her memory eventually yielded the one thing that he wanted to keep buried.

Amanda and Hayley walked a little ahead of them. Hayley wore a white coat with a fur-lined hood, and her jeans were tucked into tiny red wellingtons. Amanda's long caramel-colored coat skimmed the tops of dark suede boots and from behind, with their matching blonde heads, Evan thought that mother and child looked like an advertisement for an exclusive children's clothing catalogue.

He smiled at their backs and held onto Ailsa's hand, navigating the pavement; steering her around passersby and keeping his eyes peeled for hazards.

She'd insisted on walking to the bistro and while progress was slow, she seemed to be enjoying the fresh air, despite the frigid temperature. March was a tricky month in Glasgow, and today, Mistress weather had chosen to whip away the tease of spring they'd seen over the past few days, just to spite them.

Ailsa's grip on his arm was tight, despite the thickness of their combined coat-sleeves creating a numbing bulk between them. She'd been quiet for most of the walk, content to soak in the Sunday lunchtime activity along Byers Road, smiling at people who made eye contact with her.

As they passed the rows of three and four-level sandstone buildings, housing high-ceilinged flats atop the retail stores and restaurants beneath them, Evan felt at home in the bustling space. He glanced over at a kitchen store that Ailsa liked and wondered if she'd recognize it, then caught himself mid-thought. He needed to stop constantly guessing which memories would come back and which were gone. It was wearing.

Ahead of them, Hayley kept stopping and turning around, as if to make sure that they hadn't been lost among the throng of shoppers and diners that oozed along the road. Each time he caught the little girl's eye, he'd raise a hand to reassure her of their presence.

When they finally turned into Ashton Lane, Evan breathed a sigh of relief feeling Ailsa's grip loosen on his sleeve. The cobbled lane was significantly less crowded than where they'd just been. The pavement was dotted with a row of waist-height iron bollards and once he'd guided Ailsa inside their border, blocking anyone from getting between them and the storefronts, he knew she was safe.

A few moments later, Hayley turned again and waved. She stood next to a blackboard easel, displaying a white chalk list of the *Plats du Jour*.

"Aunty Ailsa?" The child pointed wildly across her body to the paned glass windows of the restaurant. "It's here."

Ailsa let out a soft laugh.

"I know, Pickle."

Ailsa's relaxed recognition of where she was made Evan smile. These unexpected memories, when they occurred, were like beacons of light that shot across his visual field.

"Do you remember it?" He looked down at her.

She nodded. "I do, actually."

The bistro was buzzing. All but one corner table were occupied and, guessing that it was theirs, Evan made a beeline for it. While he settled Hayley into a chair with a booster seat, Ailsa and Amanda went to hang their coats on the rack next to the door. The two women's heads were close together, and Evan took in the stark contrast between the waist-length, soft locks of her friend and the edgy, close curls that now belonged to his wife, sticking out from under her headscarf. He wasn't sure he'd ever get used to that.

Amanda must've said something funny because Ailsa laughed, her hand resting on Amanda's back. The gesture looked easy, and spoke of the closeness that had once existed between the two friends. Seeing even a shadow of that grabbed at Evan's throat, surprising him.

At the table, Ailsa sat next to him with Hayley on her left. The child insisted on being next to Ailsa, and Amanda had happily agreed.

"Hey, no problem. But you get the clean-up, too. "Amanda winked at them.

"That's fine. We don't make much mess, do we Hayley?" Ailsa leaned in to Hayley and nudged her shoulder, making the child giggle.

Evan picked up his menu and caught the eye of a waiter who was passing the table. The slight edge of nervousness that he'd been feeling about this expedition was easing.

"Can we have a bottle of the St. Emilion and some water please?" He flipped the menu open.

"Aye. No problem." The waiter, a stocky man in the customary black trousers, white shirt and long Parisian-style apron, nodded. "Anything for the wee girl?" He gestured toward Hayley, his eyes resting on Ailsa.

Ailsa hesitated and then, meeting Amanda's gaze, moved a curl from Hayley's eyes.

"Better ask her mum." She smiled over at Amanda.

The waiter blinked.

"Oh, sorry. So, anything for her?" He addressed Amanda now.

"Hayley, would you like an orange juice?"

Hayley nodded, her flushed cheeks pulsing as she chewed a mouthful of bread that she'd grabbed from the basket on the table.

Amanda laughed.

"Orange juice please, but not fizzy." She rolled her eyes at Ailsa. "Remember that time she had Fanta? It wasn't pretty."

Evan held his breath, focusing on the small printed list of hors d'oeuvres in front of him. *Come on Ailsa. You can do this.*

After several interminable moments of silence, Ailsa cleared her throat and smoothed her skirt over her knees. She turned to look at him and he could feel her eyes boring into the side of his face.

Across the table Amanda waited, her hands folded around the menu and her torso leaning forward, as if providing a bridge for Ailsa's memories to slide across.

Out of the corner of his eye, Evan saw Ailsa shake her head and then drop her chin.

With the movement, his frustration surged.

"Oh, come on, Ailsa. Even I remember that." He snapped.

Amanda leaned back in her chair.

"Hey, Evan. It doesn't matter." She patted the air.

He caught Ailsa's pained expression, so turned back to Amanda.

"So, what're you having? A lettuce leaf and a raw carrot?"

Next to him Ailsa was fidgeting. She'd laid the white napkin over her knees when she sat down but now had pulled it back up onto the table and was screwing it into a long twist. Her menu lay unopened, and Evan could feel the tiny vibrations of her heel tapping the floor under her chair. The movement irritating, he reached over and placed his palm on her twitching thigh.

"You O.K.?"

Ailsa withdrew her leg and clamped her knees together.

"Yes. I'm fine." She dropped the napkin, turned and slid her handbag from the back of the chair. "I'm just going to the ladies."

Amanda made to get up. "I'll come with you."

Ailsa held her hand up. "I can manage."

Looking stung, Amanda settled back in her chair.

Ailsa waited a moment, then, as her face began to crumble, she turned slowly, and using a series of chair-backs to steady herself, walked away.

Evan's moment of peace had been cracked wide open and he stared at Amanda, who was watching Ailsa's back weave between the packed tables.

"Well. That told me." Amanda whispered.

Hayley reached out for another piece of bread.

"Mummy, where's Aunty Ailsa going?"

Evan leaned back to let the waiter pour some wine into his glass. He took a sip and nodded to the man who filled his glass, and then Amanda's.

"Does the other lady want some wine?" He gestured toward Ailsa's empty chair.

Evan swallowed his mouthful, enjoying the burst of grape, and earthy tannins at the back of this throat.

"No." He frowned.

Seeming to sense their discomfort, the waiter nodded, left the bottle on the table and retreated.

Amanda lifted her glass and took a sip, then her eyes filled up.

"Evan, sometimes I don't know how you..."

"How I what?"

Amanda's eyebrows jumped.

"I mean, it must be so hard..."

He shifted in his chair. He couldn't bear sympathy.

"Don't. O.K.?" He thumped his glass onto the table sending a spray of wine across the white cover. "We don't need pity, Amanda. That's no use to anyone."

Amanda bit down on whatever she was about to say, and Evan instantly felt terrible. Amanda had stuck by Ailsa, and accepted having become nothing more than a ghost in her closest friend's life, without complaining. She'd brought Hayley around more often, simply because it was good for Ailsa. She'd made a point not to talk about work or their mutual friends at the company and, more than all of that, since this whole shit-show had begun, she'd not brought up the Marie scenario once, when he knew she knew it all.

He reached across the table and squeezed her fingers.

"Shit. I'm sorry. You didn't deserve that."

Amanda withdrew her hand and wiped her face with her napkin.

"It's all right." She sniffed.

"No. It's not." Evan sat back. "It's far from all right."

AILSA

Ailsa waited until she heard the front door close before opening her eyes. She didn't want to talk to Evan about what had happened at the restaurant the previous day, and the pretense of sleep, while ridiculous, was all she could come up with.

Sunday night had been silent and awkward after Amanda and Hayley had left. Evan had taken his laptop into the bedroom leaving her staring at the muted TV screen, her feet wrapped in a blanket. She'd waited until he'd gone to bed before she padded into the kitchen and served herself a bowl of ice cream, letting the milky, rich vanilla flavor wash away the sharp taste of disappointment in herself. She had been making such great progress, and then had let Evan's frustration at her not being able to pull up a particular memory take her down.

Now, as the light spread across the bedroom, she pushed herself up against her pillows. The day stretched ahead with nothing on the calendar except time. Her mother-in-law wasn't coming by, as she had other commitments on Mondays, and for once Ailsa was glad of it. Diana was wonderful, but even the prospect of her cheery manner, and uncomplicated conversation, felt intrusive today.

Ailsa stretched, careful not to graze her head on the head-board. The surface wound had healed, but her scalp remained hypersensitive to pressure and cold. She ran a hand over her hair, twisting a curl at her temple, and could feel the distinct trough in the bone and the four bumps under her fingertips. It had initially revolted her to touch them but now, as she moved her finger from one to the next, the associated tingle of pain felt like a rite of passage. Each time she pressed down she winced as her scalp tightened, sending zaps of electricity across her temple and face, as if the fine mesh of a spider's web was being stretched over her features.

Half an hour later, with a cup of tea and a slice of buttered toast next to her, Ailsa settled on the sofa. She had been working on an email to her mother for a while, but the words just wouldn't form themselves as she wanted them to. Sutherland had said that she needed to keep writing and reading, and he even recommended that she read out loud as often as she could, but today her fingers were sluggish, and while she had never been a speed typist, she felt like a clumsy beginner wrangling with the keys.

The chill outside had been keeping her indoors much of the time, but being boxed in was becoming wearing, so she walked across the room and opened the window. Her mind was cloudy this morning, like the March sky, and frustration tingled along her spine, settling at the base of her neck.

She slid her feet apart, pressed her heels together and folded at the waist, feeling the pull of her taut hamstrings as her finger-tips brushed the floor. As she straightened up, her arms forming a circle around her head, she halted. The forward bend called for a subsequent movement but, as she stood still, staring out of the window, she couldn't remember what it was. She sighed, drop-ping her arms to her sides.

Outside, the garden was beginning to come back to life, and as she looked at the dark green of the heather that crouched close to the low stone wall, the wonderful music that she'd been hearing recently tugged at her attention. The melody was incandescent as it seeped in through the open window, and the subtle notes, like gilded dandelion seeds, floated on the breeze that chilled her cheeks. Ailsa closed her eyes and breathed deeply, letting the soothing sound soak into her skin.

She knew that the flat above theirs had a new occupant, as of a few weeks ago, but she hadn't met the mystery tenant yet. She had heard the floorboards creaking above their bedroom a few times, but other than that had put it out of her mind.

The soft music continued, and she thought she recognized the melody, but couldn't place it exactly. Was it Prokofiev? She spoke it out loud, the word feeling like a chunk of chocolate on her tongue—sweet, rich and guttural. *Prokofiev*. Suddenly, she knew she was right, the notes speaking to her like they were addressing her personally. Her heart lifted as she closed her eyes and let herself wallow in the moment of absolute, irrefutable knowledge.

The flat above would be a duplicate of theirs, in terms of size and layout, and as she moved forward and leaned out of the window, Ailsa tried to visualize the person upstairs doing the same. As she craned her neck, she noticed the upstairs window was also opened wide to the garden.

Now, a different piece of music drifted down to her, the beautiful melody rising and falling in sultry waves, carrying her away from the window and back into the room, and then Ailsa found that she was swaying. Enjoying the freeing feeling rising within her, she moved carefully, her arms lifting at her sides, and as she reached out toward the surrounding walls she began a series of balancés, turning in slow steady circles as she alternated her arms in opposition to her feet. This piece of music was in three four timing—she knew that too.

Ailsa let the easy momentum take her up and she turned in time with the lilting notes, losing herself to them as she moved around the furniture, gathering speed. Catching sight of herself in the mirror, she stopped to get her breath, then strained to hear the music, which was becoming softer, and when the piece faded away and ended, she felt the dip of disappointment.

Her breathing was labored, and a layer of sweat had gathered across her breastbone. She glanced at the clock above the fireplace, then over at the front door, wondering if 11:45 am on a Monday was a respectable time to turn up uninvited at a new neighbor's door. The idea of getting out of the flat shone brightly as she assured herself that Evan wouldn't mind her going upstairs alone, as she was so much stronger now.

Walking into the kitchen, she opened the cabinet above the stove and as she scanned the contents, she heard her mother's voice in her ear '*You can't visit people without something in hand.*' There were various canned foods stacked neatly, some coffee; a box of tea bags, half a sleeve of crackers and a jar of raspberry jam—none of which would make an inspired 'welcome to the neighborhood' gift.

Next to the teabags sat an unopened bag of Evan's Viennese Whirls. Momentarily, she considered opening the biscuits, sneaking a couple out then putting the remainder on a plate as her offering, but annoyed at the greedy notion, she reached in and took the packet out.

Looking down at herself, she assessed her faded jeans and sweat shirt, but impatient to be gone she turned, grabbed her scarf from the dining table and tied it on. Picking up her keys, she nodded at her reflection in the hall mirror then walked out into the cold hallway.

The stone stairs felt icy through her socks, reminding her that Evan would have told her to put on shoes.

The door of the flat above was freshly painted a bright red, highlighting the shabbiness of their own faded blue door.

After a few moments she heard footsteps, and a soft shuffling sound accompanied by a cough, indicating that the occupant was standing close to the other side.

"Hello?" Ailsa bent down and spoke into the letterbox flap. "I'm your neighbor from downstairs, Ailsa Campbell...uh, Macintyre. Just wanted to say hi."

The heavy lock clunked and she straightened up quickly to see a young man standing in the doorway. He was tall. As tall as Evan, but a narrower frame. His jaw was comic-book wide, his eyes a startling green and his shoulder-length hair, glossy and blonde, was tucked efficiently behind his ears.

Smiling at her, he stepped backwards.

"Hello to you too." He had an accent—not Scottish, but perhaps Scandinavian.

"I don't want to disturb you." Ailsa hesitated.

"You're not," he said, beckoning her in.

Questioning for only a second the wisdom of entering a stranger's home alone, she stepped over the threshold and into the bright flat. Though just one floor up from their own, this room was significantly lighter than its twin below.

"It's good to meet you," she shoved the packet of biscuits toward him. "Welcome to the building."

"Thanks." He looked at the offering in her hand and without introducing himself, took it from her and turned toward the kitchen. She watched him go, as an immediate sense of him being somehow familiar held her on the spot.

"Cup of tea?" He called from the kitchen as Ailsa, tentatively moved deeper into the room.

"Please. If it's no trouble."

The room was empty of furniture except for a beautiful grand piano, sitting in front of the large window overlooking the garden. Its lid was propped open and a small stool was pushed in close to the base pedals. Drawn in by the lustrous wood, she walked over to the instrument.

"This is a beautiful piano," she called in the direction of the kitchen.

"Thanks." There was a pause. 'It was my grandmother's."

After a few minutes the young man walked back in to the room. He held a tray with a small teapot, two mugs and the packet of biscuits.

"Appropriate biscuits," he said, smiling.

"Oh really?" She looked around, aware that there was nowhere to sit other than the piano stool.

He gestured toward the floor and Ailsa, nodding her assent, nimbly curled her legs underneath her and sat on the bare boards.

"So why are they appropriate?" she asked as he sat down opposite her, crossing his legs pow-wow style.

"Viennese whirls, I mean…I was just playing a waltz." He looked at her, as if expecting her to grasp the reference.

"Which?" She picked up the mug closest to her and blew on the steaming liquid.

"Strauss," he replied.

Strauss. The name shifted something in her memory, but her focus was being pulled by the man in front of her.

"So, what's your name?" Ailsa shifted on the hard floor, eyeing the still unopened biscuits.

"Oh, sorry. I'm Sam Lindstrom."

The air around her shifted as she looked at the angular face, the magnetic eyes.

"And you're a pianist, obviously?" She cringed at the inane statement.

"I am." He nodded. "Just moved here from Stockholm. I've joined the Symphonia."

Ailsa swallowed the scalding tea and watched his lips as he spoke, his mouth forming a perfect circle.

"You know, the Symphonia?" There was a slight frown as he scanned her face.

Ailsa felt her face grow hot.

"Yes, I know it." Her heart jumped under her ribs. "I'm a dancer." She blurted the words, blinking furiously, unsure if the one thing was necessarily connected to the other.

Sam's eyes brightened as Ailsa began to feel lightheaded. The floor seemed to be shifting under her tailbone and the chill of the room was gone, leaving her aware of her clammy armpits under the heavy sweatshirt.

"What kind of dancer?" Keeping his gaze fixed on her face, Sam reached for the biscuits. "Classical?"

Ailsa carefully placed the still-full mug back on the tray.

"I should go." She knelt up. "Evan will be calling soon."

Sam frowned. "You just got here." He watched her get up. "Is Evan your husband?"

Ailsa, beginning to feel nauseous, nodded.

"Yes. Evan's my husband." She moved toward the door. "You'll have to meet him." She tried to smile. "I've been ill. He worries. I mean…" She swallowed.

"I'd like to meet him." Sam was up and following her. "I'm sorry you've been ill." The green eyes were full of concern, bringing a lump to Ailsa's throat.

He stood behind her in the doorway.

"You're sure you can't stay to drink your tea? I'm not dangerous you know?"

Ailsa released her breath.

"I know." She said. "It was nice to meet you, Sam." She extended a hand.

"You too." He shook her hand; his long fingers cool around hers. "Come again soon."

As she was turning to go, he touched her arm sending a spark bouncing across her skin.

"Shall we exchange numbers?" He was smiling. "It's always good to have a neighbor to call, in an emergency."

Flustered, she nodded. "Sure. Do you have a pen?"

Downstairs, Ailsa slid the key into the lock, her breath

coming fast and her chest aching. She should not have gone up there. Sam probably thought she was a lunatic, arriving uninvited then behaving like a freak and leaving five minutes later.

I am a dancer. She walked into the flat and closed the heavy door behind her. Leaning her back against the wood, she closed her eyes. *I am a dancer.* She'd finally said it out loud, as if the fact had a will of its own, no longer accepting being buried in her subconscious. While she had been keeping it prisoner, by sheer willpower, its release was undeniably freeing, and that it had happened while talking to a total stranger made it all the more liberating.

The window was still open and the room had become frigid, so moving steadily across the floor, she made to pull it closed just as a piece of glorious music floated down to her once again. She knew this piece, it was the ballroom scene from Romeo and Juliet. The knowledge, another gift this day had given her, made her smile. Leaving the window slightly ajar, Ailsa turned to face the living room and as she counted the phrases, so the hairs on her arms rose. Her entrance was coming up.

She assessed the leather sofa and coffee table, wondering if she could move around them and as the melody filled the room, her feet clenched. Excited, she slipped her socks off and spread her toes wide against the wood floor, but this was wrong. Her feet were too free.

Looking down she took in the bulbous toe joints, both big toes slanting unnaturally toward the other toes, all of which had dark pink calluses dotted across the joints. She leaned down and ran her finger over the bumpy skin. Her feet were as lumpy and messed up as her head. Seeing the irony in the parallel, she snorted and stood up, then something tugged sharply at her subconscious and she headed for the bedroom.

She flung the wardrobe door open, knowing that there should be a bag. At least she thought there should be. Her feet were now freezing as she pulled out several pairs of boots, Evan's running shoes, two pairs of flip flops and a backpack. This wasn't right. The bag should be here. Her whole life sat on a seesaw, at the mercy of her dented brain, and it was infuriating that it was so hard to tug certain memories out of the shadows, into the light of day, when others revealed themselves to her with no inducement.

Frustrated, she made her way back into the living room just as the musical phrase was repeating. She'd missed her entrance.

EVAN

E van sat in the car. The temperature outside was dropping quickly, and the outline of the building ahead of him was fading into the evening light as he shifted his weight to the opposite hip. He could see his breath, but didn't want to go inside. Not yet.

Ailsa had been asleep when he'd left for work that morning, and he'd been relieved not to have to speak to her as he slid out of bed, got dressed and let himself out of the flat. As he'd watched her sleep, this newly complex creature, her face smooth of the frown that he'd seen a little less of recently, and her short curls stuck to the side of her face, he'd realized that he missed his wife.

A bicycle swept past the car making him jump, and Evan checked his watch. He'd been sitting outside for twenty minutes, so should go inside before one of their neighbors saw him and thought he'd lost his mind.

Ailsa was sitting on the sofa with the TV on mute, as usual. She dropped her book into her lap and smiled at him.

"Hello."

"Hey, what're you reading?" Evan dumped his laptop and coat on the hall table.

"Did you have a good day?" She lifted her face as he approached.

Evan leaned down and pressed his lips to her forehead. He was aware of her mouth, so close and yet still feeling inaccessible to him, clamping shut.

"It was fine." He stepped back and then flopped onto the sofa next to her. "What did you get up to?" He glanced at the TV screen where a large white horse was ostentatiously sidestepping in a packed arena. "What on earth are you watching?"

Leaning back from him, Ailsa tucked her legs underneath herself.

"Dunno. I wasn't really watching. I just like having it on."

"So, what did you do today?" Evan tried again.

She jammed her fingers into her eyes and brutally rubbed them.

"Nothing much. I did some laundry."

"Well done, you." Evan smiled and then checked himself, unsure whether he was supposed to praise her for conquering that simple task, or if it would it be perceived as condescension. The notion that he was second guessing himself constantly these days was irritating. "What else did you do?"

She was winding the bottom of her sweater around her finger like a tourniquet.

"I went upstairs. Met the new guy in the flat above us." She jabbed her thumb at the ceiling.

Evan hesitated. Had he heard that right? He tried to imagine his now semi-reclusive wife venturing out of the flat, mounting the uneven stairs and introducing herself to a perfect stranger. The mental image was odd, and incongruous based on Ailsa's erratic behavior of the past few weeks. However, he was pleased at her taking the initiative like this.

"Really? So, what's he like?" He rose and went to the cabinet to pour himself a drink.

"Nice. Young. He's a pianist." Ailsa was up and moving toward the window. "I heard him playing again." She drew the heavy curtains, and Evan caught what looked like a smile as she turned.

"Playing?"

"I told you I heard music the other day." The smile was gone. "I did tell you, didn't I?"

Ignoring her question, Evan went on.

"How young is he?" He twisted the top back onto the whisky bottle and circled his shoulders to relieve the tension that was creeping up the back of his neck.

"Probably early thirties. We had tea." She lifted the blanket from the back of the sofa and wrapped it around herself. "Well, he made tea but then I bolted."

Evan swallowed his mouthful and sank back onto the sofa. "Bolted?"

"Yeah. He's got no furniture. Just a grand piano. So, we sat on the floor." She wrapped the blanket tighter around herself and sat down next to him. "His flat is so bright." She glanced around the room. "Much lighter than ours."

Evan felt the weight of her head as she leaned in against his shoulder. She smelled of jasmine as he kissed the top of her hair.

"You should meet him. His name is Sam." She said, wistfully.

Evan lifted the dishes from the table and deposited them in the kitchen. Ailsa had cleared her plate of the pasta bolognese he'd made and was curled up in the armchair again. The book she'd been reading lay on the sofa and, as he passed, Evan picked it up. It was Allegra Kent's autobiography, *Once a Dancer*, that he'd bought for her the previous Christmas and the distinct black and white cover photo of the Balanchine prodigy was starkly beautiful.

"Is this good?" He waved the book at her.

"Yes. I'm just getting into it." She nodded. "It really was artistic torture, the way Balanchine singled dancers out and then worked them to the point of exhaustion—like he wanted to deconstruct them." Her eyes were wandering around the room and her voice was dreamy, as if she was not fully present in the conversation.

Taken aback, Evan slid the book onto the coffee table. This was the most she had spoken about anything dance-related since her surgery, and afraid to stem this unexpected flow of consciousness, he stayed quiet and sipped his drink.

"I mean he was a genius, there's no doubt about that, but his methods..." She extended a leg from under the blanket, pointed her toes and lifted her foot toward the ceiling. It was a movement that she used to make regularly when they were sitting chatting, and Evan would tease her about it. Seeing her perform this familiar action, even subconsciously, sent a jolt of hope through him.

She lowered her leg and turned to look at him.

"I don't know much about Balanchine." Evan said. "Tell me more." He crossed his feet on the coffee table and balanced his glass on his stomach.

As he moved, Ailsa's eyes became shrouded.

"I don't want to bore you." She stood up and carefully placed a new log on the sputtering fire.

"It's not boring." He sighed. "That's why I asked you."

She hunched over and stared at the flames beginning to lick the sides of the wood.

The conversation, such as it was, being clearly over, Evan stood up. Deflated, he drained his glass, lifted his laptop and coat and walked into the hallway.

"I'm going to take a shower."

As he moved away from her, Ailsa walked over and lifted the book from the table.

"Evan?" Her voice was little more than a whisper.

He turned.

"Where's the bag?" She eyed him as he shifted the laptop up against his chest.

"What bag?" For a moment he was unclear what she was asking him.

"The bag with all my shoes. My ballet shoes." Her face was smooth, devoid of clues.

He couldn't get a read on her mood, and the inability to know her mind anymore was something new that made him distinctly uncomfortable. Taking a moment to gather his thoughts, he took a deep breath and stepped back into the living room.

"I moved it."

He watched as her brow wrinkled then he waited as she moved slowly and deliberately back to the armchair. Suddenly something popped in his jaw as he bit down. This was not her fault. He knew that. But all this going back and forth was exhausting.

"You asked me not to put pressure on you about dancing. I saw the bag a while ago and thought it'd be better to move it, just until you felt more like yourself again." He spoke deliberately, then licked his lips and slid the laptop onto his hip. "I'll show you where it is, if you want?" He watched her run a hand over her hair, letting her fingers settle on the side of her head.

After a moment or two of silence, he sighed and stepped toward the fireside cupboard.

"Wait." Ailsa stood up slowly. "I'm not ready yet. Don't show me."

Anger pressed back into the space where hope had been, and before the pinprick of light could be completely extinguished and darkness sweep back into the room, separating him from his wife again, he leaned down and pulled the cupboard door open.

"Evan, stop."

"No, Ailsa. It's time." He pulled the soft bag out and shoved it across the floor toward her feet. "You are a professional dancer. It's who you are."

Ailsa wrapped her arms across her body and stared down at the bag.

"It's who you are." He turned and walked into the hallway, so she wouldn't see his face.

Evan pressed the phone to his ear. It was cold in the outer hallway, but he didn't want to risk Ailsa hearing him.

"I don't know what to do, Mum." He tucked his free hand under his armpit. "She's just so up and down. Like she's here—I get a glimpse of her—and then she shuts down again." He tried to control the whine which was threatening to take over his voice. "I screwed up tonight. I think I was cruel."

"That doesn't sound like you, Son. Listen, all you can do is your best." Diana's voice was soft and steady. "She has a long way to go, but she needs you to be patient."

Evan shivered.

"Jesus, I know that."

He could hear his mother sigh.

"You're doing a wonderful job. Just keep her talking and let her guide you. If she's not ready to dive back into the studio, so be it."

Evan nodded to himself. "I know. But she needs to at least talk about it."

Diana tutted. "What do you want me to do?" There was a pause. "How can I help?"

Evan stared at the tiled wall. The space around him was frigid and he could see his breath.

"I wish I knew, Mum." He shook his head. "I suppose all she needs is time."

"Yes. And she needs you to be who you are—love her, have faith in her—and call your mother when you need to grumble." Diana chuckled, then paused. "I'm always here, Evan. You know that."

Evan stared into the night feeling guilty about the unconditional support his mother was giving him, her being unaware of how badly he'd let Ailsa down just a matter of months ago.

He closed his eyes and sighed.

"I do." He slid his hand into his pocket and felt the softness of the semi-crushed cigarette box. He'd given up a several years earlier, at Ailsa's urging, but this past few weeks he'd been slipping out of the office occasionally to smoke behind the building. So far, he hadn't smoked at home, but tonight might be the exception.

He pulled the box out and flipped the top open. Sliding one of the cigarettes into his mouth, he clamped his lips around the familiar shape. Even its presence was calming as he bit down on the filter.

He spoke through his teeth.

"I'd better go inside. Don't want her to hear me out here." He patted his pocket, feeling for his lighter.

"Is that you smoking, Evan MacIntyre?" Diana's voice was sharp.

Evan balked and snatched the cigarette out of his mouth.

"No. I'm just..." He coughed.

"Well don't just. Do you hear me?" Diana tutted again. "You know you can't kid your mother. You never could."

Evan laughed. "Shit, well I'll keep that in mind."

"You do that." She sniffed. "And give Ailsa my love." Diana

hesitated. "Is it still all right for me to pop over tomorrow? I've made gingerbread."

He tucked the phone under his jaw and slid the cigarette back into the packet.

"Of course. She's looking forward to seeing you." He nodded. "You might be the only person that applies to, at the moment."

Diana tutted. "That sounds distinctly self-pitying, to me."

He felt the sting in her words as he recognized the truth in them.

"Not very becoming, Evan."

AILSA

With each visit to Sam's flat, Ailsa's confidence was growing. His gentle, inquisitive manner, easing information out of her without her feeling interrogated, had allowed her to share more than she'd imagined she would with a relative stranger, and the sense of having found a confidante lifted her spirits away from the constant worry that she was now somehow less than whole.

This was the second time she'd come upstairs in a week and each time she appeared at his door, the air between them became increasingly comfortable. Sam appeared to have no agenda other than to play piano and enjoy her company, and being welcomed so unconditionally, and simply for being herself, was a gift.

As Ailsa's trust in this enigmatic man grew, so their conversations had gradually begun to delve deeper, broaching their pasts and family backgrounds, their experiences as only children and their mutual love of music, and reading.

One subject that Ailsa had steered away from so far was her surgery. The idea of sharing that with him sparked the concern that he would see and possibly treat her as damaged, his natural acceptance of her becoming marred by sympathy. As she'd considered it, the knowledge that she would undoubtedly share the truth with him when the time was right, felt comfortable.

This morning, over a pot of coffee and half a crumbly madeira cake, they'd been comparing notes on their favorite composers. Sam was now sitting on the floor opposite her with his back against the wall under the window, his legs forming a wide V shape and his hair raked away from his face.

"So, you're marooned on a desert island for the rest of your life." His eyes twinkled. "You can only take one book, one movie and one music CD with you." He paused, a smile tugging at his mouth. "What do you take? Don't think. Just go." He pointed at her.

Ailsa laughed, her stomach fluttering.

"Oh, right." She straightened her back, willing her memory not to let her down, but before she could filter her thoughts she blurted, "The book, The Unbearable Lightness of Being. Movie, Love Actually and the music, definitely some Vaughn Williams." She slapped her thighs, the thrill of having her mind cooperate making her face tingle.

"Nice." He nodded. "Good choices." His eyes flicked to the side as she crossed her legs under her.

"O.K. Now you." She grinned. "No thinking. Go." She pointed back at him.

"O.K. book, Beowulf. Movie, Back to the Future." He hesitated.

She nodded. "And the music?"

He rubbed his chin with his palm. "God. That's hard."

Ailsa's face was warm, her broad smile making her cheeks ache.

"Come on, this is your game." She tipped her head to the side. "Music." Coaxing him, she turned her hands in small circles toward her middle.

"But it's like asking a parent to choose between their children." He shook his head.

She narrowed her eyes.

"O.K. fine." He grinned. "Then it'd have to be Rachmaninoff, Concerto number 1." He spread his fingers. "Happy?"

Ailsa's heart was so buoyant it threatened to slip right out from inside her body and float up to the ceiling.

"Yes. You've no idea how much."

Sam's eyes were warm, taking her in.

"Good. My work here is done then." He dipped his shoulders forward in a mock bow.

Ailsa still sat crossed-legged on the floor, now with a cup of hot coffee in front of her, as Sam leaned in toward the piano and started to play. The bright, almost comical notes were familiar, their lightness lifting the corners of Ailsa's mouth.

As the music continued, an image of a blue tutu, and circles of red painted high on her cheekbones flashed vibrantly, surprising her.

"Is that from Coppelia?" She sipped her drink and rocked gently back and forth in time with the music.

"Yep." Sam smiled over his shoulder at her. "Do you know it?"

Ailsa nodded. There was suddenly no doubt in her mind that she had danced in Coppelia, and as the melody surrounded her, and not for the first time, an image of a dressing room filled her head. Gripped by the clarity of the vision, but open to its company, she closed her eyes and let it come.

She could smell the musk of dust and sweat and see the dark-colored walls, the overcrowded clothes rail behind the low wooden chair, the deeply notched dressing table and the splotchy mirror surrounded by lights. The mirror's battered frame had a selection of photographs tucked under its edges and if she concentrated, she could picture them. Scanning from left to right there was one of Hayley and Amanda in a studio, and two of Evan, dark eyes shining under a mass of curls. There were several of her in various roles, Odette in Swan Lake, Princess Aurora in Sleeping Beauty, Cinderella and Carmen. As she walked through the images in her mind, the names of the roles came easily, no bolts of lightning this time, rather the slow easing of a door opening.

There was also a photo of her parents giving her flowers after her first performance as Juliet, her mother elegant in white, still every inch the prima ballerina, and her father beaming as she curtseyed to them both.

As the images swam under her eyelids, where Ailsa struggled was to place them in time—Juliet before Odette, or had Carmen been her first role as a principal? Principal. That was her history. That was her truth. Principal. As she played with the word it felt slippery in her mouth and yet, it didn't scare her as it had a matter of weeks before.

While she had chosen not talk to Evan about it, even after he'd showed her the bag full of shoes, the more time she spent absorbed in music, either singing with Hayley, up here listening to Sam play or even walking around her home with earbuds in, now that she could tolerate them again, the more the dark curtains surrounding her dancing career were rising. The more she remembered, however, the heavier her conscience became.

Now, as she pressed her eyelids tight, she tasted the tang of that guilt at the back of her throat. The longer she kept this gradual re-emergence of her memories from Evan, the crueler it seemed, and the longer she stayed away from dance, from what had been the largest part of her world for so long, the harder it would be to get back to it.

Her body was changing, rebelling, her new, softer shape making her clothes feel tight. Each time she buttoned her jeans and felt the unaccustomed pressure against her stomach there was a flutter of panic deep inside her. And yet, as the days rolled by and she tucked her concern away behind toast, ice cream, butter and chocolate, she was able to hide from the fact that for some reason she wasn't sharing her progress with the one person she should—her husband.

If she tried to summon what was feeding her secretiveness, there was nothing to see but a handful of images that had been redacted, large black swaths still hiding behind a dark curtain.

Ailsa opened her eyes. The music had stopped and Sam had spun around on the stool and was watching her.

"What're you thinking about?" He smiled. "You look miles away."

Ailsa put her cup down and got up.

"Can you do me a favor?"

"Sure."

"Can you play Juliet's variation, from act one, at the ball?" Her heart began pattering as she slipped her socks off. "I heard you playing it a few days ago."

Sam's eyebrows jumped. "Um, yeah. O.K." He nodded. "So, you *are* a professional?" He stood up, flipped the top up on the piano stool and rifled through a pile of sheet music. "I thought so."

Ailsa nodded. "I was." Once again, hearing the statement out loud was liberating.

Sam placed the music on the stand and settled himself back on the stool.

"Ready?" He looked over his shoulder at her.

"Yes."

Ailsa walked to the far side of the room and tucked her right foot behind her left ankle at the coup de pied, her arms formed a soft demi seconde.

The music started. It was clear, melodic, no strained or stretched tones to distract her as it carried her arms and lifted her feet, moving her forward. She lightly touched the toes of one foot at the opposite ankle, rose onto the demi-pointe and then lifted her leg in a feather-light developpé à la seconde, unfolding it up close to her shoulder. With the movement, she felt the flutter of her non-existent skirt and the pressure of the ballet shoe that wasn't there.

Next, she stepped onto demi-pointe and raised the other leg behind her, bending her knee to form a curved Attitude. Lifting through her hips, she spun on her supporting leg to face the window and as the music's intensity increased she leapt into a grand jêté, splitting her legs apart as she hung suspended in the air, her arms extended in opposition. The leap sent a zap of tension through her tight hamstrings, but the pain felt right, fulfilling and satisfying.

Sam played on as she moved carefully through the choreography, completing a series of posé piqué turns. When she began the sautés and cabrioles, the small, neat jumps that as she was executing them she remembered she loved, she had no thought other than the way this made her body sing. Her lungs heaved, her face glowed, and as the movement gradually drew to a close she stopped in the center of the room, stepped to the side and slid into a deep curtsey.

She straightened up and looked over at Sam who was staring at her, his mouth slightly open.

"God, you're wonderful."

Ailsa's stomach lifted with joy as her breath came in quick spurts.

"Thanks. It's been a while." She padded over to her socks and sitting down on the floor, slipped them back onto her warm feet.

"Who are you with? What company?" Sam walked toward her.

"Ballet Scotland." The words came easily as Ailsa scooted over and leaned her back against the wall and, just as naturally, she continued. "At least I was, before this." She cupped her temple.

Sam settled on the floor opposite her.

"Talk to me."

An hour later, the wine bottle sitting on the floor between them was half empty. Sam lay flat on his back and Ailsa, still leaning against the wall, scanned his profile. He was undeniably handsome, in an angular, Nordic way, and as he stared at the ceiling she found herself wanting to touch his golden hair, run her finger down the bridge of his aquiline nose.

"Wow. So, you had a brain tumor?" He turned to look at her. Ailsa nodded.

"Yes. Temporal lobe." She tapped the side of her head. "Benign. If there is such a thing."

Sam shifted to his side and propped his head up on his fist.

"What do you mean?"

She cautiously leaned her head back against the wall, lifted the glass to her lips and took a sip.

"Well benign by definition means beneficial, harmless even." She said. "Tell me how a bunch of shitty cells that get together in order to screw up your brain, muddle your memory and leave you significantly less than you were, can be called harmless?" She set the now empty glass on the floor. "I've been changed by this. Diminished somehow."

"I hadn't thought of it that way." Sam was wide eyed. "But you're not diminished, Ailsa. Maybe changed, but from what I just saw, not diminished." He pushed himself up and lifted the wine bottle, waving it.

She placed her palm over the glass.

"No. Thanks, I must go. Evan will be home soon."

Sam nodded and set the bottle down.

"After everything you've been through, you are truly remarkable. You're such a beautiful dancer too."

"Thanks." She smiled.

"I'm not just saying that." He shook his head. "I mean it."

She tucked her feet under her and stood up then, surprising herself, she blurted.

"He doesn't know."

"What?" Sam frowned.

"Evan doesn't know that I remember, the dancing. Being in the company." She felt her throat narrowing, unable to believe that she was telling him this. She didn't know Sam well enough to cry in front of him, and yet she was risking that by sharing this personal confidence, which in itself felt like yet another betrayal.

Sam sat up.

"He doesn't know your memory is coming back?"

She shook her head.

"He knows I'm getting some things back, but not the company, the career part." She hesitated, painfully aware that the knowledge she was sharing could color Sam's impression of her. "He doesn't know I remember that." Her face grew hotter.

Sam stood up and walked toward the piano.

"Can I ask why you're keeping it from him?"

Ailsa noticed that his voice had altered, not becoming judgmental exactly, but a touch distant making her want to snatch back her confession.

"He's so..." She swallowed. "He just wants things back the way they were. The way I was." She paused. "He's very good to me, but he's so keen that I remember that part of my life." She watched as Sam reached out and closed the open window, then stood with his back to her and stared down at the garden.

"And that's bad, why?" He turned back to face her.

The touch of accusation in his tone felt like a thousand needles pricking her face, and as the piercing green eyes sought hers across the room, she felt naked, exposed as the deceiver that she was. She considered taking flight again and yet, something in Sam's expression held her, so she took a breath.

"Evan is so focused. He knows what he wants, no question, and he wants me back, but the me before this." She patted her head again.

Sam's eyebrows jumped.

"But what do *you* want, Ailsa?" He frowned. "Not Evan, or your parents or the company or anyone else."

"I don't know yet." She paused. "But I feel that Evan wants me to dance again more than I want it myself." She held her palms up. "What if I didn't dance professionally anymore? What if there's something else I should be doing? Something more meaningful." She licked her lips. "If I tell him I'm remembering, he'll push me back there." Hearing herself say it, give life to a fear that she'd been holding inside, made the reality of it more overwhelming. She watched Sam's face and waited for the inevitable judgment. Instead, she saw only mild confusion.

"Why can't you do something else, more meaningful to you?" His eyebrows pulled together. "Why do you have to do it professionally again if you don't want to? Can't you just dance for the joy of it."

The seemingly simple question floated around her, like vapor. The notion that she could possibly make this decision, to dance with no expectations tugging at her heels, no external pressure or agenda, wasn't something she'd considered, and the realization was like an awakening. Then, as she began to play with the idea, the weight of her reality dragged her back. How could she take that decision knowing how badly Evan wanted their old life back, a life that included her being a principal dancer?

"But, I owe Evan so much." She swallowed over the knot that was gathering in her throat.

Sam stood still for what seemed like an age, then shook his head.

"Sorry if this is too personal, but I think I can speak honestly with you, Ailsa."

She nodded, the anticipation of what he might say making her breath hitch.

"You are your own person, and you shouldn't feel obligated that way. He's your husband. What he's done for you in the past shouldn't have a price, or some kind of account attached to it." He blinked. "I mean, love isn't a transactional thing." He shrugged, his eyes darting to the window.

Taken aback, Ailsa let his words sink in. What he'd said made so much sense, it was as if a veil was being lifted from her perspective allowing light to pierce the dark corners of her angst, but even as she focused on Sam's words, light or no, as time went by and the force that was Evan was re-emerging from her memory, she was very much afraid that he could make things far less simple than Sam was suggesting.

Sam was eyeing her from across the room, his jaw ticking.

"But, I suppose I get how you feel, to a certain extent." He held his palms up. "I sometimes felt the same way about my wife. She was my biggest fan. Worked to support me through music school, paid our rent for three years so I could study and practice." He paused. "Then I'd sit at the piano in some concert hall or other, sweating in my tuxedo, and wonder if this was where I wanted to be, or whether I was just living out her ambitions for me."

The word *wife* had struck Ailsa in the chest.

Sam sat down heavily on the piano stool.

"You were married?" She made her way over and stood next to the piano.

He nodded and then slid sideways so that she could sit next to him.

"Yes, I was."

The pain in his voice was clear.

"What happened?" She sat on the stool, careful not to make contact with his leg. "Divorce?"

Sam shook his head.

"She died."

His sadness was obviously still raw, grabbing at her heart.

"Oh, I'm so sorry, Sam."

EVAN

E van sat opposite Mark, two glasses and an open bottle of wine standing between them on the sticky table top. The noisy wine bar was crowded, and not somewhere they'd have naturally gravitated toward, but Mark had limited time to meet before heading home and this place was close to the theatre.

"It's good to see you, Evan." Mark smiled. "So, what's going on?" He pulled the scarf from around his neck and slung it over the back of his chair.

"She's doing pretty well." Evan nodded. "Overall."

Mark poured the wine. "And?"

"A lot has come back, and she seems to have accepted some of the things she's forgotten. I mean she didn't remember that we were married." He paused as Mark, seemingly impassive, focused on his mouth. "I think we're O.K. there though. She's taken that in now, even though things are still strained some-times." Dangerously close to over sharing, Evan drew himself up. "It's just that there are some things, some of the most impor-tant, that aren't coming back." He leaned back in his chair feeling the legs wobble on the uneven floor.

"You mean ballet?" Mark's usually expressive face was

abnormally serene, as if he'd been practicing especially for this meeting.

Evan held his gaze, the deliberate lack of emotion in his friend disconcerting. This was a man who could control an entire studio full of dancers with the tick of a single eyebrow. Evan had seen him silence total chaos with just his index finger, and he'd occasionally seen him lose his cool, which wasn't pretty. He'd also witnessed Mark have the whole company in hysterics at his exaggerated impressions of them, hanging them each out to dry for their bad habits, stagey-superstitions and personal quirks. He could home in on tiny individual character-istics, and make fun of them, but in a way that managed to engender such loyalty and devotion from the dancers that imag-ining the company without his presence was, well, unimaginable.

Evan nodded. "She seems to have this block whenever the subject comes up. I just don't get it."

Mark lay his palm over the base of the glass.

"Do you think it's just time she needs?" He eyed Evan. "Or is there more to it?"

Evan shook his head.

"I wish I knew. Sometimes there's a spark, like she remem-bers, then just as quickly it's gone."

Mark nodded.

"There are theatre programs all over the flat. We've even looked at old photos of her in costume. But she just tells me she doesn't remember it all. Then a couple of weeks ago, out of the blue, she asked me where her shoe bag was, like she'd been looking for it."

Mark leaned forward on his elbows.

"Is there anything I can do?"

Evan shrugged.

"Dunno. I'd say talk to her, but honestly, I don't know if that's a good idea yet."

"What does her doctor say about this selective memory stuff." Mark took a gulp of wine.

"He warned us that it was a possibility, but even so..." Evan looked over at the bar where a group of young women were letting out a series of whoops as one of them worked her way down a line of shot glasses, tossing each one back to raucous applause. "I haven't spoken to Mr. Sutherland for a couple of weeks. Perhaps I should give him a call?" He raised his voice to be heard over the escalating noise.

"Might be a good idea." Mark blinked several times then continued. "Have you considered that she might not come back from this, Evan?"

"What do you mean?" He squinted at his friend.

Mark beckoned him closer as the women's voices rose in intensity.

"I mean, what if she doesn't find her way back to dance, to the company?"

Evan stared, suddenly aware that his mouth was open. Then, he shook his head and pressed his elbows into the table, his face only a few inches from Mark's.

"It's who she is, Mark. Ballet is her entire life. All she's ever wanted, or worked for." Evan licked his lips. "She has to get back to it."

Mark lifted the bottle and topped up their glasses, assessing Evan all the time.

"You know we love her, Evan." He smiled. "There's a place for her in the company, but if she isn't well enough, I mean there's a lot of pressure in our world. It's hard at the best of times, and if she's not..." Mark's voice trailed.

"If she's not what?" Evan realized that he'd just shouted and instantly felt his face grow hot.

"Take it easy." Mark leaned back and patted the air. "I'm just saying that she might find performing again too stressful. She's had brain surgery, Evan. Aside from the enormous physical effects of that, there's undoubtedly other things going on, emotionally." Mark's face was now a mask of concern, the practiced calm gone.

"I'm sorry, Mark. I think I'm just tired. Running on empty, you know." He shrugged as Mark, signaled for the bill.

"You need a break, darling boy. It can't be easy."

Half an hour later, Evan pulled his coat on as the heavy wooden door of the bar slammed behind them. Mark looped his scarf around his throat several times and tucked his hands into the pockets of his jacket.

"I'm taking the dogs and heading to the Loch house on Wednesday. Don't suppose you and Ailsa want to come?" Mark raised his eyebrows as if surprised by his own suggestion. "There's plenty of room. Loch Awe is quiet as the grave at the moment, and the change might do her good."

Evan shuffled his feet, considering the kind offer. A change of environment might well be a good thing.

He watched as Mark waved at a taxi rounding the corner of the street.

"Think about it and call me. It'd be easy to arrange if you want to come. You two could stay on a few days after I leave, if you want?" He opened his arms and Evan accepted a hug from the wiry man.

"Thanks, Mark. I'll talk to her and give you a ring."

Evan waved as the cab pulled away then turned down Hope Street, his legs suddenly heavy as he headed for Cowcaddens station.

AILSA

Amanda had stopped in for coffee and then gone to the hairdresser leaving Hayley with Ailsa. As Amanda was leaving, she'd given the child a warning.

"Remember no shouting, and do as Aunty Ailsa says, O.K., Munchkin?"

Hayley had nodded, her cheeks pulsating as she chewed a slice of apple.

The little girl was now sitting on the rug using a pair of round-ended scissors to cut stars out of flimsy tissue paper, and the more she concentrated so her rosy tongue protruded farther. Ailsa's second cup of coffee steamed on the table as she sat cross legged on the sofa, an illustrated anatomy book balanced over her knee.

Amanda had brought a couple of magazines for her; celebrity gossip rags Amanda had called them. Ailsa had thanked her and set them on the coffee table, wondering if she'd enjoyed that kind of thing in the past. She supposed Amanda knew that she did, them having been such close friends.

There were still many grey areas surrounding Amanda.

While enjoying her visits, Ailsa was frustrated that she couldn't remember the details of their relationship. She knew that Amanda was younger by one year and Evan had told her that after she'd had Hayley, Amanda had had to battle her way back to performing.

As she watched Hayley cutting a fresh piece of paper, Ailsa frowned, suddenly flooded with a disturbing dose of recall. It was true that the road back to peak performance after having a child was brutal, the dancer's body having been stretched and challenged in entirely new ways. It was a harsh reality that the majority of female ballet professionals faced and, consequently, few of them returned to work after starting their families.

When Jennifer had had Ailsa, there was little to no precedent for ballerinas returning to the stage, and so Jennifer's illustrious career had been cut short at just thirty. The irony of Ailsa's circumstances suddenly struck her, her being almost the exact same age her mother had been when she'd stopped dancing.

As the incongruous image of her svelte mother's stomach, distended by pregnancy, floated in front of her, Ailsa blinked. Then, from nowhere, the dialogue of a past conversation with Evan materialized. She couldn't place it in time, but the exchange was now clear in her memory. She'd asked him if he'd thought any more about when they might have children and his answer had left her feeling empty.

Now, as she re-ran the script of it in her mind, a distinct pang of loss made her close her eyes. Then, another memory followed closely on the tail of the first.

As Ailsa had begun to taste a little success, her mother had taken her aside and warned her against giving up her spot in the company.

"You can have babies well into your forties now-a-days, Ailsa. Put it out of your mind. Evan agrees with me, too." Jennifer had patted her cheek. "Let it go, darling. This is your path."

Ailsa could hear her mother's voice, semi-whispered but intense. The words had been cold, advice given from a place of regret, but at the time Ailsa had not heard it as such. She'd heard it as confirmation that the combined force that was her mother and Evan, were in league on this, and so she had once again stepped back from the subject.

"Aunty Ailsa?" Hayley's high-pitched voice made her jump. "Is this O.K.?" Hayley held up a sliver of pink paper.

"That's great, Pickle. You're getting really good at this." Ailsa smiled at the earnest little face. "Can you make a bigger one?"

Hayley nodded. "Yep. What color?"

"Yellow please." Ailsa laid her book on the cushion and slid down onto the floor. Her feet were bare, and she was aware of Hayley watching as she tucked them under her knees.

"When I'm big I want toes like yours." Hayley's bright eyes took in Ailsa's face.

"What do you mean, sweetie?" Ailsa frowned.

"All bumpy and pink. Like Mummy's too." Hayley grinned. "She says her toes are like sausages." She let out a peal of laughter as once again, the memory of her, Ailsa, and Amanda, floating and watching their own toes, flashed brightly.

Ailsa laughed. "Well, who wants ugly sausages for toes?" She poked Hayley in the ribs.

"I want to be a dancer, like you and Mummy."

Ailsa watched Hayley rummaging through the sheets of tissue on the floor.

"Here's the yellow." She handed a piece to the little girl.

"Thanks." Hayley smiled. "I want to dance in the theatre and have long hair in a bun, and wear ballet shoes like yours." She paused to take a breath. "And I want to get flowers on the stage, and do rehearsing and have a tutu and be famous." She exhaled, as if satisfied that she'd remembered everything she needed to say.

Ailsa reached over and tucked a curl behind Hayley's ear, suddenly picturing Amanda, in a calf length tulle skirt, her head encircled by a Les Sylphide headdress.

"Well, your mummy is a wonderful dancer, and I'm sure you will be too."

Hayley let the scissors drop to her knee.

"Mummy says when you get better you'll be dancing again." Hayley smiled and reaching out a chubby hand, patted Ailsa's thigh. "Are you better now?"

Ailsa's eyes prickled. The innocent lack of a filter was disarming.

"I'm getting better every day, Pickle. And you're helping me." She reached over and pulled Hayley into her arms, the golden curls smelling of apples and baby shampoo.

"Am I?" Hayley spoke into Ailsa's shoulder, her arms sliding around Ailsa's waist.

"Yes, because we read books and sing, and make stars together." Ailsa picked up the slice of pink tissue.

"You feel cuddlier than Mummy." Hayley squeezed Ailsa's waist.

"Oh. Do I?" She leaned back from the child's embrace. "Am I getting fat?" Frowning, she patted her stomach.

"No. I like you like this." Hayley grinned. "Can we play with your shoes again?"

Ailsa's moment of anxiety dissipated as quickly as it had appeared.

"O.K. Go and get the bag and I'll put on some music."

As Hayley tiptoed theatrically toward the bedroom, her arms flapping like wings, Ailsa flicked through the list of songs on her phone. Hayley's favorite was Prokofiev's Peter and the Wolf so finding the piece, Ailsa slid the phone into the wireless speaker cradle. The first notes of the overture floated into the room as Hayley, dragging the shoe bag, made her way across the floor.

"Wait for me."

"I'm waiting." Ailsa laughed. "Slow coach."

Hayley dropped the bag at her feet.

"Can I wear some?" Her eyes were wide.

"Yes. We'll put padding in the toes like last time, O.K.?"

Ailsa rummaged in the bag and pulled out a well-worn pair of soft shoes. The backs were malleable, they were dirty and the satin torn around the toe, but the ribbons were clean and still securely sewn to the cotton binding around the edge. She pulled out a wad of soft animal wool and stuffed a fistful into the toe of each shoe before putting them on Hayley and tying the ribbons. They looked ridiculously big on her, but Hayley beamed as she knelt and then stood up, staring down at her feet.

"Don't stand up on your toes, all right?" Ailsa warned. "You know you can't do that until you're older."

Hayley nodded.

"I'm just like you and Mummy." Her eyes glittered. "Put yours on, Aunty Ailsa." She pointed a finger at the bag. Several pointe shoes were now spread across the floor. The ribbons of a black pair were tangled in the weave of predominantly pink strips. Ailsa stared at the knotted satin trying to remember what ballet the black shoes were for, but the name escaped her.

"Wear pink ones. Pink is my best color." Hayley was moving awkwardly toward the window.

On a reflex, Ailsa reached out and lifted a shoe, wrapped her hands around either end of it and then bent the back to check its stability. The sole crackled as it moved, feeling flexible and yet sturdy. As she absently played with the shoe, bending it back and forth, she was overcome by knowing categorically that she loved them in this state, soft enough to have taken on the shape of her foot, but not so soft as to make it impossible to work in them.

As she watched Hayley negotiate her way back to the fireplace, Ailsa flexed her foot knowing that she liked to feel the stage through the toes of her shoes. She felt rooted, connected to the earth that way. She smiled to herself, as this was something else that she knew to be true, and that in itself was a gift.

There were still so many things that remained dark, shadows of memories hovering just out of her grasp, but now, crystal clear, she also remembered that she disliked to hear the clop of over-hard shoes when a dancer ran on stage. Mark called them clod-hoppers and she would laugh, agreeing with him. Mark. Thinking about the forceful man who's face now flashed clearly in her mind, she missed him.

She slid her foot into the shoe and crossed the ribbons around her ankle before tying them and tucking the ends neatly away. Her foot felt tightly constricted, her toes mashing into each other. This felt right.

Having made them sandwiches for lunch, Ailsa now sat on the bench in the garden. Hayley, wearing her pink coat, sat next to her, a book in her lap. It was the first time that Ailsa had been out to her reading spot since getting out of hospital and now the garden was bursting back to life. The heads of delicate, lilac colored hellebores hung toward the ground and behind them a thick hedge of golden forsythia served as a backdrop. Snowdrops and crocuses formed a multi-colored carpet around the bases of the few cherry trees that lined the rectangle of grass, and soft pink petals had dusted the ground, confetti-like against the darkening green of the musky lawn.

"It's pretty here." Hayley closed her book and sighed. "I wish we had a garden."

"Yes, it's nice." Ailsa nodded. "Your mummy and I like to sit out here and chat." Her eyes flickered with the splinter of a memory. The experience was becoming more regular now and yet, whenever she was gifted a tiny slice of clarity, it still surprised her.

"I know." Hayley slid off the bench and began walking away, heel to toe across the grass.

Checking her watch, Ailsa picked up her book and began walking toward the building. As she turned to call to Hayley, she heard someone shouting. It wasn't clear what the person was saying, but the panic in the voice was obvious.

Ailsa picked up her pace.

"Come on, Pickle. We've got to go in."

Hayley turned and skipped after her.

The voice was getting louder and now Ailsa could hear another sound, like thumping, so she picked up her pace and headed for the external corridor. As she turned into the tiled close, Amanda was standing at her front door hammering the wood with her fist, her face crimson.

"Amanda?" Ailsa stopped short. "What's wrong?"

Amanda whipped around, her eyes wild.

"Where's Hayley?" She dipped to her left craning to see behind Ailsa, in the dim corridor.

"She's here." Ailsa indicated over her shoulder, her stomach knotting. "What's going on?" She made to step toward Amanda, who spread her palms in front of her chest.

Ailsa felt the gesture like a slap.

"Hayley's here. She's fine."

At that, the little girl appeared behind Ailsa, and squealed.

"Mummy. We were in the garden." She launched herself at her mother who scooped her up and hugged her into her chest.

"Mummy, you're squashing me." Hayley struggled, pushing herself back from Amanda's grip. "Are you crying?"

Ailsa reached out to steady herself against the door frame, trying to figure out what could have happened to send Amanda into such a state of panic.

Amanda swiped at her cheeks and released her daughter.

"Why were you outside?" She spoke pointedly to Ailsa. "I

rang and rang. You didn't say you'd be going anywhere." She sniffed between words, elongating the confusing sentence.

Ailsa was struggling to make sense of what she was hearing. Why would she not go out and sit in her own back garden? She took another step toward Amanda, who this time didn't flinch.

"I'm sorry. It was such a lovely day and we wanted to read." Ailsa held her hands out. "I'm sorry." Even as she said it, she wasn't sure exactly what she was apologizing for, just that it seemed the only thing to do at this moment.

Amanda's chest was visibly rising and falling under her jacket as she closed her eyes.

"It's O.K. As long as she's..." her voice trailed.

The situation beginning to clarify itself, Ailsa felt the slow crawl of hurt across her chest.

"What?"

Amanda opened her eyes.

"Safe. As long as she's safe." She gave a weak smile.

Ailsa stepped back, rocked by the implication.

"Of course she's safe." She reached down and took Hayley's hand. "Why wouldn't she be safe with me?" Ailsa's voice cracked, betraying her hurt.

Amanda pushed her hair away from her forehead and, seeming to rally, spoke quietly.

"I'm sorry, Ailsa. I don't know what I meant. I don't know why..." She stared at Ailsa, her cheeks flushed and damp.

Ailsa raised her palm.

"Never mind. I get it." She took in the creep of embarrassment across Amanda's face. "You don't trust me anymore."

Amanda's eyes flashed to her daughter who was gripping Ailsa's hand.

"It's not that." Amanda shook her head.

"Yes. It is." Ailsa swallowed. "I see it in your face."

Hayley yanked at Ailsa's hand.

"Don't you cry too." Her face was crimson, her lower lip

beginning to tremble. "Mummy, why are you angry with us?" She looked over at Amanda, who was rubbing her hands over her eyes.

"I'm not angry, love. I was just a bit worried about you."

"But why?" Hayley persisted, winding her free hand around Ailsa's wrist. "I was here. With Aunty Ailsa." The simple statement felt like vindication to Ailsa, and she let herself exhale.

"I know." Amanda spread her arms out wide and locked eyes with Ailsa. "I know that."

As soon as Amanda had taken Hayley home, Ailsa checked the clock to see if there was time to go upstairs and see Sam, before Evan got home. She'd heard the piano earlier, while they'd been in the garden, but there was only silence now.

The incident with Amanda had shaken her, and as the hurt burrowed deeper into her middle, Ailsa needed to talk to someone about what had happened. Rather than call Evan, all she could think of to do was rush upstairs and find Sam, the impulse making her eyebrows draw together. Sharing her hurt feelings with someone she'd only recently begun confiding in seemed wrong, and yet innately right at the same time.

She walked over to the window and pushed it open, hoping to hear the notes that would be her invitation to climb the stairs. As she stared out at the garden, Sam's face floated in front of her, his gilded hair, the mossy eyes and lop-sided smile, and as she let his features absorb her thoughts, her phone buzzed on the table behind her. Sighing, she walked over and picked it up. A text message bloomed on the screen and her heart leapt. *Making tea. Can you come up?*

Without even checking herself in the mirror, she picked up her keys, switched off the overhead light and made for the door.

Sam was wearing long shorts and a Symphonia T-Shirt, and

before she could speak, he surprised her by giving her a spontaneous hug. As his arms went around her the objective of her mission was forgotten and she let herself be held, for a moment or two, her bruised feelings fading as she breathed in his scent.

"God, you smell good." She covered her mouth with her hand. "Sorry. I…" she sputtered.

Sam laughed, gently leading her into the room. "It's probably the strudel." He closed the door behind her. "Do you want some?" His eyes were sparkling, and the thought of eating something decadent like strudel, with no judgment attached to it, was irresistible.

"Absolutely." She nodded, followed him into the kitchen and watched him cut two generous portions.

With a plate of the flaky dessert each, they settled on the floor near the piano.

"I'm so glad you came up." He nodded at her plate, encouraging her to eat.

Ailsa forked a piece into her mouth, the still warm pastry disintegrating on her tongue.

"Oh, that's incredible." She widened her eyes. "Is it a family recipe?"

She saw Sam's face darken slightly as he placed his fork on the plate.

"It was my wife's, actually."

Ailsa set her plate down and wiped her mouth with her palm.

In all their time together, Sam hadn't talked much about his wife, and Ailsa hadn't felt comfortable asking too many questions. All she knew was that her name was Olivia, she'd been a teacher and had passed away from ovarian cancer nearly two years earlier.

Ailsa inched closer and touched her fingertips to Sam's arm.

"I'm sorry. I didn't mean to pry." She felt his palm close over hers and her pulse quickened at the contact, her visceral response to him so much more powerful than anything she felt when Evan touched her.

"You didn't." He met her gaze. "It's part of the process, remembering, then learning to accept the loss." His voice was steady as he focused on Ailsa's mouth. "When you lose someone they're always with you, like a molecule of something you've breathed into your soul."

His touching words, so sage and insightful, made her eyes fill.

Seeing it, Sam released her hand.

"Oh, don't cry." His mouth turned down at the corners. "I never want to be the cause of that."

Embarrassed at the rush of emotion, she sniffed.

"It's just the way you said it. It's such a perfect way to describe loss." She patted her sleeve, checking for a tissue.

Seeming to catch on, Sam stood up and walked toward the kitchen. The sight of his back moving away from her left Ailsa bereft, that the precious moment they'd just shared had ended so abruptly, and she was rocked by the compulsion to open herself up to this relative stranger in a way that she couldn't with Evan.

Sam's being widowed by age thirty was heartbreaking, and as Ailsa waited for him to come back, she was rewarded with a flash of clarity. His loss could be something that was drawing her to him, creating that undeniable pull. Here she was rebuilding a life, starting over with fragments of memories that often made up a less than complete picture, and Sam was rebuilding too.

As she considered this, it was clear that there was more to it. He'd felt familiar to her—from the first time she'd stood at his open door—familiar in a way that even her own husband didn't. Her and Sam's incomplete lives were complementary, their creative souls linked in some cosmic way that felt entirely fitting. All she sensed from him was his open acceptance of her, warts and all, and that made her feel brave for the first time in as long as she could remember.

When he walked back in, he held a piece of kitchen paper folded in half and was smiling.

"Sorry. No tissues." He held the paper out to her. "Will this do?"

She gave a breathy laugh, taking it from him.

"It's perfect. Thanks." She wiped her nose.

Sam sat down and lifted his plate.

"So, now I've officially made you cry, we can have no secrets." He put a forkful of strudel into his mouth then, surprising her, closed his eyes and groaned.

"Shit, that is good." He rocked back on his hips then opened his eyes and fixed hers with his. "Want to take some home for Evan?"

Hearing Sam say Evan's name was jarring. She didn't want her two worlds to meet, not yet anyway. What she wanted was to enjoy this separation from what went on downstairs and to savor it, like the fragrant dessert she was eating, letting it settle on her tongue and fill her with such comfort, such simple enjoyment, that she might never let it go. Being able to be herself up here, with no need to over think, edit, or sense that she was constantly disappointing, was priceless.

Sam was still watching her, and realizing that she'd been staring at him for a few moments, she laughed.

"I'm sorry. I was completely lost in thought there." She scraped the last of the strudel up with her fork. "What did you say again?" She caught the smile.

"I said, do you want to take some home for Evan, or for you, for later?" He set his empty plate down and put his palms on his washboard stomach.

"No, but thanks. He doesn't approve of me eating sweet stuff." She instantly felt a twinge of disloyalty.

Sam's smile slid away as he ran his fingers through his hair.

"Doesn't approve?" He cocked his head to the left,

reminding Ailsa of a lovable dog, trying to reason out what was being said to it.

"I think he's worried about me still eating so much." She patted her thigh, feeling Sam's eyes on her. Compelled to go on, she leaned back on her hands, stretching her legs out in front of her. "I was on steroids for a while, before and after surgery." She tilted her head toward the damaged side. "It messed with my appetite so much that I gained quite a bit of weight."

Sam frowned. "God, how tiny were you before, then?" He shook his head.

"Well, it's part of the deal, with dancing professionally." She pulled her shoulders forward, feeling her face warming under his scrutiny.

"I know, but it's not healthy." He stuck his bottom lip out. "Why would you let someone else tell you what to eat or not eat? You're perfect, just like this." He pointed at her. "And why on earth do you have to be skin and bone to dance? It's draconian."

She nodded, once again taken aback at his candor. There was something so deeply genuine in this man, it almost shimmered around him like an aura.

Amused at her momentary fantasy, Ailsa laughed.

"Well, if I go on like this," She nodded at the empty plate. "I'll never get back into a single one of my costumes." She held her breath, willing herself to stop. This wasn't Evan, or her mother, she didn't need to play the part here. Seeing his quizzical look, and feeling safer than she had in weeks to speak her mind, she took a breath. "I'm still not sure I want to."

He held her gaze.

"Would it be so terrible if you didn't, after everything you've been through?" He nodded at her head. "Sometimes a new path is the best medicine."

A swell of comfort in his simple philosophy moved her to share what had been eating her up for weeks.

"Evan and I are struggling a bit, to be honest." She bit down on her lip, afraid she'd gone too far, but seeing his open expression, she continued. "It's like we're re-learning one another, but there's so much that I don't know or remember about him, about us. It feels like I'm living with a stranger." A knot began forming at the back of her throat. "I know that sounds awful, but it's the truth. And to make it worse, he's been really patient with all this…" she flapped a hand over her temple, "and all I can feel toward him is grateful." Unable to help herself, she gulped down a sob, pulling the soggy kitchen towel from her sleeve and wiping her nose. "I'm trying to get back to the love." She saw Sam's eyebrows lift, but she was too far into this to stop herself now. "I know I loved him, I mean I wouldn't have married him otherwise, would I?" She searched Sam's face for some reassurance, but he simply bobbed his shoulders. "I look at his face sometimes and wonder what it was about him that I loved, what made me fall, make him my future." Her voice was ragged.

Sam shifted closer, his eyes full of sympathy.

"I don't know, Ailsa. You might never know." He paused. "But if you fell in love once, and he is the same man you knew back then, maybe you'll find that feeling again." His voice was low as he leaned forward and took her hand. "You'll just have to trust your instincts and let that lead you."

His touch was a panacea to her confusion, and the mass of conflicted emotions that were tugging her to and fro, each strained feeling draining away simply with his skin on her skin. The sensation electric, she let her hand linger in his.

"I just think that I'd be feeling it, or something like it at least, by now." She sucked in her bottom lip. "Something's holding me back, I just don't know what it is." She fixed her eyes on Sam's, craving more of whatever it was this man had to offer her.

Snapping her out of her suspended state, he sat back, withdrawing his hand, an unasked question seeming to tug at his brows.

"Well, that's was all my pocket-sized gems of wisdom, for now anyway." He gave a slightly forced laugh.

She liked the way his face creased when he smiled, the skin around his youthful eyes instantly forming troughs that disappeared just as quickly when the smile slipped away. As her face began to color, she rolled her shoulders back.

"Thanks." She mock bowed. "And how much do I owe you for that insightful advice, doctor?"

He pushed out his lips, his head dipping to the side again.

"How about having lunch with me. Tomorrow?" He raised his eyebrows. "I'll cook."

She considered her options for the following day, walking to the local store to pick up a can of soup and some salad, or coming up here to sit in this airy space, listen to Sam play, let her guard down and her body and soul breathe freely.

Pulling her legs under her, she stood up.

"What can I bring?" She smiled down at him.

"Nothing. Just yourself, and an appetite." He grinned. "Twelve thirty O.K.?"

She nodded. "Perfect."

The following day, Sam made her jump, pulling the door open before she could knock. He held an old-fashioned picnic basket and his freshly-washed hair tipped the shoulders of his scarlet Polo shirt. His jeans looked crisp and his leather flip-flops revealed the tanned tops of his feet.

"You scared me." She pressed her palm to her chest. "What's with the basket?"

"We're going to dine al fresco." He grinned. "While the weather holds."

Ailsa pressed her lips together, her mind darting to a scenario where she would be wandering along the road with Sam, and

Evan, whom she'd omitted to tell what her plans were for the day, would drive by and see them.

"Thought we could walk to Victoria Park, maybe sit by the pond?" His warm eyes were taking her in.

As she hesitated, torn between desperately wanting to say yes, and heeding the little voice inside telling her she was asking for trouble, he grabbed her hand, pulled her into the corridor and shut the door with a bang.

"C'mon."

They talked constantly for the duration of the twenty-minute walk, about Sam's move to Scotland, their impressions of living in Glasgow, about music and the composers they both gravitated toward. He told her about his upcoming concert series and the challenges of playing Shostakovich and then, he asked about how she felt her recovery was going.

Touched by his interest, she exhaled.

"Overall, I'm feeling good about it." She side-stepped to let an elderly man walking a massive dog pass them.

"Mornin'." He touched a wrinkled hand to his forehead and gave a gap-toothed grin. "Lovely day."

She nodded. "It's beautiful."

As the old man walked away from them, his awkward gait a telltale sign of him having dealt with years of pain, Sam took her elbow and guided her closer to his side.

"You were saying." He steered her left into Westland Drive, heading for the entrance to the park.

"Oh, yes. Some days I'm great, then the next I can still feel a bit weary, but I suppose it's all part of the journey."

"So, what's the chance of a recurrence?"

His question startled her, this being something she'd been afraid to confront even when Sutherland had told her there was that possibility. Taking a moment to compose herself, she watched him move slightly ahead of her, his hand trailing behind him like an invitation to hers. With all her will power, she resisted slipping her fingers into his, and picking up her pace, moved up next to his side.

"There's always a chance." She skipped over a pothole in the pavement. "But with regular checks, I'll be able to act fast, if it does recur."

He nodded, keeping his eyes ahead, the picnic basket now a buffer between their thighs.

"Were you very scared?" He turned to look at her, a frown wrinkling his forehead.

The candid questioning was a relief. She felt no awkwardness or desire to shy away from what was, after all, her history. As she considered her past, once again she was pricked with guilt at savoring this freeing experience, when Evan and she were in such a difficult place.

Something indefinable was drawing her to Sam, in a way that was almost impossible to resist, and as she considered her answer, he pointed to his right.

"Here's the way in." He turned into the entrance to the park then stopped at the ornate red and gold gates, waiting for her.

"I probably was scared but, to be honest, that piece of time is gone." A memory of the day she'd woken up with no clue how she'd come to be in the hospital, let alone that she had a husband she barely remembered and an entire career that was lost to her, materialized. "The worst part was right after I got home." She walked through the wide gate and into the park. "I was in this fog all the time, not sure what was old and what was new. Which memories went where in the timeline I was able to piece together. I had to take so much at face value, accept it as fact, that I got overwhelmed with it all sometimes." She paused, reveling in this seismic download. "Even seeing pictures of myself in the theater programs, in costume etcetera, it brought nothing back." She paused. "It was pretty terrifying, actually."

"I can't even imagine." He looked over at her. "You're really inspiring."

His easy smile brought a film of sweat to her palms, and Ailsa felt her face begin to color.

"No. I'm just doing the best I can." She flapped a hand, "and making quite a hash of most of it."

"No, Ailsa. You are remarkable." He'd lost the smile and now his eyes had an intensity that made her blink, like Icarus staring at the sun. She was overcome with wanting to bring him closer, have him swim inside her head with her.

"It was really overwhelming, until I heard you play." She dipped her chin, focusing on the ground.

Without stopping their progress, Sam looked over at her. "Really?"

She nodded. "Yes. It was the music, your music, that acted as a bridge. It brought things back, my body recognized it as part of my story, and then I started to move."

He reached over and squeezed her shoulder, warmth blooming on her skin under his fingers.

"That's so good to know." He leaned his head in toward hers. "The healing powers of music, eh?"

"Well, it's not just the music." She hesitated, her heart beginning to skip.

He looked at her and smiled.

"That's good to know too."

They walked on in silence along a dense avenue of trees, the gnarled trunks almost obscuring the view of the park that lay behind them. Ailsa tried to picture the place they were heading, the pond he'd mentioned at the far side of the park, and without the panic that usually accompanied her search for context, she wondered whether she'd been there before.

The April weather was being kind, a gentle breeze at their backs and the sky mainly clear of clouds. She could smell wet grass, and with it came a new memory of sitting on the lawn in the walled garden opposite her parents' house, making daisy chains with her mother, and as Sam led her forward, with gentle tugs on her shirt sleeve, she let the peaceful image float, trying to place it in time.

They found a spot on the lawn near the edge of the pond, and watching the swans glide in gentle circles, ate the sandwiches Sam had made. Ailsa hadn't realized how hungry she was until she bit into the crusty bread, then they both laughed at the speed with which she devoured it.

Now, with the lunch things tidied back into the basket, they lay next to each other on the blanket Sam had brought, their shoulders just touching as they examined the smattering of clouds sliding by.

"There's a nose." She pointed to her left. "And see the beady eyes right above it? Just like my mum's."

He laughed.

"Well, that's flattering." He turned his head and Ailsa sensed his eyes on her profile.

"Your mum's hard on you, isn't she?"

Ailsa hesitated, a flock of birds skimming the clouds above her.

"She's a tough cookie. Not your classic mother-hen, I suppose. But she worked so hard, and accomplished a lot. She was a principal with The Royal Ballet."

Sam whistled softly.

"She had to give up when she had me, and I think that's why she pushed me so hard." A memory of Jennifer, sitting at the front of Ailsa's ballet class, when she was eight, miming a correction to her from behind the teacher's back, flickered. "She's put everything into supporting me." Ailsa's throat began to lock up.

Sam shifted onto his side, propping himself up on one arm.

"Can I say something?" He waited for her to look at him. "I don't want to over step."

"Go ahead." She sat up, catching the beginnings of a frown.

"It sounds like you have people around you who like to drive you." He halted as Ailsa's eyebrows lifted. "You say that they do so much for you, etcetera."

She nodded.

"But I wonder if they don't bully you a little." His eyes moved back and forth across her body, as if trying to focus on a moving target.

The word bully was jarring, and Ailsa shook her head.

"No." She sucked in her bottom lip. "They just have high expectations of me." She watched him study her. "Which isn't a bad thing."

Sam sat up, his shoulder leaning gently against hers.

"O.K., but I think there's a difference between that and pushing you into things you don't want for yourself."

Even with the little information she had shared with him about that part of her life, he seemed to see right inside her soul. No words she could find adequately fit the moment, so she reached for his hand and after a few seconds, she whispered.

"I do have a voice of my own, you know." She squeezed his fingers.

"I've no doubt about that." He smiled at her.

Seeing his eyes crease at the corners, the flash of his teeth against the light tan of his summer skin, made her limbs tingle and overcome by an immense sense of peace, Ailsa closed her eyes, willing the memory of this day to stay etched in her mind as clearly as it was right at this moment.

Heading back toward home, they walked past the children's playground that had been quiet on their way in. There were a handful of children scattered across the various sections, two on a climbing frame and several running in and out of the maze that sat at the center of the area.

Just as they were passing the climbing frame, a boy, perhaps a little younger than Hayley, was dangling from the bars, his mother standing underneath him holding his hips. His face-cracking smile made Ailsa's heart clench.

"He's having a ball." Sam spoke to the woman who rolled her eyes, a sudden breeze picking her long hair up into a blonde sheet across her round face. She shook herself free and smiled.

"Yeah. He loves these things. Can't get him off them."

Ailsa recognized the same surge of need that made her breathless whenever she was around Hayley, and suddenly, without warning, her eyes were full. Embarrassed, she dropped her head, but Sam was already moving in close to her side.

"What's up? Have I over-tired you?" He frowned.

"No. I'm fine." She pinched her nose. "Just getting sentimental in my old age." She pulled a face. "Silly really."

He lifted her hand and tucked it around his forearm.

"There's nothing silly about that." He lifted his chin in the direction of the climbing frame that was now behind them. "I totally get it."

There was a soaring in her chest, a dozen birds taking flight under her skin.

"Do you?" She searched his face as he guided her on toward the red gates.

"Yes. Olivia and I were trying, when she got diagnosed." Sam swallowed, the skin pulsing at his neck. "That's how we found out about the cancer."

"Oh, Sam." She leaned in to his side. "That must've been so hard."

He nodded, steering her on.

"Yeah, it tore her up. Both of us, actually."

The pain was evident in his voice.

"I'm sure it did." Ailsa followed him around the corner and back onto Westland Drive, and suddenly unable to contain the question she'd been burying, she leaned in toward him.

"What was she like? Olivia." The name was somehow ethereal, bringing to mind a willowy maiden with bare feet and long flaxen hair. As she said it, she felt Sam's arm jolt under her fingertips. "Sorry, should I not have asked?"

He shook his head. "No. It's fine. I haven't exactly been holding back on you today." He smiled, his mouth lopsided. "She was tall, and clever, and a great sportswoman. Loved baking, football, swimming," he paused, "and she could ski like a champion." He nodded to himself. "Very opinionated, and her voice was loud. So loud that we'd sometimes have people in restaurants complain." He laughed now, raking his free hand through his hair. "She was a character."

Ailsa nodded, caught between wanting to hear more and not, but like a moth to a flame she continued.

"So, when she got sick?"

"Yeah, she didn't handle it well." His shoulders bounced. "Sounds stupid to say it, but she wasn't used to being weak or vulnerable." He looked down at Ailsa. "She was angry for most of those last months, which made it harder somehow."

Ailsa nodded. "I can understand that. You'd have wanted her to suck life dry, right? Value every second."

His eyelids flickered.

"Exactly. I knew that whatever I said or did couldn't ultimately change things, but I wanted her to find the joy in the time we had." He swallowed. "But then I realized that that was what *I* wanted for her." He released his arm from Ailsa's. "It took me ages to accept that anger was her coping mechanism. The only way she knew how to deal with death." His voice caught, sucking Ailsa in closer to his side.

"I'm sorry. That was too personal." She ran her hands into her hair, searching for the familiar bumps on her scalp.

"No. It's good to talk about it, actually." His eyes were glinting, the sun reflecting off the green pools. "People are often afraid to ask the tough questions, so I appreciate it." He smiled. "It's brave of you."

"Thanks." Relieved, she looked down at her feet, the rosy-pink toenails shining glossily against her matt skin.

He held his arm out for her and they walked on.

"So, what about you two? Any plans for kids?" He glanced at her profile.

At this, she dropped her chin again. The question was a simple one, but she didn't have a simple answer for him.

"I'm not really sure. I think we want different things." She met his quizzical gaze.

Just as she was about to continue, Sam gently tugged her to a standstill, moving them up next to the wrought iron fence that held the park in and the street out. He held her shoulders, his face close to hers.

"Ailsa." His eyes were hooded. "Don't let decisions like that slip away. Life's short, and family is too important." He looked suddenly shaken. "God. I'm sorry, I don't mean to…"

She shook her head.

"No. It's all right. You're right. I need to man up." She swallowed. "I'm finding my feet. It's just taking me a while."

At this, his frown slipped away and with his forefinger he swept the hair away from her forehead. "You are so much stronger than you think." He nodded. "I really admire you."

Her face began to glow, the thumping under her breastbone matching the pace of her breaths.

"Thanks, but I'm not sure why." She dropped her gaze to the ground, feeling his fingertips slide under her chin.

He raised her head and looked into her eyes.

"Because you're literally discovering new territory, every single day. Memory by memory." He moved closer. "You can achieve anything you want. I have absolutely no doubt."

She smiled as an image of her summiting a mountain and planting a flag in the snow sent a surge of happiness through her. She closed her eyes and then his mouth was on hers, cool, insistent but gentle, sending sparks directly into her bruised brain. She let herself fall into the kiss, her mind clearing itself of everything except this moment, this man, this sense of her life beginning to fit together.

EVAN

E van knew that while he was at work, Ailsa had been going
upstairs to see their new neighbor, Sam. The fact that Evan
had yet to meet the guy bothered him, but Ailsa hadn't suggested
it again after the first time and he had neither pushed the point
nor made any specific effort to go and introduce himself.

Something told Evan that this development, this venturing
forth, was important to Ailsa as part of her recovery and, despite
disliking the thought of her forming a friendship with a man he
knew so little about, he had decided to respect that. After all, he
wasn't exactly in a position to object, but, as the days went by
and she began to talk about Sam more frequently, Evan was
finding the hanging back more difficult. He wanted to get a look
at this amazing pianist who had captured his wife's attention.

He stood at the living room window and looked out at the
garden. Ailsa was sitting on the bench, a blanket over her knees
and a book in her lap. She'd been home for over four months
now and April was in full bloom. Any other year, she'd have
been putting in long days rehearsing the summer program in the
studio and then performing at night, and as he watched her flip a

page of her book, Evan frowned, nostalgic for that newly vacant piece of their lives.

The gaps in their relationship, rather than closing, were widening. He'd known that it would take time for her to fully reclaim her life, but as the days and weeks went by and he saw no hint of her returning to dance, Evan was afraid that she'd been permanently altered, becoming somehow less than the woman he'd known all these years, and that as a result, his role in her life was becoming fainter.

Now, as she stood up and walked away from the bench, there was a trail of sadness hanging in her wake. Ailsa had been shaken by the recent incident with Amanda, and had become newly withdrawn. She'd stopped answering the phone if Amanda called and consequently, she and Hayley had not come over since that day. The absence of the little girl seemed to be taking a toll on Ailsa, her often sitting in silence as they ate their meals or slipping off to bed while Evan was reading.

When he thought about their bed, he frowned. While they slept in it together, there might as well have been a brick wall separating them, their way of relating almost fraternal rather than any semblance of a marriage that he was interested in having.

Frowning, Evan tapped on the glass to get her attention but Ailsa, unaware, continued walking across the grass. The blanket hung from her left hand dragging on the ground as she passed the edge of a flower bed, picking up several leaves and a twig in the fringes.

His phone rang in his back pocket, making him jump.

"Hello."

"Hi Evan. How's things?" Amanda sounded cheerful. "How's our girl?"

He watched as Ailsa bent down and picked up a paper bag that someone had left on the grass.

"Pretty quiet. A bit sad, I think."

"Look. If she won't talk to me I can't apologize anymore."
Amanda's bright tone was replaced by one of exasperation.

"I know. I don't know what to tell you. She's sort of shutting
down again. It's like Hayley is the only one who can make her
smile these days."

Amanda sighed.

"I'd bring her over, but Ailsa won't talk to me." She hesitated. "I know I screwed up, but when I couldn't get an answer at
the door I just panicked."

"What did you think had happened? That she'd run off with
your daughter?" He laughed.

When Ailsa had explained the events of that afternoon Evan
had been confused, not understanding Amanda's reaction to what
appeared to be a simple misunderstanding.

"It's not funny, Evan."

Surprised at the edge in Amanda's voice, he turned from the
window and sank down onto the sofa.

"Hayley is it for me." Amanda was crying now. "You don't
understand."

Evan leaned his head back on the cushion. This was beginning to make sense.

"Amanda, don't cry." He scanned the ceiling, the chandelier
casting a rainbow across the cream-colored paint.

She sniffed. "I've never been the jealous type, Evan."

"I know that."

"I've never resented her success. I was the first one to…" she
stopped.

Evan's eyes narrowed. So, this wasn't just about Hayley.

"To what?" He frowned.

"To encourage her. To be there for her. To support her
promotions and celebrate with her." Amanda paused. "Hayley is
the one thing…" her voice trailed again.

Evan sat upright and pressed the phone tighter to his ear,

instinctively knowing the end to Amanda's sentence as clearly as he knew his own name.

"Is the one thing you have that she doesn't?" He held his breath.

"Yes." Amanda exhaled the word. "O.K. Yes."

He nodded.

"I love Ailsa, you know that. She's a natural, so gifted, but it's like she's turning her back on it all." Amanda's voice cracked.

Evan nodded. "I get it, Amanda."

"And now, the more time they spend together the more Hayley talks about her. Which is fine, but I'm being shut out, and Hayley is taking my place as Ailsa's friend. I know that makes me sound like the pettiest child around, but that's how I feel. I feel like I'm losing them both." Her voice caught.

If there was anyone who could understand being locked out by Ailsa's elusiveness these days, it was him.

You're her best friend." He pushed himself up from the sofa. "That'll never change. You're Hayley's mum, and there's no substitution for that. It's just that she's a bright light in Ailsa's fairly mundane days. She makes no demands on Ailsa, other than to spend time with her." He stretched his neck to the side and winced at the resulting loud crack. "You and I have our own agendas. We're full of expectations, have stuff we want her to remember, and we're disappointed when she doesn't." Saying it out loud was something of an epiphany. "She probably senses that." He caught sight of himself in the mirror. His eyes had dark shadows under them and he needed a haircut.

Amanda was silent, as if letting his words sink in. He heard her breathing slowly, her crying now under control.

"I hate to say this, when you're such an arse hole, but when did you get to be so wise, Evan MacIntyre?"

Recognizing the spiked olive branch that she'd extended, he smiled.

"Yes, I know. It's a terrible burden to bear." He laughed. "But I do what I can."

~

Ailsa closed the door behind her, slipped her shoes off and dropped the blanket on the armchair.

"How was it outside?" Evan patted the cushion.

She settled next to him, careful not to disturb the newspaper that was draped across his lap.

"Lovely. Just getting a bit chilly now, but the garden smells so good I didn't want to come in." She reached for the cushion next to her and shoved it down her back.

Evan draped an arm around her shoulder and pulled her closer, ignoring the slight tightening of her muscles.

"So, Amanda called again." He spoke above her head.

Ailsa nodded.

"I think you should talk to her." He waited. "She feels really bad about what happened." He leaned away as she met his gaze. "She wants to make it right."

Ailsa frowned.

"I don't know. She thought I couldn't be trusted with Hayley."

Evan removed his arm and shifted to face her.

"She doesn't think that."

Ailsa made to get up.

"No wait, I want you to hear this." He held her wrist until she settled back onto the seat. "I think she is a bit jealous of all the time you've been spending with Hayley." He saw her eyes widen. "Amanda misses you, and Hayley being around you so much just makes her feel left out."

Ailsa licked her lips.

"Think about it. You've always been a few steps ahead of Amanda. But she's supported you all the way."

She frowned.

"Then along comes Hayley, and Amanda's career is temporarily torpedoed, right?"

She nodded.

"Hayley is everything to Amanda and now, she has to share *her* with you too."

Ailsa looked up sharply.

"I never…"

"I know. I'm just saying think about it from Amanda's perspective. Hayley worships you, she always has." He paused. "Now all she talks about is you."

Ailsa's eyes filled and she released herself from his grip.

"I love Hayley, but Amanda's her mum." She looked at him. "I can never be that to her."

Evan heard the longing in his wife's voice.

"Why not give her a call?" He lifted Ailsa's hand from her thigh and squeezed her fingers.

"I will. Tomorrow."

He frowned. "Why not do it now?"

She stood up and walked to the window.

"Did you and I ever talk about having children?" Her face was impassive, but her question rocked him, and he sensed the agenda behind it.

"We did. But we agreed to wait until you were closer to retiring. A few more years." He lifted his eyebrows, hoping that he'd sounded convincing.

She assessed him, her fingers flexing and bending as if preparing to make a fist.

"How old did we say I'd have to be?" She emphasized the word we, sending Evan's stomach into free-fall.

"No specific age, just closer to taking a step back from principal roles." His nerves were now giving way to irritation, his voice taking on an edge that made her eyebrows gather.

"Really?" She squinted at him as she pulled at the bottom of her T-shirt.

"Yep." Evan resented feeling cornered, and struggling to control his rising anger, stood up and walked to her side. "Let's not worry about this at the moment." He made to touch her arm, but she took a single step back, enough to put distance between them. "You've got enough on your plate, for now." He gave her a smile.

Her eyes flashed, as if an image had lit them from behind. "Yes. You're right about that."

AILSA

S am sat at the piano and Ailsa lay flat on the floor, her hands behind her head and her sides pulsing. She'd just danced a long variation from Carmen and her feet were throbbing inside her pointe shoes. Every muscle and sinew vibrated as her legs jumped with the expended energy, and her full heart thumped under her T-shirt.

They hadn't talked about the impromptu kiss, and he hadn't kissed her again since, but it was all she could think about when she was around him.

"That was wonderful." Sam grinned at her. "What's next?"

Ailsa's breathless laugh turned into a cough as she sat up.

"Nothing. I'm exhausted." She shook her head. "What time is it anyway?"

She glanced over at her flip flops and the watch that she'd discarded two hours earlier.

"It's almost four thirty." Sam was up and rifling through the pile of sheet music inside the piano stool. "How about some of Odette?" He waved a sheet of music at her. "Just the developé solo?"

Ailsa stretched her legs out in front of her, pointed her feet and then folded over, feeling the satisfying stretch in her hamstrings as her forehead brushed her shins. The new lightness she held inside was making her feel invincible.

"The developé solo?" She laughed. "You mean the short variation, from Act two, the one with all the Attitude turns?"

Sam nodded, sat on the stool and opened the music.

"O.K., but give me a few minutes." She patted her stomach. "Let the batteries recharge."

Sam pushed the stool slowly back from the piano, then glanced out of the window.

"I know this is a bit random, but can I ask you something?" He sounded tentative as he watched her sit up. "You can tell me to bugger off if you want."

Seeing his expression, a trickle of concern made Ailsa frown. "No. Go ahead."

"Remember when I asked you about children, and whether you and Evan had planned on having any." He hesitated. "I don't mean to pry, but you said you didn't know for sure." He frowned. "Do you just not remember or …?" He leaned forward on his elbows, his eyes intent on hers.

Ailsa was transported back to her recent conversation with Evan on the subject and then, comparing it with the shadowy memory she'd had of a previous confrontation, felt a sinking certainty that he had not told her the truth. He'd been distinctly evasive when she'd brought it up, and her gut had been whispering at her to ask more, push more, but rather than follow her instincts, she'd let it go.

Seeing Sam's face, she felt safe to confide in him.

"Apparently, we agreed to wait until I was closer to retiring."

"Apparently?" He frowned.

"So I am told." She held her palms up. "What can I do but believe him? I have no way of knowing for sure."

Sam sat upright, his arms folded across his chest.

"I suppose so." He shook his head. "Look, I know it's none

of my business but isn't what you talked about back then kind of irrelevant? I mean, isn't the really important point what you want now?" His face was coloring.

Ailsa felt his struggle with perhaps pushing her too far, but his concern for her was deeply touching, and with that came a flash of resolve.

"Yes. You're right." She smiled, seeing the corners of his mouth lift. "That is the important point."

He nodded, taking her in.

Wanting to get them back to the light-filled place they'd been a few moments ago, Ailsa swung herself up from the floor and grinned at him.

"Come on. Last one." She pointed at the piano. "The developé solo."

Snapping back to life, he smiled, shifted the stool in closer and flexed his fingers, then spread them across the keys and picked out a chord from the introduction. As his long frame curved over the keyboard, his hair fell into his eyes and he tucked it behind an ear. His outline was lean, and the muscles of his shoulders were clearly defined under his shirt, drawing her eye.

Her visits up here were the highlight of her day, her waiting for Evan to leave so she could tidy herself up and climb the stairs. The more time she spent with Sam, inside the depth of his caring and calm optimism, it was hard for Ailsa to imagine that he'd been through so much.

Aside from the trust and mutual affection developing between them, what she treasured about spending time with him was his genuine interest in her whole being. With Sam, she felt like an adult, worthy, heard, and her opinions not only sought but valued. There was no hidden agenda or emotional tally being kept, and the clearer that became, the clearer it was that she felt the opposite way with Evan. Sam had, however unwittingly, become her refuge from the confusing world that was her life and the more at ease she became with the dynamic between them, the more uncomfortable she was growing at home.

Feeling her hamstrings easing, she walked to the far side of the room. Sam had left the windows and front door open to create a draft, but the heat of the day had filled the flat and her face was glowing.

As the music started, she sank into a plié preparation then rose onto pointe, extending her right leg at the side in a high developé. She then lowered her working foot to the floor and crossed her arms delicately over each other. Moving into a posé turn in Attitude, her arms in fourth position, she turned full circle to face the piano again. The slow momentum of the turn, the precision with which she executed it, and knowing that she was in total control of her body, were energizing forces.

Sam was smiling at her as she stepped back and repeated the combination, her heart brimming with the knowledge that she was once again one with the music and the choreography that she'd interpreted so many times.

"Gorgeous." He called over the music. "Keep going."

She filled her lungs and stepped forward onto pointe, her left leg rising behind her in an Arabesque. As she glanced over at him, Sam looked suddenly alarmed, then he lifted his hands away from the keys and stood up abruptly.

Deciding he must have finally tired of playing, Ailsa finished her next posé into Arabesque and then did a series of châinés turns toward the piano. Holding her arms in first position and spinning with an abandon that had been missing from her life for months now, she focused on the blond flash of his hair as her spotting point. Halting at the side of the instrument, she laid her two hands flat on top of the lid.

"What's up with you? Did I tire you out?" She panted. She was close to Sam's side and could smell the citrus of his soap. "You only get paid for the hours you work you know?" She laughed, breathlessly.

Sam continued to stare behind her and Ailsa noticed a rope of tension roll over his shoulders. Spinning around she saw Evan, standing in the open doorway, his face ashen and the bottle of wine he held dangling at his thigh. His expression was almost childlike, and as he blinked several times, as if not believing what he was seeing, the bottle fell to the floor shattering across the wooden boards.

"Oh, Evan." With a sudden rushing in her ears, Ailsa darted toward him. "Why didn't you say you were coming home early?" She stopped short as her shoes crunched on the broken glass.

"Don't." Evan held a hand up. "Just don't." He stepped backwards and bumped into the door frame.

Ailsa couldn't form a word. Her throat was closing and the breath had gone out of her.

Sam appeared behind her.

"You must be Evan?" He spoke quietly as he extended a hand. "Ailsa's told me so much about you."

The gentle offering sounded hollow as Evan stared, his mouth still open, while the wine seeped into the floor around his shoes.

"Let me get a cloth. Don't want anyone to cut themselves." Sam turned and walked toward the kitchen as Ailsa, took a pained breath then reached out once again for Evan's hand.

"Evan?" She squeezed his cold fingers. "Say something." Tears began to cloud her vision.

"What do you want me to say, Ailsa?" His eyes flashed now. "Well done. Nice work. Great that you're dancing up here with a fucking stranger, while I worry myself sick about you all day, every day." He snatched his hand away. "You're a class act, my love."

Ailsa felt the floor tipping beneath her. The pointe shoes that recently had started to become like a second skin again, now felt as if they were filled with nails. White hot, they had contributed to her betrayal of this man who deserved better from her.

Evan stepped backwards into the hallway. "Tell him I'm sorry about the mess." He jabbed a finger at the floor, turned and bolted for the staircase.

"Evan, wait." She shouted as he disappeared down the stairs.

Turning back into the room, she sank onto the floor. Her hands were shaking so badly that she couldn't untie the knotted ribbons and frustrated, she yanked at them.

"Shit."

Suddenly Sam's hands were over hers.

"Slow down." He whispered. "I'll do it." He knelt down in front of her and pushed her trembling fingers aside. He worked the knots until the satin released and then he held each shoe at the heel as she slipped her feet out of them.

Ailsa felt the contact of his fingers on her skin and it sent a spark up her calf. No. She needed to think about Evan now. Evan was hurt, furious and justifiably feeling deeply deceived. She needed to focus on that—fix that.

Sam stood up and taking her hand, pulled her to her feet.

"Breathe, O.K.?" He eyed her with those green magnets. "Just talk to him. Explain things as you did to me. It'll be all right."

Ailsa saw his cheeks twitching as he tried to smile.

"It's not all right, Sam. This is the worst possible thing I could've done to him." She swallowed a sob. "I have to go." She lifted the shoes and her watch from the ground and turned to the door.

Sam was behind her, his hand on her wrist.

"What can I do?" He whispered.

"Nothing. I have to go." Ailsa pulled away and ran out into the hall.

EVAN

Evan strode across the living room and lifted the whisky bottle from the cabinet. A vice was gripping his wind pipe and his heart was thumping in his ears.

Ailsa was dancing again. Dancing, upstairs in the flat of some guy she barely knew while he, her husband, was totally unaware that she even remembered *how* to dance. How stupid he'd been to spend his time worrying about the possibility that she might never get back to her life as it once was. She was there —but the most devastating part was that this time, it was without him.

He slammed the top back on the whisky bottle and took a gulp from his glass. The burn was comforting but as he closed his eyes, the image of Ailsa upstairs, completing a perfect Attitude turn, her arms framing her face, was blinding. Her body, even in its new, softer form, was still perfect, but what had struck him most was the expression of sheer bliss as she'd moved. The recent look of concern, conveying the sense that she'd misplaced something important, had been wiped away by a beatific smile that had stung him to see, because he'd had nothing to do with generating it.

The door flew open behind him and Ailsa spilled into the room, breathless and still flushed.

"Evan." She panted. "Please." She threw the ballet shoes onto the floor. "Let's talk about this."

"What's there to talk about?" He swung the glass across the space between them. "You've obviously found what you need. Someone else to talk to," he gulped, "and to dance for."

Ailsa let out a sob.

"Please don't say that. It's not like that." She grabbed his hand.

Despite his anger, and the hurt that was now threatening to choke him, Evan couldn't bring himself to pull away from her. They'd had so little physical contact recently that even this was worth something.

"What *is* it like then?" He watched as her chin quivered. "Tell me." He sighed. "I'm just so tired, Ailsa. And I don't get it." He pulled away from her and sank into the chair at the fireside.

Ailsa followed him and knelt in front of the brick hearth. As she looked up at him, Evan couldn't help but see her in one of her roles. There was the sorrowful expression of Giselle, the wide eyes of Aurora, then Juliet begging for approval.

"I don't know why it happened. Why I could dance up there." She swiped at her cheek. "It was the music."

Evan pressed his head back on the cushion and closed his eyes. If he wasn't distracted by her face, then maybe he could make more sense of her words.

"I kept hearing him playing and then, eventually, the pieces were familiar. One day it was a movement from Romeo and Juliet, and before I knew it, I was marking out the variation." She paused. "I couldn't remember everything, but it was as if the music was peeling back layers of the nothingness and suddenly, there were the steps. My body knew what to do, Evan."

Evan opened his eyes. She looked genuinely surprised by her

own words and, seeing her expression, his breathing began to return to normal.

"Go on." He took another swallow of whisky and waited.

Seeming to be grateful for his attention, Ailsa continued.

"I started down here, just moving a little, working around the furniture, and then doing some basic barre work. Then, after you showed me where the shoe bag was that day, I couldn't stop thinking about it." She slid her legs out from under her.

Evan nodded, letting her continue.

"I heard him playing Strauss one morning, so I decided to go up and introduce myself." She blushed. "It was rash, I know, but he was kind and easy to talk to..." She caught herself and Evan felt a pinprick of hurt return to his chest.

"Well that's great. He was easy to talk to." He spat the words, seeing tears trickling down her face.

"That's not what I mean." She sniffed. "Why can't I say what I mean?" Both hands were on her head now.

Evan ran a palm around the back of his neck. This was like being held in some kind of semi-reality. The outline of his world had cracked, and the innards of his life were oozing out, escaping as he watched—unable to contain them.

"It's like, he's just Sam and he expects nothing of me. He listens to me, he asks me how I'm feeling. He lets me be scared, or happy, or just myself."

Evan scanned her face.

"And I don't let you be you?" He shook his head. "That's rich." He laughed more harshly than he'd intended. "Really, Ailsa? After everything I've..." He stopped himself.

She dropped her head, the short, girlish curls looking somehow incongruous inside the piercing tension of the moment, then she raised her chin and looked at him with clear eyes.

"Even when you don't say it, Evan, there's an air of disappointment, and a constant need for control in you. I didn't remember it right away, but now I do. I feel the pressure of it coming back, along with the memories. It's like I'm never quite good enough." She hesitated. "It's the same with Mum."

Even as a rush of fresh anger threatened to close him off entirely, hovering under it were the shadows of his own recent acts of betrayal keeping him from saying what he wanted to. He did have high expectations of her, but being compared to Jennifer in this way felt unjust.

Before he could interject, she went on.

"I feel like I'm watching my life taking place, but I'm in the audience." She shook her head. "There are so many things I've lost, so many gaps in time, sometimes it's like this life doesn't belong to me anymore." She spread her arms wide, taking in the room. "Like I'm a visitor."

"I'm sorry you feel that way." His response, while flat, was the best he could manage.

He watched her face contort. He didn't like to see her cry, but this time he held back the comfort he would ordinarily have given her. Raising its ugly head again was the fear that what was happening was karmic, that even if he kept it from her now, his affair would somehow find a way to separate them.

Feeling like a victim of a cruel, divine justice, he sighed.

"Perhaps you need a break?" He pushed himself forward on the chair, placing the empty glass on the coffee table.

"What kind of break?" She wiped her nose with the back of her hand and stared at him.

Evan, rose and stood at the fire with his back to her.

"A break from me."

Diana set the coffee cup next to Evan and settled back in her armchair. His mother's flat, though high-ceilinged and bright, was stuffy, but the smell of freshly baked bread was a pleasant reminder of his childhood.

"So, what happened?" Diana looked at him expectantly.

Evan picked up his mug and held it close to his chest.

"I just need to stay a few nights, if that's O.K.?"

"Of course you can stay, but what happened?"

Evan began to explain and as he talked, Diana stayed quiet, nodding occasionally, tacitly giving him the time he needed to continue. Eventually, as he fell silent, she set her empty cup down on the coffee table.

"So, she was dancing all this time?"

"Yeah, it looks like it." Evan paused. "Basically lying to me, well, by omission, anyway. Here's me thinking that she can't, or won't remember dancing, or her entire career, for God's sake, while she's upstairs prancing around like nothing ever happened." He swung the mug away from himself splashing liquid on his jeans.

Evan had always found it easy to read his mother's expressions and now, as he waited for her to support him, tell him he'd been justified in throwing some clothes in a bag and storming out of the flat, Diana was frowning.

"First of all, is she all right?" She folded her arms across her chest. "She probably shouldn't be alone."

Evan nodded.

"I called Jennifer and suggested they come over for a few days."

"Do they know what happened?" Diana's eyes widened at the mention of his parents-in-law.

"Not exactly. I just said we needed a little space from one another. You know, too much time in close quarters etcetera."

Diana unlaced her arms and leaned forward, her elbows on her knees.

"And you don't think they'll figure out that you two have fallen out?" She twisted her mouth and stared at him, the way she did when she disapproved of something he'd done.

"What was I supposed to do, Mum?" He knew he sounded

petulant. "It's like I don't know her anymore. The person I loved went away." As he considered what he'd said, he knew that this applied to him too. He'd effectively gone away—left her—the first time he'd chosen to kiss Marie.

Diana got up from the chair and walked to the front window overlooking Huntly Gardens. She lifted the net curtain away from the radiator and, on a reflex, ran a hand over the sill checking for dust.

"Look, Son, I'm not judging you." She turned to face him. "But I wonder if this isn't just another stage in her recovery."

Evan balanced the cup on his damp thigh.

"Or, perhaps the whole forgetting ballet thing was just a symptom of something else going on?" She opened her arms. "All I know is that that wee girl won't get better without you." She smiled. "You two are like scones and jam. They're fine on their own, but so much better together."

Evan looked at his mother. She could usually make him feel better about whatever was worrying him. Her homespun philosophies had pulled him up numerous times in the past but this time, everything she was saying sounded hollow, simplistic under the circumstances.

"It's not that simple. She found it easier to talk to and spend time with someone else, a damn stranger, than to tell me the truth about her memory coming back. How do I not take that as a slap in the face? She's purposely keeping me out."

Diana made her way back to her chair.

"I understand, Evan. But why does it matter so much to you that she danced for someone else?"

Evan stared at his mother, her question knocking the wind from him.

"What do you mean?"

Diana laced her fingers in her lap.

"I mean," she stressed the words, "isn't it just good that she's dancing at all?"

Evan swallowed the last of the coffee. The look on Diana's face was making him doubt himself.

"Well, I suppose so." He pulled his mouth down at the corners. "But she went out of her way to hide it from me."

Diana shook her head.

"I know. But she must've had a reason for not telling you. It's not like her to be secretive, or unkind."

He shifted in the chair. There was no one else on the planet that he could share his innermost thoughts or the workings of his marriage with, but what he had to share was painful to regurgitate, even to his mother. Looking at Diana's expectant face, he spoke quietly.

"She said she felt that she constantly disappointed me or something, like she did what she did for me, and Jennifer, rather than for herself."

Diana nodded.

"What? You agree?" Evan was shocked.

"Well, that mother of hers is nothing short of a bully." Diana crossed her legs. "The way she's pushed and manipulated Ailsa, all her life. I don't know…"

Evan hefted himself out of the chair.

"So, you're saying I was doing the same thing?" He eyed his mother as she focused on her hands, twisting her wedding ring in circles around her finger.

Catching him watching her, she folded her hands in her lap.

"You did push her, Evan." She held her palm up as he made to interrupt. "I know you thought you were being supportive of her career etcetera, but sometimes I wish you'd listened to her a bit more."

Evan's mouth had gone slack. Was he hearing this correctly?

"If you thought that, why did you never say anything?"

Diana shook her head. "It wasn't my place."

∼

That evening, Evan lay down on the single bed in his old room. The curtains, the ones Diana had made for him when he was in high school and into astrology, were dark blue and covered with clusters of yellow stars. The shelves along the wall opposite the bed still held some of the I.T. and engineering text books from his A level courses, and the one and only rugby trophy he'd ever won, before injuring his shoulder.

The walls that used to be covered with posters of Queen and Pink Floyd had been cleared and painted a soft grey, the color now feeling cold in the insipid light coming from the bedside lamp.

He stretched out his feet, extending them six inches beyond the end of the bed. This was certainly not ideal, but he couldn't be at home right now and he certainly couldn't be around Ailsa. Not at the moment.

Feeling isolated and unsure of what he'd done by walking away—or what he should do next—he rolled onto his side, picked his phone up from the bedside table and dialed Marie's number.

AILSA

J ennifer and Colin had arrived from Edinburgh the previous
day, and Ailsa was getting used to the dynamic of having
her parents staying in her home. Jennifer had been jittery
that morning, finding things to dust and checking the fridge for
dinner ingredients. Colin had been his usual mellow self, and
Ailsa was grateful for the hooded winks he'd given her as
Jennifer fussed around in the kitchen.

"So, love, what's the story with Evan being away?" Her
father now sat in the chair, his ankles crossed on the coffee table.

Ailsa tried to clear her mind. She needed to sound plausible
while avoiding the details of what had happened.

"He needed a little break—just from taking care of me. He's
exhausted."

Colin nodded.

"Well you can be a handful." He grinned. "A lot of trouble in
a small package."

Ailsa gave a half smile. "That's truer than you think." She
turned and stared out of the window.

"Is everything all right?" Colin leaned forward in the chair.

She nodded. "It's fine, Dad. Honest."

~

The following morning, the second day Evan had been away, her parents had walked to the shops on Byers Road. Ailsa watched them leave, having said that she was too tired to go, but as soon as the door closed she went into the bedroom and got dressed. Pulling on leggings and a clean T-shirt, she grabbed her ballet shoes and headed for the door.

After a few moments of her knocking, Sam opened his door. He wore jeans and a vest T-shirt, and his hair was wet.

"Hi." He seemed surprised to see her.

"Hi." Ailsa shuffled her feet. "Am I disturbing you?" She moved back from the door and tucked the shoes she was holding, in behind her hips.

"No. I just had a shower. I'm making coffee." He stepped back and beckoned. "Come in."

She dropped the shoes by the door and followed him inside. Across the room, the sheen on the piano caught her eye, the instrument perfectly backlit by the bright window. She walked over to it and ran her hand along the edge of the raised lid. As she felt the smoothness of the lacquered wood, she remembered how much she deeply admired the group of talented pianists that she'd been lucky enough to work with. To be able to create beautiful melodies, with the complex combination of fingering, timing and creative expression the scores demanded had her in awe. A good pianist, like Sam, could make her hear the entire orchestra, and this was what happened when he played for her. She became lost inside the score, as much as she did in the choreography, the piano being the platform for all the other instruments that she could hear in her head.

Sam came up behind her, standing so close that she could feel his breath on her shoulder.

"Ailsa, I need to talk to you."

She turned to face him, her breath catching at his frown.

"What is it?" She laid her palm on his arm and was jolted when he stepped away from her touch.

"I'm afraid I have to ask." He cleared his throat. "What's going on, with you and Evan?"

Hearing him say Evan's name was once again jarring, her and Sam's untainted moments of intimacy exploding into dust. Shaken, she walked over and picked up her ballet shoes.

"He's gone to his mum's for a few days." She kept her back to Sam. "Things aren't good between us, and he needed a break."

Sam was behind her again, and putting his hands on her shoulders, he turned her to face him.

"Really? Was it him who needed the break, or you?" He held her gaze and Ailsa felt the warning prickle of tears.

"We had a terrible row. I mean, he was gutted by what he saw up here." She waved the shoes as her eyes began to blur. "Can't blame him really." She gulped. "I screwed that up badly."

Sam stepped back, his hands dropping from her shoulders.

"So, what is this about?" He opened his arms wide, presenting himself. "Am I some kind of consolation prize?"

The sudden hurt in his voice took her by surprise.

"No. What on earth do you mean?" Her knees threatened to buckle.

"So, he's moved out, for now, but you're still his wife, Ailsa." Sam blinked as if confirming the situation for himself.

Not being able to stand the distance he was creating between them, Ailsa moved in closer. There was something in his eyes that she hadn't seen before, a vulnerability that made her want to wrap her arms around him and whisper that everything would be all right.

"It's just that..." He scanned her face. "I don't trust myself around you. I know the timing stinks, but this is happening so fast." He traced a line in the air between them. "I've never felt this kind of inevitability before." He swallowed. "Not even with Olivia."

At the mention of her name, Ailsa's heart pinched.

"I can't take it if I end up being some kind of transitional thing that just leads you back to your husband." He held his palms up. "After losing her, I just won't survive losing you too, Ailsa."

That he'd made this comparison to his wife, took her breath away.

"I can't get any further into this if it's not real." Sam dropped his gaze to the floor.

"I understand, and I would never…" Her voice caught as she saw a flash of fear cloud his eyes.

"You say that, but in reality, we can never say never when it comes to love."

It felt as if the ground was tipping, as if she were on a seesaw, as she lunged forward and took his hand.

"But that's the point." She wound her fingers through his, panic filling her chest. "I don't love Evan." The words out, Ailsa felt the truth of them slice through her, letting months of soul-searching and self-doubt seep away.

Sam gently released his fingers and turned toward the piano.

"I want to believe that. I just think that we need to give ourselves some time for things to settle. For you to figure out what you really want." He closed the lid on the piano, his jaw rippling.

Ailsa's heart was thundering in her ears, the danger of losing him closing in on her. As she racked her brain for the right response, the perfect way to say that she couldn't bear being away from him, she saw his face again. There was conflict there, such honest pain, that rather than cross the room, she pulled her hands into fists, willing her breathing to slow down enough to let her speak.

"Don't you understand? This is the only place I feel like me." She pressed her palm to her chest. "When I'm with you." The tears she'd been holding at bay overtook her.

Sam's jaw was taut, his eyes boring into hers.

"Do you mean that?"

"Yes, I do."

"Are you sure?" His eyes were glistening.

"I don't fully understand it myself, but yes." She hesitated. "I know that I hardly know you. That we've only spent a handful of days together, but this…" She drew an arc between them, "us being together is the only thing that makes total sense to me right now. I'm wholly alive up here, with you." She let her hands drop to her sides as he closed the distance between them, pulling her close and kissing her.

She lay on her side on the floor, her hand tucked under her cheek keeping her tender head off the wooden boards. Her clothes were scattered over the piano stool and Sam, was curled tightly into her back. His arm encased her bare ribs and his hand, curved like an inverted question mark, was lying under her chin. He was breathing softly, and each time he exhaled she felt it wash across the nape of her neck.

She was afraid to move. If she moved she'd shatter this moment—this spoonful of peace that she had just found would be spilled, washed away by the guilt that was already beginning to lap at her heels.

Sam shifted and, slowly releasing her, rolled onto his back.

"Are you O.K.?" He looked over as she turned to face him.

Ordinarily she'd have been anxious about her nakedness but now, she focused on those mesmerizing eyes and smiled.

"Yes. I'm fine."

He touched a curl at her temple.

"You're sure?" His eyes sought hers. "This wasn't what I intended…"

Ailsa shook her head.

"Me neither." She leaned in and kissed him. "You did nothing wrong, Sam. Nothing."

Sam got up, pulled on his jeans, lifted her clothes from the stool and handed them to her.

"Do you want to shower?" He gestured toward the hall.

"No, I think I'll just go." Wanting to leave while the memory of what they'd just shared was, for the most part, unsullied, she slipped her leggings on and pulled the T-shirt over her head.

"Ailsa?" He took her hand.

"Please don't say anything." She shook her head. "Let's just be right here, right now, in this place." She pointed at her feet. "Because this place is perfect."

"Where were you, darling?" Jennifer was wearing Evan's cooking apron and stood in the living room with the phone in her hand. "I was worried."

Ailsa, feeling freshly shamed by her disappearance and by the thought that she might have just made a colossal mistake, blushed as she used to as a child.

"Sorry, I just went to see a neighbor."

Her mother frowned.

"Well wash your hands. Dinner is almost ready." She dumped the phone back in the cradle and walked into the kitchen.

Colin was reading the paper and as Ailsa passed, he reached out a hand. She took it and smiled at her father.

When he was sure that Jennifer was out of earshot, Colin whispered, "Whatever's going on with you and Evan, you need to talk to someone." His pale eyes were watery. "Don't go through this by yourself." He squeezed her hand and then dropped it as Jennifer walked back in.

"Right you two. To the table please."

Dinner was excruciating. Jennifer wanted to talk about Evan, and Colin kept trying to guide his wife away from the subject of their son-in-law.

"I think it's—shall we say—unexpected that he'd just up and go, regardless of how tired he is." Jennifer assessed her fork full of risotto. "It's not like him. Did you do something?"

Ailsa shoved the rice around her plate.

"He's just wiped out, Mum. Simple as that."

Colin slid the casserole closer to himself and spooned more onto his plate. Jennifer tutted. "Do you really need more?"

Colin rolled his eyes and winked at Ailsa.

"I really do, yes."

That night Ailsa spent half an hour in the shower. No matter how hard she scrubbed and soaped herself she couldn't get clean, the tacky film of her guilt sticking stubbornly to her body. When she stepped out onto the bath mat her skin was bright pink, her fingertips wrinkled and white.

She pulled on a long-sleeved T-shirt and crawled into bed, the empty side staring back at her accusingly as she pulled the duvet over her head and pressed her eyes closed.

There were still so many blank spots in her mind, whole sections of her past that might never have existed, but the image of what she had done today was searingly clear, and she was sure it would remain so forever.

As she willed her tight throat to relax, the gravity of her decision to go to Sam filled her head. She tried to conjure Evan's face but in its place were moss-green eyes and thick blonde hair.

For weeks now, she'd been struggling with her inability to feel close to Evan, in the way that she should—as a wife to her husband. He had been kind, mostly patient, and generous with his time, seeming to understand the perplexing and undulating nature of her recovery. Regardless, when she dug deep, asking the hard questions of herself, something significant had been holding her back from giving him the love her conscience told her he deserved.

As she pressed her eyes closed, once again searching for the truth, she fell into a fitful sleep.

EVAN

Amanda walked into the restaurant on Great Western Road, and Evan spotted her before she saw him. She wore a long floral skirt and her hair was caught up in a loose pony tail—her big sun glasses and gypsy-style shirt making her look younger than her years.

The long bar in what had formerly been a railway station was packed, and as Amanda wove through the crowd, Evan rose and waved at her from the booth he'd snagged. She had agreed to meet him for a quick lunch, and as he watched her approach the table, he wondered what she must be thinking about his odd invitation.

"Sorry I'm late. Had to wait for Mum to arrive, and Hayley was playing up."

Evan sat down.

"Sorry to intrude on your weekend. How is the munchkin?" He lifted a menu and handed it to Amanda.

"Oh, she's fine. I got her one of those light things for her room. You know—those LED contraptions that casts a rainbow across the ceiling?" She looked at Evan. "Of course it really only works if it's dark," she laughed, "so she keeps going in there and drawing the curtains and then she gets angry if we try to get her to come out."

Evan smiled.

"She's a cracker."

Amanda nodded and opened the menu.

"So, what do you recommend?"

"The salmon's pretty good."

Half an hour later, Evan pushed his empty plate away and leant back against the buttoned leather bench. Amanda had asked mercifully few questions since arriving, but he sensed that her curiosity was piquing.

"So, I'm sure you're wondering why I called you?" He shoved his napkin to the side and tidied the salt and pepper shakers into a neat line.

"Well, it's Saturday and I have a show, so I did wonder." Her clear eyes focused on his.

"Ailsa and I—we had a row." He pushed some grains of salt into a small heap and then brushed them off the table.

Amanda looked only mildly surprised. "O.K."

"I found her upstairs, in our neighbor's place." Evan hesitated.

"Oh?" Her eyebrows lifted.

"No, not that." He patted the air. "God, no."

Amanda exhaled. "Yeah, she's better than that." She looked pointedly at the door, as her jab struck him exactly as intended.

Undeterred, Evan shook his head.

"She was dancing."

Amanda's brow folded.

"Dancing?"

"Yes. Something from Swan Lake I think. I'm not sure. But, she was on pointe. The works. She looked amazing, actually." He cleared his throat. "The guy who lives up there is a pianist. Seems she's been going upstairs regularly to dance."

Amanda gaped at him.

"But I thought the whole subject of ballet was still taboo?"

"Yeah. Me too." Evan felt anew the rush of hurt he'd felt standing in that open doorway.

Amanda looked incredulous.

"So, she remembers—and she's actually dancing—but in secret?"

"Correct." Evan nodded and pulled his pint closer. "The whole thing's bizarre." He tipped his head back and emptied his glass. "This guy Sam, plays with the Symphonia. She's been talking about him for weeks now. I just didn't put two and two together." He licked his lips. "Feel pretty stupid, I can tell you."

Amanda was pale.

"Well, how would you know?" She drained her glass of water. "That's a tough way to find out, Evan." Her manner seemed to soften slightly.

Evan signaled to the waiter to bring the bill.

"I just needed to see a friendly face. I hope you don't mind?"

She blinked several times.

"No. I'm just… I'm not sure what to say." She sucked in her bottom lip. "All I can think is that she must have a reason."

Evan's mouth dropped open.

"What reason could she possibly have?"

When Amanda didn't respond, he slumped back in the seat.

"I'm staying at Mum's. I just had to get out of the flat." He tapped his glass with his fingernail.

"You've moved out?" Her eyes widened.

"No. Well just for a few days. I think we both needed some space." He dropped his gaze to the table. "Well, *I* needed a break, at least."

Amanda leaned forward, her eyes on fire.

"You needed a break?" Her voice was low and dangerous. "She gave you a second chance when you did the dirty on her, but you need a break, now, when she's rebuilding her entire life? You're incredible, Evan."

Evan felt his face grow hot.

"Look. I didn't expect sympathy." He paused. "I just needed to tell someone."

She put her sunglasses on then pushed them up into her hair.

"Well, I'm sorry you're feeling sorry for yourself, but I'm afraid you came to the wrong person. I'm team Ailsa, all the way." She assessed him. "And you know what? I could say the same. I'm her best friend and she didn't tell me about any of this dancing, or Sam stuff." She circled her arm between them. "But instead of pouting, my first thought was about her, what's motivating her to hide it." She eased out from behind the table.

Realizing that he had misjudged the situation, Evan followed her.

"Look, I'm sorry. I didn't think."

She nodded, hauling her bag onto her shoulder.

"Yeah, that's becoming a habit with you."

Seeing his shoulders slump, Amanda's expression softened again.

"Listen, Evan. I know I'm tough on you these days, but I just have a hard time getting past what you did." She started moving toward the door.

"I know that." He spoke to her back. "But if Ailsa can forgive me, why can't you?" The whine in his voice grated.

Amanda turned to face him, her cheeks crimson.

"Have you talked about that, since she got home?" Her eyes were piercing.

Evan felt his stomach flip-flop as deep down, he'd been afraid of this coming up again. He shook his head, stepping back to let a waitress carrying a tray get past him.

"Not really."

Amanda gave a wry smile.

"Not really, as in no?"

He shook his head again.

"It's not exactly been top of the priority list, Amanda." He snapped. "There's been a lot going on."

Amanda turned her back on him again and walked out the door.

Outside, the Great Western Road was busy and as they mumbled their goodbyes, Amanda held her bag in front of her, like a shield.

"Listen, I know it's not my business, but if you hope to have any chance of an honest relationship, moving forward, you can't pick and choose what she remembers." She paused. "I'd say your communication would have to be one hundred percent open, or it'll never work." She stepped toward the curb, scanning the road for a taxi.

Evan was embarrassed, regretting confiding in Amanda, whom he knew was Ailsa's staunchest ally. As he took in the angular face, that had once looked on him kindly, he thought he saw a hint of empathy creep back into her eyes.

He pulled his hat on.

"Sorry. I'm a bit of a disaster at the moment. I shouldn't have called you."

Amanda flapped her hand.

"It's O.K. I'm just sorry I can't say what you want me to. I can't make you feel better, Evan." She eyed him. "Just be honest with her, and what will be will be."

He nodded as Amanda, spotting a taxi, waved frantically. As the cab pulled up in front of her, she turned to him.

"Do you want to share a taxi?" She glanced behind her at the steady flow of traffic.

"No, thanks. I think I'll walk a bit. I could do with the exercise."

He waited for the taxi to pull away from the curb, then made his way down the Great Western Road. The tree lined footpath was dotted with people, the warmer weather drawing them outside to enjoy the smattering of outdoor cafés and parks. The

Georgian sandstone terraces, set back behind the trees, reminded him of his mother's home in Huntly Gardens. The bay windows on either side of the front doors were like elegant, welcoming eyes and as a child, he'd thought his house was smiling at him as he climbed the front steps.

AILSA

E van had still not moved back home. They'd been talking
on the phone occasionally but it was six days since he'd
gone to Diana's and he hadn't mentioned when he'd be back.
Though she had no reason to think that Evan would turn up, each
night after her father locked up and went to bed, Ailsa—her guilt
creeping in as she lay in their empty bed—tiptoed out to the front
door and slid the safety chain off.

Her parents were planning on going back to Edinburgh at the
end of the week, as Colin had a board meeting to attend and, as
Jennifer's had said numerous times, her ballet students and
charity work wouldn't wait forever. They had stopped asking
when Evan would be home, and Ailsa was sure that was thanks
to her father's intervention.

Now, Amanda and Ailsa sat opposite each other. Their table
was tucked in a corner against the back wall of the bistro, and
consequently the general buzz of voices around them had not
prevented them from talking quietly to one another.

The first thing they had tackled was the incident with Hayley.
It had been awkward, and they'd both been emotional, and while

Ailsa was still hurt by Amanda's reaction, Ailsa had made a conscious decision to let it go.

What Evan had said about Amanda had sunk in, but besides that, so much was in flux that she had no wish to drive a bigger wedge between her and her only friend.

Amanda had been visibly relieved when Ailsa told her to put it behind them.

"It's in the past now. Just forget it."

"You know I trust you with her, more than anyone in the world." Amanda had wiped her nose with a crumpled tissue. "I think I just got a bit wobbly, not sure how you were really coping. You'd been pretty up and down, and then when you weren't where I expected you to be..." She paused. "You did have brain surgery." She grimaced. "Sorry, but..."

Her friend's discomfort was obvious, and it hurt Ailsa to see it.

"Please, let's just move on, Amanda."

Amanda was checking her phone for messages as Ailsa split the remaining sparkling water between them.

"I'm so glad we did this." She smiled as Amanda slipped the phone back into her bag.

"Me too. I hate when we fall out." Amanda eyed her. "We mustn't do that again. O.K.?"

Ailsa nodded, and flooded with affection for the woman opposite her she blurted,

"I'm sorry that I'm different now."

Amanda frowned. "Don't apologize."

"No. I need to." Ailsa paused. "There's so much I don't...I can't. I just wish..." Her voice faltered.

Amanda leaned forward.

"Stop it. The most important thing is that you're here. You're healthy and the rest, well, the rest we'll figure out in time."

Ailsa looked at her friend's face. It was a kind face. A face that made you trust the person behind it. Ailsa hated that her inability to pick up the friendship, from where she understood it had once been, had been hurtful to Amanda. However, the more Ailsa tried to chase the memories, pin them down and examine them, or follow their trail, the more elusive they became.

She now had some memories of Amanda when they'd first worked together, but then there were blank swaths that slashed across their chronology. Much of their time together in the company was gone, and Ailsa was doing her best to cover up the gaps whenever she could, but Amanda was perceptive and, ultimately, it had felt more respectful to tell her the truth—however painful.

"Let me get this." Amanda reached for the bill.

"No. Let's split it." Ailsa dug in her bag for her wallet.

"So, what's happening with Evan?" Amanda laid her credit card on the table.

Ailsa shrugged.

Amanda was studying her.

"Is he back?"

"Not yet."

Amanda's mouth dipped.

"Have you asked him to come home?" She folded her napkin into a square and straightened it on the table.

Ailsa's conscience twinged.

"I'm not sure he'd want to."

"What do you mean?"

The waiter swept past them, picked up the two credit cards and headed back to the front desk.

"Why wouldn't he want to?"

Ailsa's fingers went up to the side of her head and she slid her fingertips into her hair, searching for the now familiar bumps. Finding them, she pressed down until a bolt of pain shot across her scalp like a legion of ants marching in spiked boots.

"I've done something I shouldn't." She swallowed. "Let myself down."

Amanda lifted her glass and drained the last of the water.

"What are you talking about? Everyone argues, especially when they've been through the kind of traumatic…"

Ailsa cut her off.

"I'm not talking about the row." She had no idea if this was the right thing to do, but there was a force deep within pushing her to share this burden, and there was no one else she could tell.

Amanda was staring at her, her lips pulsing as she chewed her cheek.

"I slept with someone."

The tainted words tasted sour and foreign, and the moment she'd spoken them, Ailsa wanted to wash her mouth out.

Amanda was silent, her face contorting.

Blood thumped in Ailsa's ears, drowning out the ambient noise of the restaurant as Amanda's lips continued to move, no sound coming out.

"Say something, please." Ailsa's voice cracked. "I know I'm a shitty person."

Amanda slowly shook her head, as if denying the legitimacy of what she'd heard.

The pounding in Ailsa's ears was reaching a dangerous crescendo.

"Does he know?" Amanda's voice was brittle. "Have you told him?" She looked stricken.

"No. Not yet."

"Was it the guy upstairs?"

Ailsa gulped.

"Um, yes. Sam. He's a…."

"Evan told me about him." Amanda's eyes softened.

"When did he tell you?"

"The other day. We had lunch."

Ailsa nodded, a pinprick of jealousy surprising her. What did it matter if they'd had lunch? They were all friends, but why hadn't Evan mentioned seeing Amanda? Ailsa had been hiding so much from him that she knew she had no right to object and yet, the knowledge hurt.

"What did he tell you?" She tried not to sound petulant.

"Just that he'd come upstairs and seen you dancing," Amanda paused, "and that you'd had a fight and he'd gone to his mum's."

Ailsa nodded.

"What did he say about the dancing?" Her heart was racing.

"Does that really matter now?" Amanda shook her head.

Choked by shame, Ailsa dropped her gaze to the table.

"There's no explaining what I did, and I'm not looking for forgiveness. It's just that Sam doesn't know the old me." She swallowed. "There's no pressure to remember anything, or to be who I used to be." She paused, catching the hint of a nod from her friend. "He's not trying to rescue me from anything either. When I'm with him I'm whole and the world's in full color, then when I go home it goes back to black and white."

Amanda's eyes widened.

"You really care about him then?"

Ailsa nodded.

"I just needed to tell someone, and there's no one else I trust." Ailsa felt the press of tears. "I'm sorry for everything, Amanda. I'm constantly bloody sorry these days." She wiped her eyes with her palm.

Amanda's face melted.

"Listen, I'm the last person you need to apologize to, and honestly, you have to stop beating yourself up about what's happened with Sam." She paused. "After what Evan did…" her voice trailed.

"What do you mean, what he did?"

Amanda raked a hand through her hair, her fair complexion coloring slightly.

"Look, you know I love you, right?"

Ailsa nodded.

"When I saw Evan the other day..." She halted. "I told him that if he really wanted to help you he needed to be totally honest —about everything."

"Go on." Ailsa leaned in, her palms growing clammy.

"Please understand why I'm telling you this. I want to protect you from painful things, but I can't let you go on believing..."

"Amanda, please just say it."

Amanda eyed her for a second then cleared her throat.

"A few months ago, when we were out in Asia..." She rolled her shoulders back. "Evan had an affair with someone at his work."

Ailsa's hand went up to her mouth, the impact of the statement sucking at her breath.

"You found out because he got careless. He'd taken the woman to the flat." She frowned. "And you found a hairband in the bathroom."

Ailsa's head was thumping now, all the moisture having drained from her mouth. As she stared into Amanda's eyes, a shard of memory appeared and suddenly the feel of a lumpy elastic-band in her fingers and the sickly smell of vanilla came back to her. Of all the things that she had forgotten, and still remained closed off to her, this was something she would have given anything to un-remember.

Amanda reached across the table.

"I'm sorry, but I had to say something." She wiped at a tear that was sliding down her cheek. "He was feeling all hurt and sorry for himself, and it just made me want to slap him."

Ailsa reached for her glass and gulped down some water, the visual of Evan with another woman swirling in front of her. As she tried to regain her equilibrium, she realized that what she was feeling was not simply shock, or even hurt. Drowning everything else out was a dawning of recognition, a nugget of understanding forming at her inability to allow Evan to get close to her.

Seeing her friend's flushed face, she reached out and squeezed Amanda's fingers.

"You know, I think I remember."

Half an hour later, they sat in silence, empty coffee cups in front of them. A combined sense of relief and dread had left Ailsa feeling numb.

Amanda was pale, her fingers twitching as she twisted a napkin into a linen rod, and just as Ailsa was about to ask her if she was all right, Amanda turned to her.

"Why didn't you tell him that you'd remembered, that you'd been dancing again?"

Ailsa ran a hand over her head, searching for the bumps again, sending a fresh shot of pain across her scalp.

"Because I was afraid that if I danced again I'd be sucked back into a life that didn't always make me happy."

Amanda's brow creased.

"What do you mean?"

"If he'd known, then I'd have had to go back to that life. Do you understand?"

Amanda shook her head.

"Dancing again felt wonderful. But underneath that was a dark memory."

Amanda was focusing on her mouth, as if lip reading.

"I remembered how hard Evan pushed me, like my career was more important to him than it was to me." She paused. "It reminded me of my mum, doing the same thing."

"I get that." Amanda nodded.

"He's only ever known me as a dancer. Think about it, Amanda." She scanned her friend's face. "From the moment we met, that was my life."

Amanda seemed to be processing what Ailsa was saying.

"He never got to know the me that wasn't totally focused on ballet, and all that comes with it."

"O.K." Amanda looked puzzled now.

"It was always all consuming. The focus one hundred percent on my career, at the expense of everything else. The crazy lifestyle, the weird hours, the touring, the constant injuries, the competition, the stress, the inability to let up even for a second." She took a breath. "Or to stop and have a baby." She closed her eyes briefly. "It's obvious now that despite his driving me on, Evan felt neglected, and that he resented giving up things that he wanted, to support me—so if I didn't go back to ballet, that'd all have been for nothing in his eyes." She paused. "The more the memories came back, the more I realized that I'd lost the joy and begun to feel obligated to dance. I'd forgotten that, but this past few weeks it's come back to me." She paused. "Getting to know Sam has made me see it."

Amanda shook her head.

"But you love dancing. I know you do."

Ailsa nodded.

"I do. I did. It was everything."

Amanda stared at Ailsa's mouth.

"I wonder if it hadn't been for Mum pressuring me, just assuming control, if I'd have even chosen to do it professionally."

Amanda's eyes narrowed.

Ailsa took in her friend's expression and steeled herself before she went on.

"When was the last time you went out to dinner on a Saturday night, or ate something you really fancied without feeling guilty? And what about all the things that we were never allowed to do like ice skating, gymnastics, horse riding, skiing, the list goes on and on?" Ailsa coughed and reached for her glass. "I can't remember a time when ballet didn't dictate my every action or reaction." Ailsa sighed. "Maybe it's time I focused on something else?"

Amanda sighed.

"So, what're you saying? That you want to get back to it, or that you don't? I'm completely confused."

Ailsa considered the question and as she ran her thumbs over the two edges of the dilemma, one as sharp as the other as regards the consequence on her life, she shook her head.

"I'm not sure yet."

Amanda pursed her lips. "So that's the reason you kept it from Evan?"

Ailsa nodded. "He's woven into the fabric of that life. They're intrinsically linked, and I don't know if I can separate them."

Amanda stayed quiet.

"The dance stuff aside, I've been holding back from him. I know I must have loved him, and I've been telling myself that I *should* love him now. I really tried to find those feelings again, Amanda. He's been so good to me. But the problem is that I don't remember what made me love him in the first place." Ailsa felt her chest heavy. "It's all so full of holes."

"And now you know about his affair?"

Ailsa picked up her credit card from the table.

"It all makes so much more sense. Something was stopping me letting him in." She swallowed. "Even though I couldn't put a finger on it, something was getting in the way."

Amanda leaned forward on her elbows.

"Your subconscious. Or just some deep-seated sense of self preservation, maybe?"

"Whatever it was, I let it guide me." She bit her lower lip. "So, you mustn't feel bad for telling me this, because some-where, deep inside, I knew."

EVAN

E van slid the key into the lock. It had been almost three weeks since he'd walked out of the flat and it almost felt like an invasion to be letting himself in now. He fought the impulse to knock and pushed the door open.

Mark hung back in the corridor as Evan stepped inside.

"Come on." He beckoned to his friend.

"Are you sure about this, Evan?"

"Yes. No." He shrugged. "Not really sure about much these days."

The living room was empty, the afternoon sun bouncing a prism of light off the chandelier, casting golden shafts across the rug. The place was tidy, newspapers folded neatly in the basket at the side of the chair, the tartan blanket draped over the back of the sofa and fresh flowers sat in a vase on the coffee table. The normalcy of the space felt odd to him as Evan walked over to the window and looked out, expecting to see Ailsa on the bench.

Mark stood awkwardly in the middle of the room, his sun glasses shoved onto the top of his head and his hands deep in his pockets.

"Is she here?"

"Dunno. I'll check the bedroom."

Evan walked down the narrow hall and opened the door to the master bedroom. The bed was made and a towelling robe he didn't recognize was lying on the small chair in the corner. Jennifer and Colin had given the chair to them as a wedding present, and Evan had always disliked its bulbous frame and old-fashioned floral fabric.

There was no sound, and despite the efforts of the weakening sun hitting the window, as he turned to leave he shivered.

When he walked back into the living room, Mark was holding a picture frame.

"This is a good one." He wafted it at Evan.

Evan glanced at the photo. It was of Ailsa in Paris. She was sitting at a small table in a street café in Montmartre and smiling from under a broad brimmed hat.

"Our honeymoon." Evan's voice was flat.

Mark nodded and replaced the frame on the sideboard.

"So, no signs of life?"

"Doesn't look like it."

No sooner had Evan spoken than he heard the sound of a key in the lock. He glanced over at Mark and jerked a thumb toward the door.

"Here she is now."

Waiting for her to walk in, Evan felt his pulse quicken. He had been calling her now and then to make sure she was coping, particularly since her parents had left, and she'd been chilly to say the least. He knew that she'd seen Amanda, and other than that he had no idea what she had been doing to fill her time, but he had no doubt that she'd been going upstairs to see Sam, and dance.

The unaccustomed degree of separation from her everyday life had been uncomfortable but now that he was back inside their home, the distance that he'd created by leaving felt wholly unnatural.

Ailsa was carrying a shopping bag. Her face was flushed, her short hair wind-blown, and her flimsy cotton dress clung to her curves. She was breathtaking.

"Evan. You should've said..." As she dumped the bag onto the floor her eyes darted to the corner of the room where Mark stood, leaning against the drinks cabinet.

"Hello, darling girl." He stepped forward and opened his arms.

Evan held his breath as, after only a moment of hesitation, Ailsa walked into Mark's embrace.

"Mark." She shot Evan a questioning look.

Mark stepped back and held her hands.

"Well, look at you all summery and relaxed." He grinned. "The time off has been good for you."

Ailsa smiled, ran a hand over her hair, then smoothed her skirt. Evan caught the gesture, a reminder of the young girl he'd first met.

"If I'd known you were coming..." She looked back at Evan.

Mark led her to the sofa.

"I wanted to surprise you." He sat down and patted the seat next to him. "Come and talk to me. How are you feeling, darling?"

Evan walked into the kitchen and filled the kettle. The idea to bring Mark here had of course been his, and despite Mark's trepidation, he had agreed to play along. Two days earlier, Evan had stopped by the theater and told Mark about walking in on Ailsa dancing.

"You mean she's hiding it?" Mark had been shocked. "Why on earth?"

Evan had held his palms up.

"You tell me."

Now, with a tray of tea and biscuits, Evan went back into the living room. The twosome was talking quietly, their heads inclined toward one another, the sight of them together making him nostalgic.

He set the tray down.

"Mark, milk, right?"

Mark nodded. "Thanks, Evan."

He handed a cup to Ailsa.

"Biscuit?" Evan offered the plate to Mark, who shook his head.

Ailsa reached out and took a Bourbon and Mark's eyebrows twitched as she bit into it, and both Evan and she caught the tiny, telltale gesture. Ailsa blushed, put the remainder of the biscuit on the tray and sat back in the seat.

"So, are you ready to come back?" Mark sipped his tea. "We've all missed you so much."

She shook her head. "I'm not sure." She glanced at Evan, her eyes glittering.

She looked like a faun with its leg in a snare and, for a split second, he regretted springing Mark on her this way.

"The longer you leave it the harder it'll be to get back to form."

Ailsa was fidgeting, plucking at her skirt and then stretching her neck out, looking like a frightened child next to Mark's sharp, purposeful frame.

"Are you stretching daily, doing any classes?" The older man took another swallow from his mug and then set it on the table. "Why not come and do class with us tomorrow? Ease back in gently." He smiled over at Evan, looking for endorsement.

Ailsa's now appeared completely distraught and, despite himself, Evan jumped to her rescue.

"Perhaps if she's feeling up to it she could just come and watch a class or two first?" He nodded encouragingly at Ailsa, as the tension visibly eased from her jaw.

"Yes, I could watch. See how it goes." She gave a half smile as Mark frowned.

"Well, if that's what you want, of course. Come in tomorrow and then we can talk after class." Mark made to get up. "We need to discuss timing and plan your triumphant return."

Ailsa's eyes were hooded as she pushed herself up from the seat. She followed Mark to the door and hugged him goodbye.

The door closed behind the company director, leaving Evan alone with his wife. Her back was to him and as she stood still, staring at the space where Mark had been, Evan had no idea what to expect. When she turned around, her face was ablaze.

"How could you do that?" Her voice was ragged. "Just bring him here." As she pushed past Evan, he saw tears streak her cheek.

"I just thought it was time you saw him. How much longer did you think you could avoid him?" He followed her into the kitchen. "This is your career we're talking about."

She stood at the sink, her shoulders quivering as she stared pointedly out of the window.

"Ailsa, look at me." He reached out and touched her back.

"Don't." She spun around, jerking away from his hand.

Evan lowered his hand and stepped backwards.

"O.K. Just calm down."

"You fucking calm down." Her face was crimson.

The impact of the word was like a physical blow. He'd never heard her use it before, and that, combined with the foreign look on her face, made him realize that he didn't know this version of Ailsa, at all.

His breathing was labored as he walked away from her. He couldn't take this. He had obviously screwed up by bringing Mark over unannounced, but he hadn't deserved that outburst.

He heard her coming up behind him, and as he opened the front door to leave, she touched his arm. Her voice was more controlled now, but her face was blotchy and her eyes were like lasers on his.

"You need to let me figure out what I want, in my own time."

He took in the stricken expression, the shallow breaths she was taking and the way her hand quivered at her side. At any other time he would have back-tracked, and maybe apologized, but instead he took a deep breath, lifted her hand from his arm and walked out of the door.

Turning to face her, he spoke as he would have to Hayley, if she was having a tantrum.

"It seems to me that you've already figured out what you want, Ailsa. You're just not ready to acknowledge it."

She crossed her arms protectively across her middle, her face a miserable mask.

"You go up there and dance your little heart out for someone you've known for five minutes, and yet you hide it from the people who love you the most, who've supported you all these years."

She stepped back as if he'd struck her.

"You know exactly what you want. You always have." He spat. "You've just never been honest about it."

Her body was shaking violently now, and Evan realized that he'd gone too far. Her tried to reach out to her but she batted him away.

"Don't touch me. You can't talk to me about being honest when you lied to me. You betrayed me, betrayed us, and now you're trying to blame me for the way things are between us." She sobbed. "I know it all, Evan. The whole thing."

He gulped in some air, feeling as if he might choke.

"So just think about what you're saying." She forced a swallow. "Because you're the one who actually broke us."

"You don't know what you're talking about. Ever since your…" He grappled for something, anything to delay the inevitable.

"No. Don't do that. Don't make this about me, or my tumor." She tapped her temple. "You don't get to do that anymore."

Knowing he had been exposed, and that he had to diffuse this situation before it became any more explosive, he held his hands up.

"O.K. Enough."

Evan stood back, watching her shoulders quivering as the tears continued to come. He wished he knew what exactly had changed between them—in that he could be cruel to her now.

AILSA

The studio in the arts complex smelled musty, a mixture of rosin dust, sweat and damp wool. Ailsa sat on the floor at the front of the room with her back pressed against the wall of mirrors. It had been months since she'd been here and strangely, it was the smell that was the most comforting part of the space.

Despite her anger at Evan for springing Mark on her, the thought of stepping back into the ballet studio, and how it might make her feel, had kept her awake the night before. As she'd stared at the ceiling, the one thing she had been certain of was that if she did go, it would be on her terms.

Now, she was surrounded by a sea of bags and back packs, marooned among pools of ballet shoes spilling out around her. She reached out and stroked a shoe that brushed her calf, the satin feeling cool to the touch.

The welcome she'd received when she'd walked in with Amanda had been overwhelming. The company members had circled around, hugging and kissing her cheeks, telling her how worried they'd been and how much she had been missed. Many of the faces were unknown to her, but there were some she recognized, so she had focused on those as she moved between the touching hands, the pressing bodies and mouths that crowded in on her.

A fair-haired man with kind blue eyes had grabbed her hand.

"Welcome back, sweetie. I've missed my Aurora." He'd bowed and gallantly kissed the back of her hand.

She'd smiled at him, having no memories of him to rescue her, then stammered something unintelligible, seeing the frown split his brow, until Mark had mercifully come to her rescue.

"All right Steven, everyone, don't smother her. Let her breathe." He'd positioned himself between Ailsa and the group and ushered the dancers away to the barre.

"Ailsa's just here to watch today, so be on your best behavior." He'd laughed, handed the class over to the wiry ballet mistress who kept turning back to smile at Ailsa, then told her to find him when the class was over.

The pianist in the far corner was grinning and nodding at her. Ailsa knew the face but frustratingly, the name escaped her. She was a tiny woman, so short that her feet only just reached the pedals, and with hands that were childlike. As she began to play for the pliés exercise, Ailsa marveled at the reach of those miniature fingers. Sam's hands were broad and long fingered, by comparison. Sam. She hadn't seen him in a couple of days and she missed him like she would any element of survival.

Amanda was half way down the barre on the right side of the studio. She smiled at Ailsa and gave her a thumbs-up and Ailsa fanned her fingers at her friend. Things had been better between them since their lunch, but Amanda had been busy, and Ailsa had hardly seen Hayley at all.

While she was tortured by not knowing, she was afraid to ask Amanda if she'd said anything to Evan about her, Ailsa's, transgression. She was sure that if Amanda had, Evan would have confronted her when she'd called him out at the flat, but the uncertainty was still weighing on her.

As she watched, the barre exercises continued, and when the

music began for each combination of movements, the familiar melodies allowed the exercises to unfold in her mind like scenes from a movie. She could almost feel her foot pressing through the floor as she pointed her toes in a tendu, her thighs bracing as she brushed the ball of her foot away from herself extending into a battements frappé and the pull of her hamstrings as she picked her leg up in front, to the side and behind her in grand battements.

Ailsa's feet were twitching, longing for the confinement of her shoes, her spine aching to arch into a back bend, so when the dancers moved into the center of the studio, unable to contain the impulse to move, she stood up and slipped to the back of the class. There she marked the ports de bras, her arms moving through a combination of positions—first, third, fifth, and then she lifted up and back into a graceful back bend trying to avoid the stares as some members of the Corps glanced over their shoulders at her, smiling their encouragement. It felt magical to put pressure on the parts of her body that she knew now she'd used so expertly for so many years.

Soon, she was moving through an adage, a test of her strength and balance as she completed a grand ronde de jambe en l'air, gracefully circling one leg around herself in a high arc. Then, Amanda was at her side.

"How does it feel being here?" Amanda whispered, as two girls Ailsa didn't recognize practiced pirouettes next to her.

"Weird." She whispered back, as the ballet mistress scowled at them over the heads of the class, placing a finger across her lips.

As soon as she heard the music begin for the petit allegro enchainément, the quick, tightly controlled jumping combinations that Ailsa excelled at, her body went onto autopilot. She stayed as close to the back of the room as she could, but the momentum of the music and the intricate footwork carried her forward into the group in front of her.

Unaware of drifting, she was soon working in the middle of the studio, her bare feet bouncing on the sprung floor and her heart tapping rapidly in her chest. Her mind went to the rhythm, the beating of her feet against each other, the crisp feeling of the brisés, cabrioles, the êntrechats and the pas de bourées forming a map that she was compelled to follow without questioning her destination. As her feet repeatedly found and then abandoned the floor, and her heart pattered in time with the staccato notes filling her head, Ailsa willed the music not to stop until suddenly, it was over.

Without her noticing, a space had cleared around her. The other dancers had moved aside to give her room and now, as her ribs heaved and sweat ran down between her breasts, there was a soft ripple of applause. Ailsa blinked, re-entering the studio from her own mind space. The circle of faces around her were smiling and nodding, as suddenly embarrassed, she moved to the back wall. As the gentle clapping continued, she dipped into a shallow curtsey with as much grace as she could muster.

The cluster of faces looking at her made her face burn, as she worried that she'd made a fool of herself, getting lost in the combination, her sense of her surroundings slipping away as the music lifted her up and transformed her into a performer once again.

She was overcome by the sudden need to be alone. She wanted to dance, not here where people were watching, but for herself, somewhere she could find the freedom she had found in Sam's empty flat, where the next movement and all the time before her was her own, to do with whatever she chose.

Among the faces was Amanda, her smile as broad as the others but, underneath it, Ailsa thought she saw a flicker of recognition, as if her friend was reading her mind. She nodded at Amanda, and then made her way to the front of the studio. All she wanted now was to go home, take a hot shower and go upstairs to see if Sam was home.

Thinking about him sent her pulse up a notch. Picturing the line of his face and the tapering fingers deftly running up and down the piano keyboard, and then her body, all caused a seismic shift inside her. Then, paradoxically, Evan's face appeared to her confirming, with startling clarity, what she had to do.

EVAN

E van walked into the coffee shop on Byers Rd. It was over a
week since they'd had their last confrontation and he'd
elected to meet on neutral territory for their next encounter. He
had been away from the flat for four weeks and while part of him
wished to be back there, back in his life, he was reluctant to take
the step away from the unexpected peace that he had found at his
mother's house.

Ailsa was waiting at a small outdoor table when he arrived.
She had a coffee cup in front of her, the thin strap of her T-Shirt
had slipped off her shoulder and her face was flushed with the
heat of the unusually warm day.

Glasgow seldom got seriously hot, but the past week had
provided some of the warmest weather on record, for June. Evan
was glad of the comforting heat on his shoulders as he inched his
way between the tables to sit opposite his wife.

"Hi." He smiled at her as she made to get up to greet him.
"Sit still. I'm going to grab a coffee. Do you want anything?"

She shook her head and picked at the raw skin around her
thumb.

A few minutes later, holding a cappuccino and a pastry, Evan settled himself opposite her.

"How are you? How've you been?" He cut the pastry into narrow slices and shoved the plate into the middle of the table, wondering if Ailsa would take a piece. Instead, she held up a palm and shook her head.

"O.K. Coping."

Evan noticed the roundness of her cheeks, the softer line of her shoulders and how well she looked.

"So, what've you been up to?" He kept his tone light.

"Just much of the same." She said. "Working through stuff."

He nodded and sipped the frothy coffee.

"I saw Amanda. Then I went to the studio, to watch a class." Her expression was giving nothing away.

Surprised, he smiled. "Good. That's good that you went."

"I watched the barre, then ended up doing some of the center work. I couldn't help myself." Her shoulders twitched.

Evan nodded. "How did it feel?"

She pushed her cup away.

"It was good, and disconcerting. I felt like I wanted to be there then I couldn't wait to get out." Her brow creased.

Evan leaned back.

"So, have you been upstairs much—I mean dancing up there?" He instantly wanted to snatch the question back.

Ailsa slid her fingers into her hair and appeared to be pressing on her scalp. He'd noticed her doing that frequently before he'd moved out, unsure what it was about. Her cheek was twitching as if she was clenching her teeth and he wished that he could rewind just a few moments.

She was staring at him intensely, as if trying to read the map of his face.

"What is it?" He frowned.

The heat of the afternoon now felt as if it was gathering on his skull, pressing on his fatigue. She looked uncomfortable in her skin as she shifted on the seat and then shoved her cup from side to side between her palms.

Unable to stand the suspense any longer, Evan reached out and placed his hand over hers, stopping the movement of the empty vessel.

"Ailsa?"

As she pulled her hand away, he caught a splinter of fear in her eyes.

She folded her arms across her front and pulled her chin in, as she always did when she had something difficult to say.

His pulse quickening, Evan waited.

"I need to tell you something." She held his gaze. "It's not good, Evan."

As he went through a number of possible scenarios in his mind, what she said next was nowhere close to what he expected.

"I've been with Sam. I've…we've been together." She clamped her mouth shut.

Evan instantly felt himself floating, leaving his body as if a vacuum was sucking him up out of his bones. He hovered above the table looking down on himself and Ailsa, sitting opposite each other like any other couple out enjoying the summer afternoon. *Been with Sam.* Despite his inner voice telling him that this was no more than he deserved, he still wanted to have misunderstood her.

As he slowly drifted back into his body, Evan fought to make his mouth work.

"What…what do you mean?"

A tear broke from her lower lid.

"You know what I'm saying. Don't make me say it again." She gulped.

Evan's chest felt as if it were being slashed, but as the weight of the truth pressed in on him, beneath the shock was the realization that deep inside, he'd suspected this. Perhaps that was why he'd been so cruel the last time—punishing her for the ultimate act of revenge, before she'd even confessed to it.

He closed his eyes. He couldn't look at her face, knowing that someone else had kissed it more recently than he had. This Sam person had held her body, felt her skin next to his, and Evan couldn't bear knowing it.

"Evan, I'm so sorry." She spoke in staccato bursts, punctuated by sniffs. "Regardless of the past, there's no excuse."

He kept his eyes closed, the pressure of the lids shutting out this reality was all that was keeping him from losing control.

"Evan?"

His eyes flew open and he took her in. Her nose was red, her short curls were twisting away from her perfect face and her eyes were red-rimmed and swollen. Even in this distressed state she was beautiful, another tragic heroine but, this time, one he had lost.

Evan felt his heart falter. He needed to focus on getting through this moment. Whatever came next for him would undoubtedly be brutal, and possibly unbearable, but for now he just needed to keep breathing.

After a few moments he cleared his clogged throat.

"You slept with him?"

She nodded and dropped her head. "It is inexcusable."

Unable to move, Evan focused on her mouth. Her face was contorting, the fine features morphing, shifting in a way he didn't recognize. The wife he knew, the woman he'd loved, would never have done this, and yet perhaps he'd never truly known her. She'd been a child when he'd met her, struggling under the weight of her mother's expectations for her life. He'd recognized that and had tried to guide her, but in doing so he had just become a different kind of bully, taking Jennifer's side, time and time again.

He shoved the image of Ailsa with Sam out of his mind, and what came to fill its place was the picture of her dancing in the flat upstairs, the joy, the carefree abandon and the blissful look on her face as she completed a perfect, graceful Attitude turn.

"You know what's strange, Ailsa?"

A flicker of what looked like hope lit up her eyes.

"You dancing for him was more of a betrayal than the cheating."

AILSA

Ailsa's room at her parents' house had remained fundamentally untouched since she'd last lived there. The wallpaper, the bed cover and the kidney shaped dressing table all took her back to her youth and the hours she'd spent lying on the floor surrounded by ballet books. She'd close the door, put on a record and sort through her collection of black and white photos of her favorite performers that her mother had bought for her in a dusty shop on London's St Martin's Lane. When she'd been in the hospital, this room had been the place that had come to mind when she'd thought of going home.

Now, as her father set her suitcase on the bed, there was an overwhelming sense of hollowness—a longing that she couldn't identify. Whatever she'd been hoping would be here to greet her was long gone.

Ailsa dropped her handbag and before she could thank her father, she let go of the torrent of pain that she'd been holding in since he'd picked her up in Glasgow that morning. Her knees gave way and she sank onto the carpet, and burying her face in the quilt cover, she let all the months of fear, frustration and confusion flood into the feathers under her face. As she grabbed the quilt, her insides quivering, she felt her father's hand on her back. She could sense his concern through his fingertips, but she couldn't hold back the tide.

She wasn't sure how long they'd been sitting on the floor, but when she opened her eyes her head was on a pillow and her father was next to her, leaning against the side of her bed.

"Dad?" Her voice was rough. "What's the time?"

Colin twisted his wrist to look at his watch.

"Nearly five." He shifted. "Mum'll be back soon. Do you feel up to a drink?" He hefted himself up as Ailsa rolled onto her back and stared at the ceiling.

One thing she'd always appreciated about her father was that whatever mess or conundrum she found herself in, he never interrogated her, or tried to force a confidence. Even when she'd called him that morning and said nothing more than *please come and get me*, he hadn't pressed her as to why. Three hours later he'd simply walked into the flat and asked where her bag was.

He paused at the door.

"Perhaps you should wash your face, love."

She nodded.

"Thanks for coming for me." She tried to smile.

"Just come down when you're ready." Colin gave her a thumbs-up and then closed the door softly behind him.

Ailsa got up from the floor and sat at her dressing table, the three paneled mirror catching her reflection from all sides. Her face was scarlet, her eyes blotchy and inflamed, and her hair was standing up at the back, so she smoothed it down with her palm.

Walking into the bathroom she took a washcloth, ran it under the cold water and pressed it gently over her eyes. After a few moments, she dropped it in the sink and raked her fingers through her hair. Her fingernail caught the edge of the uneven bone above her ear and she winced, a tingling sensation trailing across her scalp. Breathing through it, she dabbed on some eye cream and pulled her shoulders back.

Downstairs, her father had poured her a glass of wine. He was sitting in his favorite chair and Vaughn Williams's *Lark Ascending* was playing softly in the background.

"Come and sit." He smiled at her. "You look better."

She accepted the glass and settled on a chair opposite him. She loved this room with its tall windows, the wide stone fireplace with the floor to ceiling bookshelves either side and the tasteful Iranian carpets scattered across the wooden floors. Her mother had always made her take her shoes off to come in here, and as she looked down at her bare feet, the callouses and oddly angled toes looked ugly and distorted against the soft silk of the shimmering rug.

Her father sipped his whisky then leaned his head back against the chair.

"Are you going to tell me what's going on?" He spoke to the raised panel ceiling as Ailsa, taken aback by the unexpectedly direct question, swallowed some wine.

Her hands were shaking as she set the glass down on a side table. While she desperately wanted to confide in him, her shame made it impossible.

"Evan and I..." She faltered.

Colin continued to study the ceiling.

"We had a terrible row. We both did things. We've made mistakes. He ..." She couldn't go on.

He sat forward in the chair.

"He what?"

She felt the press of fresh tears and seeing it, her father reached into his pocket and handed her a white handkerchief. He was the only man she knew who still used cotton hankies and, as she accepted it, she smiled through her misery at this endearing eccentricity.

She wiped her nose and offered the hanky back to her father, who screwed his face up.

"Em, no thanks. Keep it." He grimaced as she stuffed the cotton square into her sleeve. The cold dampness against her wrist brought back the day in the car, outside the hospital, when she'd done the same thing with a tissue and she and Evan had laughed about it. She could see his face, all concern, and then the release as he'd joined in her amusement.

"I can't imagine that either of you did something so terrible that you can't work it out. How bad *was* it?" He assessed her over the rim of his glass.

"Worse than you can imagine." She felt like a guilty child. "Pretty much the worst."

Colin balanced the glass on his stomach.

"Do you want to tell me?"

She took a mouthful of wine and forced herself to swallow it. "Not really."

He nodded slowly and set his glass down on the table.

"Well, then you'll just have to keep trying to work it out— whatever it was."

Ailsa shook her head, the need to set the scene for what now felt inevitable, overwhelming.

"I'm not sure we can, Dad. Too much has changed."

Jennifer sat across from Ailsa at the dinner table. The casserole dish was still half full of coq-au-vin as her mother replaced the lid and moved it to the end of the table.

Ailsa had no appetite, despite eating next to nothing all day, but having drunk her glass of wine she was feeling calmer.

When her mother had arrived home from teaching a ballet class, she'd been full of the news of her day, relating step-by-step the combination of exercises that she'd put the students through.

She'd been pleased, but apparently only mildly curious as to why her daughter had arrived for an unplanned visit—and alone. Colin kept winking at Ailsa, letting her know the nature of her arrival was a secret that was safe between them.

"So, what's Evan up to this week? Working I suppose." Jennifer sipped her water. Her fair hair was twisted into a coil at the base of her long neck, and she fingered her pearl earring. "You're staying a week, you said?"

Ailsa dipped her chin.

"If that's O.K.?"

"Of course, darling. Stay as long as you like." Jennifer patted her hand. "As long as it's not a problem for your work?" A frown split her mother's forehead and she looked over at her husband, as if waiting for an endorsement. "Have you decided when you're going back?"

Ailsa watched her mother drain her glass, seemingly oblivious to the almost imperceptible shaking of her husband's head.

"I wanted to talk to you both about that, actually." Ailsa folded her napkin and set it on the table.

"Oh, wonderful. It's about time you got back in the saddle." Her mother beamed at her. "You're looking so much better."

Ailsa widened her eyes at her father.

"You should at least be doing a daily class by now, getting your stamina back." Jennifer frowned. "That's the first thing to go you know, when you miss so many."

Ailsa closed her eyes, trying to block out the disapproval that was clouding her mother's face.

"Ailsa, I'm talking to you."

Jennifer's tone caused something to snap inside Ailsa, and her eyes flew open.

"Yes, I know. I know." She placed her hands carefully on the tabletop and locked eyes with her mother. "Actually, you're not talking to me, Mum, you're talking *at* me." She spoke softly, but there was no mistaking her intention.

Jennifer's jaw slackened as she flicked her eyes to Colin, who stared at his daughter, his eyes wide with warning.

"What do you mean, exactly?" Jennifer's voice was cold as she turned back to Ailsa.

Ailsa felt her pulse quicken and recognized the rush of adrenaline, which in the past had posed the question—fight or flight. This time there was no debate to be had, it was clear to her what she must do, and it was long overdue.

"I mean that all my life you've been this voice in my ear—wear this Ailsa, go that way Ailsa, do classes with this teacher not that one, audition for that role, request this partner, live here not there, eat this not that."

Ailsa was shaking and as she watched, the color drained from her mother's face.

"I'm done, Mum. I'm finished letting anyone tell me what's best for me anymore. I'm tired of being maneuvered, molded, by you and Mark, and even Evan. I want to make my own decisions, finally." Her voice cracked.

Jennifer blinked, her frown deepening.

Colin cleared his throat. "Ailsa, I think your mother..."

She cut him off. "No, Dad. Please. This needs to be said."

Colin dropped his napkin on the table and gave a single nod.

Apparently having regained her momentum, Jennifer hissed at her.

"Don't speak to me like that. All I've ever done was protect you, advise and want the best for you like any mother would. Colin—you know that's true?" Jennifer looked at her husband for back-up.

Colin remained still, his eyes on Ailsa.

Feeling her resolve gathering, Ailsa took a deep breath and leaned her elbows on the table as her mother continued.

"All I wanted to do was share my experience with you. I know your world, the ballet world, better than you do. I've lived it, Ailsa. I've been in your shoes. It's a constant struggle to stay on top, a competitive minefield, often thankless and heartbreaking. And as for the..."

"Stop." Ailsa whispered. "That's exactly my point."

An expression of non-comprehension overtook her mother's face.

"All those warnings and lectures, the doom mongering and constant reminders of the price of your own success, you took the joy out of dancing for me, Mum. I didn't realize it until recently, but I was scared all the time." She swallowed. "Not scared of dancing, but of letting up for a second, of failing or not coming up to your standards—of disappointing you."

Jennifer tutted and plucked at the table cloth, refusing to meet Ailsa's eyes.

"There's so much more that I might've done if you hadn't pushed so hard." Ailsa felt a clog of tears at the back of her throat.

Jennifer looked stricken.

"What are you talking about? Professional ballet was all you ever wanted to do."

Tears now slipping freely down her cheeks, Ailsa shook her head.

"No, Mum. I just wanted to dance. Being a professional was all *you* ever wanted for me, and I was too timid to protest." The surge of liberation was like a vice being released from around her heart.

Jennifer's eyes bored into hers. The room had become silent aside from the low ticking of the clock on the mantle, marking the seconds passing one at a time. Ailsa flicked her eyes to the clock then back to her mother's face, which was frozen in a mask of disbelief.

Colin pushed his chair back from the table.

"I think we all need to stop now."

Ailsa wiped her nose on her napkin.

"I'm sorry, Dad."

Colin shook his head.

"No. We never need to apologize for the truth."

Later that night, as Ailsa lay in bed reading, her phone buzzed on the side table. She picked it up and a mixture of relief and joy sent her hand up to her temple.

Are you doing O.K.? Sam's text was brief, but all she needed, to know that the door was still open.

She tapped out *Yes. I'm O.K. You?*

Moments later his reply came. *Fine. When are you coming home?*

Sam had been understanding about her need to get away for a few days and had been keeping in touch via a daily text. Seeing his words, while removed in their form of delivery, was confirmation that she did still have a home to go back to. It might not be a particular space, per se, so much as a place where she knew she was loved, and that, to Ailsa, felt like the epitome of home.

She typed *Soon. So much to tell you x.* After a few seconds a reply bloomed on the screen. *You're the bravest person I know.*

She pressed her eyes closed, letting the image of the words burn into her retina, then switched off the light and slid down under the covers, knowing that for once, sleep would come easily.

Two days later, Ailsa left her parents' house on Carlton Street and headed down Dean Terrace on her way to the bridge across the Water of Leith. The atmosphere had been strained since her outburst and the prospect of time alone was intoxicating. She and her mother had finally reached the point of being civil with one another, after her father had gently encouraged Ailsa to take her small victory and try to make peace.

The previous evening, after a relatively relaxed dinner, Ailsa had told her mother that she wanted to talk to her. They'd sat in the small sunroom that extended from the back of the kitchen, and Jennifer had made them some Chamomile tea.

Ailsa had felt surprisingly calm, as Jennifer settled opposite her and eyed her over her cup.

"I wanted to say that I know why you did what you did, Mum. I know you had the best intentions."

Jennifer's eyelids had flickered.

"Of course I did."

Keen to get her thoughts out before her mother could divert her, Ailsa had ploughed on.

"I think that if I'd had a bit more backbone, a better sense of what it was that *I* really wanted, it would've been easier to forge my own path."

Jennifer, seeming to sense the need to let Ailsa speak, simply nodded.

"That said, you're a tough force to resist, Mother." Ailsa had smiled at Jennifer, seeing that her words were hitting home.

Jennifer had huffed and set her cup down.

"I know I can be tough, but I had to be, in the world I chose." She'd traced an arc across her body. "I wanted you to have all the tools and insights, all the help I could give you." She'd paused, her mouth twitching. "It wasn't easy to hear what you said to me. It hurt me deeply, Ailsa, but I accept that I might have pushed too hard sometimes." She'd paused, "While I don't regret much, I think I just assumed you wanted the same things I did for you."

To her surprise, Jennifer's eyes had begun to glitter and the sight of it had made Ailsa's heart ache.

"Mum…"

"No, Ailsa. Let me say this." She'd run her palm over her

silky hair. "Your father's been telling me for years to back off, and I might have made mistakes, all parents do, but I knew you had what it took to get to the top." She'd nodded to herself. "I saw it in you from an early age. The potential. The raw talent. And I was right." A flash of the old Jennifer-determination had allowed Ailsa to release her breath. "However, I concede that I should have talked to you more, asked what you wanted." She'd dipped her chin. "And for that, I'm sorry."

At this, Ailsa had stood up, moved over next to her mother and, as Jennifer smiled at her, Ailsa eased herself into the same chair, their slim bodies turned toward each other like two sides of a clam shell.

"Thanks, Mum." Ailsa had held her palm out and Jennifer laid hers on top. "You don't know how much that means to me." She'd leaned in and kissed her mother's cheek.

"Well, you know how hard that was for me to admit." Jennifer had widened her eyes comically.

Ailsa had laughed, a lightness filling her.

"Yes, I do."

Now, as she paced out toward the bridge, however tenuous their peace treaty was, it had been cast, and Ailsa was glad of it.

She loved walking around Stockbridge, enjoying the village feel of the enclave where she'd grown up, just north of the city. With its curved Georgian streets and cul-de-sacs, picturesque mews and the old Stockbridge Market, complete with original Victorian archway, it felt separate from the city. The proximity to the Botanic Gardens and the river made Stockbridge feel rural, despite being only a ten-minute walk from the center of Edinburgh.

It was Sunday, and she was looking forward to passing under the familiar archway and wandering through the market, with no agenda other than to browse at the stalls lined up under the rows of yellow tents. She would look at antiques, count the braces of pheasants hanging from overhead railings, listen to the merchants calling to passersby, sniff briny oysters and sample fragrant local cheeses. She wanted to lose track of time, flip through boxes of old photographs, handle blocks of handmade soap and taste the rich ethnic foods that she been avoiding for years—and have no one tell her she shouldn't.

As the weeks had gone by, she had begun to cope better with being in public places and even, to a degree, with crowds. The energy of the market was always electric, the vendors welcoming and friendly, and just for today she craved the anonymity and sense of solitude that being among strangers offered.

The market was busy with groups of people crowding around the rows of stalls, waiting their turn. The queue at one of the bakery tables was particularly long, and the smell of freshly baked bread made Ailsa's tongue stick to the roof of her mouth as she moved past the back of the line.

At the next stall was a silver-haired man selling Dunkeld smoked salmon. Knowing her father loved it, she took up her place behind a young couple with a baby, to wait her turn. The child was in its father's arms, looking over the man's shoulder at her. Golden curls bubbled around pale-blue eyes and the ruddy cheeks were glistening with something sticky as the child happily slapped its father's back with a chubby palm.

Ailsa smiled, and as the baby responded, she held out her index finger, as if beckoning a baby bird. The child reached for her and feeling the movement, the father turned around and nodded at Ailsa.

"He's flirting with you." The man laughed. "He's a wee lady killer."

Ailsa felt the small fingers wrap around her own, the child's simple reflex bringing a hard lump to her throat, and then the little boy's face cracked into a gummy grin.

"He likes you." The young woman standing next to her smiled. "Do you have any?" She stared at Ailsa.

"No, not yet." Ailsa squeezed the little fingers again and then let go.

The couple stepped up to the table and began talking to the vendor as Ailsa, rocked by a bone-deep longing, moved silently away into the crowd.

EVAN

E van stood in the doorway and assessed the compact space.
A friend had offered him the use of his studio-flat above a
bar in Ashton Lane, while he was in Australia for three months,
and as Evan had no idea when, or if, he'd be going home, he had
agreed to sub-let the place for a few weeks rather than stay too
long with his mother.

The living area was small but cleverly designed. The small
kitchen had a breakfast bar that separated it from the living
space where a slim, contemporary sofa sat along the exposed
brick wall behind him. There was a bathroom on the main level
and a spiral staircase twisted up from the far corner of the room
to a platform, where the bed sat behind a wrought iron railing.
The retro, bachelor-pad vibe was obvious but the place suited
his needs, for now. Not only was it tiny and easy to manage,
but it was close to both his work and to home, on Dumbarton
Road.

He hadn't seen Ailsa since the day she'd cracked his heart
open. She'd left him a couple of voice messages, but he hadn't
called her back. Every time he thought about her he fought with
an image of that carefree smile—and then he'd see Sam, kissing

her neck, stroking her back, lying on top of her, and it sickened him to his stomach.

Diana had been a rock. She hadn't pressed him for too much information, even when he'd stumbled into her house that night, drunk and spewing vitriol about his darling wife. She'd helped him to bed, stayed up all night in the living room knitting and then made him coffee when he surfaced in the morning, without a single probing question.

It had taken him four days to tell her what was going on with Ailsa, and even then he'd held back, leaving out his own role in their breakdown.

"I'm so sorry, Son." She'd looked pale. "I had an inkling the other night, but I didn't want to jump to conclusions."

"I still can't take it in, Mum." He'd been pacing around the room, his jeans hanging loose around his hips and a glass of whisky in his hand.

Diana had taken her time to consider before persuading him to sit down, then she'd taken the glass from his hand.

"Hear me, Evan MacIntyre. When someone is seriously ill they don't think clearly. They sometimes make bad decisions." She'd stemmed his attempt to protest with her palm. "I'm not excusing her—but she's been through something far beyond your average illness. Agreed?"

He'd nodded.

"However, I think she knew what she was doing." Diana's mouth had twisted.

The next moments of silence had dragged, as he suppressed the rising guilt at hiding his own culpability, but Evan had seen his mother's face and knew to wait before he reacted.

"Obviously she's still struggling with memory issues, and there's a deep-seated confusion there, but there was also something resolute in her deciding not to tell you what was happening."

Evan had nodded.

"There must be a reason she did that and I think, until you understand that reason, you won't know what kind of future you have—with or without her."

He'd known then that he must stop the conversation if he wanted to retain a modicum of his mother's respect.

Now, as he stood in the bright little studio, Diana's words echoed around him, making more and more sense each time he played them back. The last thing he wanted to do was see Ailsa, but until he did he would be treading water.

He picked up his backpack, climbed the metal staircase, and dropping the pack on the floor he flopped onto the bed. It felt good to be in a place where Ailsa had never been, and it might be easier to sleep without missing her presence here.

He pressed his head back on the pillow and noticed a small round, stained glass window in the wall above the bed, so twisted around to better see the design. It was a tree, reflected in four different seasons, each in a separate panel. The low afternoon sun was seeping through the glass, sending a kaleidoscope of color crawling up toward the ceiling as Evan closed his eyes and let sleep take over.

AILSA

Having got home from Edinburgh three days before, the flat had become oppressive, and Ailsa found that she could spend less and less time there. She was taking longer walks, staying out after picking up groceries, wandering along Byers Road just to people-watch, or sit in a café with her book.

When she was at home, she busied herself with tidying, rearranging photographs, shifting piles of books and papers, then shifting them back, and as each day passed without any contact with Evan, so his presence began to fade from the place.

One bath towel hung on the rail, one toothbrush stood in the glass on the sink, and one mug, plate and fork sat on the kitchen draining board. As she wore and then put away her clothes and shoes, so Evan's were gradually being shoved further and further back in the wardrobe.

So much was changing, and each time she remembered new slices of her past, which was happening more frequently, she was momentarily sad that Evan wasn't around to share the unearthed memories. Each dusty image, sentence or experience as it was revealed to her, felt like a prize she'd won.

That morning she had put away a clean shirt of his, and as

she smoothed the soft cotton into a drawer, she'd tried to calculate how long he'd been gone. The fact that the number of days and hours wasn't etched on her brain was enlightening. Later, when she checked the calendar in the kitchen, it had been over five weeks since he'd packed a bag and left.

Since their devastating confrontation, and her subsequent week with her parents, she'd been going upstairs to see Sam every day. He'd given her a key so she could come and go while he was rehearsing, and she'd spend hours sprawled on the floor, drinking coffee, surrounded by books on dance, and the anatomy of dancers. Her interest was growing in the nuts and bolts of the marvelous machines that kept her kind moving, and the more she read, the more fascinated she became with every small miracle that went on under the surface.

While she was becoming used to the new, more fluid structure of her days, and allowing herself to relax into them, seeing Evan again soon was inevitable.

That morning, she'd been to a class at the West End dance studio and having taken a shower, she locked her door and climbed the stairs to Sam's flat.

He was at the piano, tidying a pile of sheet music, and as she was about to cross the room and kiss him, a dark shape flashed in her peripheral vision. She glanced over, surprised to see a large armchair sitting at the side of the fireplace.

"You got a chair." She spun around as Sam was pushing the stool in to the base of the piano.

"Yeah. I thought it was time. You can't sit on the floor forever." He smiled. I want you to feel comfortable here."

"I do." She smiled. "You have no idea how much."

The chair's presence felt like a significant step forward, a move toward him making this empty space a home, and one she was welcome in. Overcome by a sense of peace, Ailsa circled it and sat down.

"Super comfy." She patted the soft fabric arm and scooted

into one corner of the chair. "Plenty of room for two." She grinned as Sam crossed the room to join her. He squeezed his lean frame in next to her and pulled her into his side.

"I feel so grown up." He widened his eyes comically. "Real furniture." He dropped a kiss on her head.

Ailsa nodded against his shoulder, breathing in the fresh, soapy smell lingering on his skin. This was all she needed, Sam, and this corner of the universe. In a world where she had felt so discombobulated, for so many months, she now felt at one with everything around her.

"Sam, I want to make sure you understand something." She put her hand on his shoulder, feeling the broad strip of muscle under her fingertips.

He looked down at her.

"This is the only place I want to be." She swallowed over a nut of emotion.

"You asked me before, if I was sure, and I am. More than ever. I want to be here."

His mouth widened into a smile.

"Well, good. I'm glad we cleared that up."

She poked his rib.

"But if I change my mind, is there a statute of limitations on this relationship?" Mischief glittered in his eyes, making Ailsa's heart flip-flop.

"Absolutely not. You're stuck with me." She placed her palm on the side of his face, drawing his mouth to hers.

An hour later, when she went downstairs, Amanda and Hayley were standing at her door.

"Hello there." She knelt down and hugged Hayley. "I've missed you so much, Pickle."

Hayley's arms squeezed Ailsa's neck.

"Where have you been? We've been ringing your bell for ages." The little girl wriggled out of her grip.

Amanda gave a mock grimace and took Hayley's hand.

"We've not been here ages, love. Don't be cheeky."

Ailsa patted the air, dismissing the child's rebuke. It had been close to two weeks since she'd seen Amanda, and she was so glad to see them both that nothing would get in the way of that.

"Come in. Can you stay for tea?" She opened the door and ushered them in ahead of her.

Ailsa tossed her ballet shoes on top of the bag in the hall as Amanda slipped Hayley's jacket off.

"We've got an hour or so before her gym class."

Ailsa's eyebrows shot up.

"Gym?" Ailsa was fairly confident that this wasn't something Amanda had mentioned.

Hayley tiptoed over to the bookshelf and began shuffling through the selection of books that Ailsa kept for her, on the bottom shelf.

"It was something you said." Amanda flopped onto the sofa. "About us not doing the things we wanted to, because of ballet."

Ailsa nodded. "I remember."

"I didn't want Hayley to ever say to me Mum, why didn't you let me do this or that, you know?" She chewed the skin around her index finger. "If she takes the ballet route eventually, then that's fine. But at least she'll have had other experiences—options, so to speak." Amanda crossed her ankles on the coffee table. "I'm just not telling her ballet teacher." She tapped her nose. "Mum's the word."

Ailsa laughed. It felt good to let go.

Hayley pulled out a book and sat on the rug.

"Can we sing, Aunty Ailsa?"

"Not yet, love. Aunty Ailsa and I need to chat for a bit." Amanda smiled at her daughter. "Just be a good girl for a few minutes and then we'll all sing together."

"O-kaaay" Hayley puffed up her cheeks and exhaled, elongating the word dramatically.

Ailsa, taking the cue, beckoned Amanda into the kitchen.

"What's up?" She faced her friend.

"How did it go with Evan?"

Ailsa leaned back against the counter,

"Awful."

Amanda grimaced.

"You told him everything?"

Ailsa nodded.

"God. How did he take it? I haven't heard from him for a while."

Ailsa described the meeting at the café and Evan's gut-wrenching response to her confession.

"He said that? That the dancing was a worse betrayal?" Amanda whistled softly. "Considering his role in all this, that's a bit melodramatic, don't you think?"

Ailsa watched Amanda fill a glass of water from the tap and take several gulps.

"I've tried to contact him a few times, but he won't speak to me." Ailsa pressed her fingers into her eyes. "I didn't plan any of this you know?" She stared at Amanda. "I never wanted to hurt him, or take some kind of evil revenge." She could feel the weight that she'd just shed upstairs, settling back on her chest.

"Hey, I know that." Amanda held her hands out. "I'm sad for you." She paused. "For both of you, actually."

Ailsa ran her fingers through her hair searching for the tender trough. Finding it, she pressed down on her scalp. There were so many emotions channeling through her that she was still struggling to identify them all.

"This might sound crazy, Amanda, but along with the sadness, it's kind of freeing, letting go of something that's been such a huge part of your life."

Amanda caught her breath.

"Do you mean ballet, or Evan?"

Ailsa wiped her nose with her palm.

"Both."

They settled into a comfortable calm, talking in low voices as the kettle boiled, and just as Ailsa was about to pick up the tea tray, Amanda patted her pocket.

"God, I almost forgot." She pulled out an envelope.

"Is that for me?"

"Yes. It's from Mark."

Ailsa took it and slid her finger under the flap—no idea what to expect as she unfolded the single sheet of heavy paper. It was written by hand with a thick pen and as she read it, Ailsa felt a swell of what could only be described as relief. She refolded the paper and handed it to Amanda.

"Read it." She nodded. "Go ahead."

Amanda frowned. "Are you sure?"

"Please, read it."

Amanda dipped her head, her lips moving slightly as she read.

"Oh shit, I'm so sorry." She was holding the paper away from her middle, as if it were smoldering.

Ailsa took it and tossed it onto the counter.

"He was angry that I didn't go and see him after class that day. I should have, really. And I haven't called him since."

Amanda hefted herself up onto the counter, her feet dangling in front of the cabinet below.

"But what he said, about you not coming back." She halted. "You are coming back, right?" She shoved her hair from her forehead and studied Ailsa's face.

"He's given me another week to decide. I think that's more than reasonable." Ailsa blinked. "Although, I don't think I'll need that long."

Amanda stuck her chin out.

"Well?"

Ailsa picked up the tea tray.

"I think I'm done."

"You can't mean that?"

Ailsa turned to face her friend.

"I do."

The letter now sat on the bedside table, and Ailsa wasn't sure why she'd brought it to bed with her. It was brief, and totally Mark. He'd said that while he'd been glad to see her at the studio, he was disappointed that she'd left without talking to him. He went on to say that despite his fondness for her, and the length of their personal friendship, he was now faced with the difficult task of deciding what to do with her spot in the company. As she had given him no indication of her intentions, he needed her to confirm by July 20th whether she would be returning to work. If he did not hear from her, while it would break his heart, he would have no choice but to terminate her contract.

There were plenty of talented dancers patiently waiting in the wings for their time, their chance to step into her shoes, and there was a time when that knowledge would have terrified her, but with all that had happened over the past few months, she clung far less tightly to much of what had made up the foundation of her life, before.

Mark's words were white-hot and yet their intention hadn't affected her as they should have. Rather than inciting panic or anxiety, his ultimatum had paved her way as beautifully as if he'd rolled a red carpet out for her to walk away on.

EVAN

E van walked down Dumbarton Road. It had been weeks
since he'd seen Ailsa and even longer since he'd been
inside their flat. The studio on Ashton Lane had begun to feel
like home, and the ease with which he'd adjusted to living with
so few of his possessions was astounding.

All the things that he'd been collecting over the years, his
clothes, books and music and the two decent paintings that he'd
splashed out on when he'd got a raise, had all been relegated
from his life and he didn't miss them at all.

As he stepped to the side to allow a woman pushing a stroller
to get past, the little girl held a teddy bear whose ear she was
furiously chewing. Dark chunks of hair framed her round face,
and icy-blue eyes flicked between the street and Evan's face.

"Thanks." The woman smiled as she passed.

Evan touched his forehead.

"She's a wee doll."

He turned to watch them walk away and the little girl had
twisted around and was looking over her shoulder at him,
holding the bear out at right angles to the stroller. He waved. The

child's coloring was exactly how he'd imagined his and Ailsa's children might look—pale skin and eyes, with that dark curly hair—a classic Gaelic combination. He shook his head, another of his many regrets resurfacing.

Reaching the building, he turned and walked down the external corridor, then stopped short. The front door to the flat was red. Evan frowned, taking in the new paint color as he pulled the keys from his pocket. He held them to the lock then stopped. This time, he put the heavy ring away, lifted the brass knocker and smacked it sharply.

Within a few moments, he heard footsteps and then Ailsa opened the door. Her hair was still cropped short, making her eyes seem huge, her dark skirt skimmed her bare calves and the outline of her shoulders curved softly under her blouse. Her face was slightly more angular than the last time he'd seen her, and she was clearly anxious.

"Hi." She smiled. "Come in."

Evan followed her into the living room. Aside from his armchair which still sat at the fireside, all the furniture had been moved. The sofa now faced the window, and the dining table had been pushed up against the wall clearing a large space in the middle of the room. The rugs were gone and in place of the coffee table, a small trunk sat in the corner with the TV remote, a pile of magazines and a pair of glasses he didn't recognize on its top. While in some ways it was fitting that the place looked different, as he felt no particular affinity with it right now, his jaw tightened at the changes.

"What've you done in here?" He watched the smile leave her face.

"I just moved things around. It's all still here."

"Looks a bit odd, that's all." He licked his lips. He'd known that this would be difficult, but being here with her was like breathing in glass shards. He smoothed his hair and moved deeper into the room. "So, how've you been?" He hovered at the chair unsure whether he should sit or if this was now someone else's spot. "Can I?" He gestured toward the chair.

Ailsa's face flushed.

"Of course. Why are you asking me?"

He sat down.

"Well, you never know. Things change so quickly around here." He paused. He hadn't wanted to be nasty, but his hurt was losing the battle with his resolve. "And what's with the brothel-red door?"

Ailsa stepped back as if she'd been struck and then her face darkened, her hands finding her hips as she fixed him with her stare.

"Look. I just want to get through this."

He watched her move to the window. Her back was to him and he could see her sides heaving.

"Ailsa?"

She turned to face him.

"I wanted to keep this civil." She paused. "Can we do that?"

He nodded. "We can."

Twenty minutes later, Ailsa sat on the floor with her back against the sofa. Evan had joined her there rather than talk to the top of her head. While it was difficult to be near her without touching her, he'd fought the impulse to reach for her hand or brush a curl away from her eye, as he would have done once.

"So, you're still dancing?" He tried to sound disinterested. She nodded.

"Yes. I've been going to a new studio—trying out a few different classes. I'm enjoying them…" Her voice trailed away.

He watched her cross her ankles, her bare feet as tiny and malformed as ever. There were fresh looking red blotches on her toe-joints, and her calves looked even more defined than they used to.

"Mark terminated my contract last week." Her voice was soft, but he heard no trace of angst in it. More, it was matter of fact, as if she'd been reading the items on a shopping list.

"What?" Evan leaned forward, and on a reflex his hand slid across the floor toward hers. "Why?"

"He gave me an ultimatum, but he'd been more than patient."

Evan shook his head, disappointment tangy on his tongue.

"So, you're all right with it?"

She shifted onto one hip to face him.

"I am."

He heard the words, but they carried no weight. They floated past him like smoke as he tried to focus on her face.

"So, what're you going to do now?"

"I'm not sure." She pushed her skirt down over her knees. "I thought about teaching, but I'm not sure it's for me." She eyed him. "Evan, before we talk about that, we need to talk about us."

Of course she was right, but Evan's stomach tilted. Her statement was shoving him toward Pandora's box and he wasn't sure he wanted to lift that particular lid.

"O.K., let's talk."

She pushed herself up from the floor and walked to the window.

"First of all, I've given this a lot of thought, so please let me get it out. All right?"

He blinked his consent as she linked her hands low behind her hips, as Juliet might.

"Ever since the surgery I've felt cut off from myself, and my own life. It was like I was watching but not participating." She eyed him. "I've been working with small pieces of the past, fragments of time, here and there, trying to fill in gaps and make things whole—and I've been aware of hurting you, and others, with my half-memories and by seeming distant.' She swallowed. "All I could think about was what I couldn't remember."

Nothing she was saying was news to him, so Evan remained silent.

"I spent so much time trying to find the pieces of myself that'd been lost and get back to life the way it was, that I didn't realize two basic things."

Evan couldn't contain himself, so cut in.

"I know there are a lot of holes, Ailsa, but we can still grow around them." He held his hands out, like an open book.

She frowned and closed her eyes.

"Evan, please."

"Sorry. Go on." He sighed.

"First thing I realized is that I'm not the same person I was. Those pieces of me aren't lost. I've changed. Perhaps even grown. And second, when I was brave enough to be honest with myself, I knew that I didn't want life to go back to the way it was."

Evan felt the cold slap of her words.

She held her hands out at her sides.

"I realized that I was tired, Evan. Tired of being managed, coached, and steered into a life that was so unforgiving."

Evan stared at her mouth.

"Don't get me wrong, I loved being a dancer, whether I truly chose it for myself or not. At least most of the time I loved it. I'm always going to dance, in some shape or form, but now there's so much more that I want to do." She paused as Evan tried to piece together the cumbersome chunks of information.

"I want to eat butter. I want to keep my hair short. I want to be present in my life, every day of it. I want to stop sacrificing for my art, making it the be all and end all of my existence." Her eyes filled. "I want to open my mind, learn more about the human body, what makes it work." She made an odd, hiccupping sound. "When I stood back and looked at everything I'd achieved, and everything I'd given up for ballet, I was really proud, but also a bit resentful."

Sensing everything slipping away, and unable to take the distance between them any longer, Evan stood up and walked to her side.

She was trembling.

"It's O.K., just breathe." He took her hand and pressed his lips into her palm.

"Evan. Listen to me, please." Tears were trickling down her cheeks as she took her hand back.

"When I asked myself what I really wanted, all I could come up with was, something different." She shuddered, wrapping her arms across her body.

"How different?" His breath was now coming in sharp spurts and his palms were growing clammy.

"I tried so hard to get it back. The love. You did so much for me." She hesitated. "But I couldn't remember the us that you knew."

Her face was scarlet as she wiped her nose, and although Evan knew precisely what she was saying, he said nothing.

"I want all those things I just said." She paused. "But the thing that I want the most is to be a mother."

The list of her wants had been fairly succinct but now, as he tried to recall everything she'd said, Evan felt the air around him thicken. Nowhere in the list had he featured—not his name, his presence or even the concept of him had been mentioned in her desires for the future. This was everything he had dreaded—the worst potential reality.

He had one last chance.

"If that's what you want, you can have it." He shoved his hands in his pockets. "We can get it all back. And we'd intended to have kids eventually." He'd put himself back in the equation. Now he just needed to hear her say that she saw him there too.

Ailsa looked up at him and, with the quiver of her chin and the film across her eyes, there was no need for her to say anything more. Evan heard the truth in the sickening silence and dropped his chin to his chest.

"So, it's just me you don't want anymore."

She stared at him as he stepped back from the window and headed for the door.

AILSA

T hree days had gone by. Their meeting had been agonizing and Evan had taken her declaration as badly as she'd feared, adding the painful knowledge that she had shattered his heart to the burden of guilt she already bore. She knew it was hers to carry but the sight of his face when he'd left the flat that afternoon would be seared on her own damaged heart forever.

Ailsa wasn't remotely surprised at Evan's silence, but her concern for his state of mind was blaring—annihilating all other topics or things she tried to focus on. She was surviving on two or three hours of sleep a night, and her healthy appetite had been replaced with a sickly bird's. Her head ached and rather than resort to aspirin, she bore the discomfort with a masochism that helped to take the edge off her guilt.

Regardless of what Evan had done, the knowledge that she had hurt him so deeply was gnawing at her, and her taking some time to be alone seemed like the only way to acknowledge everything that had happened, and what they'd each done to the other.

When she explained how she felt to Sam, he had been understandably concerned.

"I get it, Ailsa, but it does make me nervous." His eyes had glistened. "Are you sure that's all it is?"

"Of course." She'd wound her fingers through his. "I'm moving forward, every day, but I need this time to process everything." She'd paused. "I think it's a way of paying respect to what I had with Evan, somehow." She'd seen his eyebrows lift. "But nothing has changed between you and me. Trust me."

He'd held her close, breathing into her hair.

"Then take your time. I'm not going anywhere."

Sam had only been downstairs three times since she'd met him, not wanting to be inside the place where she and Evan had lived together. As she looked around her, she totally understood. They had both contaminated this well and even she didn't want to drink from it anymore.

With the new, slight distance between her and Sam, Ailsa had been spending more time alone. The solitary nature of her days was, however, providing some reward. Her memory, while still patchy, was yielding more morsels of the past. It would catch her off guard when she'd taste something, see an image on television or listen to a particular piece of music.

The previous day she'd been clearing out some books to take to the charity shop when she'd pulled *The Old Man and the Sea* from the shelf. While handling the battered red cover, running her finger over the faded gold lettering, she'd been overcome with a memory of her honeymoon. Evan had bought her the book from Shakespeare and Company, the tiny bookstore crouched on the banks of the Seine where Hemingway had borrowed books as a penniless young writer. She'd been romanced by the author's story, and after they'd visited the shop, Evan had snuck back and bought her the book. He'd given it to her later when they'd been sitting in a café, on Boulevard Haussman.

Sitting on the floor, as she'd turned the book over in her hands, she'd remembered every detail of how it became hers, but she couldn't remember if she'd read it. The tiny hole in the new memory was fitting—this laciness was something she was becoming accustomed to.

The book was now safely stored on her bedside table and her bookmark nestled under its cover. As she lay in bed that night turning the curling pages, each one felt as if she were honoring the memory, solidifying it in her chronology. Evan deserved that, at least.

Now, Hayley and Amanda were coming over to have lunch with her and the flat was devoid of food. She opened the fridge and closed it again then checked the cupboards, seeing that there was nothing the child would eat. As she considered phoning the Italian restaurant around the corner, the doorbell rang and as she approached the door, she could hear Hayley's voice, high pitched and giggly.

She pulled the door open.

"Hi, Pickle." The little girl trotted in and wrapped her arms around Ailsa's waist. Her hair was getting longer, and Amanda had tried to put it in a ponytail, but several stubborn short pieces coiled around Hayley's Botticelli cheeks.

"I love your hair." Ailsa smiled at her and winked as Amanda grimaced.

"We *had* to have a ponytail today." Amanda dropped her bag on the floor and checked her phone.

Hayley pushed past them both and went into the living room.

"Aunty Ailsa, where's all your furniture?" She stared at the sparsely filled room and a crease split her narrow brow. "Did you sell it?"

Ailsa laughed.

"No. I just moved it around and put away the rugs. I wanted to clear the decks a little."

Hayley beamed. "So you can dance?"

Ailsa nodded. "And that."

Amanda shoved her phone in her pocket.

"So, what's going on with you?" She scanned Ailsa's face. "Any changes?"

Knowing that Amanda was asking about Evan, she shook her head.

"Radio silence. Don't suppose you've heard anything?"

Amanda shook her head. "Nope. Not a word."

Hayley turned around. "From who?"

"Never you mind, nosey parker." Amanda smiled at her daughter, then turned to Ailsa. "Shall I put the kettle on?"

Ailsa bit her lip.

"I'm sorry. I've got nothing in to eat." She grimaced. "Want to go out?"

Twenty minutes later, the threesome walked down Byer's Road. Hayley held one of each of their hands as they flanked her, swinging her between them every few steps, whenever there was room on the pavement. The sun, while weak, was shining and the warm breeze smelled of garlic, making Ailsa's stomach rumble.

"You're looking a little peaky." Amanda glanced over at her. "Are you sleeping?"

"Not much." She side stepped to avoid a hole in the pavement.

"Hmm, I wondered. It'll take time. You just have to take each day as it comes, and try not to look too far forward, or back." Amanda reached down and wiped a dark smudge from Hayley's cheek.

Ailsa nodded.

"Difficult to make any progress if I can't look backwards or forwards." She smiled at her friend, and Amanda stuck her tongue out.

"You know what I mean. Just let things come. Let the days take their own shape."

Ailsa nodded.

"Yes, sensei."

"Oh, shut up."

Amanda shoved her shoulder and laughed as, overcome with emotion, Ailsa grabbed her friend's hand.

"I don't know what I'd do without you, and Hayley." Her voice cracked.

Amanda returned the pressure of Ailsa's fingers.

"Just as well you don't have to find out then."

Ailsa pulled the tape taut over the top of the box. The last of Evan's books and CDs were carefully wrapped in paper and the final thing she'd added to the box was a selection of their wedding pictures. He hadn't been back to the flat to pick up his clothes or belongings, and after a month of unanswered calls and messages, Diana had finally phoned to tell her that she should pack whatever she thought he'd want and that someone would come round to pick it up, at some point. Ailsa had tried to talk to her mother-in-law about everything that had happened, but, the conversation hadn't gone well.

The flat was growing chilly as Ailsa worked, and despite the heat that she'd generated from her labors, she shivered. September was closing in and autumn's musky smell was settling on the garden.

She'd been outside to read that morning, while Sam was at rehearsal, and she'd noticed that the trees were already turning. The lawn was regressing, its dullness highlighting the glow of the heather, now in its element, a mass of soft pink and purple along the base of the stone wall.

As she sat with her book, she'd looked up at Sam's window, now firmly closed. So much had gone on behind those mottled panes of glass. So much change and self-expression, so much sharing, rediscovered freedom and joy. But on the back of all that there had also been fear, uncertainty and of course the pain that she'd caused Evan.

As she'd squinted up at the glass, a bird had flitted overhead and then smashed headlong into the window. She'd been so startled that she'd shouted out loud and dashing over to the building she had pushed her way into the spiky shrubs growing under her living room window. She'd searched among the branches, eventually finding the sparrow, its neck twisted at an awkward angle and its tiny eye fixed on the sky. She'd lifted the small pile of feathers and carried the bird inside, and finding a little box, had wrapped the bird in tissues and taped the box closed, all the time letting her tears plop onto the cardboard.

She had no idea why it had affected her so deeply, but later, as she took the spade from the communal shed and buried the tiny creature under the heather, she'd felt a lightening of her spirit as if by scattering the dark soil on top of the battered box she was laying to rest so much that had plagued her over the past eight months.

Now, the doorbell rang, startling her from her daydream, so she wiped her hands on her thighs, walked over and opened the door.

Diana was standing in the outer hall and the sight of the familiar face, a woman whom she truly loved and yet had alienated, made her heart skip. Diana was pale, her face drawn and thinner than Ailsa remembered.

"Diana. I didn't know…"

"I didn't call. I should've called." She throttled the handles of her handbag.

Ailsa stepped back, widening the door.

"Please, come in."

"I can't stay long." Diana followed her inside the flat.

Ailsa's nerves were tingling. "Would you like a coffee?"

Diana shook her head and then hesitated. "Actually, a hot drink would be nice."

Grateful for any opportunity to keep Diana on her territory, Ailsa turned and walked into the kitchen.

Diana followed her into the room and leaned against the cabinet by the window. She looked exhausted.

"How are you?" Ailsa filled the mugs from the warm kettle. "We're O.K."

Ailsa registered the inclusion of Evan in the statement, grateful that Diana had done that.

"How is he?" She handed a mug to Diana and gestured toward the living room.

"Shattered, but he's coping."

The obvious emphasis on only Evan's hurt, was disappointing. She'd never asked him if he'd told Diana everything, but a part of her had assumed he'd have been honest with his mother.

In the living room, Diana slipped off her jacket, perched on the edge of the sofa and balanced the cup awkwardly on her knee. Ailsa sat in the arm chair and watched her mother-in-law assessing the newly arrange furniture.

"So, you've made some changes?" Her voice was emotionless. "Spartan." She sipped her coffee.

"Yes. It's a bit bare, but I like it." Ailsa crossed her legs, suddenly self-conscious of her faded yoga pants and baggy T-shirt. "It's fine for now."

Diana nodded and cupped the mug in her hands.

"I've come to give you a letter, from Evan's solicitor." She reached into the pocket of her coat. "I didn't want to play the messenger, but he asked me to because he didn't want it to be too official." Diana held a slim brown envelope out to Ailsa, her face a mask of misery. "I still can't believe this is happening, Ailsa." Her voice was tremulous.

Ailsa eyed the envelope, set her cup down and took it from Diana.

"What is it?" She held the slice of brown paper in her hand and turned it over. There was no writing on it, no name or identifying marks of any kind.

"It's notice that he wants to sell the flat, if you're agreeable."

Diana looked embarrassed. "He said that there's no particular rush, and presuming you don't want to buy him out, he'd like to put it on the market as soon as possible." She nodded. "He needs to move on." Diana wiped her eye with her thumb.

Ailsa set the envelope on the arm of the chair. It made sense that Evan had done this but not communicating in any way with her, still felt unnatural. The suggestion of her buying him out took her aback, not being something she had considered, but as she did so now, she knew that she was ready to move on too.

"He won't answer my calls." She eyed Diana. "I do understand this," she laid her palm on the envelope, "but he and I need to talk. There's so much to sort out."

Diana set her cup on the floor and stood up.

"I'm sorry. I can't make him talk to you."

It was the first time she'd been curt since arriving, and Ailsa winced.

"I think he's perfectly within his rights to work through a solicitor." Diana crossed her arms over the jacket she now held across her stomach.

Ailsa stood up.

"Diana, I know you're hurt. I can't tell you how much it kills me to know that he…"

Diana made a choking sound.

"It kills *you*." Her eyes were full. "How do you think *he* feels? You took away everything. You spoiled everything."

Diana's voice broke and in an instant, Ailsa jumped up from the chair and crossed the room. As the older woman dipped her face into a tissue, Ailsa wrapped her arms around the stooped shoulders and pulled Diana in close.

There was little resistance as Diana leaned on Ailsa's shoulder and let the tears come, and with each heave of her mother-in-law's shoulders, Ailsa swallowed the impulse to defend herself. Diana had been through enough, and to diminish her son in her eyes now would be the ultimate cruelty.

Ailsa wasn't sure how long they'd been standing there but gradually Diana recovered herself. Taking her glasses off, she wiped them on the bottom of her blouse.

"I really didn't want to do that." She spoke quietly as she replaced the glasses and then moved some silvery tendrils off her forehead.

"Do what?" Ailsa indicated the sofa. "Please, Diana, sit for a bit."

"I didn't want to cry, or to shout at you." Diana sniffed. "I was going to be all business-like. Straight to the point and then out the door." She glanced at Ailsa. "But when I saw you, this place…" she swept her arm around the room, "it all just went to pot."

Ailsa nodded.

"I know. It's hard for everyone." She paused. "Diana, I'm so very grateful for everything you've done for me, and I can't tell you how sorry I am."

Diana wiped her nose and then shoved the tissue into her pocket.

"Sorry is really no use though, is it?" She sat back down. "Evan told me not to ask you any questions, but I have to." She glanced at Ailsa. "What made you fall out of love with him?"

Ailsa's insides folded over. If only it had been as simple as that. Somehow the idea of just falling out of love would have been less random, and much easier to explain than the truth.

"Part of me will always love him, but I just couldn't get back to who we were." She swallowed. "All he wanted was for us to go back to our life before this." Her hand hovered over her ear. "But there *was* no going back."

Diana nodded.

"I tried to explain." She hesitated. "That I'd finally figured out what I wanted for myself. And what I wanted—have wanted for a while—wasn't what Evan did." She paused. "I tried, Diana, I really did. But it felt dishonest being with him and yet not being truly *with* him." She glanced at her mother-in-law. "Do you understand?"

Diana was staring at her, her face having regained its pale calm.

"I suppose I do. But does Evan?"

Ailsa lifted her shoulders. "I don't know. I hope so."

Diana crossed her legs. "He's leaving, you know." She stared at Ailsa.

"Leaving where?"

"He's going to New Zealand."

Ailsa sucked in her breath, but even as she felt the spark of shock, underneath it was a sliver of acknowledgement. Evan had often talked about them going to visit his cousin Eric, in Auckland, but there had never been a good time for her to be away from work that long. Her rehearsal schedule, class timetable, touring and performance requirements meant that they really hadn't had a proper holiday since their honeymoon. She'd felt bad about it, but then they had both been re-consumed with the hectic pattern of their life together.

"Is he going to see Eric?"

Diana nodded. "He says he'll be gone a year." The older woman's eyes filled again. "I won't see him for a year." She looked accusingly at Ailsa.

"He's always wanted to go there." Ailsa smiled, despite the ache in her chest.

Diana's eyebrows lifted.

"This is exactly what he needs, Diana. My career held him back from things *he* wanted to do too."

Diana reached into her pocket and pulled out the mangled tissue.

"Maybe this tumor was the best thing that happened to us both?" Ailsa tapped her temple. "A twisted gift of some kind." She blinked. "This bastard thing forced us to step back and really look at who we were, where our lives were going."

Diana sniffed. "That's a dark way to look at it."
Ailsa nodded. "Maybe, but it could still be true." She paused.
"Do you think he'd see me, before he goes?"
Diana shook her head. "I don't think so."
Ailsa nodded. "Would you ask him for me, please?"
Diana eyed her as she rose from the sofa. "I can't make any promises."
Ailsa smiled. "I don't expect any."

EVAN

E van stuffed the last of his T-shirts into the backpack and
zipped it closed. The studio looked tidy—exactly as he'd
found it and as if he'd never been there—and as he lifted the
keys and turned to leave, it struck him that this impersonal space
was a pathetic metaphor for his life.

It had been five weeks since he'd been back to Dumbarton
Road and he was growing tired of the pit of self-pity that he'd
allowed himself to slip into. Having made the decision to go to
New Zealand, there was finally a light ahead and he intended on
keeping his eyes on that, for now.

His company had been shocked at his resignation but had
agreed to allow him to do some work for their affiliate in
Sydney, which he could do remotely from Auckland. The
arrangement worked for him, being a free agent while staying
with his cousin, and if it resulted in a few trips to Australia—all
the better.

As he'd emptied his cubicle at the office, shaken a sea of
hands, exchanged personal email addresses with a few
colleagues and left the building the previous Friday, he'd been
filled with a mixture of relief and anticipation. The only blot on

the landscape had been Marie, who'd been noticeably absent on his last day. He'd been hurt, but overwhelming the feeling had been his excitement at finally being able to spread his wings and see a part of the world that fascinated him.

The general lightening of his own mood had cheered Diana, but knowing that he wouldn't be back for twelve months, it had been difficult to tell her what he was planning.

"A year?" Her face had crumpled. "Why so long?"

Evan had put his arm around her shoulder.

"I need a fresh start, Mum. Far away from here and all things Ailsa."

She'd sniffed as he'd hugged her.

"It'll go fast. Before you know it, I'll be back, driving you mad."

Diana had gripped his hand. "I know you need to go. But a year?"

"I'm sorry. I know it's hard, but I need that time to fully reset."

She'd nodded, holding on to his arm until her breath had returned to normal, each hiccup poking at Evan's conscience.

Having gone back to her house on Huntly Gardens, he'd persuaded her to put on her coat and go with him to the Botanic Gardens so they could eat doughnuts and drink hot chocolate outside on the terrace. Now, the fresh September wind was picking at their backs as they enjoyed their drinks and watched people milling around them.

"So, we'll talk, and do those video call things every week, at least twice?" She lifted the cup to her lips.

"Yes, at least twice." He smiled at her. "Maybe more." The effort she was making to be strong was typical, but nonetheless touching.

"Well, all right then." Her eyes were full, but her shoulders were back and her chin high.

Diana set the cup down and sighed.

"I went to see her yesterday, like you asked." She eyed him, as if gauging whether to continue.

Rather than submit to the compulsion to ask what happened, he took a bite of the sugary doughnut.

"It felt so strange to be in the flat. It looks quite different." She pulled her mouth down at the corners. "*She* looks different too. Calm." She frowned, meeting Evan's eyes. "Perhaps centered is the word?"

Evan, still trying to banish the images that came into his head when he thought about Ailsa now, nodded and took another bite of doughnut.

"She wants to see you before you go." Diana drained her cup, leaving a tiny blob of foam on her nose.

Evan tapped his own nose and laughed as Diana tutted and swiped the milky fluff away.

"So, what do you think?" Her eyes were intense.

He stared above his mother's head for a few moments, considering if whether to refuse to see Ailsa would be cowardly, and possibly even cruel. He was tired of being disappointed in himself, and if seeing Ailsa helped her, after everything that had happened, he wouldn't deny her that.

"I could, I suppose."

To his surprise, Diana looked pleased.

"I think it's the right thing to do, Son." She nodded decisively. "I think it'll be good for both of you."

The following afternoon, as he walked down the steps from the studio and out onto Ashton Lane, Evan checked his watch. He had half-an-hour to make it to the University Café, and from there he'd go back and stay the night with Diana, his last in Glasgow for the foreseeable future.

The café was as lively as always as he ordered and made his way to a table. Evan's stomach was churning as he shed his jacket and positioned himself across from the door. He wanted to see her coming, give himself the maximum time to prepare, and as he lifted a newspaper that someone had left on the table next to him, he saw her outside the door.

She was wearing a soft hat he didn't recognize and a long red jacket, the brightness of which was unlike her customary, muted choices.

He pulled his shoulders down and forced himself to breathe slowly, as Ailsa shoved the heavy door open, looked around the café and then spotting him, walked to the table.

"Hello." She looked nervous.

"Hi, I didn't see you come in." Evan cleared his throat of the lie.

She slipped off her jacket, threw it onto the spare chair next to her then sat opposite him. She then tugged the hat off, the static electricity instantly coaxing her short hair into a soft halo around her head.

Evan felt his heart tug.

"Is this for me?" She asked, sliding one of the cups on the table toward herself and smoothing down the crackling halo with her palm.

"Yep. Skimmed latte—right?"

"Perfect." She lifted the foamy liquid to her lips then set the cup down on the saucer. "Thanks for coming. I know this wasn't easy."

Evan stirred his coffee and kept his eyes on the circling foam.

"It's fine. We needed to talk before I go. It just took me a while."

She nodded. "I totally understand."

An hour-and-a-half later the café was emptying out. They'd had a second round of coffee and shared a toasted cheese sandwich which, rather than irritate Evan, had amused him. As he watched her chewing with gusto, her rounded cheeks working on the food, he'd been surprised that he liked this new face of his wife and now, as she wiped crumbs from the corner of her mouth, he allowed himself a moment of regret that he hadn't had the chance to know this more carefree version of Ailsa.

"So, what are you going to do now?" He asked, as she sat back and lay her hands in her lap.

"I'm not a hundred percent sure—which is a first." She smiled. "I was thinking about trying my hand at teaching some ex-professional classes, and maybe going to University."

Evan's eyes flicked up from the table.

"Uni? To do what?" To the best of his recollection, she had never mentioned a desire to study anything other than dance.

Her eyes dipped to the side as if avoiding the sun.

"Anatomy and physiology—possibly train as a physio-therapist."

Evan took in what she'd said and let the idea percolate. He could picture her carrying a pile of books, wandering around a campus looking the part with her edgy haircut and youthful face.

"You always did love to read anatomy books. Any idea where you'd go?"

She nodded.

"Glasgow is ranked pretty highly actually. They have a course for mature students that'd be perfect and, apparently, I might even get some credit for my experience." She lifted her shoulders. "Seems they think a professional, um, former profes-sional dancer might know a thing or two about anatomy." Now she was smiling again. "Amazing, eh?"

Evan smiled back. Seeing her light up, her eyes widening as

she talked about something that excited her, brought back good memories. He'd missed this face.

In an unwise moment of bon homie, he leaned in.

"And Sam? Are you two…" The moment he'd said it he wanted to cut his tongue out, wondering what possible good this knowledge could do now.

Her eyes clouded over, and she leaned back against the chair.

"Never mind." Evan cleared his throat.

"No." She held his gaze. "You deserve an answer."

His pulse was picking up.

"We are together." Her face twitched as she fiddled with her napkin.

Evan held his palm up.

"I don't need to know. I shouldn't have asked."

He licked the spoon and watched as she ran her hand up into her hair, the gesture he'd seen numerous times since her surgery.

"Why do you do that?" He frowned.

"What?" She looked puzzled.

"You keep touching your head. Is it still sore?"

Ailsa let her hand drop to her lap. "It is." She pulled the cup closer. "But I do it to focus."

Evan shook his head. "Not getting you."

She leaned forward, her elbows on the table and her shoulders forming a half circle under her sweater.

"When I touch the scar, the screw heads etcetera, it's painful."

He nodded.

"But the pain reminds me of where I was, and where I am now." She stared at him. "I sound insane, don't I?"

Evan shook his head.

"Actually, no. It makes sense." He smiled at her anxious face. "Like a rite of passage."

"Exactly." Her eyes lit up. "It's like a medal of honor or something—a reminder of a battle—something that qualifies everything that's happened." Now her smile was gone. "Not that it excuses anything though, that's not what I'm saying." She scanned his face. "Just a macabre reminder of how I got here, and how fortunate I am."

Evan nodded. He watched her blush and then lift the cup and sip her coffee. The café hummed around them and for the first time in months, he felt close to her—she'd allowed him in—and the irony of the timing struck him, as he smiled at her.

"What?" She looked puzzled.

"Nothing. Let's talk about selling the flat." He patted the table with his palm, and with the simple movement, took another step away from the past.

AILSA

Since telling her parents what had happened, Ailsa hadn't been back to Edinburgh. So much was swirling around inside her, and in her newborn life, that coping with their shock and disappointment at her separation from Evan, was difficult. They'd been calling her every couple of days and, despite their protestations, she'd persuaded them that she could cope alone with whatever came next.

With everything involved in selling the flat, getting her application paperwork in order for the University and attending regular dance classes at the new West End school she'd been frequenting, her days were full and flying by at an alarming rate.

Sam had been caught up in intense rehearsals at the concert hall for the past few weeks. He was to play a Rachmaninov piece that he found extremely challenging, and she'd been touched when he'd asked her to listen to him practice, all the while looking anxiously at her over his shoulder as he'd repeat any phrase he was having trouble with. She loved that he wanted her in the room and to Ailsa, the music he created was as perfect as what they were creating together.

She'd been sleeping upstairs ever since Diana's visit, gradually packing and moving her clothes and belongings in, along with the few pieces of furniture that she hadn't sold to the new owners. Now, she had only a few days left to vacate the premises.

Evan had been in New Zealand for six weeks and other than a text or two from Diana, with his feedback on the sale of the flat, Ailsa had had no news from him. Each time she went to pick the mail up from the doormat she expected to see something in his distinctive hand—perhaps a large envelope with divorce papers inside or a flimsy airmail letter—but so far nothing had come.

She pressed the top down on the bulky suitcase she'd been filling and tugged at the zip. This was the last of her winter clothes and then the wardrobe would be bare. She slid the case off the bed and wheeled it up against the wall. Next to it, the bulky bag with her pointe shoes spewed a web of pink ribbons onto the floor so she leaned down and gathered them up, pushing them back inside. As she zipped it closed, the image of Evan, shoving the bag across the living room toward her, flashed starkly. A picture of his face, twisted with frustration, and then his words came back to her. *It's time, Ailsa. It's who you are.*

Giving the bag a soft kick, she left the room.

The kitchen was bare aside from a few last items in the fridge, and her breakfast dishes. She emptied the fridge contents into the bin and picking up the bowl and mug from the draining board, wrapped them loosely in a tea-towel and put them in the open box behind her.

As she stood back and assessed the empty room, she flipped through several memories, like record albums stacked in a box. She was sitting on the counter while Evan cooked, her picking at the salad leaves before he could wash them. Then he was scolding her when she burned something, or poking her with a wooden spoon, laughing as he shooed her out of the room.

She remembered that their conversations had often gone long into the night when she'd been working through nerves over a new role, insecurities about an injury, or her stamina holding out through another season. He'd always dismissed her fears, and she'd let him.

Next, she saw him helping her walk, bathing and dressing her, teasing memories from the dark spaces in her mind while shrouding others, in order to protect himself. She pushed down a swell of sadness and as she took in the newly blank canvas that had been their home, putting aside the remnants of her hurt, she felt once again immensely grateful to him for everything he'd done for her.

Aside from the struggles and tension, she knew there had been laughter in their time together, and she wanted to remember that. More importantly, there had been love, and that she would never turn her back on.

Dragging the suitcase down the hall, Ailsa spotted the mail on the mat. Under a colorful circular for a new Indian restaurant, and an electricity bill, lay a glossy postcard. She flicked the other items aside and lifted the card. On the front was a bird with a creamy chest, a dark mask over its eyes and iridescent blue speckles around the edges of its wings. The background of the card was artfully blurred but looked like a forest of lush green ferns.

She studied the front, her hand trembling, then flipped the card and read the wording on the back. "The Kookaburra bird, native to New Zealand." Below the stamp there were nine words. 'I'm sorry. Doing O.K. Keep dancing. Be happy. E.'

Ailsa's throat knotted as she lifted the card to her forehead. The relief was so overwhelming that she reached a hand out to steady herself against the doorframe. The recent wall of silence was broken. Evan was all right. She could finally allow herself to breathe more freely, to move forward with this path she'd chosen and not feel responsible for his happiness anymore.

She swiped at her eyes, picked up her shoe bag and the remainder of the mail, tucked the postcard into her waistband and pulled out the extendable handle of the suitcase. She hesitated only for a moment, took one last look over her shoulder, then walked out into the hall and closed the door behind her.

EPILOGUE

GLASGOW, AUGUST 2021

The theatre was in darkness as Ailsa felt the brush of warm air against her face, and the weight of the silence— waiting for the final moment before the music began. Her stomach fluttered as she closed her eyes and breathed deeply into her chest and as she concentrated on the slow, controlled filling and emptying of her lungs, the tease of nerves eased.

Cutting into her calm, a distant bell rang to warn the audience that they needed to take their seats. The familiar sound sent the hairs on her arms to a prickly attention. It had been so long since she'd been here, in this theater where she'd spent a significant proportion of the last few years, that being here now was both exhilarating and laden with nostalgia.

As she focused on the tiny white speckles that began to appear in the blackness beneath her eyelids, images flashed on and off like the prompts inside the MRI machine. She saw the countless hours that she'd spent sitting in the chilly auditorium during technical and dress rehearsals, stretching behind the rows of seats, trying not to crush her costume and wrapping her legs in wool to keep her muscles warm. She could almost feel the edges of crisp rows of tulle scraping her inner arms, the shift of soft chiffon against her thighs as she walked, the feel of her partners' hands firm around her waist as she spun in a series of pirouettes. She was being inundated with sensations, each presenting her with a memory of its own.

Allowing the picture show to take her in, she pressed her eyes closed even tighter and flexed her feet inside her shoes, feeling for the ground.

The orchestra was whispering its warm up, strings wailing and airy woodwind notes tangling together in a lilting melody that deepened her smile. This felt wonderful.

A small hand grabbed her wrist and Ailsa's eyes shot open. Hayley sat in the seat next to her, in the Orchestra section of the auditorium, Hayley's now long hair pulled into a tight bun and her toes tipping the floor as she leaned into Ailsa's side.

"When will it start?" She spoke in an exaggerated whisper.

Waiting for her equilibrium to rebalance, Ailsa squeezed Hayley's fingers.

"Soon, Pickle. The overture's about to begin." She nodded toward the orchestra pit in front of the stage, where the heavy red curtains bulged, keeping their secrets safely inside.

"Will she be on first?" Hayley's breath smelled of chocolate.

"Yes." Ailsa nodded and then flicked her eyes to the empty seat on her other side.

Hayley extended her legs, kicking the seat in front of her, and Ailsa smiled apologetically at the young man who spun around and scowled over his shoulder at them.

"Don't do that, love. It won't be long." She pressed Hayley's leg down and lifted the girl's hand in her own. "Patience."

The lights in the auditorium dimmed, the rise in anticipation tangible as the audience quieted and settled back in their seats.

Just as the music began, Hayley grasped Ailsa's arm again.

"Aunty Ailsa, look." She pointed across her body to Ailsa's right.

"Shhh." Ailsa scolded.

"No, look. It's Uncle Evan." Hayley's voice rose to a raspy croak.

Ailsa snapped her eyes in the direction the child was pointing and there, walking down the side aisle was the unmistakable figure of Evan. He was leaning forward, carefully watching his feet as he moved in the dimness. His profile was sharp, his hair shorter than she'd ever seen it. A jacket was slung over his arm and his shirt was tucked tidily into his trousers. Behind him a woman followed, her finger hooked into the back of his belt. She was tall, Ailsa guessed around five-feet-seven, and even in the dimming light, she could see that the woman's hair was long, a mass of fiery red waves. She wore a fitted dress that revealed just enough of her shape—her narrow waist, lean frame and long legs.

Ailsa swallowed.

"Can he see us?" Hayley was waving wildly as Ailsa reached over and gently pulled the girls arm back down to her lap.

"Hayley. Not now, love." There was a tight knot in her throat.

"But…"

"Not now. O.K.?"

Evan was edging along a row to her right, as the people he passed pushed up in their chairs just enough to let him and his companion slip by. Reaching their places, they both sat down then the red-head leaned in and whispered in Evan's ear as the lights dimmed further and the curtain began to lift.

Ailsa's heart was clattering, and her lungs felt like overfilled balloons. He was back. Evan was here—and with someone. As her mind filled with a cascade of images, she calculated that it was almost eighteen months since he had left for New Zealand.

Controlling her hitching breaths, she focused on the back of his head. The redhead was now nodding, and Evan's shoulders moved, a slight shake that sent a shiver of recognition through Ailsa. She knew that movement well. He was suppressing laughter.

Ailsa dragged her eyes back to the stage.

A chair sat in the middle of the simple set. A blue light cast a ghostly shadow across the lone dancer sitting with her back to the audience. As the violin and clarinet cut dulcet lines through the murky light, the dancer turned to her left and stepped out of the chair. The characteristic blue dress with a white pinafore swirled around her knees, and the long blonde hair was held up in a girlish, half pony-tail.

Hayley audibly drew in her breath.

"There's Mum. She's Alice." She leaned against Ailsa with such force that instinctively, Ailsa wrapped her hand protectively over her rotund stomach, her fingers feeling for the reassuring edge of a tiny foot, or the point of an elbow.

"Yes, Pickle. Doesn't she look beautiful?" Ailsa massaged the taut mound under her fingertips as she spoke in Hayley's ear.

In front of them, Amanda rose onto pointe and lifted her arms above her head, as if reaching for the sky. As she watched her best friend bourré soundlessly across the stage, Ailsa felt numbness creeping along her thigh, so shifted her weight to the opposite hip.

As she fidgeted, trying to smooth her skirt which had wrinkled up underneath her unaccustomed bulk, she caught a movement out of the corner of her eye. At the end of the row someone was edging past the seated audience members. The broad shoulders and blonde hair were distinct in the half-light now seeping off the stage, and as he approached, Ailsa felt a rush of joy move up into her chest.

Sam slipped into the seat next to her.

"Sorry. I couldn't get parked." He whispered against her cheek, his hand instantly going to her bulging stomach. "How are we all?" Reaching across Ailsa, he tapped Hayley's arm.

The child looked over and smiled, her eyes snapping quickly back to the stage.

Ailsa slipped her arm underneath Sam's, wound her fingers

through his then leaned in and kissed him, inhaling the sharp scent of his cologne.

He pulled her closer and squeezed her fingers, then nodded at the stage and whispered.

"Doesn't Amanda look amazing?"

"She does." Ailsa smiled as he twisted around in his seat and cupped her face.

"Not as amazing as you two, though." He let one hand fall to her stomach again.

The weight of his palm, and the warmth it generated permeating her skin, sent waves of contentment rushing through her. Ailsa leaned into his side and gently sighed, focusing on the stage. This was exactly where she'd been heading, for so long. This was where she belonged.

THE END

ACKNOWLEDGEMENTS

Heartfelt thanks to the many people who supported me in the creation of this book. I am extremely fortunate to have every one of them in my life.

I firmly believe that I would not be here today if it wasn't for my husband. I am so grateful for his love, support, irrepressible humor, scary intelligence and unwavering belief in me every single day.

Special thanks go to Peggy Lampman, my dear friend and fellow author, who writes beautiful, thought-provoking books and gives such invaluable feed-back.

Heartfelt thanks to Bette Lee Crosby, Rochelle Berger Weinstein, Amulya Malladi and Heather Bell Adams, all incredibly accomplished authors, for their support and generosity with their time, and to my co-hosts in the Blue Sky Book Chat group on Facebook, I am privileged to be included in such a talented and uplifting group of writers.

Sincere thanks to Kelli Martin and Bev Katz Rozenbaum. I am grateful that I found such wise and insightful editors to help me marshal and bring this story to life.

Thank you to Rasheeda Syed for her staunch friendship, willingness to read my early drafts, and for listening to me fret about each and every book I write, and to Sharon Erksa, for her encouragement and constant support.

A simple thank you seems insufficient for Dr. Daniele Rigamonti, for his incredible skills, the depth of his kindness and humanity, and for literally giving me back my life. I will be eternally grateful.

A very special thank you to Dr. Andrew McCarthy for his tremendous support in answering my myriad questions, but mostly for his compassion, and insights into the intricacies of the brain and the sensitivity required in dealing with someone recovering from brain surgery. I consider myself blessed to call him a friend.

Heartfelt thanks to Lesley Shearer, my ballet guru, for her staunch support, sage advice and stellar professional expertise. A special thank you to Carly Guy for her enduring patience with me sending her draft after draft, and her faith that this story would find its way into the world. And to my parents, for, well, everything.

The work of the late Dr. Oliver Sacks, on neuroscience and the effects of music on the brain, was an essential resource in researching this book, specifically *Musicophilia, Tales of Music and the Brain, 2007*. Dr. Sachs was a remarkable human being whose intelligence and clinical insights will be greatly missed.

Last but by no means least I'd like to thank all the friends, readers, reviewers, book bloggers, my fabulous ARC crew and members of my Highlanders Club, who support me on social media, specifically Susan Peterson of Sue's Booking Agency, Linda Levak Zagon of Linda's Book Obsession, Elizabeth Silver Reviews, Tonni Callan and Kristy Barrett of A Novel Bee, Denise Birt of the Novels and Latte Bookclub, Annie Horsky McDonnell of The Write Review, Samantha Alvarez, Wendy Clarke and the team at The Fiction Cafe Book Club and Janelle Madison of Green Gables Book Reviews. Thanks also to Chloe

Jordan, Bambi Rathman, Tina Hottinger, Pam Vogt, Lori Beam, Jackie Shephard, Sue Baker and all the wonderful Instagram bloggers on the book tour: @katerocklitchick, @readabookplz, @whatkelreads, @babygotbooks13, @megsbookclub, @nikkisbookshelves, @lostinastack, @rwbookclubgoodreads, @ReadingGirlReviews, @samalvarez823, @my.boys.mom, @novelsnlatte, @tina_readsbooks, @wildsageblog, @books_with_bethany, @littlebookpage, @cassies_book_reviews, @iwanttoreadallthebooks, @DustjacketReviews, @musingwithmeirys, @bibliolau19, @DeborahMurrill, @thebook_spa and @Hemysbookclub. Every one of you made the journey more enjoyable.

A special thank you to Kate Rock, for her book-smarts and outstanding promotional skills. There are too many people to name, so I say another sincere thank you to all those not mentioned individually. It really does take a village.

FROM THE AUTHOR   ·

This book is very personal to me. Not only am I a former professional dancer but I am also a brain tumor survivor.

I want to point out that while I have those two things in common with Ailsa, that is where our stories part. I never made it to the heady professional heights within the dance world that Ailsa did, but putting much of her experience down on paper transported me back to 2009, when I was undergoing my own surgery and recovery.

Dance was a passion for me for many years and now writing has taken its place, and I feel honored to bring this tale to life.

A percentage of all sales of this book will be donated to braintumor.org to support the critical research and invaluable care they offer brain tumor patients and their families.

ABOUT THE AUTHOR

Originally from Edinburgh, Alison now lives near Washington D.C. with her husband and dog. A former professional dancer and marketing executive, she was educated in England and holds an MBA from Leicester University.

The Art of Remembering is Alison's fifth novel. For more information on upcoming books go to www.alisonragsdale.com.